# THE RED CROSS ORPHANS

## GLYNIS PETERS

One More Chapter
a division of HarperCollins*Publishers* Ltd
1 London Bridge Street
London SE1 9GF
www.harpercollins.co.uk
HarperCollins*Publishers*
1st Floor, Watermarque Building, Ringsend Road
Dublin 4, Ireland

This paperback edition 2022
1
First published in Great Britain in ebook format
by HarperCollins*Publishers* 2021
Copyright © Glynis Peters 2021
Glynis Peters asserts the moral right to be identified
as the author of this work

A catalogue record of this book is available from the British Library

PB ISBN: 978-0-00-852379-4
HB ISBN: 978-0-00-852378-7

Printed and bound in the UK using 100% Renewable Electricity
by CPI Group (UK) Ltd

*To Lynda Lane, a fan and loyal reader of my books.
We formed a friendship which I will always treasure. Your passing
during the pandemic saddened me. RIP you 'crafty' lady.*

# Chapter One

'Bye Auntie Lil. Oh, don't cry. Come here, silly bean,' Kitty Pattison said.

Her stomach lurched as she pulled her aunt in for one last hug before she left home. The home she'd lived in for all her twenty years. This was not an easy parting. Her five-foot-nothing aunt's plump arms gripped tightly around Kitty's midriff and Kitty kissed the top of her head. Words were no longer required; the hugs expressed the love they shared. The mother figure, who'd taken her in when Kitty was orphaned after a ferryboat disaster took her parents and baby brother from her when she was four, adored her and received Kitty's undying love in return.

At five feet nine inches tall, Kitty towered a good nine inches over the woman who had encouraged her to join the Red Cross, and then retracted her enthusiastic claims when

1

she found Kitty was to be moved to Birmingham for further training. News of the enemy's relentless bombing attacks around Britain heightened her concerns.

'Don't ever not come home for want of a bob or two for the train fare. Do you hear me? Promise? Telephone the grocery shop with your message and we'll get the ticket sent to you. You hear me? All those miles between us, I can't bear it.'

Closing her eyes to the sound of her aunt's muffled tears, Kitty squeezed her tightly.

'I promise. It will be all right, auntie. At least it's not another country.'

Kitty's journey meant she would be near on two hundred miles away from her home town of Parkeston, near the Essex port of Harwich, but, determined to support her country, Kitty tried not to allow her voice to give away the knotted-gut anxiety she experienced deep inside. Emotion after emotion punched out messages, intensifying with each moment she waited before stepping outside the door.

They fought her each time she tried to suppress them; the sadness of parting, along with a fear of failure, and the guilt-drenched ones suggesting she stay home, continue to be a good foster-daughter doting on her middle-aged guardians. She tried to ignore the one which told her she was selfish, but no sooner had Kitty suppressed it, the thought welled up and tugged at her heartstrings once again. The world might be at war, but Kitty had battles of her own to fight. The sense she would always be beholden to the couple who had taken her in during the worst time in her life often played on her mind, but she knew part of winning a war was not to give in at the first battle.

Lillian Pattison argued day and night that Kitty should withdraw her voluntary aid application, and tried to persuade her to find something worthwhile to do closer to home. Her aunt had caved when she realised she could not persuade her niece to give up her desire to fulfil a dream, and voluntary first aid would pave the way for her to qualify as a trained nurse further down the line. Today, Kitty staved off the guilt and blasted any negative thoughts from her mind. This was the time to prove to herself she was able to cope alone. Her aunt and uncle were overprotective, which under the circumstances was understandable, but Kitty couldn't remain a girl – she was a young woman with much to learn.

Kitty's uncle Frank, her father's brother, walked into the kitchen,

'Hello, Lil off again?' he said, giving Kitty a smile.

He stood behind her aunt, his voice huskier than normal as he held back his true feelings. He puffed and sucked on his pipe. Kitty noticed a twitch shimmy down the right-hand side of his face, an emotional habit Kitty often witnessed during times when he became stressed or upset. Kitty leaned forward and gave him a gentle kiss on the cheek. She had his side of the family's genes when it came to their tall and trim athletic build, chestnut hair, and grey-blue eyes. Eyes which glistened when he turned to look at her, framed with damp lashes. Kitty watched her uncle struggle with her decision to leave.

'Why they are sending you to the middle of England

3

when there are places to be filled in this area is beyond me. Got everything?' he asked, glancing around the room.

'Yes, uncle. You know Lil, she's panic-packed for me. I've even got a kitchen sink in there,' Kitty said, and pointed to his old kitbag sitting to the right of the back door.

'You take care of that lot. It cost me a week's wages,' her uncle teased.

Kitty sent a wide smile his way. Despite his teasing she was aware he wasn't referring to his kitbag from when he had served in the British forces. Her new uniform and shoes had cost him a lot more than a week's wage.

Every payday, her uncle had taken great pride in placing funds into her savings jar, a project she'd undertaken since she'd seen the poster recruiting Red Cross nursing trainees.

Her meagre wages from washing up at the local holiday camp – a temporary base given over for the Kindertransport children – would never have purchased the many dresses, aprons and caps she needed, plus her living allowance for the years she volunteered.

Her uncle had found her the job for the year leading up to her leaving. The place had been transformed into a refugee camp for the children whilst she worked there, and when on duty Kitty witnessed the sadness of the young Jewish refugees brought to the town from Germany via Holland. The first group of children had arrived the previous December, and they had made Kitty look at her life a little closer. She intended to leave her family willingly, but these little ones had been sent away by parents for their own protection, not knowing if they'd ever meet again, and it made Kitty want to do more than just work in the kitchen washing their dishes. At the end of each working day, she read to them, despite knowing many couldn't understand a word. She would hold them close when they cried, and whisper words of comfort, just as Lil had when Kitty was missing her own parents. One of the matrons there told her she had a kind heart and that she definitely had a future in caring for others. She had pushed Kitty to recognise what she could offer others, and now the day had arrived to prove herself.

'Time to go,' she said, and embraced Lil and her uncle once again.

'Be safe, Kitty. Come home to us when you can,' her aunt said, sniffling back a river-flow of tears.

Her uncle puffed even harder on his pipe, his hands gripping it so tightly his knuckles turned white. The emotional tension in the air was overwhelming and it hurt Kitty to witness her family in such distress, but she wanted to commit to her war work and say she had at least tried. She often confessed to her friend Helen how she struggled with the way her aunt and uncle suffocated her with their overprotective love. Now, a flash of guilt for those thoughts washed over her. She shook them off and widened a smile of courage.

With one last glimpse around the kitchen, Kitty walked through into the front room and stepped out into Hamilton Street – the place where she'd played as a child, gathered with schoolfriends after chores, and celebrated many community moments with the other forty-plus families who lived in the small, terraced railway houses. She would always be grateful to her aunt and uncle for moving into the house. It made sense; her uncle had stepped into her father's job on the quay, and the house was reallocated to them, plus it was a place they felt Kitty needed to remain for stability, with the school a few feet away at the end of the street.

Residents stood or sat on their polished steps, waiting to cheer her on her way. Much as they'd waved other children away to war, or mourned their deaths together, just as they had supported her family when her cousin died in June during the Dunkirk evacuation. Once again, guilt tried to force her to retreat back indoors, to stay at her aunt's side so she would never suffer a bout of nervous depression alone. Kitty's uncle always withdrew into his own black silence whenever her aunt's mood slid into uncontrollable sobs and wailing. Both drew upon Kitty's strength to see them through, and it often took its toll, but Kitty never complained. Forever the dutiful niece.

Two doors down, the matriarch of the street, known as Widow Johnson, sat as she always did, upon a small stool, legs akimbo, hair bound by a headscarf turban, whilst she peeled potatoes, her stern voice berating the young children for taunting each other as they ran back and forth across the road playing What's the Time Mr Wolf. The woman muttered as she offered Kitty a farewell smile and handed her an apple.

'For the journey,' she said. 'Don't rush back 'omesick. Get away, girl. Make a life. She'll suffocate you. We'll take care of them. You do your bit, poke that 'itler with a stick, but make sure you come 'ome in one piece when you do come back. God bless you, gal.' Her head bobbed back down to the task in hand as if she'd never spoken. The twang in her tone and classic dropped h, defined her as Harwich born and bred. Like many in the parish, her family were original residents, a solid community of friends and fighters, whose present aim was to rid the country of an enemy destroying their next generation.

A bemused Kitty continued walking to the end of the road, grateful for a dry day, which meant she'd not sit on a train for hours in a damp outfit, and that her chestnut hair stayed in its neat curls. The little ones of the street ran around her shouting *good luck* in happy voices; some cried and begged her not to leave. To them she was family: the big sister some never had; their babysitter when Mummy went to work in the uniform factory or on the land. Kitty turned, gave a final wave, and tried to ignore the welling tears as she entered the shortcut to the station, avoiding the feral cats protecting their kittens. Walking across the small no-man's land, Kitty felt a twinge of sadness. She'd played there as a child, and now her childhood was behind her and only war and the unknown lay ahead. What she'd give to play hide-and-seek with her cousin once again, or sit on a large rock pretending they were on a desert island and eat sticky sandwiches made by their grandmother. She gave herself a shake and a telling off for focusing on the past. Now was time to head forward towards the station with no regrets.

The train for London pulled alongside the platform and, with one last glance behind her, Kitty climbed onboard. A few sailors brushed too close as she eased her way along the corridor in the hope of finding a seat in one of the compartments, but with one withering look from Kitty they soon got the message and made way for her. She found a seat beside an elderly woman and a small child. The little boy she recognised from playing with the refugee children where she'd worked. His mother was part of the housekeeping team.

'Hello, Gerald.'

The boy gave her a toothless grin.

'My goodness, you've lost another one.'

His head nodded with great enthusiasm, and the woman beside him laughed.

'You know this ruffian, I take it?' she asked.

Kitty smiled at her. 'I certainly do. I work... worked, in the same place as his mummy.'

The woman held out her hand, 'I'm his gran, Christine's mother. He's coming to stay with me in Gloucestershire for a while, to give her a break – isn't that right, Gerry?' She ruffled the boy's hair, and he gave her a loving smile in return and clambered on her knee.

'Grandma lives on a farm.'

His grandmother gave a slight shake of her head. 'It's a smallholding, nothing so glamorous as a farm, but it needs another working pair of hands and this little man volunteered to come and feed the chickens.'

Gerald grinned and Kitty thought him one of the lucky ones. His new home as an evacuee was a place where he'd thrive and be loved; she'd witnessed the many children from her small community leave for unfamiliar towns to live with strangers hundreds of miles away. With a sudden jolt of nerves as the train puffed its way towards London, she realised her own journey to an unknown home amongst strangers had begun.

## Chapter Two

Standing on the concourse, Kitty looked around the busy station. Her skin tingled both with fear and excitement, and her clammy hands gripped the handles of her kitbag until her knuckles could no longer find another shade of white.

For a brief moment she thought back to her uncle and his attempt to hold back his sadness and fear that morning. Kitty shook off the image and braced her shoulders. This was a moment to remember, a time to make him proud. She was standing in the city of London and had made the first part of her journey intact; now she needed to find her connection for Birmingham. A panic set in. Where was she to pick up her connection? Where was her paper with the details? How did she get to the next station?

As she watched people stride by with confidence, Kitty's insecurities rose. If she couldn't manoeuvre from A to B, how on earth was she going to find courage enough to care for the wounded? A trickle of sweat meandered down the back of her neck and cooled as it journeyed beyond her collar. She dropped the bag to the floor and bent with her hands supporting her on her knees. Fainting was not an option.

'Pull yourself together, Katherine Pattison. This is not you; you are organised and in control.' Kitty muttered the words mantra-like until her pounding heart settled to a natural beat and her breath eased from a choke to normal. She stood upright and tugged her luggage close. She pulled out the paperwork giving guidance to her final destination.

First, she needed to head for King's Cross station. 'Excuse me,' she called out to a uniformed guard.

'What can I do for you, young lady?'

'King's Cross. How do I get to the station from here please?'

With a slow, exaggerated swing of his head from side to side, the man frowned. 'You'll have to walk it today. Just under an hour but a straight walk from here. Underground out of action. Lucky it's not raining. Exit that way.'

Kitty followed the direction of his pointed finger and pondered on his use of the word lucky. She considered it an unfortunate choice as there was nothing lucky about walking an hour through the centre of a new city carrying a heavy bag.

'Thanks. I think,' she replied, and headed towards the exit.

Her stout shoes proved to be comfortable and supportive as Kitty strode towards the station; her heeled ones lay in the bottom of her bag and she thanked the sensible side of her personality for making the right choice.

Evidence of previous bombings lay around, and Kitty prayed there would be no further delays to her journey forced upon her by air raids. She arrived on the appropriate platform with six minutes to spare and delighted in the moment. Kitty gave herself a virtual pat on the back for making it despite her aching legs.

The train, packed with people crushed into every corner, pulled out from the station on time. Its slow chug and lurch forced Kitty into the bodies also trying to stabilise themselves. She pushed herself into a space at the end of the row and eased her kitbag in front of her feet. Kitty clung onto the handrail and stared out of the window as they sped towards her next stop. Daylight would soon slip into twilight and she hoped to reach Birmingham before dark.

After three hours of standing, Kitty's back ached. She was hungry and thirsty and unsure when she would find another opportunity to eat, so Kitty reached into her bag for the small thermos and cheese sandwich her aunt had wedged into the corner before she left. With care, and using a number of balancing skills, she added to her triumphant achievements and managed to sip tea without slopping it over herself or her travelling companions.

'Cleverly done,' said the soldier standing beside her.

Kitty laughed. 'I've eaten all the sandwiches, but I've another cup if you'd like some tea. I won't be drinking any more.'

The soldier inched himself sideways to face her. His blue eyes sparkled as his smile widened. Handsome was Kitty's first thought. Her second was – romance-novel hero. 'I wouldn't say no. Very kind of you. I'm parched.'

Kitty poured the tea into the small tin cup and passed it to him. She begged her knees not to give way when he ran his tongue across his lips.

'Where are you heading?' he asked.

With a silent reminder to herself not to stare too much, Kitty replied, 'Birmingham. I'm signed up to the Red Cross – nursing. I'm heading for my training at the Queen Elizabeth Hospital. You?'

'Visiting family in Derby before I head further north.'

Kitty nodded. Not having a clue where Derby was, she gave a simple response.

'Nice. Enjoy your family.'

Handing back the cup, his hand touched the back of hers by accident, and she pulled it away as if scalded by hot coals.

The soldier smiled. 'I'm planning to. It's my wedding day tomorrow. A quick turnaround, not what we'd really planned, but Julie, well she's, um, keen shall we say.' The flush across his cheeks told Kitty all she needed to know: the man was to be a father. She gave the cup a wipe around before packing it away.

'I wish you all the luck in the world. Have a wonderful wedding day.'

'Thanks. I think I need it. Now, had I met you earlier, pretty nurse …'

'Cheeky.' Kitty laughed and gave the soldier a light tap on the arm. He made the journey a shorter one with his light-hearted chatter.

With a sudden jolt the train came to a standstill. The guard called out the name of the station and Kitty realised it was time to leave the train. The soldier helped her with her bag and from the platform she waved him goodbye, noting with amusement that she knew the name of his fiancée but not his own, although she felt it wise to put him to the back of her mind; he was far too handsome to have at the forefront – a distraction. To her surprise he blew her a kiss. 'Thanks for the tea, nurse. If ever I need medical attention, I'll come and find you. Good luck.'

A few faces grinned at her as she glanced around, and when she looked back at the soldier, he gave another wave.

'You're welcome, and yes, do that, soldier,' Kitty called, over the sudden hiss of steam from the train as it slowly pulled away, taking her acquaintance homeward. She giggled to herself over his cheekiness and tucked it away as a memory from her first journey to her new career. Kitty headed for the exit where she hoped the promised transport would be waiting to take her to her accommodation. Across the road she spotted a truck sporting the familiar symbol of the Red Cross parked up and surrounded by several young women. She took a deep breath; this was it, her moment to join the other trainees and head for pastures new.

'Name?' Kitty looked up at the tall man holding a clipboard. It was a few seconds before it registered that he was addressing her as she approached the side of the truck where she debated which of the two groups of women she ought to join.

'Katherine Pattison – Kitty.'

She waited whilst he ran a grubby, well-chewed fingernail down the list and ticked a box beside her name. Kitty felt a sense of relief. She was on the list; she was in the right place. 'Right, Kitty Pattison, it says here you are for group two – over there.'

A well-dressed young woman waved her arm with great enthusiasm at Kitty.

'Over here. We're group two.'

Group two consisted of three young women of around her age, and Kitty walked over to join them. The one who had waved, eager to make her acquaintance, was standing beside a large, smart suitcase in red leather. Kitty couldn't help but notice the girl wrinkle her nose at Kitty's bag when the driver told them to move their things nearer the truck. To Kitty's relief, she saw the other two had minimal luggage the same as her, and leaned their well-worn brown suitcases against the wall. Kitty had an overwhelming sense of pride over her kitbag. Her luggage represented all that she stood for and her reason for joining the Red Cross: British pride and service of one's country. The kitbag might well appear shabby and worn to some, but Kitty knew with one glimpse that the others in the group understood she was not about glamour and making an impression with her worldly goods. The Great War and the past year of another war had taught many the true meaning of respect. She pushed her shoulders back and addressed the attractive auburn-haired girl who had beckoned her over.

'Thanks for the welcome. I'm grateful. I'm Kitty Pattison, from Essex,' Kitty said, lowering her shoulder bag to the floor.

The girl held out her hand. Kitty noted the neat manicure and softness of her hands. A privileged girl who didn't appear to have washed a dish in her life and who was groomed like a film star.

'Annabelle Farnsworth, but you can call me Belle. It annoys the heck out of Mother when my brothers do, so as she's not here I'll do what I ruddy well like. I'm from Surrey. With a toss of her immaculate curls, indicating an air of defiance, she pulled out a packet of cigarettes and offered one to Kitty.

'No thanks. I don't,' Kitty said.

The other two girls had formed their own huddle and Kitty made a mental note to get to know them better later that evening. For now, she would enjoy listening to the plummy tones of Belle, grateful for the company and not having to put effort into a conversation. The journey had exhausted her.

'Mother said I'm to cut down as they are not easy to purchase nowadays, but the hypocrite smokes two or three after drinks in the evening. Lord knows how she manages to lay her hands on so many. She won't allow me the odd shot of brandy either.'

Belle gave a dramatic sigh, and it took all Kitty's courage not to giggle.

'I told her, I am to help in the war effort you so greatly want me to join, therefore I'm entitled to enjoy a drink of good brandy, but no, she still tells me I'm to fund my own as it is an expensive treat. She hides the darn bottle! Do your parents nag?' Belle asked, and drew on her cigarette.

Kitty thought about it for a moment. Her aunt and uncle encouraged, discouraged and protected as well as any parent she knew.

'No, my, um, parents are …' At that moment Kitty decided not to share the fact she was an orphan as it often brought about awkward moments of sympathy.

These strangers didn't need to be privy to her personal life. 'They are supportive – and care for me. Although, they have been a little overprotective ever since my, er, my brother died at Dunkirk. They are—'

Belle cut into the sentence when she held up her hand, waved and called over to the others. 'Oh, I say, how horrid. Hear that, girls? Kitty lost a brother; Dunkirk.'

The three faces looked at Kitty, each one wearing a mask of pity, the one look she'd tried to avoid by not sharing she had lost parents and a brother – and a cousin. Belle patted her chest as a gesture of sympathy. It choked Kitty and she wanted to correct the statement to cousin not brother, but then felt it was best left. Besides, Brian had been like a brother, and she'd known him longer than her own. Kitty stood in awkward silence, never meaning to draw attention to herself. A short girl with neat pixie-fairy features and jet-black hair curled at the neck walked over and touched Kitty's arm. Her voice, soft and sweet, became breathy with emotion. 'I'm Trixie Dunn. Trix for short. You must be devastated.'

Unsure whether she was expected to respond or not, Kitty gave a simple nod. The tallest girl of the three moved in for a handshake. She had cropped brown hair and a pair of tortoiseshell-rimmed glasses perched on the end of her nose. Kitty immediately thought of a male scientist – an intellectual. She also had the deepest voice Kitty had ever heard in a girl. 'Joan Norfolk, but always known as Jo. My uncle came back injured. In a fishing boat. There were so many heroes, not just soldiers,' she said, and followed it through with a low whistle. 'What a coincidence we all use shortened versions of our names. Where are you from? I'm from Bristol and Trix here travelled from Somerset; we're practically neighbours, which is why our accents sound alike.'

'I'm from Surrey and Kitty's from Essex, and we sound nothing like each other,' Belle said, to which Kitty agreed.

Belle's upper-class tone was definitely nothing like her semi-rural Suffolk border with a touch of East End London accent.

Belle jiggled about and looked over at the driver.

'I do hope we move on soon; I'm dying for a pee.' The group giggled, and Belle gave a curtsey.

Kitty observed Belle's love of being centre of attention. Trix smiled all the time, and Jo stood back as if awkward in her own skin. One of Kitty's favourite things was to watch people, to follow their body language, a discreet habit which helped her sense the needs of others, and today, she had three new people to observe. She stored a few things in her mind to jot down in her leather-bound notebook – a gift Brian had given her before he left home. She used it to write down her own feelings in short diary notes, and the words and actions of other people. Kitty would sit for hours deciphering the emotions and thoughts, reassuring herself she was normal for experiencing some of them in relation to those loved ones she'd lost. Her aunt guided her in a modern way with some things in life, but Kitty took what she wanted to base her own life upon to another level. She knew she was not meant to stay in a small village, marrying a local lad and producing children. She'd learned her father had had a deep-seated urge to travel but never did, and Kitty wondered if she'd inherited his restless spirit. Inside her notebook she'd written short passages of possible adventures to be had in the future, but then the previous September, when war was declared, Kitty no longer wrote about them. Instead she worked on a more emotional journal dealing with the present rather than a future she was no longer sure would exist.

She wanted to write to Brian and tell him of her fears, new colleagues, and hopefully, new friends. It was then she had the small moment of realisation that Brian would never receive another letter from her, when the pain of loss kicked in and she had to pull up her protective shield to prevent the ever-threatening tears.

'Time to go, ladies!' The driver of the truck called them over and saved Kitty from embarrassing herself. She watched as he threw their bags into the rear. Belle berated him for not taking care of their worldly goods, to which he made a sarcastic comment which more or less told her to do it herself at the other end of the journey. He jumped into the driver's seat with the threat to leave with or without them. Group two clambered into their seats and chattered their way to their destination.

## Chapter Three

**M**uch to the surprise of the girls, the truck pulled into a narrow street with a row of terraced houses either side. The street could only be described as drab. Grey and drab. Tell-tale signs of where there were once metal railings added to the shabbiness.

'This cannot be where we are staying!' Belle's voice squealed so high the others winced.

'It's temporary, so I'm told,' the driver said as he unloaded their bags, giving Belle a smirk of a smile.

Kitty had a feeling he enjoyed seeing Belle's jaw drop when he pointed out a house at the end of the terrace with an alley dividing it from a public house which had seen better days.

'Temporary for how long?' Trix asked.

The driver shrugged his shoulders and dropped the last bag onto the pavement. Clambering into his vehicle, he waved a hand from the driver's window.

'Well, let's find out shall we girls?' Jo said.

Jo picked up her bag and the others followed as she made her way up the four steps leading to the front door of the property.

'I can tell you for how long. One night. Tonight. I'm not staying here any longer than I have to,' Belle declared in a voice which to Kitty sounded as if she meant business.

Pointing and flouncing back and forth from them and the bags, Belle found every fault she could up and down the street and mentioned them out loud into the twilight, not caring who looked at them, or the feelings she might hurt with her spiteful words.

Kitty disliked the slight Belle cast on her surroundings; a lot of places had succumbed to lack of paint and the seconding of metal for the war effort, leaving them looking tired and unloved on the outside – it wasn't always the fault of the owners.

'It's probably very nice inside,' Kitty said. 'Our house looks a bit like this; tidier than some I'll admit, but inside Li — Mum keeps it pristine.'

Again, she spotted the wide-opened mouth of shock from Belle.

'You live in a house like this? So small, with no garden?' Belle asked in a shocked whisper.

'As I said, tidier and well-maintained by my – um, dad – when he's lucky enough to find paint, but yes, similar style.' It irked her to see Belle's snobbery so public. She wasn't keen on the shabby state of the property either, but good manners told her not to judge until evidence to warrant judgement presented itself.

'Well, as you are so desperate for a pee, maybe it's time

to find out if it is bucket in the cupboard or a hole in the ground at the end of the yard,' Jo said, her voice steeped in sarcasm as she stepped aside with an arm outstretched for Belle to knock on the door.

The colour paled from Belle's face, and before any of them could say another word, the front door opened, and they were face to face with a five-foot-nothing plump woman with a wild thatch of greying hair. Her eyes peered with suspicion at them from narrow slits, then she gave a half-smile.

'All you girls from the Red Cross? I said I'd got room for two. Weren't expecting four. Welcome to Birming'am.'

Kitty listened to the drop and fall of the woman's nasal accent, one she assumed was native to Birmingham. It fascinated her the way the woman said yow instead of you, and oy instead of I.

Belle stepped forward.

'So, where do you propose the other two sleep?' she asked with a voice loaded with indignation. Jo looked at Kitty and Trix, all three sharing disapproving frowns towards Belle's attitude.

'I've got room for two. I was told two,' the woman repeated.

Kitty peered above the woman's head and into the hallway. It looked tidy, and the smell wafting from the house gave the hint of disinfectant, indicating a clean house, plus something pleasant was cooking and her stomach grumbled with appreciation. It was time to stop dithering on the step.

'Dare I suggest we top and tail?' She looked to the

woman, Jo and Trix, who both nodded to the positive. 'I'm game,' Jo said.

'Me too.' Trix threw a grateful look at Kitty as she spoke.

Relief in their faces told Kitty they were just as tired as she was; she didn't bother looking to Belle for approval.

'It's getting late, we're tired, and well, Mrs – I'm sorry, we haven't been introduced, I'm Kitty, and this is Jo, Trix and Belle.' She held out her hand.

The woman gave Kitty's hand a warm shake. 'Smith. Known mainly as Ma Smith around here. I've been paid for the rooms. I'll take two shillings for two more suppers and breakfast. It's no extra work to muster up a couple more pillows. In the morning you can find out where there's other boarding rooms for two of you. It was a housing officer who spoke to me. No name I'm afraid. Anyway, top and tail all you like, just don't make a row.'

Belle's face was a picture of confusion and reluctance, but Kitty was no longer prepared to stand around debating the two who'd be lucky enough to get the rooms, or the two who'd have to walk the streets looking for overnight accommodation.

'You'd best come inside then,' the woman said before Belle had the opportunity to agree or object.

The layout of the house was very much like her parents' house, and Kitty knew upstairs would be laid out to three bedrooms; one large, one medium and one small box room. She suspected the medium and box room were theirs, which would mean a tight squeeze. They climbed the narrow staircase with Belle muttering to herself at the rear.

Kitty dared not ask her to share her thoughts, for she had a feeling they would not be complimentary.

Ma Smith pushed open the door to the main room.

'Two in here, and two in this one,' she said as she led the way to the medium room.

'I sleep downstairs in the front room. The back room is the parlour where you'll eat in five minutes. That small room is the bathroom.' She looked at them with a grin. 'Oh, don't look so surprised. I know what people think when they see the house. I had it changed when my Jim passed away. I made the home an investment for widowhood. The last war took him, and I had to survive. There's a privy outside; feel free to use that too.'

Belle pushed her way from the back of the group and along the small landing. She peered inside the master bedroom and flounced inside, flinging her suitcase on the bed.

'This is my room,' she declared.

Kitty could see by the expressions on the faces of the others that not one of them was surprised by her choice.

'Jo, you or Trix with Belle?' Kitty asked in the hope one of them said yes.

With a devilish grin and staring Kitty right in the eye, she slowly shook her head. 'Not at all. You were the clever one suggesting top and tail, so deserve the privilege of the larger room.'

Trix gave a small cough and Kitty knew she smothered a giggle.

Giving them both a wry smile and clenching a fist in a silent threat to seek revenge, she entered the room. Ma

Smith closed the door and the laughter from Jo brought a smile to Kitty's face.

'Well, Jo's happy to have a room for the night,' she said to Belle, who walked the room wiping her finger along furniture and inspecting it for dust.

'The woman keeps a clean house – that's a blessing in disguise. Let's hope the bathroom is as clean. I'll wait for you all to use it first. This place is not at all what I expected.'

Kitty chose not to respond. She pulled her wash things from her kitbag and tugged open the bedroom door, and to her relief the bathroom was free. Like the bedroom, it was fresh and clean. After a swift freshen-up, she headed back to the bedroom where she found Belle pulling covers from the bed.

'What on earth are you doing?' Kitty asked, completely bewildered as she watched Belle smooth out the remaining bedding on the mattress, leaving a mound of top sheet and blanket under the window.

'I do *not* top and tail. Where you come from I …'

Kitty stared at Belle. Who did this girl think she was, royalty? How dare she belittle everything she came across.

'*Where* I come from? What exactly do you mean by that? You know nothing about me.' Kitty tried to contain the anger she felt flare inside. Suddenly it dawned on Kitty that she was to sleep on the floor and Belle had claimed the large double bed for herself.

'You said yourself your house was like this one. I assumed you would be used to unusual sleeping arrangements when you have visitors, given such cramped conditions. Sleeping on the floor must be a common occurrence in a house this size,' Belle said, and the superior tone she used forced Kitty to take a deep breath and leave the room before she fired out words she'd regret. She headed to Jo and Trix's room and tapped on the door.

'Ready to eat?' she called out.

Jo opened the door. 'We are. Lead the way. No Belle?'

Kitty felt it safe to say nothing and headed downstairs.

Ma Smith gave them a beaming smile when they entered the small parlour. She pointed to a table draped with a green cloth and set for four diners.

'Take a seat. It's mutton broth with bread I'm afraid, but I wasn't sure what time you were arriving, and as it is 8.30 now, the evening is drifting away fast.'

The three girls sat at the table and each took a piece of bread from the plate.

'Belle not eating?' Trix asked Kitty.

Kitty shrugged. 'She's probably still finding a hole for me to curl up in for the night.'

Her words were bitter, and it upset her that she'd let them slide out with an edge of annoyance.

Jo and Trix stared at her in question.

'On the floor. My bedding is on the floor. Madam has claimed the bed.'

Trix stared at Kitty with her mouth wide open, and Jo gave an inward gasp.

'She's done what? She can't do that. How unfair. We barely know each other, granted, but we all need somewhere to sleep.'

Kitty shrugged. 'I've got somewhere, it's just not on a bed.'

Their hostess peered into the room. 'I thought I heard voices. The other one not coming down?' Ma Smith asked.

'I'm not sure,' Kitty said.

'Well, you must be starving, so we won't wait.'

Ma Smith brought a tray to the table with three steaming bowls of cloudy broth with cabbage and carrot bulking it out. The smell filled the room, and all three girls exclaimed their thanks.

A clip of heels along the hallway told them Belle was on her way.

All four women in the parlour turned their heads her way as she entered the room, overpowering the mutton aroma with an overdose of a heady floral perfume and cigarette smoke. Belle stood in the doorway examining her surroundings, whilst Kitty, Jo, Trix and Ma Smith stared at the taffeta pink dress with contrasting pink stole draped across Belle's shoulders and forearms.

She'd dressed for dinner. A full top-to-toe outfit of clothing Kitty could only dream of owning. Items she'd stared at on display in the large, luxurious stores in Colchester.

Three out of the four women in the room froze. The fourth took control, but not without rendering the other three into a state of unanimated gratitude.

'Sit yourself down, young lady. Mind the skirt on my floor – I've not swept it today.'

With one wave of her arm, Ma Smith had reduced Kitty, Jo and Trix into spluttering guests, all three grabbing their napkins to smother their mouths.

Belle, oblivious to the fact Ma Smith had taken the

opportunity to mimic and amuse herself at Belle's expense, waited until Ma Smith pulled out the chair before she sat down. Kitty dared not look at Jo or Trix for fear of crying with laughter at their hostess's antics. She sensed once they'd started, they'd never stop. From the moment they'd pulled up at the house and the woman had opened the door, she'd set a path of no return. Belle was the outsider whom they'd watch and at times ridicule, but some days envy.

She watched Belle place the napkin in her lap and braced herself for whatever happened next.

'I'll be glad to eat and sleep,' Jo said and broke away a piece of bread and dipped it into her bowl.

Kitty and Trix spooned mouthfuls of the broth, nodding their approval.

'What on earth is that?' Belle asked.

'Mutton broth,' Trix mumbled, wiping away a drip from her chin.

'It's good. Tasty,' said Jo.

Kitty sat in silence; Belle's face had a tendency to share her opinions as loudly as any voice.

Ma Smith entered with Belle's bowl and placed it before her, and the mischievous glance she gave the other three warned them not to eat more before she'd spoken.

'It was too late for venison. Being's I'm the only chef in the kitchen tonight it's a simple supper, but should fill your belly well enough.'

Belle stared down at the bowl. With slow, deliberate movements she lifted her spoon and stirred the contents. Kitty, Jo and Trix watched on as Ma Smith stared her down, defying her to object. Kitty had a feeling Ma Smith had taken a dislike to Belle and would not hold back with putting her out onto the street.

'Enjoy it while I go and find those extra pillows,' Ma Smith said as she brushed past Belle and out of the room.

'Disgusting mess,' Belle said after more stirring.

'It's actually tasty. Just eat it, Belle.' Jo's voice, loaded with irritation, snapped across the room. Like Kitty, she'd had her fill of snobbery.

'I'm not paying a shilling for this muck,' Belle said, and placed the spoon back onto the plate beside her bowl.

'Try it – you'll be surprised. There's a lot of folk who'd give their right arm for this feast right now. Besides, you'll be hungry during the night,' Trix said.

Kitty sensed no amount of encouragement would get Belle to eat the broth and it annoyed her when the girl pushed it aside with a disapproving grimace. Kitty looked at her in disgust.

'I'll pay the shilling, and I'm sure one of the others will pay their way. If you are not going to eat your share, then we will. I'm not going to waste food; goodness knows it's hard enough to get nowadays. Jo, Trix?' Without waiting for a response from Belle, Kitty picked up the bowl and offered it around the table. Each girl took a share and Kitty placed the empty bowl back in front of Belle.

'Do what you want. If this is how I'm expected to live, I'll have to rethink my options.' Belle said and lit another cigarette.

Jo's face turned a deep shade of red, and Kitty, like Trix, concentrated on eating their extra portion. Kitty guessed Jo also came from a less fortunate background than Belle, and resented her statement.

'Probably for the best,' Jo muttered. 'Rationing is going to get worse. If you can find better *options*, I'd take them and do us all a favour.'

Belle sat upright in her chair and stared at Jo.

'And what do you mean by that? Do us all a favour?'

Trix flinched and Kitty guessed that, like her, she disliked conflict of any kind, but she wasn't prepared for the likes of Belle to make the three of them feel uncomfortable.

'I think Jo means extra portions. If you opt out, we might get extra food. Didn't you, Jo?'

Jo shoved her spoon into her mouth and slurped the contents in a loud and unsavoury manner. Kitty felt the tension in the room and forced a laugh.

'Really Jo, you are the joker.'

To her relief, Ma Smith came back downstairs and bustled her way into the room, her face glistening with sweat.

'I don't know what you two girls were doing in that room,' she flicked her face to Belle and Kitty, 'but I've remade the bed. Top and tail style. Why half of it was on the floor is beyond me; it's not that warm around here.'

With a shrug, Kitty spooned the last of her broth into her mouth.

Jo and Trix looked to her and Belle with frowns on their faces.

Belle stubbed out her cigarette into an ashtray nearby and rose to her feet.

'Well, I'll go and un-tail it. I am not, I repeat not, sleeping in that bed with anyone else.'

Ma Smith's hand landed on the table with a slight thud. Kitty felt the woman had controlled it for their sakes.

'I will not have my bedding on the floor. Understand?' she said, and the challenge in her voice said it all. Belle was not going to get her own way.

'Very well, then find me another bed to sleep in. Maybe those two could move into the large room with Kitty. The bed will be big enough for three and I've no doubt they've experienced it all before, but you have to understand, I have not and will not. I have standards.'

Belle's voice was high-pitched and whining. Kitty began to stack the bowls and cutlery; she was not happy to bring confrontation into Ma Smith's home, and with someone she barely knew.

'Although I don't understand, and I also have my standards, I'll sleep on the chair. It's only for a few hours and the chair is a sturdy one. Shall I take these through to the kitchen, Mrs Smith?' she said.

Trix and Jo both jumped to their feet and began helping Kitty.

'Thank you, girls. It will help while I sort out the sleeping arrangements for madam here,' Ma Smith replied. 'You come with me miss, and we'll go upstairs and organise something.'

At the sink Kitty nudged Jo. 'Do you think she'll make the course?'

Jo picked up a tea towel and began wiping dishes dry, handing them to Trix.

'Not sure. She's not cut out for life outside a castle by the sounds of it. Spoilt to the core. Not a care for anyone but herself,' she said.

Trix gave a tut. 'I don't like her. She looks down her nose at everything and everyone. Mrs Smith is so angry; you can see it in her face. Belle's rude. Horrid.'

A bang and clatter from the hallway halted their conversation and they ran through to see what was going on. The front door was wide open and the darkness outside threw back only shadows. Ma Smith's voice echoed into the street.

'Good luck to you. The Ritz might be open.'

The three girls looked to one another and then back at the door.

'She hasn't?' Kitty whispered.

'I think you'll find she has,' Jo replied and laughed.

Trix pushed past them to get a better look.

'She has. Belle's case is in the street and it's burst open.'

'Move over. This I've got to see,' Jo said.

Kitty also squeezed her way forward and all four of them stood on the step watching Belle snatching up her belongings. Mrs Smith stood with her arms folded and a determined stance.

'You'll regret this. I'll report you,' Belle yelled at her as she scrabbled around for her clothes draped across the bottom step.

'Try it. I'll tell them what sort of person you are,' Ma Smith yelled back.

'Kitty. Jo. Trix. Say something,' Belle called out.

Jo stepped onto the next step and called out before

stepping back inside. 'Bye, Belle. Hope you find somewhere comfy.'

Belle clamped the case shut and rose to her feet. Her perfectly coiffed hair was now hanging limply around her face. A smidgen of sympathy for her caught Kitty unaware, and she touched Mrs Smith's arm.

'Give her another chance. I'll sleep on the chair. I don't mind.'

Ma Smith patted Kitty's hand. 'I offered to make her a bed in the bath, or downstairs on the truckle bed I've got out back, and that wasn't good enough. She's demanding all three of you sleep in one room and she has one to herself. My home isn't good enough for her, so she'll have to learn the hard way. Don't give in to her; she'll never survive if you do.'

She eased her way past Trix and stood on the lower step with her hands on her hips.

'Top and tail or go, those are your choices. The others are tired, I need my rest, and you are creating a scene in my street. This world hasn't got time for the likes of you anymore, so get a grip on your hysterics and make a decision.'

Belle looked one way down the street and then the other. She took a step forwards towards the house.

'I'll sleep on the chair,' she said with a clipped voice.

Ma Smith turned around and climbed back up the steps.

'I think you mean, "*May* I sleep on the chair please, Mrs Smith?"'

She ushered Kitty, Jo and Trix down the hallway.

'Get yourselves to bed. Madam will follow. Night now.'

The clip clop steps of Belle followed through, and the door clicked shut.

'I'd like a word, young lady,' Ma Smith called to her.

Jo stopped outside the middle bedroom.

'Good night Kitty, and good luck.'

Once inside the bedroom, Kitty smiled when she saw the bed. Ma Smith had placed cushions down the centre of the bed as an attempt to create two singles. The woman was wise and thoughtful. She had every right to ask two of them to leave, considering the agreement with the Red Cross was to take in two girls, but she'd put up with the extra work and rudeness from Belle. Kitty made a note to find a small gift to give her as a thank you when she could. Rushing to the bathroom before the other girls took their turn, Kitty changed into her nightdress and brushed her hair. As she brushed, she thought of ways to handle Belle until they reached their permanent base. Once there, she hoped not to have any further dealings with the girl. Bad manners and discourteous remarks were not something she was prepared to tolerate any longer.

## Chapter Four

'**M**orning.'

Kitty slid from the side of the high bed and addressed a dishevelled Belle sitting on a chair across the room. The girl glared back at her. Kitty had given her three chances to sleep on the bed but had received only biting remarks, so eventually she gave up and curled up under the paisley eiderdown.

With a stretch and a yawn, Kitty inhaled and exhaled to settle her nerves. Today was one of the most important in her life and the pouting Belle was not going to ruin it for her.

'Are you using the bathroom first, or am I? That's if Jo or Trix aren't in there already,' she said.

Belle huffed. 'Do what you want. It's far too early. I'll lie on the bed now you are out of it and get a few comfortable hours of rest.'

With a loud laugh, Kitty looked at her and grabbed her washbag. She crossed the landing and tapped on the bathroom door. To her surprise, Jo pulled it open, toothbrush in one hand and white around her mouth. Kitty gave an apologetic smile.

'Sorry. I'll come back.'

Jo shook her head.

'Mmm,' she mumbled and pointed to the hallway. 'Pee, then I'll finish.'

A grateful Kitty swung her a smile. Her bladder had reached a limit of comfort and was threatening levels beyond Kitty's control.

'I'll be quick,' she said and dashed inside.

Finishing, and washing her hands, she handed back the use of the bathroom to Jo.

'Thanks. That was considerate of you.'

Jo nodded and grabbed a towel to wipe her mouth.

'Where's her ladyship? Did you sleep?' she asked.

Kitty gave a snort of a laugh. 'I slept well enough, thanks. Her ladyship slept in the chair and is now sleeping on the bed. It seems she didn't get enough sleep and is going to enjoy a few more hours.'

Jo leaned back in amazement.

'I take it you told her it was six o'clock and we have to get to HQ by 7.30?'

With a shrug of her shoulders, Kitty gave a sly grin.

'You think I'm brave enough to come between Belle and sleep? No, she had the same information as we did, so she will have to sort it out for herself. I'm done with her and her tantrums.'

As the words left her lips Kitty was amazed by her bold statement. If someone had told her she'd be outspoken to and about relative strangers before she'd left home, she'd have laughed. Kitty was far from timid, but she didn't like conflict and tended towards the keep-things-calm side of life. She let out a sigh and Jo patted her on the shoulder.

'I thi—'

A click of a door interrupted whatever she was going to say to Kitty, and they turned around. Both giggled as Trix came scuttling from the bedroom and made a dash for the bathroom, offering only a nod for acknowledgement.

'See you in five, and good luck,' Jo said.

Kitty raised her hand. 'Will do and thanks.'

Entering the bedroom, she saw Belle had made herself comfortable on the bed and offered soft snores through pouty lips. Tiptoeing around the room, Kitty dressed and gathered her things. She hesitated at the door as to whether to wake Belle, but opted to leave her sleeping. The waft of toast from downstairs meant breakfast was underway, and she was not going to get caught up in any disputes with Belle and ruin the start of the day.

Downstairs, Mrs Smith was bustling around Jo and Trixie, and gave Kitty a beaming smile.

'Morning. Sit yourself down and tuck in. Tea's mashed and in the pot.'

Kitty sat down. She looked at the pile of toast and pot of jam in the centre of the table.

'Thanks, Mrs Smith, I'm ready for this …'

Before she could say any more, Mrs Smith deposited soft-boiled eggs in egg cups onto the plates in front of her three guests, and Kitty stared at the welcome treat.

'An egg?'

She looked across at Jo and Trixie. Both looked down at theirs wide-eyed.

'I've chickens at the bottom of the garden. Collected six this morning. Enjoy them. You've a long day ahead of you. By the way, where's her ladyship?'

Kitty glanced at Jo, who offered back a smile and wink.

'Still asleep when I came down,' Kitty said and focused on her plate.

Mrs Smith stood with her hands on her hips and stared at her. 'Asleep? Didn't you wake her?'

Kitty dipped a strip of toast into the deep-yellow egg yolk and popped it into her mouth. She chewed and savoured, before answering.

'Delicious. I did speak with her when we woke up this morning, but she insisted on moving from the chair to the bed for a few more comfortable hours' rest.'

With a loud harrumph, Mrs Smith marched from the room. Kitty, Jo and Trixie returned their attention to their eggs and waited for the aftermath of Belle's eviction from the bed. All they heard was the odd creaking of a floorboard above them. By the time their plates were cleared, Mrs Smith had reappeared and put her hand to the teapot.

'Still hot enough. I think you've got time for one more and then you'd best make your way to headquarters.' She busied herself topping up their cups. Kitty looked across the rim of her cup and gave the other two a quizzical look. They returned theirs with raised eyebrows.

Jo gave a shoulder shrug and stood up.

'Well, I'm done Mrs Smith. Thank you for breakfast – it will keep me going for a month, I think. The eggs were a real treat, thank you. I'll catch up with you two in a minute and then we'll head off,' she said.

Both Kitty and Trix nodded whilst sipping their tea. The only noise they heard after Jo left was Ma Smith humming in the kitchen.

'She's a good stick, isn't she?' Trix asked Kitty and gave a flick of her head towards the kitchen.

Kitty nodded and drained the last of her drink before standing up. 'She is, and I'm glad we made the choice to stay. Right, ready?'

Before they left the room, Jo burst in, puffing for breath. 'You should see what Ma's done.'

The three of them raced upstairs and Kitty stared at the heap of clothes and suitcase blocking the bathroom doorway.

'Good job we don't need a pee!'

'Your bags are in our room, Kitty,' Jo said, 'I think Belle is in for a bit of a shock when she wakes up. Should we wake her? She's going to be late for our arrival sign-in.'

Trix put her finger to her lips and shook her head. She pointed down the stairs with the other hand. Kitty and Jo grinned.

Ma Smith stood at the bottom of the stairs with her hands on her hips. Her flushed face beamed up at them. All three burst out laughing.

'What are you like, Mrs Smith,' Kitty whispered.

'Innocent until proven guilty, so don't look at me with those pretty brown eyes all accusing. I can't abide bad manners.'

Mrs Smith hitched her bosom and straightened her back.

'You three will always be welcome. Come and see me for a cuppa if you ever need a chat or feel homesick. Now get going and don't worry about madam; she's got choices to make in life and one was to put herself above others. Not a good look on anybody in my eyes. No fancy frocks can cover up selfishness. Got everything?'

Walking towards the front door, Ma Smith pulled it open and the fresh air wafted through. The smell of damp morning dew heralding the start of autumn mingled with the smell of toast still lingering inside the house, giving it a homely feel. Memories of leaving her own home for school as a little girl flooded back to Kitty. Today felt much like the start of a new term and a flip of excitement and anticipation rushed through her veins.

'I'm not sure what Belle will be like when she comes to, but I hope she isn't rude to you, Mrs Smith. Here's my shilling, and again, thank you.'

Ma Smith pushed her hands into her pinafore pocket. Her lips sealed in a silent act of determination.

'Put your money away. I'll get my two shillings, don't you fret. Off you go, and good luck to you all.'

Giving a last wave to her as they turned out of the street, Kitty, Trix and Jo strode at a steady speed towards Queen Elizabeth Hospital in Bath Row. Kitty and Jo walked in silence with Trix chatting in her high-pitched voice, her nerves evident, and Kitty sensed out of the three people she'd spent the evening with, Jo would be the one who'd she'd be inclined to lean towards for calm and solid friendship.

## Chapter Five

As they approached the large hospital building, Kitty's nerves fluttered, and she set down her bag for a brief moment to collect her thoughts.

'No turning back now, girl,' Jo said, and gave Kitty a friendly pat on the back.

Kitty gave a frown. 'Aren't you nervous?'

'What of? A bunch of puffed-up men who think the world revolves around them, or the blood and gore?' Jo said with a loud laugh.

'Shhh, one of the doctors will hear you,' whispered Trix.

'Too late. Rudeness will not be tolerated.'

A loud male voice echoed around the large entrance, and all three froze on the spot. Jo was the first to turn around and, to Kitty's surprise, burst out laughing. She dropped her bag and ran towards the tall male approaching them.

'Smithy!' Jo shouted and flung her arms around him.

'Hello Jo, old girl. I promised I'd be here, but if I'd

known you were going to be rude about me and my colleagues, well …'

Jo gave him a gentle punch on the arm. Trix and Kitty stood waiting.

'Do you think it's her man?' Kitty asked.

Trix shook her head.

'She said last night she had a friend from home working here. He's rather good-looking,' Trix said, and giggled behind her hand. Kitty nudged her and gave a low laugh. Jo turned to them both with a grin.

'Girls, meet trouble. My best friend. Gordon Smith, meet Kitty and Trix.'

Gordon gave Kitty a brief nod and she noticed his attention lingered longer on Trix.

'Nice to meet you. I've got to fly, we're busy in theatre. Find me later, Jo.'

As Jo's friend walked away, a woman in uniform approached them.

'Ah, our new recruits. Welcome to the Queen Elizabeth. Only three of you – where's the fourth?'

The woman looked around for their fourth, her voice deep and commanding.

Jo shook her head and gave a left-shoulder shrug, Trix dipped hers, and Kitty felt a warmth flush over her cheeks. An awkward silence followed.

'I take it from your faces and silence there is a problem.'

Kitty was the first to speak.

'I think Belle's been delayed.'

Jo coughed and the woman swung her a shrivelling look.

'I see. Tardiness is not something we condone. Well done for arriving on time. We'll not wait for ...' she glanced at a clipboard in her hand '... I'll assume Belle is short for Annabelle, and we are waiting for a Miss Annabelle Farnsworth.'

Jo stepped forward and held out her hand, but the woman gave a slight eyebrow raise, and their position to this woman was duly noted.

'You are, and I'm Joan Norfolk, this is Kitty Pattison and Trixie Dunn,' Jo said.

'And I am Senior Sister Barker, in charge of new nursing recruits. Our circumstances require extra hands, and you as volunteers are most welcome. As promised, you will receive all basic training offered to our regular recruits. Once through your training you will earn the title nurse. You will address me as Sister or Sister Barker.'

As she spoke, Sister Barker gave them a quick glance and ticked their names against her list with an efficient flick of her wrist.

'Follow me.' Her brusque manner sent flutters of anxiety to Kitty's stomach. She pulled her bag from the floor and fell in line behind Jo, with Trix following at the rear. Each time they passed a nurse in uniform they received a smile. Kitty wondered if it was one of pity. She glanced at a clock on the corridor wall. Eight o'clock and her new career was about to commence. They stepped outside and walked across the yard. Sister Barker pointed out places of importance as they kept pace with her large strides. A breeze rustled leaves across the yard and it amazed Kitty that the sister's cap stayed in place, starched and upright, on her crown of black curls; she guessed it was pinned in place, as it never moved once. Her own soft hair would no doubt present a challenge when she wore hers for the first time. Wild and untamed if not controlled with a full head of rollers, Kitty often cursed the baby-soft mane. Before she'd left home, her neighbour had cut four inches off the length so it could sit on her shoulders or in a neat bun. She thought of the many items of uniform waiting for her to wear, and a shiver of excitement and nervous anticipation ran through her body.

'Your accommodation. Nuffield Nurses' Home. House Sister will show you which section you are in and anything else relevant to your stay with us. Meet me in two hours at the front entrance in full uniform.'

For an hour Kitty unpacked her personal items into cupboards in her room, which overlooked a small courtyard. The room allocated to her was twice the size of her one at home, clean and furnished with her basic needs, with a shared bathroom further along the corridor.

She placed two photographs on the bedside cabinet beside the single bed pushed against the wall – one of her aunt, uncle and Brian, and the other of her with her parents and brother, taken on their last day out together – and a little trinket box which had once belonged to her grandmother, none of which made the room look as cosy as her bedroom at home. Stark walls and plain brown blankets over white sheets starched to a crispness like nothing Kitty had seen before, didn't invite her to lie down and rest. No doubt after a few hectic shifts she'd look at the bed through different eyes.

She heard Jo moving around in her room next door, and Jo obviously had heard her when she knocked on the wall to let her know she was ready to leave for their uniform instruction. Kitty knew she'd found a friend in the down-to-earth girl and was thrilled they were neighbours. Unfortunately, Trix had been allocated a shared room for a temporary period for a week, which set her into an anxious flutter that it might be with Belle, but she settled once she found out it was with a different girl. Jo had offered to change places, but Trix chose to step outside her comfort zone and embrace the new adventure.

The house sister was a short, plump, motherly figure with an infectious laugh, although Kitty was in no doubt that the woman was as strict as she was friendly. She taught them the art of wearing their hair and settling their caps into place with the skill of a well-practised tutor. Back in her room, Kitty spread out her uniform on the bed, and had a quick strip wash using a precious bar of rose-perfumed soap given to her by her aunt as a parting gift. The soft perfume rising from the warm water gave her a moment of homesickness, but Kitty suppressed it before it took hold. She was on a time deadline and moping with regrets was not part of the agenda.

She slid on the dress, pinned the pinafore in place, readjusted her warm stockings, laced her shoes, and tackled her hair and cap with half a packet of hairpins. Eventually, she was satisfied with her reflection. She smiled at the black woollen cape draped around the upright wooden chair in the corner of the room. Lifting it from its resting place she settled it around her shoulders and gave a deep sigh of satisfaction. Giggles outside her door told her Jo and Trix were ready to meet and, with one last glance in the mirror, Kitty stepped out into the corridor.

'Look at us ready to take on the world,' said Trix.

'So long as this cap stays in place, I'll be happy,' replied Jo.

## Chapter Six

At the entrance of the hospital stood another six girls in uniform and Kitty guessed they were the rest of her group. Shy waves and bold greetings were shared, but silence soon fell when Sister Barker appeared on the scene.

'All here? Dare I hope your missing fourth has arrived?'

Sister Barker turned to Kitty, Jo and Trix. All three shook their heads.

'We've not seen her, Sister,' Kitty said.

A deep growl-like sound of disapproval from Sister Barker lingered in the air. All the girls stared at her, waiting for her red face to explode into some form of angry outburst, but instead she turned her attention to her clipboard.

'You will all spend time in classroom three before taking a lunch break of an hour. There is a tour of objects to be made before anything else happens. I warn you now, you will need strong stomachs. If asked to leave the room do not argue; simply do as asked. Remember who is in charge and who has experience in their field. Follow the signs and do so quietly, I—'

'Jo. Kitty! Woo hoo, I'm here at last. Where were you?'

Kitty, Trix and Jo stared at Belle as she flounced through the main entrance. Her heeled shoes clipped out loud, tinny echoes and her suitcase clunked across the tiled floor.

Wide-eyed, Jo looked at Kitty.

'They were here and on time, Miss Farnsworth. Which leads me to ask why you are over two hours late?' Sister Barker said.

Belle tiptoed forward and stood in front of Sister Barker holding out her hand. Realising it was not going to be taken by the nurse, she gave a flick of her hair and shared a forced smile.

'I'd had so little sleep last night. Our B&B was just dreadful. I simply knew I couldn't arrive here in a morning grump. Besides, the landlady was a dreadful bore and muddled my suitcases. Have I missed much? I see you are all in your uniforms,' Belle said and turned to face the group waggling her fingers up and down in front of them. 'Not very flattering, are they? Jo, the size of your hips ...'

Kitty felt sure her jaw trailed the floor as she stared at both Belle and Sister Barker. Two complete opposites. One oblivious to the fact the other had reached boiling point, and Kitty felt certain the woman was about to express more than Belle wanted to hear. However, Sister Barker impressed her with her cool command and firm tone; she'd never have remained so calm faced with Belle.

'Miss Farnsworth. The group were just heading to room three for their first lesson. As you were so tired and enjoyed a nap, it is good to know you will be refreshed and ready to attend along with them. Sadly, there is no time for you to change from your pretty outfit into uniform. Shall we? Oh, I suggest you remove your shoes and carry your bags. We enjoy a quiet environment at the QE, and they are rather noisy – thank you.' Sister Barker watched as an exasperated Belle began removing her shoes.

With a flick of her wrist, she pointed ahead to the group and they fell in line, following her along one corridor and up three flights of stairs.

Belle could be heard huffing and puffing behind them as she struggled barefoot up the steep stairs. Sister Barker opened a door further along a corridor and pointed inside.

'Stand around the edges. I'll be back in a moment. Keep the noise to a minimum; there is a lecture taking place next door.'

The group watched as Belle staggered into the room, bags banging against tables and chairs nearby. She lowered herself into a chair and massaged her feet.

'What is that dreadful smell?' she asked, wrinkling her nose.

'Formaldehyde. A preservative. Get on your feet girl and stand with the rest. I won't ask why you are not in uniform or why you are barefoot, but I will write it on your attendance report.' A tall, wiry man with a moustache wider than his face walked into the room, and Kitty watched his jawline firm with annoyance when Belle tried to argue as to why she should sit and of how she came to not be wearing shoes. He frowned then pointed to Kitty whilst talking to Belle.

'Get up and stand beside this student, and I suggest you remain quiet.'

A reluctant Belle did as instructed just as a young man brought in two large jars and placed them on a table in front of them.

'My name is Dr Blackthorn, and it is my pleasure to introduce you to the collection of items which you may come across during your training.'

Belle leaned forward and peered into the first jar and squealed.

'My God, is that a hand?'

Dr Blackthorn nodded the affirmative and addressed the rest of the group.

'I suggest you take a moment to think about how close you might like to get to the objects you will see today, and at any point you feel sick at the sight, leave the room or take time to consider the poor soul who no longer has the hand on the end of their arm. This is from a female, a bomb blast victim. The other a male's foot from entrapment in a caved-in building. One was amputated and the other blown off. Note each one and the differences you see. My assistant will bring out more specimens and I'd like you to record your observations. Pen and paper are over there. You, hand them out.'

The doctor pointed at Belle. With her mouth open in readiness to object, Belle was given no time to speak.

'Do it. Mouth closed, if you please.'

For the duration of an hour, specimen after specimen was presented to them. Kitty took in the objects with the view that she was there to learn. Others larked about, and three left the room. She, Jo and Trix compared notes, whilst Belle found a seat after the doctor and assistant left the room, declaring she had no intention of looking at body parts in jars. It was not connected to her idea of nursing handsome soldiers back to good health.

'But if we know more about these things, the better understanding we'll have. Besides, they are only here to find the weak-stomached amongst us. Smithy told me. We're going to see worse than this, and this is part of our study session. I bet we'll have grades and targets,' Jo said, and Kitty heard the annoyance in her voice. Belle was becoming a distraction none of them needed.

'Don't be ridiculous. I've not unpacked nor eaten lunch yet – I'm not ready to start studying. Surely, they are obliged to give us a day or so to settle in – do you not think, Jo?'

Jo turned away from her and studied an eyeball in a jar. Trix and Kitty gave each other a semi-smile and continued their observation of a tongue. Without speaking, all three had made their choice. Belle was to be ignored when not engaging or distracting during study periods.

The specimen session finished, and those with the stamina to do so enjoyed lunch in the staff canteen. 'Anyone for a stroll around the area to get our bearings when we've finished? Before it's too dark? I need fresh air after what we've seen today. How I'll manage to eat is beyond me,' Trix said.

'I think that's a great idea, Trix. At least if anything happens tonight,' Kitty pointed to the sky, 'we'll have an inkling of where to go. I think we're expected at the main entrance for evacuation instruction at six, which gives us time.'

Belle left them in a huff, bemoaning the quality of the food, and headed to her room to unpack and rest after the morning's ordeal. She also declared she intended to telephone her mother to send supplies of decent food. Jo tried to explain to Belle that there was nowhere to cook it – and worst of all, no one to cook it for her – and this heightened the uptight anger and indignation in Belle, so Kitty, Jo and Trix took a step back from her company for the rest of the day.

The three friends left the hospital and headed left towards what looked like a large green park. From there they found a small newsagent and a hairdresser. All in all, by the time they returned to their new home, they'd walked a mile, discovering several shops, two halls with bunting and notices of pending dances, and to their joy, a cinema.

'Well done for the suggestion, Trix. I'd have gone back to my room. Now I feel as if I've a place to describe when I write home,' said Kitty, as they stood chatting in the corridor outside her room.

Jo nodded her agreement.

'Trix is my hero too – a hairdresser to keep this messy crop in order!'

Jo wore her hair short, almost masculine in style, and Kitty felt it would drive her crazy trying to set a cap on such short hair, but Jo found a way with her hairgrips, and Kitty swore she'd never have the patience.

A voice called out to them, and unconsciously they all sighed and made a face as Belle headed their way. She wore her uniform and had brushed her hair to her shoulders with her cap sitting to one side in an attempt to look fashionable – she looked more glamorous than ever. Kitty stared at Belle's feet. Dainty cream ballerina-style slippers completed the outfit.

'Where are your shoes?' she asked.

All four looked at Belle's feet. She shuffled them around and lifted them in admiration.

'I cannot possibly wear those heavy old things Mummy purchased. Gracious, I'd have blisters with them on my feet. I move much faster in these.'

With a grump of disapproval, Jo tapped her watch. 'Time to get changed ourselves.'

Belle walked away leaving Trix and Kitty watching, staring at Belle's feet.

'She'll never get away with it,' Trix said.

'She'll have a damn good try. We'd better get a move on and get ourselves ready. We don't want Sister Barker on our case,' Kitty replied.

After changing and regrouping, the three friends walked into the main hallway of the hospital, where they saw their group, and headed towards it. Sister Barker called from behind them before they joined the others.

'Neat and tidy, that's what I like to see, ladies.'

Kitty and Trix turned around. Kitty felt her face flush with embarrassment at being praised.

'Thank you, Sister,' she said.

'Yes, I, um, thank you, um, Sister Barker,' a flustered Trix replied.

'Confidence girls. Confidence. Build upon it and you will go far.'

They watched as she swept past them and greeted the rest, instructing them to form a line, and to do so every time they were together during instruction sessions. Kitty nudged Trix.

'I can't wait for when she spots Belle's shoes!' She pointed to Belle at the end of the row.

They stood patiently as Sister Barker adjusted caps or aprons or offered praise where it was due. Kitty, Jo and Trix craned their necks and watched as Sister Barker walked the line-up, stopping in front of a smiling Belle.

'A novel way to wear one's cap, with a tilt. Interesting, Miss Farnsworth – and the shoes – such dainty embroidered flowers.'

Belle lifted her feet for more admiration.

'They are so comfortable, Sister. You would benefit from a pair. They might help hold off bunions – unless of course you already suffer, in which case they would relieve the pressure.'

A loud gasp filtered along the row. Sister Barker leaned her head to one side as if considering Belle's words.

'You are considerate. A pair of dainty shoes for my weary feet will, at some point in my life, become my prime focus, Miss Farnsworth. In the meantime, I think I will concentrate upon yours.'

A giggle snickered inside of Kitty as she heard the heavy sarcasm in their mentor's voice. A bubble of anger brewed too, for the way Belle never took anything seriously.

'Miss Pattison.'

Sister Barker's voice was firm and loud as she called out to Kitty.

'Sister?' she asked.

'Escort your colleague back to her quarters and explain to her the reason why she is to scrub the main bathroom clean before joining us at 7.30 for a fire-at-night instruction from another colleague of mine. You may use the words, rules, regulations, and the point of a uniform.'

Kitty's heart sank – why Sister Barker had chosen her was beyond her. Time with a whining Belle was a waste as far as she was concerned, but she had a feeling this was a character-building exercise for both of them and it was probably not in her best interest to refuse.

'I will do my best, Sister.'

Belle swung her a look and Kitty's stomach flipped with nerves. Not wanting to delay the others heading to their next instruction session, she turned to Belle and indicated they should leave.

'There's a quick route to our rooms, Belle. It's this way,' she said.

Belle's back straightened and Kitty's breath caught in her throat. She'd seen the action from the girl before, and it often happened when she prepared herself to launch into a tirade of irritated objections. Kitty swiftly shook her head to warn her not to say a word, but it was in vain. Belle stepped out of the line and stood with her hands on her hips facing Sister Barker. The once jauntily perched cap now jiggled around on its soft bed of large curls, and Belle's cheeks needed no rouge to give them a hearty cherry-red glow. The girl was furious and not holding back on her anger as she pointed towards Kitty.

'I'll not be escorted by *her* or told by *her* to scrub bathrooms. I'm afraid I do not undertake menial tasks. I'm here to learn to nurse – Mother's wishes and all that.'

The indignant tone was thrown out with shrillness in her voice, and Belle made a dramatic swish of her cape once she'd had her say. The air became thick with anticipation. Feet shuffled and heads craned around the line to get a better view of what was about to happen.

'Ah, I understand what you are saying. I think it is my duty to help you,' Sister Barker said. She turned back to speak to Kitty, who waited with dread to hear what the woman's next set of instructions were.

'Miss Pattison, a change of plans. Please, join the others and take yourselves to the canteen. Have a short break, enjoy a cup of tea and I'll rejoin you once I've helped Miss Farnsworth select her wardrobe for this evening.'

Her voice was calm and in control as if she'd expected the reaction. Kitty suspected she'd come across this type of spoilt recruit before and she did not envy Belle at all for the attention she'd gained. The girl was naïve if she thought she'd become the centre of Sister Barker's universe.

The topic of conversation in the canteen became a bet on whether Belle returned with her hair pinned in place and her uniform complete, versus Sister Barker enforcing the bathroom cleaning instruction.

Introductions were made and the group dynamic altered. Nine women were disgusted by the behaviour of one and vowed to ensure she did not let the side down again. All those who remained and hadn't requested to leave after the specimen session – designed to weed out the weak-stomached amongst them – were united in wanting to do their bit, and were frustrated by Belle holding up the evening-fire instruction.

The whooshing sound of the canteen door opening and Sister Barker holding it open stopped all chatter and the group automatically formed a line. The group watched as Belle entered carrying a bucket in one hand and a mop in the other. Her face was lipstick free, her hair was bound in a blue turban scarf, and she wore blue overalls that were far too big for her. On her feet were her sturdy shoes, and her face was deadpan, emotion free. Kitty thought her eyes looked red but didn't stare long enough to confirm her thoughts.

No one said a word as Belle walked across the room and stood at the end of their line.

'An agreement has been reached between Miss Farnsworth and me that she either leaves or learns a few cleaning basics before embarking on caring for the injured. To her credit, Miss Farnsworth has agreed a trial period. Now, enough of the dramatics and onto the important task of ensuring patients are safe if we are under attack.'

Led by Sister Barker and Jo, the group left the canteen. Belle remained at the back of the group and carried her mop and bucket in silence. Once the fire officer finished his drill they were dismissed, and they were relieved of instruction for the day.

Jo tapped Kitty's arm and beckoned her away from the crowd walking back to their rooms.

'I've got to find out what old Barker said to her!'

Kitty shrugged.

'I bet Sister gave her hell in a quiet way – she's very controlled and in command. Belle deserves to be flagged up. What a selfish person, to worry about what she looks like.'

Trix exhaled in a huff.

'I'm fed up with her. The more she creates, the more attention she will bring to us. Just because we lodged together for one night, doesn't mean I want to become her friend. I see only trouble ahead with that one. What a snob!'

'We need to head back and rest up for tomorrow. Six o'clock breakfast. I suggest the three of us leave her to make new friends – there's bound to be someone who'll tolerate her snobbery, and we'll stick together, study together and get to where we want to be. I'm not losing my reputation to her, that's for sure,' Jo said.

Her tone of voice meant business and Kitty understood her grievance. She wanted to train without conflict of any kind. Belle had best behave or lead a lonely life. Kitty had no intention of pandering to her; the girl needed to learn about life and caring for the injured if she was to be of any use to the Red Cross.

'I think she should go home and make jam,' Trix said, and marched off in the direction of their living quarters.

Jo linked arms with Kitty. 'Come on, friend, let's face the foe together. She's bound to be waiting to declare her hardship to us. I think she's one we'll not escape tonight, but this is the last time I'm listening to her bleating on.'

---

## Chapter Seven

Gold-tinged leaves fell around Kitty's feet as she walked through the park. It was a peaceful walk despite the cool air and fresh wind. Kitty strode through the leaves across the damp grass. She couldn't believe how many weeks had passed since she'd arrived for training at Queen Elizabeth, and it had not been an easy time for some. They'd made it through smallpox and measles alerts, bombings and intense classroom studies.

Their lessons were not easy, but all three had absorbed what they could and helped each other when required. Kitty had held the sick in her arms, assisted medical staff by cleaning up after major bleeds, comforted relatives, and worked extended shifts until someone realised she'd been there far too many hours. Her heart bled, lifted with joy, and pounded with fear so often that Kitty convinced herself it would give up on her one day. Under the covers at bedtime, she sobbed for the dead. During the night shift she kept busy to stop thinking about air raids and constantly reading the exit regime.

She, Jo and Trix had formed a tight friendship, with Belle flitting in and out with her woes and troubles on occasion. The three friends had learned to listen, tut in the right places, and leave Belle to find something else to cry home about. All Kitty's free time was spent in the company of Jo and Trix – although, she and Jo noticed that Trix's time with them became less and less as she spent more time with Smithy.

Kitty's mood was a mixed one as she headed back towards the hospital. Today was final assessment results and allocation notice. Trix had already declared her desire to find a place on the children's unit, but Jo and Kitty had expressed an interest in the more critical areas of emergency admissions and theatre. They'd both added their names to the voluntary rescue team, and Trix had opted for fire watch. Belle had chosen to apply for after-care clinics.

'Ready?' Kitty asked and linked her arm through Jo's.

'As I'll ever be. That last assessment was a tough one. I'm sure I handed a scalpel instead of forceps when Smithy called for them.'

'Talking of Smithy, Trix is meeting him before he goes on duty and said she'd meet us this evening after results. I've also got news of a party for us all from the hairdresser across the park.'

'Sounds fun. Best get going before our nerves get the better of us,' Jo said.

The pair headed towards Matron's office, where they would learn of their fate. Matron was a stern figure of a woman, but a fair one. She'd made it clear to Belle that she was to put in more effort, and praised Trix for her ability to calm the most distressed child they'd encountered. Jo and Kitty were often praised by her for their courage in theatre or facing the worst traumas the war presented them with, and both admired the woman for running a tight ship.

The group had reduced in numbers and was now only six. There were days when Kitty climbed out of bed and wondered if she'd done the right thing. Bone-weary from scrubbing floors, cleaning equipment, studying and putting into practice the lessons taught to them, she wondered if she was cut out for the emotional and physical pull of the job. She'd seen injuries that turned her stomach, and on days when the enemy dropped heavy loads of explosives on the city and surrounding areas, Kitty drew on an inner strength she never knew she had by pushing herself forwards to assist wherever possible. She and Jo had little time to themselves and when they did, they slept soundly for hours. Today, she'd enjoyed being pampered at the hairdresser, and found herself agreeing to bring friends along to a fundraising dance. After their assessment results, she'd put it to the others. A night out would do them good. First, she had to face Matron and find out whether she'd passed enough assessments to move on to the next stage of training.

'Katherine Pattison.'

Kitty's nerves kicked in when her name was called to enter the office. Inside the room a clock ticked and showed 10.30. Matron insisted upon punctuality, and few failed her.

'Good morning, Matron.'

Kitty stood upright, feet together, wearing a nervous smile.

'Morning, Pattison.'

Matron picked up a brown envelope and opened it without looking up at Kitty. With a slow nod and a pouting of her lips as she studied the assessment results, Matron finally raised her head and smiled at Kitty.

'Well done. Full marks on all basic assessments. Keep this up and you will climb your way into a nursing role to be envied in a few years. You have a bright future ahead of you.'

Kitty let out a soft sigh and returned the smile.

'Really? You mean I can continue training?' she said.

Matron folded her arms and leaned forward on her desk. Her usual stern face softened into a partial smile.

'From today you will have the title Nurse in front of your surname and will work alongside a qualified team on the male surgical ward. Listen and learn, and you will do well. We also have an additional placement to offer you within the emergency team. It is a new set-up due to the strains on our resources.'

Matron pointed to the chair nearest the desk and indicated for Kitty to sit.

'You've proved you've the three S's required for the job: stomach, speed and sensitivity. Think about it and let me know your answer no later than four o'clock tomorrow. You will have the added pressure of ensuring you complete your proficiency tests, so long nights or extra shifts might take their toll. However, you are a wise enough young woman who is suited to this role.'

Kitty sat in a daze. The emergency team was a busy hands-on unit and worked with the ambulance and recovery teams. She had a lot of respect for the front-line staff and deep down her gut and heart told her it was the job for her. When her cousin had died, Kitty's family had learned that he'd needed immediate help, and although he'd passed away, she wanted to pay forward the gift of care the medical team had given to Brian.

'I can give my answer now. It's yes please. I'd be honoured to work with the emergency team. I won't let you down. Thank you for putting your trust in me.'

Matron raised one eyebrow and her face returned to its serious state. She stood up and put out her hand for Kitty to shake.

'Don't make promises, Nurse Pattison. Simply do your best, that is all we ask. It is a dangerous world out there, so keep calm and watch the qualified staff. Anticipate their needs and never put yourself in a position which will endanger either them or you. Good luck.'

Outside the room, Kitty looked over at Jo. For the first time since they'd met, Jo looked pensive, and Kitty wondered how much bravado her friend showed in public to protect her feelings. She walked over to her and sat down on the seat beside her, and Jo gave a weak smile.

'All right, kiddo?' she asked.

Kitty smiled. 'Yes, I get to stay here on male surgical and I've a placement on the new emergency team! Nurse Pattison reporting for duty.'

'That's wonderful news – oh, they've called my name. Stay here and we'll compare notes when I come out.'

'You'll be fine – break a leg,' Kitty said, and laughed.

Jo gave a wag of her finger as she walked a few steps backwards, still facing Kitty.

'Not good advice, nurse.'

She turned around and entered Matron's office. For what seemed like an hour, but in reality was ten minutes, Kitty waited for her friend.

Jo reappeared with a serious face and Kitty's stomach turned over. Her own excitement and achievements forgotten, she rushed to greet her friend.

'How did it go? Why the long face?'

Jo gave a body shake.

'Shock. I think.'

Kitty stared into her face. 'Come on Jo, what's going on?'

Putting her arm on Jo's shoulder, Kitty gave her a little shake.

'I'm in shock. I passed all my assessments; I stay! I'm going to work on women's surgical, how about that?'

## Chapter Eight

'Stop whingeing. You promised to come tonight. Smithy and Trix have managed a night off together and although I'm exhausted, I think it's the right thing to do.'

Kitty paced up and down in front of Jo.

'But *dancing*,' Jo said and pulled a face of disapproval.

'You don't have to dance, just smile and look as if you want to be there. I rarely got the opportunity to go to dances at home. Keep me company – please?'

Kitty put her hands together in a pleading position, and Jo tapped them down.

'An hour. I'll come for an hour.'

'Great, thank you!'

Jo lifted an eyebrow. 'You won't be thanking me when your feet ache in those shoes, your dress is damp, and mascara is running down your face thanks to the heavy drizzle out there.'

Kitty didn't respond. She'd learned Jo would keep coming up with reasons not to go to the dance, and Kitty was grateful she'd get an hour to unwind with her friend, so didn't push her luck with any more pleading.

Jo was not wrong about the walk and the weather; both were uncomfortable, and Kitty felt like a damp mess when she arrived at the community hall.

'Don't you just love it when I'm right?' Jo said and nudged Kitty in the ribs.

Pulling off her coat and fluffing up her hair, Kitty chose to ignore the teasing. The warmth of the hall and the cheerful music was to be enjoyed, and her friend would not spoil her happiness. Back home it was rare for her to enjoy a dance without her aunt and uncle present, watching her every move and tutting if she dared to dance to the latest tunes, making her skirt swing and twirl, so tonight she intended to make the most of it.

'Come on grumpy guts, let's get a drink and find a table.'

Jo laughed.

'Trix is waving like a madwoman over there, so we'd best go join her and Smithy.'

Weaving their way across the dance floor to the far side of the room, Kitty bumped hard into a couple dancing.

'I'm so sorry,' she said.

'No harm done,' the male of the pair said, and gave her a friendly smile. Kitty's stomach flipped with pleasure. His hazel-brown eyes and dark-brown hair were pleasing features shining from an extremely handsome face. Their eyes locked and neither moved. Inside Kitty's chest a double-beat and deepened breathing forced her to shake herself from the moment, unsure what had happened. How could a stranger make her heart race and make her want to push the other girl aside so Kitty could dance with him? This was a new sensation, not just a brief glance at a man who had caught her eye. They'd connected in some way. Preventing her mind from taking the odd situation into a fantasy, Kitty stepped backwards, breaking the stare.

'Thanks,' Kitty said with a shy smile, and with reluctance, she made her way to Jo, Trix and Smithy.

Her heart still pounded with what she assumed was excitement.

'Flirting with the foreigners, eh?' Smithy said with a teasing wink.

'Stop it. I was not flirting. We bumped into each other. What do you mean by foreigners anyway?' Kitty questioned, feeling her cheeks flush warm. She had not flirted with intention, but had enjoyed the moment with a handsome man staring into her eyes. She looked across the room at him laughing and chatting with a group of other men and an extremely animated young woman intent on gaining flattery and attention.

Jo leaned across the table. 'I thought some of the uniforms looked different. But Kitty's man wasn't in uniform, so what's foreign about him?' she asked.

'I thought that too,' said Kitty.

Jo gave a sarcastic laugh.

'Really? You were looking at the uniforms and not at the man in civvies?'

'Yes, the uniforms the others are wearing look different. What's different about it, Smithy?' Kitty asked, ignoring Jo's jibe, and attempting to take the attention away from the man who had made her skin tingle with pleasure just by looking into his eyes.

Smithy grinned at Kitty.

'Some are Canadian medics, and the chappy whose attention you caught is one of the civilian Canadian doctors who are working alongside me. There's around six in the hospital. They were here for exchange medical training before the war broke out, and they've all qualified. We've just finished our speciality. His is emergency medicine, and damn good he is at it, too.'

Kitty did her best to look indifferent but in reality, she wanted to learn more about the handsome Canadian. She twiddled a strand of hair and did her best not to keep looking at him across the room.

'Will they remain in England?' she asked.

Smithy shrugged his shoulders.

'I'm not sure. I know four will be leaving Birmingham in the week, but two of them are staying. The short one over there, he's due to leave and train in skin-graft surgery.' Smithy indicated with a lift of his chin towards the man standing beside the one Kitty was trying to avoid staring at; now she had little choice but to look his way. As she gave a brief glance, she saw him looking in her direction and he gave her a beaming smile. Kitty pretended not to see him and made a play of looking around the room at anything and anybody. Her cheeks burned and she was grateful for the dimmed lights, for they probably glowed enough to attract the enemy's attention. She returned to the conversation.

'That's fascinating,' Jo said.

'Mmm, I'm not so sure I'd stomach seeing that kind of surgery, but it is wonderful for the patients when so many new treatments are available,' Kitty said, and Trix agreed.

For half an hour they watched people jiving and swinging each other around the room. Kitty's feet itched with wanting to dance; no matter how hard she tried she could not stop them from tapping to the beat. She wanted to rush across the room and beg the Canadian to twirl her around just as he did with a few other girls lucky enough to enjoy his company.

'For goodness' sake, Kitty. Jiggle or dance, but don't do both. This table has two short legs and wobbles without encouragement from you,' Jo said.

'But I just want to dance. Don't you? Doesn't the music get inside and take over, 'cos it does me, and I can't stop it making me feel happy.'

Jo jumped to her feet and pulled Kitty to hers.

'Well, you give me little choice but to show you how this grumpy guts can move.'

With much laughter, they joined the other dancers on the floor filled with bodies performing athletic moves.

'I didn't know you could swing so well, Jo!' Kitty said as they sat breathless at the table.

Jo took a long drink, and as she placed her glass on the table she winked. 'There's a lot you don't know about me, Kitty Pattison. Something I've learned about you though is that you are a good friend, and we make a great team on the dance floor. Thanks to you, I now realise coming out for the evening was a good thing.'

Kitty raised her own glass and smiled.

'I've a feeling we'll be friends for ever, Jo. Here's to us.'

Smithy and Trix rushed back to the table giggling and holding hands. Happiness shone from both their faces. Kitty envied their ability to fall in love so easily, and looked around the room at others holding each other close, enjoying the last few notes of the evening or arguing over flirtatious glances with the opposite sex. The war had brought out the best and worst in couples. Girls gave themselves to eager young men far too soon, and others married for life – however long the enemy allowed it to be. Tonight, a gathering of people out to enjoy themselves would end with the inevitable fist fights, marriage proposals, and break-ups. All the time she looked around, Kitty looked out for one man and was secretly pleased to see the handsome Canadian wasn't on the dance floor.

As the last note died off into the background, another shrill sound reverberated around them and the crowd rushed towards the door.

'Sirens!' Jo called out and the four friends moved to the end of the crush to leave for the shelter.

'Drat. They're here; overhead!' Smithy said.

Kitty and Jo glanced around.

'Pull tables together and stack a couple on top. Quick!' Jo shouted above the screams of those cramming the doorway. She, Trix and Smithy pulled at tables whilst Kitty clambered onto one and shouted to the leaving crowd. If she didn't stop the panic, someone would be crushed to death.

'Make shelters inside. Everybody, please listen and turn

around. There's not enough time to get to the shelter. We'll have to stay here. Protect yourselves!'

To their relief, the crowd listened and moved into action, guided by Smithy and Kitty, whilst Trix and Jo scouted around for items to help make the floor more comfortable to sit on. They all worked as a team and soon the blacked-out room became calm and organised whilst the world outside the doors became chaotic and frightening. A member of the band pulled out a pair of spoons and tapped out a tune, another started singing, and those sheltering beneath the tables joined in, all drowning out the noise from enemy planes thundering above their heads.

Trix huddled up to Smithy, and Kitty, along with Jo, sat with three men who'd helped them with stacking tables.

'You girls really took control there. Impressive,' one said.

'I think we surprised ourselves, right Kitty?' Jo said, and gave Kitty a shoulder nudge. Unfortunately for Kitty, the nudge was a firm one, and Kitty, although seated on the floor, fell sideways onto the man she'd previously bumped into on the dance floor.

'Whoops. Sorry. Again,' she said.

'It's becoming a habit. I think I'd better move along – or will I be safer outside?' he said, and gave a loud laugh.

Hitching herself upright, Kitty thanked the semi-darkness for hiding her yet again burning cheeks.

'Listen! They've gone. It's the all-clear,' she said and leaned her head to one side. To her embarrassment it touched the man's shoulder, and she felt his hand brush against her cheek. Flustered, she moved away and was grateful to hear the room fill with excited voices and clapping as others extracted themselves from their safe zones.

'Time to go,' she said, and followed as Jo crawled out from under the table.

'Not the most dignified exit, Jo,' Kitty said, and laughed.

'Not a bad view from where we're sitting,' said one of the men behind her.

Scrabbling to their feet and rearranging their dresses, Kitty and Jo waited for the men to come out from the makeshift shelter, to help dismantle it and push the tables to one side.

Kitty stood with her hands on her hips and challenged them when the three men appeared.

'Who's the cheeky one?' she asked with a mimicking voice of a sergeant major.

The man she'd lurched into earlier stepped forward.

'Guilty as charged, ma'am,' he said, and mock saluted her and Jo.

'Fool,' Kitty said, and gave him a friendly punch on the shoulder.

'We'd better get these tables and chairs back in order,' Jo said.

As they piled the last of the chairs against the wall, the main door opened and two air wardens entered.

'All clear. It's a mess out there and we need help. Civvies, follow Ernie here, and anyone with medical knowledge, please follow me,' one called into the room.

With no hesitation, Kitty, Jo, Trix and Smithy ran towards them.

'I'm a doctor at the hospital and these are trainee nurses. How can we help?'

'Three more to help here,' one of the Canadian team said.

Kitty turned to see the concern on their faces and gave them a small smile.

Stepping outside, the scene before them was not one Kitty expected at all. The houses surrounding the community hall were badly damaged, with a row of terraced cottages in flames. Other properties lay in mangled heaps of brick and metal, with the personal contents of the homes flung around the area. The incredible sight of one house between two others razed to the ground made her realise the randomness of war.

People screamed and cried; others stood unable to move with shock. The earlier rain clouds had given way to a clear sky.

'A pilot's dream up there,' one of the firefighters said and pointed to the navy sky.

'Let's hope they don't return,' Trix said, and Kitty placed a comforting arm on her friend's shoulder.

Smithy turned to the people still inside the hall.

'Put the urns on, make tea, and we'll send the walking wounded to you. We'll do our bit out here.'

A mumble of agreements went around the room and before she knew it, Kitty was grabbed by the arm and pulled towards an ambulance arriving at the scene.

The doctor holding her arm turned her to face him.

'As we've literally been forced into meeting in one way

or another tonight, we'd better introduce ourselves. I'm Michael McCarthy. Doctor.'

'I'm Kitty Pattison, trainee nurse with the Red Cross at Queen Elizabeth hospital.'

Michael McCarthy grinned. 'Same hospital. Nice to meet you, Kitty. As I see it, we make a good team and you proved to be level-headed earlier on. I need someone to remain calm and help. Let's grab a medical kit and see what we can do. Agreed?'

Without waiting for a response from Kitty, Michael grabbed her by the hand. For a second or two, their eyes locked again, and Kitty's heart flipped with pleasure inside her chest. His firm touch startled her by the way it sent rippling shivers around her body, and she was more than happy to keep the contact. She gave a gentle squeeze of his hand.

'Yes, I'm ready,' she said, and surprised herself by sounding relatively calm.

'Come on, let's get kitted out,' Michael said, and they ran to the back of the ambulance.

Both sought out what they needed and together headed towards a bombed-out house Michael pointed out might be a good place to start.

## Chapter Nine

'Careful, you two. We haven't checked for gas leaks yet,' a member of the rescue team called out to them. Michael raised his hand in acknowledgement.

'Here, let me help you.' Michael took Kitty's hand again and helped her over loose bricks. His touch thrilled her, and the pleasurable waves of close contact with him shimmied through her veins until her skin tingled. What was it with this man? She'd held male patients' hands before and never had the same reaction.

Treading carefully in her heeled shoes, Kitty had a fleeting moment of concern.

'I've only had basic training for a few weeks. I might be more of a hindrance than any help to you and I'm wor—'

A whimper caught their attention and Michael cocked his head to one side and listened. He pointed to their right where a mound of rubble and wood had caved in.

'Listen. Hear that?' he asked.

Kitty took a step closer towards where he pointed.

Smoke spiralled from a small gap where a warming fire had once comforted the family now buried beneath the bricks.

'Help. Help me. My children. Help.'

A woman's voice filtered from somewhere below them and Michael wasted no time getting close to where she lay.

'I'm a doctor. Are you injured?' he called down through the cavity. Kitty heard his voice, calm and controlled. Taking a deep breath to reduce her rapid heartbeat, she felt her way amidst the raging firelit shadows and joined him. Someone needed help and calm, not a flustered girl panicking about making an impression on a doctor. Kitty became aware she had to become more than just a practising nurse; this was the role she'd agreed to commit to, the moment she took Michael's hand. He hadn't taken it to romance her under the stars, he had taken it because he wanted support, and now was the moment Kitty had to decide whether to prove herself capable or to go and help back at the hall or hospital.

'What can I do?' she asked. Aware she was breathless, she inhaled and exhaled as she waited for his instruction.

'Talk to her. I'll go and get a few muscles to move this lot,' Michael said, and pointed to the rubble.

Alone in the dark, Kitty listened for sounds of life. She crouched low and tried to see through the darkness.

'Hello? Are you still awake?' she called into the gap through which Michael had spoken to the woman.

'Help us. My baby. I can't find my baby. My children. Ow, the pain. Please, find my family.'

Kitty's heart lurched. A baby not with its mother would surely cry.

'How old is baby?' she asked.

'Ten weeks. I can't move. I can't hear her. Help me.'

The distress in the woman's voice rose, and Kitty made shushing sounds.

'My colleague has gone for help. We'll have you out in no time. How many of you were in the house? Which room were you in?'

'Kitchen. I'm in the kitchen. My children were in their bedroom. Three children. Five, three, and the baby. My mother was in her room, the small one at the back.'

Kitty took in the information. 'One bedroom at the front, one at the back and the kitchen. Right. Oh, is the kitchen at the front of the property or the back?'

No reply came.

'Hello? Is the kitchen at the front or the back? What's your name? Tell me all the names. Hello?'

A muffled moan of pain came from the woman.

'The back. I'm Maureen. Mum's Mary. John. Susie. Baby Daphne.'

Kitty eased herself onto a stable mound of bricks and leaned across to where the voice came from. 'Maureen. We'll have you out soon. Stay calm. Try not to fall asleep. Listen for your children. Guide me if you hear them. Did you hear that? Listen, I think I can hear a little voice. It could be one of yours; it sounds close,' she said.

'It's John. We call him Johnny.'

Kitty strained to hear the woman, whose voice grew weaker. She pulled her handkerchief from her coat pocket and laid it over a brick, placing another on the corner. A marker to find the woman now in place meant she could move and help the children.

'Johnny? Johnny? Can you hear me?' she called out above the noise of others shouting names and the injured screaming out for help.

'Mummy! Mummy where are you? I'm scared, Mummy; Mummy I'm scared.'

The voice whispered out into the night to the right of Kitty and further to the front of the street. Front bedroom. Kitty made her way crab-like towards his voice. Nausea threatened to prevent her from moving any further when she heard more cries and screams from a hole beneath her. The moans from others experiencing the end of life in pain and agony, and there was nothing she could do to help them without the support of Michael or a rescue team. She refocused her mind and knew what she could do, and that was to save a little boy. An inner surge of energy helped her block out the other noises. There was only one voice she wanted to hear.

'Keep talking to me, Johnny. My name is Kitty. I am a nurse and I've just spoken with your mummy. She can't get to you right now but has asked me to help you. Is your sister with you? Is Susie there?' Kitty said, and kept her voice soft and calm.

'She's under the cot. She's under the baby. We can't get out. I want Mummy!'

Johnny's voice grew loud and frantic, but what concerned Kitty more was that she heard nothing from the baby or little girl. She reached where the boy's sobs echoed out and she started lifting bricks away, each movement slow and deliberate as she placed them into a heap behind her, hoping it was not a hindrance for anyone else buried beneath. A noise below made her stop, and Johnny's sobs had increased into a wail and full-blown scream.

'Don't panic. It's Kitty. I'm moving the bricks to get you out, Johnny. Don't look up as the dust will get in your eyes. Tell your sister,' she instructed in a loud, firm voice in the hope of bringing him to a calmer state.

'Susie, close your eyes. Mummy's coming. Her friend is helping us; she has a funny voice.'

Kitty smiled to herself. Even in the darkest moment of his life, a little lad had spotted her accent.

'Clever lad. I'm from Essex, another county not country. I'll help you, little man. I'm a southerner, which is why I sound different. When you get out of here, we'll look at a map and I'll show you where I'm from. Right now, I live here, in Birmingham, at the Queen Elizabeth hospital. I'm here to help. Be brave and remember to keep your eyes closed. Here goes.'

Kitty continued chatting as she moved the bricks when, to her relief, Michael and four other men returned.

'We're back. What have you found?' Michael asked and placed his hand on her shoulder, giving it a gentle squeeze. Kitty had no objections to another touch from him; it was both comforting and reassuring, with the added flash of pleasure once again.

'I laid my white handkerchief where Maureen is buried below. She's an adult female, getting weaker by the minute by the sounds of her voice. She's in what was the kitchen. Where I am is the front bedroom. Two little ones and a baby are underneath. Somewhere is a back bedroom, and I'm guessing that way,' Kitty pointed to the right of what was the kitchen area, 'Maureen said her mum Mary was in bed. I've not made it over there yet.'

Michael settled down beside her and Kitty leaned into him and whispered. 'I've only heard Maureen and Johnny's voices. The three-year-old, baby and grandmother are quiet – I'm worried they—'

Johnny's distressed wail stopped Kitty in her tracks. She hoped he hadn't heard her speak about his family. Before he had the chance to ask questions, she spoke to him slowly and calmly.

'Johnny, don't cry, you are safe now. My friend Michael has arrived with his friends. Michael is a doctor, and he comes from another country, so his voice has a different accent as well. It's a friendly country called Canada. Dr Michael is here to help me get you out. Be brave. Close your eyes and be brave.'

As each word fell from her mouth, Kitty adapted it to her own mind. Open your eyes, be brave.

# Chapter Ten

*Queen Elizabeth Hospital*
*Birmingham*
*24th November 1940*

*Dearest Uncle and Lil,*

*I hope this letter finds you well. I miss you both but want you to know I am still fine and dandy here in Birmingham, although some days I could do with a replacement set of feet and legs – they are so sore and tired. The miles I walk around this hospital is nobody's business!*

*The aftermath of the bombing raids is painful to witness. Poor Birmingham is a large target for the enemy. There is no day where we do not fill the unit with injured patients from the factories. Inexperience in factory work is the problem for many of the workers, but bless them, they want to do their bit and battle on for England. Some of the* injuries are life-changing and so sad to witness. Some days I struggle but I've got good friends in Jo and Trix. Not that we see Trix as often as we once did as she is in love with Smithy, the English doctor I told you about in my last letter.

Our Canadian colleagues are still here and the doctor I helped in the night raid I told you about, Michael McCarthy, is to lead the emergency team I am part of now. We work as normal in the emergency department but drop everything if called to a disaster. The unit is covered well and when we leave it ticks along. We had to rescue someone from a cellar where freezing cold water was a problem. I was the smallest in the group and had to slide through a narrow gap – good job I'd skipped pudding! The poor man was blue around the lips and I don't think mine were the right shade of pink when we got out, either. Don't be afraid for me though, every member of the team watches my every move. I've learned so much and have no regrets in saying yes to joining both the Red Cross and the emergency crew.

I am not sure whether you will hear this on the news but just in case, to put your mind at rest, these are the facts. Sadly, the medical block behind us was hit and we had to scramble to it, with a young chap climbing up and saving the roof on his own. A proper hero, I can tell you! Sadly, yesterday the Royal Orthopaedic Hospital was hit, and news filtered through to us that nursing staff were killed. It brought sadness to the home and we tightened our *resolve to keep supporting those who are fighting for us. I do it in Brian's name.*

*Belle, the posh one I told you about, well, she lives in a fantasy world and I swear she will give Sister Barker a heart attack one day. She didn't pass her last two practical assessments and must sit them again next week. She turned up wearing postbox-red nail varnish for one of them! She is so vain. However, I have a feeling she will be back at home for Christmas. She harps on about the game shoot her father holds and to be honest with you, she is rather annoying and won't be missed very much apart from the entertainment factor. You know me, I will listen to anyone about anything, but snobbery talk I cannot deal with – especially from someone more worried about herself than the important job she's chosen to do; it's not as if we were forced to join. We had other options.*

*I'll write again soon, and as soon as I have a decent run of leave, I'll come home for a visit.*

*Stay safe and send my love as always.*

*Your loving niece,*
*Kitty x*

Almost overnight, a deep sadness had fallen over the staff, especially in their home since the news of nurses losing their lives, and Kitty felt a reluctance to join other residents in the common room for fear of losing what control she had over her emotions. Normally, she'd be happy to play a game of table tennis, sit and embroider, or update an old outfit whilst listening to someone read from a book or listen to the war news updates on the radio, but today she wanted to be outside despite the cold, damp weather. She eased the letter to her aunt and uncle into the envelope and wrote their name and address across the front, grateful she was her and not them; it must be frightening to have a child so far away and under such dreadful circumstances.

Making up her mind to slip away unnoticed, Kitty chose to spend two hours to herself and then rest up in the afternoon in readiness for night duty. It was not her favourite shift, but due to a rota alteration she had a four-day stretch with one off before she went back to day duty. Jo was on opposite shifts, Trix was home on leave for a week, which left Belle, and she'd made it quite clear she did not enjoy seeing her name on the night duty rotation. It meant Belle would be a grumpy companion should they meet, and for Kitty, time with Belle was not something she felt she could endure during nights.

She slipped out into the corridor and just made it to the end when a familiar voice called out her name. Kitty's heart sank. Belle must have been listening at her door for someone to walk past, she'd acted with such speed. Kitty inhaled and composed the irritation she knew was etched across her face and turned around.

'Belle. Hello.'

'Are you off somewhere? I'll join you,' Belle said.

Kitty pulled her letter from her pocket and waved it at

Belle. 'Nothing exciting, posting a letter home. I'll catch you later.'

Before she'd reached the front door, Belle was beside her in a navy coat with a red scarf, gloves, and shoes. On her head she wore a black cloche beret with a red flower to one side. Kitty's first thought was that it was over-kill for a walk to the postbox.

'I'll walk with you. I need some air. How are you? I haven't seen you for a few days – are you avoiding me?' Belle said and gave a high-pitched giggle.

Unable to speak for fear of asking Belle to disappear and leave her in peace, Kitty simply shook her head. Her peaceful, calming walk became a chore as she listened to Belle complain about and ridicule their establishment, the food they ate, their colleagues and patients. Kitty walked in silence only half listening, grunting an agreement when she felt necessary, when to her delight as they turned a corner near the postbox, Michael McCarthy and a friend were walking their way.

'Michael. Hello!' she called out and waved, feeling awkward after she realised she probably sounded over-enthusiastic.

'Kitty, oh, and Belle; now there's a sight for tired eyes. Ladies let me introduce you to Dr Robert Keane. Just arrived from Wales,' Michael said and joined them both.

Pushing herself in front of Kitty with the grace of a pig at a trough, Belle held out her hand to the tall, thin man beside Michael. Kitty staggered to one side and only just managed to save her footing. Unable to hide her irritation with Belle any longer, she tutted. Belle turned to look at her, flicked her hair back in a triumphant swish, and turned her attention back to the new doctor.

'A pleasure, I'm Belle.'

'Wait, your name – it rings, and please – excuse the pun – a bell. I'm Robert Keane.'

Kitty noticed Robert give a slight glance over to Michael as he spoke, which Michael returned with a brief nod.

'Pun, hmm – who's the naughty one bandying my name around then, Robert? Is it you, Dr McCarthy, you naughty Canadian you?' Belle said in an exaggeratedly flirtatious voice.

Robert moved closer to Belle, and Kitty internally thanked him for distracting her away from her moans and groans. It amused Kitty to see Belle preening and flirting her way throughout the conversation, her voice plummier than ever, and Kitty waited for the *dahling* moment.

Michael looked over at her and winked; it was then she understood. He'd told his friends the stories she'd relayed to him over a cocoa break one shift, including those of Belle and her arrival at the QE. She gave a grin back and a reprimanding tilt of her head with a frown in fun.

'The temperature is dropping; do we head back to the canteen for a cuppa?' Robert asked.

Belle looped her arms through those of the two bemused men, in what Kitty felt was an over-friendly manner. 'Splendid idea. Lead the way. Come on Kitty Daydreamer, keep up.'

The last thing Kitty wanted to do was to sit down with Belle sounding as if she'd stepped out of the local big house on a jolly jaunt. She'd much rather enjoy the company of

Michael alone; she always enjoyed her shifts when he was around. He taught her well and encouraged her to push herself harder.

'I've still to post my letter home. I'll catch up later. I'm on night duty so I really need to grab a few hours' rest,' Kitty said.

Belle swung her head and called over her shoulder. 'Please yourself. Be boring – we don't care. I'll catch you after your beauty sleep. Some of us don't need as much as others.'

Her quip, followed through with a loud, condescending laugh, infuriated Kitty. Belle always managed to belittle her or make her feel small in the company of other people. She chose to ignore her but carried the uncomfortable feeling Belle had dumped on her shoulders and turned her attention to say goodbye to Michael.

'I'm sorry for being a bore, but I really do like to rest before shift. I find my mind is more alert during the early hours that way. I'll catch you another time on duty,' she said. He gave her a warm smile and she returned it with an apologetic one.

'No apology needed. You're no bore, Kitty, I'll be grabbing sleep in a couple of hours, too. I'll walk with you to the postbox, and we'll head back together,' Michael said as he unlinked his arm from Belle and walked over to Kitty.

'Please yourselves,' Belle called out to them, and walked away with Robert Keane.

'She's happy. Robert will entertain her. Let's post this letter of yours and you can tell me more about the history of your town. Did the *Mayflower* ship's captain really live there, or were you teasing the other night when we were on duty?'

With a swift nod yes, Kitty carried on walking towards the postbox. 'He did. King's Head Street to be precise. Harwich has a great historical background and port. My village, Parkeston, is also an important port from which boats sail to Holland.'

Michael cocked his head to one side.

'Harwich? Now that is interesting. We have a Harwich in Canada. It is a place in Ontario. I know the name because my grandfather's family is buried in the cemetery there. I suspect settlers from your town gave it the name, or we gave it to yours. As they say, a small world.'

Kitty gave a cheeky grin. 'I suspect we gave it to Canada. My Harwich is older than yours.'

'Thank goodness they still have young nurses though,' Michael retorted with a laugh.

'I think someone has the gift of the gab and knows how to flatter a girl,' Kitty said, and playfully flicked her hand against the back of his.

'Do you have a boyfriend back home, Kitty? A lucky guy waiting for your letters or calls?' Michael asked as he stopped to tie his shoelace.

Kitty leaned against the wall of a narrow walkway through a cluster of houses, and, looking down at him, she was so happy to be able to answer him honestly.

'No, I don't. I've never had a serious one. Do you have a sweetheart waiting for you when you return to Canada?' she asked, not really wanting to hear the answer.

Michael stood up and smiled.

'No. I've been in England too long to expect any girl to wait for me. I am surprised about you though. My last few years have been about studies, but you've only just begun. I cannot believe a boy hasn't won your heart,' Michael said with a teasing lilt to his voice.

They continued through the walkway; with it being narrow, Kitty walked ahead of Michael.

'I've never met anyone who didn't want to tie me to a pram and an oven. My father had an adventurous nature, and my mother was quite an independent woman by all accounts. According to my aunt, she was a modern woman ahead of her times, and I think it rubbed off on me. I'm not ready to settle down, and my kind of prince charming doesn't exist.'

Michael touched her arm and gently turned her around.

'Maybe you've not met him yet. Your kind of prince charming. The one to give you all you want or need,' he said, and leaned into her, his breath soft and warm against her cheek.

'Maybe I haven't – but then again …'

Their kiss was tender and not unexpected. Kitty had felt the moment brewing inside of her and she sensed Michael had led the conversation to find out more about her love life with the purpose of letting her know his feelings towards her, given the right answers and her response.

Their conversation on the way back to the hospital became one of swapping stories of their homelands, and by the time they'd arrived at the entrance, Kitty found herself more attracted to Michael, and her mood a happier one thanks to the many kisses they'd shared before leaving the confines of the alleyway. Kitty didn't hesitate when Michael's lips demanded more from hers.

He had qualities she admired and had listed in her journal as great attributes she'd look for in a partner. Michael was witty and thoughtful, intelligent and fun. His good looks and masculine physique added to his attraction. Only one thing nagged at the back of her mind and on several occasions during their extended walk, it crossed her mind as to whether she was woman enough to draw him into her life and keep him there before another attractive, fun-loving woman captured his attention. She thought of Belle, who appeared to have no problem when it came to luring men into wanting her physically, but Kitty wanted to be the kind of woman a man wanted as a friend, possibly a wife, a man who respected her as a person not just as an object or a name on a marriage certificate, or a mother to his children. She wanted to be recognised as someone who could discuss more than the price of groceries. They might be knee-deep in a world war, and life a tad shorter than she'd originally thought, but Kitty still clung on to dreams of a soulmate. She had several dreams, some of which she wasn't prepared to devalue, thanks to Hitler, and she felt sure even Michael had a set of values scribbled down in his life journal tucked away in an old sweet tin, too.

## Chapter Eleven

D ark shadows filtered through the curtains, surrounding patients down the length of the long ward. Each patient slept soundly, and a couple snored so loudly, Kitty's senior rose from her seat now and then to nudge them into a better breathing position. A purely selfish reason rather than a medical one; it was kinder on the ears of those watching over them.

Kitty didn't mind night duty; she enjoyed the camaraderie amongst the staff and found the senior staff on duty were always friendlier than during the daytime shifts. There was a special bond between the few who sat in the dimmed wards from late evening until dawn. She did, however, prefer the bustle of the emergency department, but a request for her to stand in for someone who'd reported in sick, meant tonight she worked a male ward instead.

Humming whilst tidying the top and final shelf of the linen cupboard, a noise distracted Kitty and she climbed down from the ladder and went to the door. She heard a member of staff call for assistance and Kitty ran along the ward to help the nurse persuade a patient back into his bed, just as the haunting drone and scream of the siren sounded. Kitty froze for a moment; the blood in her veins ran cold. The planes were close, and the distressed male patients looked to the team to keep them safe.

Reassurances were uttered at each bedside and before long the anticipated and much-feared bombs hit the ground, vibrating their terror across roads and along the residential or factory floors nearby. Blast after blast sent tremors through Kitty's body as she kept herself busy. When the siren's wail finished, she knew her night shift would drift into the morning one, when she and the emergency team would be asked to seek out the missing wounded from the wrecked buildings surrounding them, and relieve some of the search party who would have been working since the first bomb dropped.

Once the all-clear was given, Kitty and her colleagues finished their workload and handed the ward over to the day staff. Kitty raced back to her room and freshened her face with soap and water, rushed to the dining room and grabbed toast and tea, gaining a scolding from the house matron for eating too fast. With a nod and smile, Kitty took large mouthfuls of tea and waved goodbye.

'No rest for the wicked,' she called over her shoulder as she left the room.

Kitty inhaled the crisp morning air and moved with haste to the emergency unit. Halfway along the shortcut back to the main building she was joined by Michael heading in the same direction.

'Morning Kitty. You're in my team. Grab an emergency kit and meet me around the front,' he said. His authoritative voice gave her clear and precise instructions despite his breathlessness from running.

'Will do,' Kitty replied, secretly pleased he'd included her in his team, She'd been worried after their kisses earlier in the day that he'd avoid her, but she realised Michael was professional, and admired him for keeping their working relationship separate from what had been a one-off fun moment. She owed it to him to do the same, and did as he asked. She watched the chaos form around her into an organised formation with Michael head of procedures, and felt proud when he singled her out to be his support nurse. It promised to be a difficult day, going by the injuries she'd witnessed still being brought into the hospital and main unit. Patients lined the corridors, and walking wounded were escorted to various parts of the hospital.

'Kitty. It's awful out there, be careful!' Trix's voice rang out from halfway down the main corridor. She pushed a trolley with a colleague towards the theatre, her tiny face pale, with a bright streak of blood across her cheek.

Kitty gave a wave, and her heart sank. On the trolley she saw the outline of a little child, and blood seeping through the top sheet. The bombs knew no boundaries.

'I'll try. See you later. Stay strong, Trix,' she said.

For over four hours Kitty worked alongside Michael and four members of the local volunteer groups. Any fatigue she felt, Kitty pushed to one side. Lives relied on their skills and ability to help. She – bomb attacks willing – could sleep later. Kitty picked up a bag filled with bloodied bandages and loaded them into a van to be returned to the hospital for boiling. As she went to collect another, Michael tugged at her arm and, out of sight of anyone, they shared a gentle kiss. They held each other tightly. Many people they'd pulled from the wrecked homes would never get the chance to express affection with a loved one again, and Kitty felt a heightened sense of gratitude.

'Put the bag down. You've done your bit for now. Time to head home. We've done all we can here. You need to get rest and be back in the emergency unit fresh and alert,' Michael said as he pulled slowly away from their embrace.

'What about you?' Kitty asked.

'I'll follow on after I've checked the old man over there. Go, before you fall asleep here. I'm a little too busy to catch you when you fall.' Michael gave a laugh and gathered his medical bag into his arms.

Without speaking, Kitty nodded. She clambered into a returning ambulance and gave him a tired wave goodbye. Falling asleep in Michael's arms appealed, but it would be a dreadful embarrassment to do so in public, so she did as she was told. Despite being desperate for a hot drink and food, Kitty opted for a bath and sleep first.

Back in her room, Kitty was thankful there wasn't a queue waiting to use the shared bathroom. She stripped off her uniform, tied her cosy dressing gown around her, picked up her wash things and placed the dirty uniform into the laundry skip at the end of the corridor, before running a hot bath to soak away the sadness of the long shift. The water in the sink when she washed her face took no time at all to turn black from the dried soot mixed with blood. Once dried and dressed in her pyjamas, Kitty hurried back to her room and curled up under the bedclothes, blotting out the horrific scenes she'd coped with, knowing she could face the same again within a few hours. Before she drifted off to sleep, Kitty re-enacted the scene of the past few hours and held onto an image of Michael's face smiling back at her, and a warm sensation of contentment shimmied through her body. She'd dreamed of a hero in her life, but never thought she'd meet one in the flesh, and to Kitty, Michael was every inch a hero. She wanted to learn more about him, his life, and to work alongside him for as long as she was able. His attention to their patients' needs was admirable. He didn't grunt and walk away as many doctors tended to do; Michael cared about the person, not just their injuries. They were human to him, not textbook models.

Turning over in her bed, Kitty made herself a promise to ensure she and Michael formed a strong friendship in any way she could possibly make it happen within the boundaries of dignity. The courting territory was new to her and she didn't want to make a fool of herself, but she wanted Michael as her boyfriend, that much she knew.

'Kitty Pattison, it's time to grow up and make a future for yourself. This is real life and Michael could share it with you. Don't let yourself down,' she whispered, before giving in to much needed sleep.

## Chapter Twelve

'What do you do for fun, apart from kissing me, Kitty?' Michael asked her when they were clearing up after another busy dawn rescue. Today was an extra tiring one, and she hoped the dark circles under her eyes didn't stand out as they weren't her most attractive feature.

The idea of always looking attractive for a man – for Michael – never really featured in Kitty's life. It seemed most times she was with him, she wore a bloodied uniform and a soot-smudged face streaked with tears. She appreciated that he never told her off for crying when they failed to revive a patient, and allowed her the tears of frustration.

'You mean when I'm not at the local dances with the girls meeting Canadian doctors? Not much, if I'm honest. Aside from studying, I go to the cinema – Jo's not a fan, but she keeps me company. You? What do you do when you are not kissing me?' Kitty asked.

Michael gave a huff of a laugh.

'Work and sleep. That's my life. I'm studying new techniques and falling asleep over my notes. I don't have many friends, but the couple I do have are in the same boat as me,' he said.

Kitty nodded. 'It's hard finding time for friends with our shifts going through constant change. Trix and Smithy are always together nowadays, and Belle, well we are like chalk and cheese, so I tend to try and avoid her when I can. Does that sound dreadful of me?'

Michael continued reading through the medical kit checklist. Kitty loved to watch him work. He had a habit of touching his tongue to his top lip when in serious study mode.

'Not at all. Belle is a forceful woman. She's gaining a bit of a reputation amongst the doctors, if I'm honest. I'm like you – I tend to steer clear.'

Loading the freshly cleaned ambulance, they climbed on board and sat side by side, their arms touching, and Kitty found it hard not to turn to stare at the handsome man beside her. Each small brush of his hand against hers sent tremors of excitement through her body. She refocused her attention to their conversation, not wanting the closeness to end.

'I like to dance, but rarely get the chance to go to one thanks to my studies, too. Back home I belonged to a small dance club – mostly women, but we enjoyed getting together in the little hall at the end of the road with a record player and orange juice. A simple life.'

Michael turned and smiled at her. 'A happy one, I'll bet. I led a simple life back home, too. My grandmother kept me on my toes. She cared for me when I lost my parents and grandfather in 1922 to a fire on the farm where they worked. It was my fourth birthday, and a terrible time in everyone's lives in the area. My grandmother was not the strongest of women due to a bad heart, but she found us a new home not far from Haileybury and put her heart and soul into bringing me up,' he said, and Kitty noticed a slight change in his mood. She saw a sadness around his eyes and watched as he dropped his shoulders.

'I lost her during the depression when all her life savings disappeared. Her heart couldn't take any more. We had nothing to buy food with, no rent money, nothing. I was eleven and a homeless orphan.'

A silence fell in the ambulance and the latter part of Michael's words hit Kitty hard when he announced he was an orphan. It was a surreal moment; he was a relative stranger and yet had opened up to her as if they were old friends. She let the moment settle in her mind and gave him breathing time to gather his thoughts, and when he looked up at her and smiled, it seemed the right moment to share something about herself other than her hobbies.

'I'm so sorry, Michael. What a dreadful thing to happen to you. You were right, I have experienced a happy life, *after* I'd allowed myself to come out of my shell. You see, my family also died. My parents and little brother were killed in a ferryboat accident when I was four, and my aunt and uncle brought me up. I'm an orphan too Michael, so I understand your sadness, your loss. I still carry a feeling of never really belonging; of looking in from the outside, no matter how much love I received.'

Michael straightened in his seat. Kitty gave a gentle smile – not of pity but of friendship and understanding. She knew he'd hate the pity smile; she found most orphans did. They needed support, not pity.

'Yes, that feeling you are missing out on something special. That's another thing we have in common,' Michael said. His voice lifted with its usual cheery tone, lightening the mood.

Kitty gave a puzzled frown. 'The other is?'

Grabbing his kitbag as the ambulance slowed to a halt, Michael headed to the back doors, talking over his shoulder using a fake upper-class English accent, much like Belle's.

'Why, scrabbling around in mud and dirt of course.'

With a belly laugh, Kitty joined him and the rest of the crew. She had a feeling Michael's friendship would definitely see her through the dark times from now on. When Jo or Trix were not around, he might be someone she could turn to and share her fears or concerns. They'd stepped into a different working relationship.

They worked their way through more trauma and horrors. Occasionally their hands touched, and they would exchange soft glances of tenderness. When the team celebrated the successes of the day with whoops and cheers, nobody commented when Kitty and Michael embraced, and it gave her a thrill to know people recognised them as a couple. It saddened her when they eventually climbed into the ambulance for the final trip back to the hospital just as the December evening shared a pink sky across the rooftops. It had been a long day and she wanted to spend more time with Michael, to curl up and fall asleep beside him, but both were exhausted, and what she wanted was impossible under the strict hospital rules.

'It's going to be a good day tomorrow. I can feel it in my bones,' Kitty said, gripping the seat tightly as they bumped their way around Birmingham.

Michael yawned and stretched. 'Famous last words, Kitty Pattison. I hope you don't live to regret them. I need sleep and can be a grumpy companion if I don't get it.'

'I wonder if I'll ever find out,' Kitty said with a coy grin.

'I wonder.' Michael said, and winked.

The brief intimate moment came to an abrupt halt when the ambulance driver parked the vehicle.

As they walked towards the hospital from the ambulance, Kitty noticed a man standing by the front entrance. His face looked familiar and when a wide smile broke out across his face, Kitty realised it was the soldier from the train.

'Ah, here's my nurse. My lovely, nurse. I knew if I stood here long enough, I'd find you. Got a kiss for a soldier?' he said, holding his arms outward as she and Michael reached him.

'I, um, I …' A puzzled Kitty struggled for words.

Touching her shoulder, Michael spoke before walking inside.

'I'll see you on shift, Kitty.' His voice was efficient, but not over friendly.

'Michael, wait,' she called after him, but he'd already stepped inside the hospital.

A confused and disappointed Kitty looked at his back and then returned her attention to the soldier.

'What are you doing here in Birmingham? I thought after your wedding in, um, Derby, you were heading to Scotland?'

The soldier shifted his body to a more relaxed one and leaned on the entrance railings.

'I'm on leave. I never married. It turned out my sister found out Julie had been seeing another man, and the baby was his. I asked her outright and she confessed. I got myself into a bit of an emotional situation and was given a few days in a cell. Not proud of that black mark on my record.'

Frowning at him, and not in the mood for a long conversation, Kitty chose to commiserate and move on. She was still puzzled by his sudden appearance, and the way he made out he'd searched for her.

'I'm sorry to hear that. I'm still not sure what you're doing here though,' Kitty said, and sidestepped in an attempt to get past him. 'I hope you have found a little brightness in your days. Now, I must go and get my meal and rest. I'm on call for emergency events, and we've worked since dawn. Take care of yourself.'

The soldier reached into his uniform pocket and pulled out a pack of cigarettes.

'Smoke?' he asked, holding out the pack to her, his arm preventing her from moving forward.

Kitty shook her head and tried to take another step towards the hospital steps.

'I'm sorry I can't keep my eyes open. I really have to go.'

Drawing on his cigarette, the soldier released the vapour with a slow exhale.

'I never forgot you, you know. You were the prettiest girl

on the train, and so kind. You told me to visit if I needed help. Well, I need the help of a lovely nurse right now, so here I am.'

His small talk began to irritate Kitty and she continued walking. Something about him didn't sit well with her, and she desperately needed to eat.

'It's kind of you to say so, but if you'll forgive me, I am walking away. I've to rest, and I'm not comfortable standing chatting to a stranger in front of Matron's office.'

The soldier moved closer and stepped to her side.

'Let me take you for a drink some time. A cuppa to repay you for the one on the train. I'd love to get to know you more before I head back to my unit.'

Irritated and confused by his persistence and not wanting to cause a scene, Kitty gave a slight nod of resignation.

'I'm due a day off tomorrow. I'll meet you by the postbox at the end of the second road on the left – that way and around five minutes away, at two o'clock. If I'm not there it will mean leave has been cancelled,' she said, and pointed to the end of the road.

'I'll be there. Eddie's my name by the way. I heard the doc call you Kitty, so now we are acquainted, I'll leave you alone. See you tomorrow.'

From a window in the long corridor inside the hospital, Kitty watched Eddie walk away. She had no intention of meeting him the following day, as she promised herself several study hours in the library. With luck he'd get the hint and leave her alone if she didn't turn up, if not she'd approach Sister Barker for advice. It irked her he'd interrupted her time with Michael, and that he'd tracked her down. How many days had he stood in front of the hospital on the off chance of meeting up with her? Kitty found it odd, but being so tired she decided to put him out of her mind and concentrate upon a large bowl of meat and potatoes, a cup of cocoa, and undisturbed sleep of several hours. Providing Hitler's men allowed it.

## Chapter Thirteen

'I can't believe he did that; how creepy,' Jo said as they headed towards the library the following morning.

Kitty, refreshed from a good night's sleep and leisurely breakfast, inhaled the fresh air and allowed herself to relax. She'd relayed Eddie's arrival and her scheme to leave him waiting to Jo over breakfast.

'Nor me. I have visions of him standing by the postbox for days.'

Jo laughed. 'At two o'clock I'll think of him and his sad face. Seriously though Kitty, you did the right thing. He sounds like trouble.'

Kitty shrugged. 'I'm sure he's fine, but just not for me. He's a good-looking chap, but—'

'Cooee!'

With Belle's sudden appearance, Kitty stopped talking. They'd all learned not to share too much with her as Belle's inability to keep a secret let her down in the confide-in-a-friend sector.

'Morning. Who's good-looking? I like good-looking,' Belle said.

'Oh, a patient we transferred,' Kitty replied with a quick glance at Jo to indicate culling the conversation with Belle around.

'Damn, I must have missed him.'

Jo gave a huff followed by a sarcastic laugh. 'Gracious, your standards are slipping, Belle. It's unlike you to miss a handsome male.'

Kitty sidestepped the conversation by changing the subject. The last person she wanted to discuss her personal situation with, was Belle.

'We had a tough few days on the emergency run. I learned a few things from Michael McCarthy, and I—'

A snort of a laugh from Belle stopped Kitty talking. 'I bet you did – learned a lot. Now there's a talk-of-the-devil moment. Ooh, he's a dish. Michael, were your ears burning? We were just talking about you, and how you've been teaching Kitty a few things.'

The high-pitched squawk in Belle's voice rang out like an over-excited schoolgirl. Whenever men were around, Belle would use a cutesy voice to draw them into her circle.

As Michael walked towards them, Kitty saw a flash of irritation cross his face. 'Morning ladies. We all learn from each other, Belle. Enjoy your day off.'

He gave a brief nod and carried on past. His voice was flat and not the usual friendly one they were used to, and Jo gave Kitty a quizzical glance. Kitty gave him a soft smile, but Michael didn't return it as usual. Something worried him. Kitty had read his expressions when they worked together often enough to be able to read his moods or concerns about patients.

'It's a study day. We know how to have fun,' she said, but spoke to Michael's back as he walked away.

'Wait up. I'm heading your way,' Belle called after him.

Another confused glance between Kitty and Jo brought about a grin from Belle.

'I'm not wasting an opportunity. The man looks down in the dumps today. I'll cheer him up.'

Another sarcastic laugh from Jo made Kitty giggle.

'You can try, but I've seen that face before, and he'll take a long time to snap out of it, I can tell you,' she said.

Belle chose to ignore her and ran after Michael. When he turned sideways to speak with Belle, Kitty saw him increase his speed.

'He won't shake her off that easily,' she said to Jo.

'Sadly, no. She's a man-eater that one.'

An unsettled flutter in Kitty's stomach screamed jealousy when she watched them walk towards the main hospital. With Belle taking his attention, Kitty stood little chance of forming a stronger friendship with Michael; Belle had a way of making men fall at her feet. The notion startled Kitty, and a thought flashed through her mind. Her feelings when around him of late were different, and she realised she was on the path of wanting to be more than a kissing friend to Michael. The other part of her wanted him to also consider her an able colleague. Unsure why the pang of what she supposed to be jealousy had reared its head, Kitty chose to suppress the feeling. Their kisses were merely that moment when you need comfort after a disaster;

nothing more. She decided to dismiss the jealousy as a fleeting silliness on her part and to concentrate on her studies.

'Come on. Let's leave them to it. We've got blood and guts to read about – far more exciting than Annabelle Farnsworth's love life,' she said, and strode towards the library block.

The hushed sounds from inside the library washed over Kitty like a soothing bandage. She was annoyed with herself for allowing her heart to rule her head.

Each time she read something she didn't understand in her research books, Kitty gave a sigh and failed to concentrate so often she lost her desire to study. She scribbled notes for a short while, and then gave up. She sat back in her chair, stood up to stretch her legs, walked to bookshelves in the hope of finding something inspirational, flicked through them disinterestedly, and returned them for more of the same. Jo gave her the odd glance across the table, but after two hours, she closed her books, tapped Kitty's hand and pointed to the exit.

Once outside, Jo confronted Kitty.

'So, what's going on with you and Michael?'

Taken aback at the question, Kitty made a show of rearranging her books in her bag, whilst she collected her thoughts. How much of what she felt about the Canadian did she want even her closest friend to know?

'There's nothing going on. We work together and are good friends. You know that, so what makes you ask such an odd question? Leave it, Jo.'

Jo hitched her bag higher across her shoulder and Kitty

did the same. They walked back to the canteen in silence. Midway through their lunch, Jo asked the same question.

'What's going on with you and Dr McCarthy? Kitty, I'm not stupid. I can see how upset you are over something. If it isn't Michael, then I'll eat my hat, so please don't tell me it is the job – one of those dreadful scenes you've witnessed. I know something is wrong between you and that man. If he's hurt you, I'll have something to say.'

Kitty bit into the last crust of her sandwich and drank the final dregs of her milk. She wiped her mouth with a napkin, folded it and placed it onto the empty plate. Jo had known her long enough, and Kitty also knew Jo wouldn't back down until she'd ensured Kitty had told her the reason for her silent mood. Jo had the kindest heart of all the women Kitty worked with; even Trix with her gentle ways couldn't compare in the friendship stakes when it came to Jo. Her friend deserved the truth, so she no longer fretted, but Kitty wasn't prepared to confide the real truth, so adapted her reply enough to put Jo off the scent.

'I thought I had a thing for him, but it's nothing. I think it's hero worship. He's amazing out there when we're in the darkest moments. Strong and dependable. The ideal person to help me learn. For a little while I thought I'd like to spend time with him socially, but it would ruin the working relationship we have. So, in answer to your question, there's nothing going on, and I'm more upset about that stupid soldier turning up like he did.'

Jo raised an eyebrow. 'Justifying your feelings by giving me a long speech doesn't convince me.'

'Leave it, Jo. I've told you, and there's nothing else to

say. I'm fine. It's been a rough few weeks. Let's go for a walk. Get away from here. Head to the park across town. Somewhere different.'

Shaking her head, Jo stood up. 'Sorry, no can do. I'm playing hockey this afternoon. Be kind to yourself, Kitty. Don't be scared of enjoying yourself. Life's too short.'

Kitty gave a smile and for the first time that day, it was genuine.

'Go, enjoy your hockey. I'll go and write up some notes, take a bath, and maybe enjoy a walk later.'

They hugged goodbye, and as Kitty headed for her room, she glanced at her watch. Two-forty. Eddie would be long gone, and she could relax for the rest of the day.

After her bath Kitty couldn't settle. She wrote a fantasy letter to Michael in her journal, and hoped by writing down the words, they would stop nagging inside her head.

As she walked along the pathway, she saw a couple with their arms linked. Belle's familiar girlish giggle rang out and Kitty's heart went out to the poor unsuspecting male the girl had captured with her charm. The couple moved into a lighter area of the walkway and to Kitty's surprise, the man wore the same uniform as Eddie, and when he moved his face towards her, she realised it *was* Eddie.

'Well, well. Crafty Belle, you overheard us, heard about a soldier who would be hanging around and was to be stood up and you went in for the kill. You are welcome to him,' she muttered to herself. A strange tremor of relief that Michael was no longer the focus of Belle's attention washed over her. In her eyes, Michael could go walking with any girl in Birmingham, just not Belle. He deserved better –

even if it wasn't Kitty; she'd accept him walking out with a different nurse each night – just not man-eating Annabelle Farnsworth.

Eddie and Belle disappeared from view and Kitty found herself in a brighter mood.

## Chapter Fourteen

'**H**appy New Year!'

The greeting rang out around the ward in a whispered chorus between staff and those patients still awake enough to see 1941 slip into their lives. Not one regretted the passing of 1940, and hope of it being the year the war ended was the whisper around the room. During December alone, several attacks on Germany, an attack on Manchester, the push against the Italians in Egypt by the British, rumours of Germany going against the Soviet Union, and an attack on London resulting in damage to St Paul's Cathedral, drained each person or brought about elation as the news filtered through the wireless on a daily basis. Emotional staff contained their concerns around patients, but were stretched to the end of their ability to cope with horrific injuries, while new ideas of treatment were introduced at lightning speed. Kitty's class were issued with regular nursing updates and studies. Their spare time was limited and spent in small study groups learning together.

Kitty felt the return of an earlier disappointment as she shook the hands of exhausted colleagues. Despite her own body feeling the effects of long shifts and emergency call-outs, she'd hoped to join Jo and Trix at a party held for staff able to celebrate the start of a new year, but a change of staff rotation meant she found herself in uniform rather than a pretty dress. She wiggled her toes in her black flats, thinking about the neat heeled shoes in navy leather she'd purchased with her Christmas postal order from her aunt and uncle. A generous gift sent with love. She'd written telling them she would not return home until the end of January, rotation willing.

Watching the clock tick around each hour and convincing Kitty it was on a go-slow to torment her, she thought of the happy faces and dancing a few streets away in the community hall where she'd first met Michael.

Michael!

In all the flap and fuss of Belle rushing to her door to report that her ward sister was on the internal telephone, and that Kitty was to ready herself and help the ward on the night shift, she'd forgotten to let Michael know she'd not make the party. They'd had a fun agreement about a dance when they were last working together.

That night, amongst the dust and rubble, she'd felt a smidgen of hope he still considered her a friend. The standoffish manner in which she felt he'd treated her in November seemed to have been an overreaction on her part, as he'd since asked if she'd be trying out her new shoes on the dance floor, after a discussion about Christmas gifts and celebrations. She'd replied to the positive and teased him with a challenge not to tread on his toes if he was brave enough to dance with her. Expecting a list of excuses, she'd been pleasantly surprised when he'd agreed to put himself at risk. She'd finished the shift happier and more hopeful of getting back on track with Michael. She'd missed his kisses, but now thanks to staff shortages she'd lost the opportunity to be held in his arms and experience them yet again – if he was willing to offer them. She felt cheated.

Looking out of the ward window, a member of staff called the team to watch the revellers returning home. A large group of people were singing in the street. The darkness made it hard to make out their features, but they all expelled joy and happiness until a warden called out for them to have respect for sleeping patients and get themselves home.

Kitty turned away, upset at missing out on the fun, and then with herself for putting herself ahead of patients who needed all the care and attention she could offer them.

During the rest of the night, a man passed away, and Kitty, along with her mentor, prepared him for the next part of his journey through the corridors of the hospital. Another moved in his bed and burst a few stitches, meaning bloodied sheets needed changing and his wound sutured in theatre.

An exhausting shift came to an end when Matron swept onto the ward to wish them all a Happy New Year. After she'd left, staff took virtual bets on how tipsy on sherry she'd get by the end of shift. The ward day sister also declared her wishes for them to enjoy a better year, and after thanking them for their work during the evening, called Kitty to one side.

A nervous Kitty thought over her work of the evening and concluded she'd followed all rules and regulations, so Sister was about to ask her to cover another shift. If so, she'd not refuse, but would remind her that she was also part of the emergency team and would be called away should enemy bombs drop.

'Kitty. Thank you for stepping in for Nurse Farnsworth. As I understand it, her mother is to recover but will need her daughter's support for a few more days – maybe longer, poor woman. It was fortunate Belle managed to get a lift home with a returning troop. Anyway, sacrificing your New Year's Eve hasn't gone unnoticed.'

A confused Kitty gave her a smile.

'I'm happy to be of help.'

All the way to the canteen, Kitty wondered why Belle hadn't mentioned going home for a family emergency, but now she didn't feel so bad covering the shift. It had helped Belle and, although she wasn't a fan of the girl, they all had to pull together during such horrendous times.

The corridors were quieter than normal with only the occasional doctor or nurse scurrying to and fro. Fortunately, the previous night was not hampered by visits from enemy planes, and most incoming injuries were minor. The canteen was also unusually quiet, and Kitty guessed the skeleton staff had eaten and the remainder were enjoying a lie-in in preparation for the late or night shift. She intended to get plenty of rest and catch up with Jo and Trix later in the afternoon to enjoy the news of the dance. She'd also track Michael down to find out if he'd enjoyed himself and to apologise for not letting him know her plans had been altered, but not by choice.

On occasion, Kitty woke to the sound of the house matron reprimanding someone for making a mess in the bathroom, or groups of muffled voices gathering in the corridor, so much so that by the end of her self-allocated sleep time, she gave up and went to the communal kitchen to brew a pot of tea. As she left the kitchen, she heard Jo's voice chatting in the common room and ventured there instead of heading back to her room.

'Ah, hello sleepyhead,' Jo said as Kitty slumped into a comfortable chair.

'Hello yourself. Good night?'

Jo rubbed her head as Kitty spoke, and grinned.

'Whisky is not my friend. A New Year's treat.'

Kitty laughed. 'If you can't handle it, guess what state I'd be in today if I'd drunk it – a darn sight worse than you for sure! Orange juice with a tiny dash of gin and I'm ready to dance the night away. Seriously, I am glad you had a good night. Mine was a tough one. A death and a bleeder kept us busy.'

Pointing to Kitty's cup, Jo stood up. 'Another? We had fun. Lots of dancing. Michael is light on his feet, a brilliant dancer. He certainly entertained us with a few modern moves.'

Kitty handed her cup to Jo and pulled her dressing gown closer around her, more for comfort than warmth.

Just the thought of Michael dancing with others sparked the little flame of jealousy once again, and no matter how she tried to suppress it, tiredness and the sense she had missed out on a special time with him, jarred a little.

'… especially when he and Belle stepped up to …'

'Belle!?'

Kitty jumped to her feet, tiredness no longer an issue. She followed Jo as she headed for the kitchen.

'Are you telling me that Belle was at the dance?'

Jo filled the kettle, lit the gas, and turned to Kitty.

'Jealous, eh? I'm sure you'll be able to grab his attention again, but yes, he and Belle danced well together. Very entertaining. They managed to find space for the Lindy Hop, and I was exhausted just watching them.'

Without warning, Kitty burst into tears. She'd felt the pressure of disappointment so forcefully, and made no effort to control her emotional outburst, the tears took their lead from her shock and upset. Belle's betrayal and lies were unforgivable.

'It's not jealousy. I'm livid. Furious – at her, not him. Michael is free to do what he wants and with whomever he wants, but she … she is a despicable liar!'

Kitty's voice had reached a louder pitch than its norm, and she saw Jo step back in surprise.

'Kitty, lovely. That's a harsh thing to say. Don't let jealousy eat at you; it can make you bitter.'

Kitty blew hard into a handkerchief and cuffed away her tears, angry at herself for allowing her upset to take over her annoyance at Belle.

'I'm not jealous and I am not bitter. I'm absolutely

furious, and she had better steer clear of me from now on. Do you know why I had to work? I found out this morning that she lied to the ward sister about her mother needing her at home after an accident or illness.' Kitty looked at Jo and she felt the burning of anger in her cheeks as Jo stared back in surprise. 'Yes. Glad to see you are as shocked as I am. Oh, and apparently she was lucky enough to get a ride home with a returning crew to be the dutiful daughter. How about that one then? She herself told me I'd been called to cover due to staff shortage and my name was on the roster for next night shift, and now I've found out it was to cover for her to go to a dance! The conniving ...'

A book hit the floor, and Jo grabbed Kitty's arm before anything else was thrown around the room.

'Calm down. I can't believe she lied like that – well, I can, but no, how could she? She did say she has leave and is going to head to her parents' holiday house in Cornwall. Maybe she missed her ride home and made the most of it before she has to care for her mother. She might have told the truth, Kitty. Think before you regret what you do or say.'

A loud laugh burst from Kitty. A harsh sound.

'This is not *Honest Trix* we are talking about; this is Miss Annabelle Farnsworth – Man-Eater Extraordinaire. She set this up, Jo. She is determined I am not to have a man of my own. Look what she did with Eddie.'

Jo gave a frustrated sigh.

'But you didn't like Eddie. You stood him up, and in fairness to Belle, you and Michael aren't a couple, you just ...' Jo stopped talking and looked over Kitty's shoulder. 'Go back to bed. This is not the place to talk, and you are tired. Calm down, and I'll see you around four as planned. Go and comfort your heart with a good cry and sleep.'

With the smile of encouragement, Jo hugged Kitty close and smiled at the other nurses filing in. 'A hard night shift. She needs sleep,' she said to the inquisitive arrivals.

Anyone crying was always watched over with concern within the home. War was not kind and many girls had rushed from the community rooms with news of loved ones lost.

Curling under her covers, Kitty did just as Jo suggested. She felt a little foolish to cry over a man – a friend. She needed to keep her strength and focus on those who needed her attention. Annabelle Farnsworth and Michael McCarthy were an emotional distraction she could do without.

## Chapter Fifteen

**P**icking up the post from her pigeonhole, Kitty was surprised to see two letters. She recognised the handwriting from her aunt and uncle on one, but the other looked more formal and was franked with the Red Cross symbol along the top centre of the envelope.

Needing the reassurance that all was well at home, Kitty settled in a chair in the canteen and, between mouthfuls of porridge, read comforting words from home.

*Parkeston*
*Near Harwich*
*Essex*
*27th December 1940*

*Our Dearest Kitty,*

*What a joy it was to receive your letter and to know you*

*are safe and well. It was lovely to read that you all managed to enjoy Christmas together. Dining alone isn't fun, so to all enjoy a canteen feast after the carol service in church reassures us you had a happy one. How we'd have loved to have been at the midnight mass service and heard you girls sing in your capes with lanterns – what a festive sight that must have been.*

*Thank you for your thoughtful gifts. Handkerchiefs and seeds are perfect and well-received. As for your own gift, you are most welcome. New shoes? Well, there's something wise and wonderful to spend your postal order on. Happy dancing days!*

*We enjoyed a street feast, and the children are all running around with rewound woollen hats knitted by me and Betty at number four. Your clever uncle made twenty spinning tops in his shed – a secret even I didn't know about and the faces of the children playing on Boxing Day brought the street alive with laughter. It had a gloominess to it at the start of December when George and Audrey Cousins received a telegram. They too have lost a son. We've offered our support and they are coping. It's the one thing we do as parents – we cling onto the knowledge their young lives were lost to offer the next generation a safer world. They did not die in vain.*

*Don't laugh, but we are now the proud owners of an apple tree. We purchased it from the orchard near the cemetery and we've also rented a small piece of land at the top of the road which we will cultivate soon. So, you can see your gift of seeds will be used there and not just the back garden. The tree gives a good yield of fruit and your bedroom now stores several boxes of apples wrapped in what newspaper we can find. Don't worry, when you come home, they will be gone as your uncle is selling them to the local grocer, along with anything else he grows in the future. Without you and Brian the house feels empty; we both needed something to keep us occupied. We are as happy as we can be and news from you is always welcome.*

*Here's wishing you a Happy New Year, darling girl, and we look forward to seeing you very soon.*

*Much love, your adoring aunt and uncle*
*xx*

Folding the letter and placing it back into the envelope, Kitty smiled. The letter had lifted her spirits and the previous day's upset seemed less heavy than when she'd first felt the pain of being used and made to feel foolish.

Finishing off her food, she helped herself to a second cup of tea and settled down in her seat to read the official letter.

To her delight it housed two certificates. She had passed another step towards her goal. The pretty certificates declared she was proficient in *First Aid to the Injured*, and *Gas Attack Efficiency*. An excited flutter ran through her body. For Kitty it meant she'd completed enough examinations to be awarded proficiency badges and wear the Red Cross pinafore instead of a plain one. This was the final stage of her entry into the next level of training within the society. Another step towards full nurse training.

Setting off on duty, she heard her name called out and Michael's voice echoed around the walls of the courtyard.

'Kitty. Wait up. Slow down.'

Kitty had no intention of slowing down. Her heartbeat banged inside her chest at such a speed it scared her. She knew it was not due to the exertion of wider strides to increase her distance, but the fact she was about to be faced with Michael. The man whose voice turned her feelings upside down whenever he spoke to her, let alone whenever she looked at him. However, images of him and Belle together tangled with thoughts of what might have been, had Belle not lied. A sensible voice told her not to become bitter, and new courage merged as she took a deep breath before turning around and acknowledging him.

'Michael. Happy New Year.'

Bending to catch his breath, Michael puffed out his returned wishes for Kitty. They fell into a slower-paced walk and for a short while were both silent. Kitty was unwilling to speak for fear she'd say the wrong thing and her moment alone with Michael disappeared, while Michael allowed his breathing to settle into an even pattern. Eventually, Kitty could no longer stand the silence.

'I take it you'd already run a fair way before seeing me. I'm certain you're not that unfit,' Kitty said with teasing in her voice.

'I'd forgotten important papers and had to run back to my room. You were missed on New Year's Eve. *I* missed you.'

Kitty gave a disgruntled huff and immediately regretted it, so followed through with a slight giggle and ended up regretting that too when it sounded like a muffled snort.

Michael shot her a glance and sidestepped in front of her to prevent her from walking ahead of him again.

'Do I detect a little bit of hostility from someone?' Michael asked with a bemused tone to his voice.

Opening her eyes wide and giving him a stare resembling Matron when not amused, Kitty took a step to one side, but Michael was too fast for her and again blocked her way.

'Oh, stop playing games. Let me past,' Kitty said. She wanted to numb the pain she felt whenever she thought of Belle making a fool of her, and of Michael enjoying Belle's company.

'I'm sorry you didn't make it to the party and didn't get to stomp on my feet, but I don't think I deserve whatever it is you are firing at me,' Michael responded with a questioning frown.

'I'm firing nothing. I'm just so miserable about the party and I'm sorry, I know it's not your fault. It's Belle's and just the thought she had fun with you after telling such a dreadful lie, I'm a little bitter I suppose. Sorry.'

Michael stepped back to allow her to walk along the path again.

'Lie? What lie?'

'She told our ward sister her mother was injured or ill

and she had to return home, but not before she'd added my name to the top of the rota cover list. I saw it yesterday, my name carefully added above the others. It was my official night off, so regardless of the fact it was New Year, I shouldn't have been on the list.' Kitty stopped to take a breath. Her anger was about to get the better of her and she didn't want to push Michael away with her temper. It took a lot to fire up an anger inside Kitty, but each time it had any connection to Michael, it was down to Belle. Kitty needed to express why she was upset to Michael, without making a fool of herself by throwing the tantrum of a jealous schoolgirl. But the resentment was too deep to not say anything and she wanted him to see Belle for what she was through Kitty's eyes.

'Anyway, she proved herself a liar by not going on the truck she allegedly managed to bag a lift home on. But you both had a good time, and I should never begrudge people being happy nowadays,' Kitty said when they reached the end of the path. 'I'll see you on the next emergency shout. Bye Michael.'

Michael pulled open the door into the main hospital. 'I'm sorry you were let down by your friend. It must hurt, but don't hate me, please. I have to go, but I'll be in touch. Have a good shift.'

Kitty heard the genuine, soft concern in his voice.

'It did hurt. I'm sorry I snapped at you,' she replied.

Kitty spent her time on the ward with her assessment mentor learning about wound infection and the latest methods of cleaning and prevention. Some of the wounds she was faced with were stomach-churning, but she never let her face show her inner feelings. It wasn't fair on a patient with life-altering injuries; they needed comfort and reassurance from someone offering a strong sense of calm and control. In between sessions of notetaking, she thought of Michael and of how she had to step off her high horse or she'd lose the microscopic thread of friendship they shared, and once again, the thought of not having any contact with him was unbearable.

Two hours after finishing her shift, Kitty felt restless. Her off-duty mind always filtered its way through a tangled mire of on-duty fears of making a mistake, and Michael. Always Michael, even if she'd had a good day with no misgivings, Michael strayed into her thoughts. She dreamed of him, invented a life with him, and played out a scene where she introduced him to her aunt and uncle.

During her shift today, a young woman, eight months pregnant, staggered into the grounds of the hospital after digging herself out of a caved-in building. She literally fell at Kitty's feet as she made her way on duty, and gave birth to a little boy within fifteen minutes of puffing her way into the emergency unit, clinging onto Kitty and swearing like a soldier confronted by the enemy. From the moment they met, Kitty had no time to think, and actioned a team to help deliver the copper-haired little girl to the young mother whom she learned was named Alice and who worked as a tram driver – although she vowed to never say hello to a sailor at the end of the line, ever again. All the way through the short labour, Alice refused to let go of Kitty and screamed out her wishes for Hitler to sink every boat he came across. By the time baby Winston slid from the womb to the outside world, even Kitty cursed the sailor who'd left Alice high and dry after promising her the world – or at least a cottage in the north of Scotland, and decided motherhood wasn't for her.

Throughout her remaining hours on duty, Kitty sensed the adrenaline still surged through her veins and rendered her restless. Instead of staying inside to study when she finished her shift, she chose a walk, making the most of the extra light of winter. The best thing the government did was not take back the summer hour and plunge them into deeper darkness an hour early. The blackout made life difficult enough as it was, and with the weather turning colder by the hour, another snow fall would make walking out treacherous underfoot, as it had done the previous year. Kitty suspected this would be the last late afternoon walk she'd have for several weeks, so added to her walking distance by paying a visit to Mrs Smith.

The girls often dropped in for a cup of tea and a chat – excluding Belle, who refused to try and redeem herself. Kitty was fond of Ma Smith, who had become a regular mother hen and greeted them as if they were her own daughters. They put the world to rights or cried in her arms after a traumatic event, and she never judged, merely waited until their tears stopped flowing and set them back on the road with a less laden heart, a belly full of something tasty, and a bucket full of tea. Kitty never failed to feel uplifted after a chat with her, and today was no different. She'd offloaded her feelings for Michael, and before the first heavy flakes of snow fell, had learned of the heartbreaks and joys Ma Smith had endured throughout her life, and of how to deal with accepting what was meant to be. If Michael was to become a solid part of her life, she must be patient, but not too far in the background or else he'd never notice her as anything other than a colleague in the trauma team.

## Chapter Sixteen

The sky darkened as Kitty made her way home. To her dismay the snow fell heavier and hampered her vision along the now dimmed streets. The late afternoon had transformed itself into early evening far too soon, and with the street names removed she didn't recognise where she was. Soon realised she must have taken a wrong turn. With no sun to guide her position and the moon not ready to shed light from behind the blanketing clouds, Kitty took a moment to get her bearings.

At the end of the long road ahead, she saw treetops silhouetted against the dark skyline. They were laden with the settling snow, and Kitty shivered. The temperature dropped as she walked, and her breath puffed out white clouds the faster she attempted to pick her way through the thickening snow mounds, towards what she hoped was a park or a central building of sorts where she could find someone to ask for assistance. She'd visited many parks within a half-hour's walk from the hospital, so if it was a park she headed for, she hoped it was one she recognised and from where could get her bearings back to the hospital. The faster she walked the more snow fell, and her lungs protested against the cold wind. She felt the freeze against her skin as snowflakes settled, and Kitty cursed herself for not wearing an extra layer of warm clothing.

To her relief the trees were central to a public park, but to her dismay there was no sign to tell her which one. Unrelenting, the snow continued to fall, forming larger flakes and swirling in every direction, blinding her vision. Had she not been lost, she might have appreciated the beauty of the snow settling in neat, thick mounds and glistening whenever the struggling moon put in an appearance. Time moved into early evening and she guessed it was around seven o'clock. Kitty stumbled, her feet sore and cold. Even her sturdy shoes were no match for the weather. Her foot stubbed against what she assumed was a large boulder and she stumbled against another, sending a jarring pain through her shin. Her foot caught on a slippery mound of frozen moss and she lurched forward, twisting her ankle.

She bent over to rub life back into the shin, wincing with pain when she tried to stand on her foot. Unable to see properly in the dark, she bent back down and ensured her shoe was firm around her foot in readiness for a difficult walk to seek help. Kitty tested the foot against the ground again, but the pain and the deepening snow proved too much.

'Damn and blast!' Kitty shouted, and listened as her voice echoed back to her in anger.

A sudden movement in the form of a shadow flickered across a virgin stretch of snow to her right-hand side and made Kitty jump. She stood upright, trying hard to ignore the twinge of pain forcing its way upwards to her knee.

'Cursing in the street is not very ladylike. You British girls are usually so prim.'

Never had Kitty been so pleased to hear Michael's voice as she was now. She turned around and gave him a beaming smile. His eyes sparkled in the darkness and as the moon gave a thirty-second burst of light, she saw him grinning back. He wore his greatcoat with the collar up around his neck and looked every inch the rescuing hero Kitty saw in him.

'Not today. Today cursing is allowed. What on earth are you doing here?' Kitty asked, and lifted her foot to relieve the pain.

'Walking home. A couple of the guys live across town and are heading out tomorrow. I killed an hour with a whisky farewell. I could ask you the same.'

'Visiting a friend and took a wrong turn,' Kitty admitted.

Michael held his face to the sky as another heavier gust of snowflakes flurried around them.

'This snow reminds me of home. Are you heading back to the hospital?'

Kitty listened to Michael's soft voice in the silence of the falling snow and heard a twinge of sadness.

'Homesick, or sad your friends are leaving?' she asked.

Michael pulled a folded handkerchief from his pocket and wiped his face dry of snowflakes.

'A bit of both if I'm honest,' he said.

'I'm sorry, it is hard to be away from the place you were born. I feel it sometimes, but I'm lucky to have good friends around me. I'm sorry yours are leaving. Anyway, yes, I am heading back to the hospital,' Kitty said, and wiped snowflakes from her own face. 'You have a choice: you could have the pleasure of my company, but if you want to walk faster, you'd better point me in the right direction and head off. I'm afraid I've tweaked my ankle on black ice,' Kitty said, and winced with pain as she tried to place her foot on the ground.

Without hesitation, Michael dropped to his knee and lifted her foot, forcing Kitty to lean one arm on his back for balance. She squealed when he touched the anklebone.

'You've pulled something for sure. Lean on me and we'll check it back at base,' he said, and rose to his feet. He held out an arm for her to lean on and they took a few steps, stopping when the pain became too much.

'You must miss home despite living here so long, and weather like this probably doesn't help. The snow is so beautiful,' Kitty said.

Michael stopped to allow her to adjust her footing.

'And so are you,' he said, his voice soft.

Kitty heard his words loud and clear but dared not respond for fear of making a fool of herself. Had he really declared her beautiful? Kitty faltered when trying to offer a response. She simply smiled, acknowledging his flattery.

'I've never met anyone like you, Kitty. You are kind, always thinking of others, and you never shy from hard work. You are fearless.'

Michael's warm hand tingled against her cheek as he

brushed away newly settled flakes of snow. Their breath clouds mingled and rose skyward, entwined on their journey, and Kitty's heart pounded in her chest. Words remained inside her head; she had no desire to speak for fear of ruining the moment brewing between them, but she wanted him to know her reasons for being offhand with him.

'I wanted to dance with you, and I'll never forgive Belle for taking that opportunity away with her lies.'

'It's in the past. Let's enjoy the now,' Michael replied and moved his face close to hers.

By the time their lips touched, all thoughts of a painful ankle dissipated, and she gave in to his tender embrace. The kiss grew in passion and Kitty felt the intensifying need for more as her body tingled.

To her dismay, a breathless Michael pulled back and shook his head. 'We must get back before we freeze to death. Not that I want this to stop, but we can't drop with hypothermia.'

Another giggle escaped from Kitty. 'After that kiss I think I'll never feel the cold again,' she said with a newfound boldness.

Michael's lips found hers again and smothered her words. He kissed her with such a ferocity Kitty was convinced her lips would be bruised. She returned her feelings with as much fierceness, and lost herself in the moment.

'That will keep you warm until we're home,' Michael said.

Kitty wrapped herself in Michael's arms, grateful they'd

found each other again and she hadn't put him off with her reluctance to put Belle's behaviour aside. A renewed energy surged through her body, and a sensation of what might be pounded through her veins, creating an avalanche of bittersweet emotions. She knew Michael could be the first man she would know intimately, but there was also the nagging possibility he might not survive the war.

If she wanted their relationship to take a new step forward, Kitty knew she had to remain level-headed and not get carried away. War cursed romance and pushed it into a corner where it either surrendered or simmered with hope.

Kitty wanted no white flag, nor had she any plans on simpering. Deep down, Kitty knew she wanted to have it all: a nursing career and Michael's friendship. A friendship to grow into more than snatched kisses. If she dared dream of marriage, Kitty's war fighting the enemy by rescuing and supporting survivors as part of the Red Cross, would end. Michael's kisses were confusing her, and Kitty floundered in her personal battle.

## Chapter Seventeen

K itty's foot no longer pained her, and the four-day rest period had ended with her rushing around a busy ward.

Michael sent her notes, encouraging her to get back on her feet and working alongside him again.

Curled up on the bed, with Trix and Jo lying on the floor, the three friends chose to have a rare evening off together in the warmth of Kitty's room.

Kitty wore large rollers in her hair to try to tame her natural curls into a more modern style, whilst Trix slathered cold cream over her face; Jo scoffed at the idea of all attempts to get her into a beauty regime. She declared herself a soap and water girl. Kitty loved the comradeship they had between them, and of how open they could be with their feelings about life. Whenever Belle barged her way into their small group, the evening never had the intimate warmth they enjoyed when she wasn't around.

The weather showed no sign of increasing in

temperature. Tonight, they wrapped themselves in blankets, and were in deep discussion about marriage and what women sacrificed for love. Kitty had shared her feelings about Michael, and Trix had confided how her love for Smithy had deepened.

Trix and Smithy's relationship had gone beyond best friends and they were tiptoeing around the idea of marriage. With Jo as a solid friend of his, Trix had also became her close friend. The three never left Kitty out of days out or afternoon walks, and she loved every minute they spent together.

Sipping at a small glass of barley wine, Kitty listened to Trix talking of her relationship, and nervous at the prospect of further intimacy with Smithy.

'We both want a future together, and have already discussed children, but this war gets in the way. Gordon suggested we just marry and have done with it, but he doesn't understand when I point out I'd have to stop training. As a married woman I'd have to stay home or go to work in a factory, and that isn't going to happen, no matter how dedicated to the war effort I am; I love this job and he thinks I love it more than him – it isn't possible. I am so sad; we had our first row over this last night.'

Kitty pulled Trix close.

'Smithy is a good man. He loves you and he'll find a way where you can both follow through with your dedicated services. I'll bet you lipstick,' she said.

Jo sat upright. 'I know how much he loves you, Trix; he tells me. He's worried you will be separated by the Red Cross if they move us on elsewhere. He spoke with me the other day. Trust him, he's got his thinking cap on and is trying desperately to find a way you can both be together.'

When Jo mentioned the Red Cross moving them, a shiver ran down Kitty's spine. She'd never anticipated moving so soon, but on reflection realised how many Red Cross and St John's Ambulance recruits had shipped out around the world and across Britain, to support the defence forces in various departments.

'Now, about this lipstick, Kitty. Where on earth would you get one nowadays!' Jo said, and brought laughter back into the room. 'I never wear the stuff. You know me, can't be doing with this girly-twirly business. Give me a car engine to tinker with, and I'll be yours for life,' Jo quipped.

'I'll never understand your fascination with cars, Jo. What's so special about them?' Trix asked.

Jo gave a theatrical sigh. 'What's so special about a car? It can get you to where you want to go without crowds. It gives you freedom, and the mechanics fascinate me. How can a piece of metal and a bit of fuel manage to transport so much? Oh, there's a lot I could tell you about my passion in life, but you'd be bored, Trix old gal.' Jo gave a loud laugh.

A deepened atmosphere of a tightened friendship gave Kitty a powerful feeling of wanting to share with the girls – her sisters-in-arms were a larger part of her life than she'd realised, and she wanted them to know why she often found it hard to become emotionally articulate.

'Girls, I'd like to share something with you both. I've held off from saying anything before, as sometimes it's easier than to explain and experience the pity I always have showered on me afterwards. So, no pity hugs, promise?'

A puzzled Jo and Trix nodded their promise.

'My parents – as you know them – are actually my aunt and uncle. My brother – the one I talk about, is in fact my cousin. My parents and baby brother died when a ferryboat got into trouble and sank with no survivors. I was four at the time and refused to talk for a year. My aunt and uncle took me in with no hesitation, and when their only child was killed at Dunkirk, it confirmed their deep love for me. I am an orphan and I envy hearing you both talk about your parents. Is it wrong of me, given I have such loving guardians?'

Both Jo and Trix had sat listening without interruption, something bordering a miracle with Trix, as she was a fixer of hearts and would most definitely be chomping at the bit to express something meaningful. But, true to her word, she kept her distance and made no attempt to embrace Kitty. When Kitty finished speaking, Jo gave a soft cough.

'I've no pity to give and will only say this. Don't always envy those with parents. My personal experience isn't that great. I talk about mine, but I doubt they say much about me. I'm an embarrassment. A tomboy, not a princess. Out of sight, out of mind is their motto when it comes to me.'

Kitty gave her friend a warm smile.

'Thanks, Jo. I'm sorry you feel so hurt by your parents. If I'd known, I would never have brought it up. Sorry.'

Trix looked at both of them.

'I'm lucky, but it doesn't mean my relationship has always been as rosy as I paint it with my parents, either. That said, I do feel lucky to have them in my life. Being an orphan must be tough. Especially when you are older with life experiences to share, Kitty. I don't pity you, but I do feel for you.'

Kitty shook her head. 'I'm not sad by it, but it's come to my mind more often since I've met Michael. Can you believe he is also an orphan? His grandmother brought him up. When we're on breaks during the rescues, we talk about those who brought us up, but have limited memories of our parents. I fear, with this war, there will be a lot of children with the same – a few years of parental love snatched away in a second.' Kitty stopped talking and stood up, stretching her legs. A sudden wave of embarrassment for opening up to her feelings washed over her.

'I'm sorry girls, I'm not wallowing, but I needed to get it off my chest. Every time we pull a child free, and I know they've been orphaned, it becomes a personal pain. The moment I was told about my own parents floods back, and it is all I can do to remain in control and regain my professional balance again.'

Trix jumped to her feet and put her arms around Kitty. 'This is not a pity hug. Just a hug.'

Also clambering to her feet, Jo gave Kitty a wide grin.

'Don't panic, no hug from me, but I will say, keep up the good work with Michael. Plus, as a new friend of yours, he's quite a catch.' Jo nudged Kitty and gave a wink, earning her a nudge back.

'Watch your back with Belle if you do take up with each other. She's been sniffing around Smithy, but Trix put her right, didn't you kiddo?'

Trix flexed her arm muscles. 'I put her off with my right hook. Seriously, I told her to walk away before her reputation became gossip in all the wrong places, and she's left us alone ever since. Thanks for listening to me bleat on about Smithy and for sharing your stories, girls. I love our time together, but right now, I think I love my bed more, so I'll wish you both goodnight.'

'I'm following. I'm shattered and have a busy day tomorrow,' said Jo.

When the girls left her room, Kitty wrote out her feelings in her journal. Listening to Trix talk about her future and concerns about giving up her career made Kitty think about her own, and tonight her journal housed her answer.

The war came first.

Her personal happiness had to be put aside as those who fought gave up theirs. If she didn't help to defend her country in some small way, she wouldn't have a place to live and follow future dreams of marriage and children.

## Chapter Eighteen

'W hen?' Kitty's voice forced out the question as she stared at Michael. Tears of disbelief and panic, of fear and loss flowed freely down her cheeks. The news he'd just given her was as forceful as a body blow.

'The day after tomorrow. Before dawn, as soon as we've packed and are ready to go. Smithy is also heading out too – not sure if Trix knows yet, so don't say anything, but he's remaining in England. Yorkshire, I believe. Closer than I'll be; I wish I could tell you where I'm heading but this particular post is TS, I'm afraid. I never dreamed I'd be called to teach emergency medicine – I applied for other positions before you came into my life and if—' Michael said, and she heard his own distress.

'If nothing. This is what you are destined to do, and it cannot be altered, Michael,' Kitty said, with more bravery in her voice than she felt, but Michael didn't need more pressure placed upon him than he was already experiencing.

Their relationship over the weeks since Kitty's accident had grown into a deeper one than expected. Every spare moment they shared was filled with passionate kisses. Both confessed they were too committed to their cause to consider a more permanent relationship.

Until first thing that morning when Michael rang the home and asked to meet with Kitty before she went on duty, she had thought of nothing but the war's end and of the outcome. Now she knew she'd become so attached to him, she wanted more from him than the short-lived romance they'd barely begun.

Any dreams of them having a future together were dashed. She and Michael had been thrust back into the cold clutches of the present day once again. Fighting for the lives of people, rescuing and tending to their wounds was one thing, being separated and reminded that they were also vulnerable to loss and fear was another. Kitty shuddered, holding back the threatening tears.

'I can't imagine life around here without you,' she whispered.

Michael reached out and touched her hand.

'We'll have this evening. I have to go now, but promise we'll meet later,' he said, offering an encouraging smile.

Kitty gave a slow, sad nod. With a heavy weight tugging at her insides, she watched him walk away. He turned by the large tree at the end of the path and blew her a discreet kiss. Kitty pretended to catch it and tuck it into her heart pocket. She was rewarded with a beaming smile and then he was gone from view. The moment Kitty caught her breath and composed herself before walking towards the hospital, a familiar voice cut into the silence and her skin tingled with irritation. Belle was behind her, and the last person she wanted to see was a self-interested adult brat.

'I said, wait up.' Belle puffed out her irritation as she caught up with Kitty. In no mood for listening to an onslaught of Belle's latest conquests, Kitty simply carried on walking without acknowledging her.

'Don't tell me you are still angry about New Year – or last week when I asked him to the community dance. He turned me down and I've apologised enough, surely?' Belle said.

Kitty stopped in her tracks and turned on Belle. She had little doubt her face shared her resentment and anger but made no effort to plaster a fake smile across it just to appease her.

'Life doesn't revolve around you alone, Belle. Lie your way through life and get what you want, but please do not keep pushing your way into a friendship which is fragile enough. Michael and I have something special, and every time I turn around you are there, trying to crush what we have. You are a jealous manipulator and I'm done talking with you.'

Kitty stormed off without looking at Belle. Her temper cooled the nearer she got to the main entrance of her ward. Working with Belle for several hours was to be a challenge she didn't need, but she had the evening to look forward to, and time with Michael was too precious to be tarnished by a spat with someone else. On seeing Belle arrive on duty,

Kitty pushed herself forward for wound dressing support, knowing this would be the last task Belle would want to do, and would be a one-to-one with a qualified member of staff, meaning Kitty had limited contact with others on duty. Her mind needed to focus and concentrate on work rather than Michael leaving, so with a wound care assessment on the horizon, she felt it the better option.

From behind the screens, she often heard Belle's name called out in impatient and reprimanding tones by her senior. It always amazed Kitty how Belle drifted through her working life oblivious to her failure to impress. Although, Kitty suspected Belle's social life was an entirely different matter. How could she ignore the implications of war?

---

Michael's abrupt departure left Kitty bereft – an unexpected feeling she'd not experienced since the loss of her family and cousin, only this time it had a depth to it she couldn't explain. Michael still lived, so why did she feel as if she were in mourning for somebody – or something? It was a question she asked Jo many times.

Trix and Smithy's relationship became a frantic whirlwind of Trix applying for a transfer to Yorkshire, and Kitty held the twinges of jealousy deep inside. She watched her friend pace the corridor waiting for the post to arrive, and held her close when Smithy left to take up his position as a temporary GP in a rural village in North Yorkshire.

Kitty spent her days working all the hours her body could spare to prevent her recalling the last few hours she'd spent lying in Michael's arms the night before he left. They'd lain fully clothed on a bed inside an unused ward. Not many knew about the small six-bed bay tucked away from the main hospital, and Michael's friend mentioned he'd slept there on occasion when he needed undisturbed sleep. The clandestine meeting added to the nervous parting, and Kitty's tears flowed readily.

During the three weeks since Michael left, Kitty had spent every night turning over his words of reassurance and love in her mind.

'We will have a life after I return home. Wait for me, Kitty. Don't ever give up on me. I love you. I'm not a man of many words, but I'm happy to tell you I'm falling in love with you.'

Taken aback by his declaration of love for her, Kitty had tried to find the words she wanted to share. She touched his cheek.

'I think I might be falling for you, too. Maybe the time apart will prove it to us. As they say, absence makes the heart grow fonder,' she said, and accepted another of his passionate kisses.

Michael had held her close as he spoke, but had respected her boundaries. Although both were desperate to explore each other's bodies, they fought the urge. Kitty knew Michael struggled with controlling himself, as did she, but admired him all the more for not taking advantage of her weakness. They lay together enfolded in comforting clutches, not wanting to part or think about what would happen next, and their silence spoke volumes. Kitty's tears were kissed away, and Michael's sighs of despair and reluctance to unwrap his arms from around her continued for several hours until eventually they caved in to the inevitable and went their separate ways.

For over a week Kitty was in a state of despair, and Jo watched her like a hawk. Slowly, acceptance crept in and Kitty climbed out of the darkness and was able to function without tears.

---

There was an eerie silence in the streets as Kitty headed for the postbox early that morning. It was a familiar route and had been every day from the day Michael left. She wrote to him during any spare minute about her day, the weather, and anything else she could think of to entertain him.

Belle gave her plenty of material. The girl had been taken to Matron after she was caught staying overnight in a junior doctor's room, caught smoking behind the medical storage building, and many other jaw-dropping incidents according to the senior staff.

Jo despaired whenever they were grouped together for assignments and projects. Kitty tried to keep the peace between her and Belle, but gave up when Trix pointed out their differences and how futile it was to try and get Belle to understand life outside of her own selfishness.

Walking alongside the tumbled housing spilling onto the pavements, Kitty mentally wrote out a request to return home for a few days' leave. She'd worked so hard and earned a break, which she knew would not be denied. She needed time to step away from the environment tormenting her romantic brain so she could return to work with a more focused one.

A noise cut into the silence and she traced it to the sky above her head. Distracted from her thoughts, she watched as two planes tossed and twirled in combat. Noise escalated when children ran from their yards and homes to watch, excited by the vision of a dogfight in the sky and cheering on the brave British pilot defending their right to live.

Smiling at their innocence, Kitty silently begged the powers that be to spare their little lives and not allow the enemy to return and create havoc. The medical staff were exhausted. She gave a deep sigh before making ready to continue her walk.

'Somebody looks a little miserable today.'

Kitty cringed when she heard Eddie's voice. Why could she never rejoice in his or Belle's company?

'On leave again, Eddie?' Kitty asked, her voice terse and tense. The man rarely seemed to be away at his barracks – wherever they were supposed to be nowadays.

'Running errands, and thought I'd call in on the parents, then make a detour to see you on the way back. Call it checking in on our volunteers and making good use of military fuel,' Eddie replied with a cockiness in his voice. He was so sure of himself, and his Jack-the-lad attitude grated on Kitty.

'See *me*? Belle was out, was she? Listen Eddie, I am not interested in a man traipsing halfway around the country using vital, precious fuel. I've never given you reason to do such a dreadful thing.'

She paused when he raised an eyebrow in mock amusement. 'But you told me to visit you if ever I was in town,' Eddie said.

Kitty drew herself up to her full height. 'I did no such thing – not in the way your mind works, anyway. My advice is to do what others are doing and start taking this war seriously. Now clear off and let me get back on duty.'

Kitty's temper was at a peak she'd never experienced before and as the planes overhead pushed and pulled against the rising wind for supremacy, she nudged Eddie to one side and pushed Michael's letter into the postbox, angry she couldn't kiss it as she would normally do with Eddie's eyes upon her, and turned back the way she had come. To his credit, Eddie didn't speak further, and nor did he follow.

Kitty relaxed. When she walked to work from the home later that day, she spotted Belle and Eddie together. She ignored them when they saw her, and tried hard to ignore Belle's loud, tinkling, singsong laugh.

'*Cooeee*, Kitty. Eddie said you broke his heart today and he needed someone to fix it for him, so I'm obliged to offer him my services. Rejecting friends is not polite, Kitty,' Belle shouted out to her.

Kitty watched as Eddie whispered something and made Belle laugh again.

She sighed. Let them have their games; she just wanted to get through the endless struggles of every day until she saw Michael again.

With April poking its head around the corner, small buds appeared on shrubbery, and birds flitted back and forth collecting nesting materials, but none of the beauty of fresh life hit home for Kitty as it usually would. A series of bombing raids battered the Midlands yet again, and staff were on edge.

Kitty admired the residents of Birmingham and their resilience, and it made her more determined than ever to play her part in their city. Her heart went out to them whenever they had to claw their way back to some form of survival, only to be beaten back to the ground another day.

Her heart also weighed heavy with Michael's absence, and his latest letter had puzzled her and broken her heart. He wrote as a friend, not a lover. It was a polite letter compared to his previous ones.

*Address withheld*

*Dear Kitty,*

*I hope this finds you well. Not a lot to say if I am honest and this is not an easy letter to write, but one I feel I must send to you sooner rather than later.*

*This war and where I am at the moment has me thinking about us and the promises we made. They were hasty and said in a frantic moment in our lives. By tying you to a boyfriend/girlfriend relationship, I feel I am not being fair to you, especially now it has come to my attention that Eddie is back in your life.*

*In many ways it's a good thing. If you are to have a relationship of any kind, it is best you choose a British man who might become a husband, over a passing Canadian doctor who thinks he will inevitably return to his own country once war ceases or Hitler's men find their target. It is too much to ask you to hang around waiting, only to be left standing on the shore watching me sail away with no idea whether I'll contact you again.*

*You have a future ahead of you as a qualified nurse, and to be fair, with your ability you could become a doctor. I cannot – will not – hold you back. I am fond of you, and our friendship was a comfort during those dark days of rescuing and recovering, for which I thank you. You brightened up the tough days.*

*I have an ego which will assume you will be upset reading this and want you to know it hasn't been an easy decision. With distance and time, we will accept this as the right thing for both of us.*

*Yours truly, your friend,*
*Michael*

Upset? Friend? Kitty concluded she was more puzzled – and angry – than upset by his assumption she was walking out with Eddie. What made him think such a thing? Kitty backtracked to the day in March at the postbox; it was the only time she had been alone in Eddie's company, and she realised it must be his and Belle's interference – a game concocted to repay her for rejecting Eddie. Belle must have asked one of her many doctor friends to get the letter to him. Their childish behaviour had destroyed something special, and she'd never forgive them.

Kitty wrote back to Michael using the postal address he'd given her and hoped it found him; with *address withheld* on his letter, he may have moved on and chosen not to receive post from her any more. With tears dripping onto the paper, and three attempts later, she pushed what she'd written into an envelope.

*Birmingham*

*Dearest Michael,*

*What a heart-breaking letter to receive! Your assumption I'm walking out with Eddie is ridiculous. The man is a creep and seeks his satisfaction from the person I think sent you spiteful hints of me meeting up with him. Annabelle Farnsworth is nothing more than a liar and a dreadful flirt – I'm not sorry for writing such a thing. She is hellbent on ensuring I do not have you in my life, so as you bluntly put it, Hitler might get you, but I will also pray Belle never does. If this reads like an angry ranting slight against her, then you have read it properly. I am so angry right now.*

*Michael, we are a couple who used the word love. Until the point you wrote this letter, I thought your feelings matched mine, but I can see they do not, or you would never have written goodbye. If, as you say, you are ending our relationship, then I will have to learn some way of living with that and try to heal the heart you have broken.*

*Stay safe, and if you return to Canada never to give me another thought, please know there is a woman somewhere in England who will remember you always.*

*K x*

All Kitty could do after posting the letter was move forward with her life. She tried to put Michael from her mind, but every day, as she dragged herself from her bed to work as many shifts as she could manage, his name entered her head.-She could not believe he was ready to give up the love they had declared for each other, and the intimate moments – the passionate, skin-tingling, over-the-blouse fumbling – they had shared. Every day Kitty was grateful for the distraction of work. The emergency unit was pushed to the limit and she often found herself heading a team. It was in those moments she switched from a crying mess to being confident and in control.

Emotionally, when on a rescue mission, she tried to push all thoughts of Michael aside, but professionally he still worked his magic and she imagined his soft Canadian voice encouraging her to pull someone free from danger, how to dress a wound, and dig deep inside for courage.

Paranoia became her enemy and she never left herself open to idle gossip. She turned down offers of trips to the cinema and parties – especially from men, who she could no longer trust. Kitty also avoided Belle wherever possible. She'd destroyed Kitty's dreams of a life with Michael, with a force more powerful than one of Hitler's incendiary bombs.

## Chapter Nineteen

One morning, Kitty noticed her mood had turned a corner. She'd experienced a good night's sleep and spent an afternoon studying with birds singing outside her open bedroom window, allowing the gentle afternoon breeze to filter around her room.

She was surprised at how upbeat she felt, given the previous morning Trix had left for a new post in the same area in Yorkshire as Smithy, and the friends parted with tearful promises to stay in touch. They had a strong bond, so each girl knew they were not false promises. Even thoughts of Michael didn't pain her quite so much.

Kitty sat on the edge of her bed absorbing a moment of calm, when she heard Jo's door click shut next door. She waited a couple of hours before inviting her in to play a game of cards, and a contentment soon filled the room. Kitty thanked her blessings for such a good friend in her life and knew she could always confide in Jo – something she intended to try and do that evening. It was time Jo learned of how hurt Kitty had been by both Belle and Michael. By sharing, Kitty had a feeling she might heal a little more. She would see what mood Jo was in and take it from there.

'Do you think Trix will survive without us?' Kitty asked with a giggle, as she laid down a killing hand from her card selection.

Jo laughed.

'I'd like to think not, but she's grown up a lot more than both of us, I think. She bustles around organising, and has turned Smithy around well and truly. He was a buffoon before she took him under her wing. He was always in trouble at school; I'm surprised he made it this far in life. Trix is good for him,' Jo said, and placed a counter-defensive trump card. 'Tah da!' she said with a triumphant air punch.

'Great game. I enjoy our quiet moments together, but not when you beat me every time we play.' Kitty conceded defeat and rose to stretch out her back and legs.

'Gracious, is that the time? It's true what they say, it flies when you are having fun. I needed tonight. There's something I need to …'

No sooner had she stretched one limb than the squealing sound of the sirens filled the building, and the call for all staff to evacuate to the wards came from the house matron. A banging of doors and a chaos ensued in the corridor. A commanding voice shouted for order, and Kitty grabbed a towel to remove the cold cream from her face.

'Crikey, wasn't expecting that!' Jo yelled as she ran to her room, grabbing her shoes and cape.

'Stay safe. See you later!' Kitty shouted out to her friend

as she rammed her feet into her shoes, cursing the laces and her fumbling fingers for refusing to tie at her speed, and flung her cape around her shoulders. Although not fully dressed in uniform, she had no time to waste and knew she would be forgiven for wearing her siren suit. Time was of the essence and patients needed to be protected from the overhead battle about to commence. She heard the first of the anti-aircraft home defence guns firing skyward as she ran out into the courtyard where a swarm of staff ran from every direction towards the main building. The familiar *rat-tat* sound rallied around the city as the defence teams made a desperate attempt to hold off the enemy.

A chilling sound of air rushing around a descending bomb hurtling to the ground forced Kitty's heart and legs into a state of heightened urgency. A cold chill coursed through her veins as she ran through the yard escorted by flashing searchlights flickering and twitching across the sky. What happened next struck fear through her, and she trembled where she stood. The ground shook and more bombs fell from the sky like leaves from a tree. One after the other they pounded the city. They were close – far too close.

Without stopping, she and the other staff ran full pelt towards the hospital, and Kitty caught up with the emergency teams to register her availability. They stood around in a gaggle of frustration. All waiting for the go-ahead when the all-clear sounded out the start of the rescue race. The moment it rang around the streets, the hospital buzzed with readiness. Kitty inhaled and waited for her allocated team to be called out. Adrenaline bubbled around her body and she felt that if she wasn't sent from the hospital soon, she would explode with nervous energy and make her escape that way. At last, she heard her name.

'Kitty Pattison. You are with me. Quick, into the next ambulance,' the familiar voice of Michael's friend, Robert Keane, called out her name. When she reached his side, his face was creased with intense, deep furrowed frowns, and Kitty didn't hesitate to do as he instructed. She stood waiting for the ambulance to pull up to the kerb, her body alert but still trembling. Both clambered on board and waited for the driver to forge his way towards the epicentre of the disaster.

'It's a bad one,' Robert said.

'I'm shaking, and that's unusual for me,' Kitty confessed.

Robert nodded.

The ambulance rocked and stalled its way to its destination. Once stationary, Robert jumped out and held his hand up to prevent her from doing the same whilst he assessed the scene before him.

'Oh, God no!' His voice cracked with emotion and it caught Kitty's attention. She pushed his arm to one side and stepped onto the street, peering into the darkness.

'It's worse than the March raid, isn't it?' she asked, not expecting an answer as she stared at the carnage before her. A loud blast forced them to take cover inside the ambulance again, and Rob pulled Kitty close.

'Michael will never forgive me if anything happened to you. Don't put yourself in danger out there, hear me?'

Easing herself from his arms, Kitty patted her protective tin hat back onto her head.

'So long as you don't suffocate me first,' she said with a forced laugh, trying to lighten the mood. Rob's mention of Michael hit hard, but it was neither the time nor place to talk about Michael breaking off their relationship.

After a while they ventured out of the ambulance again, and, gathering her thoughts as to their whereabouts, Kitty realised they were staring at the city centre. The Bullring and the surrounding shopping areas, The Prince of Wales theatre, and other large imposing buildings either lay in destroyed heaps or were damaged beyond repair. Although the enemy had returned home, their presence lingered with the threat of intent to return. Rescuing victims needed to be carried out swiftly, just in case.

'Here we go,' Rob declared in a voice so low Kitty barely heard him. It was not the statement of a hero about to leap to the rescue, but one cloaked in trepidation of what they might find.

To their relief, they only encountered minor injuries and could deal with them on the spot. After an hour in the field, they moved to the temporary injury unit in a nearby school, and continued with their care, dividing patients into varying levels of need.

Rob pulled Kitty to one side after talking with the driver of a van bringing more supplies from the hospital.

'We're needed on the outskirts. It's just as bad if not worse in some places. I could do with your skills and calm. Are you in, or staying here?'

Kitty patted the child she tended on the head and turned to Robert.

'I sense I'd be letting people down if I stayed here?'

Robert touched her arm.

'You'd never let anyone down. None of us would, but as I said, I could do with your skills. Michael said you were good, but he didn't say *how* good. You're a born natural. I don't need an assistant by my side; I need someone who can think on their feet and work independently. We're over our head out here tonight.'

Kitty opened a medical bag nearby and filled it with bandages and anything she felt would be useful to them amongst the rubble. She snatched up two torches and gave Robert a small smile.

'You have a way with words. Let's go,' she said.

---

Two hours into the search and rescue, Kitty began doubting her ability to continue. The harrowing sights began to take their toll on her tired limbs and mind. A loud voice distracted her rambling thoughts, and she spotted a man staggering around waving what appeared to be a rifle and wearing an oddly shaped tin helmet.

'Come on lads. This way. Over the ridge. Trench one,' he shouted. His commanding voice echoed above all other noises.

'Robert. I think we have help and support,' Kitty called over to him and the team of men pulling people from a collapsed building which had fallen in on itself. An explosion had forced the bulk of the brickwork to cave inward and collapse onto a converted shelter in the basement. The report came through that several hundred people were below.

'Direct them where they are most needed, Kitty. I'll stay here,' Robert replied.

Kitty rushed towards the man and, as he came closer her mistake dawned on her and she suppressed the urge to laugh. His distress and actions were not to be taken lightly.

The man was elderly and dressed in a checked brown dressing gown with a tin hat shaped suspiciously like an upturned chamber pot; on closer inspection, it was exactly that. A pot with a broken handle. His rifle was in fact a broom handle, and he wore what looked like a woman's handbag across his body.

'Sir. Can I help you?' Kitty asked once they met face to face. She reached out her hand to the man. His startled face turned to one of bewilderment.

'What are you doing on the field, girl? Where are your parents? This is no place for a child. Men! Sergeant! God damn it, where are they? Where is everyone!?'

Kitty's heart went out to the man as she watched him fall to his knees. His confusion became more and more obvious with his frantic repeat for his men to join him on the front line. He needed help, but help with the dignity he deserved. A man of the Great War brought into a state of agitation by the latest bombings. His accent was local, and she guessed his house was also a victim of the night. The man's war history was no doubt one of true bravery, as she'd learned much about the First World War and its horrors. He would have been a young lad when he was sent to defend Great Britain, and if he could endure that, then she could cope with saving lives.

'Sir, I believe they are in the medical tent awaiting your instruction. Do you live nearby?'

The man looked about him, and Kitty's eyes followed as he observed his surroundings.

'Live nearby? Are you mad? Take me to the tent. To my men,' the man said as he rose to his feet and puffed out his chest. Kitty's ears picked up a hint of hidden aggression. It was best not to agitate him further.

'Of course, sir, follow me.'

They picked their way along the difficult pathway towards the first-aid centre, and the moment they arrived, the old man became alert and demanded his men attend reconnaissance instruction. Kitty withered anyone sniggering with one stare as she escorted him towards a doctor at the end of the tent. After pacifying the man and offering him a cup of tea, the medical team took over his care.

As she walked away, Kitty thought of his distress, but knew the sight of him when she first set eyes on him would always bring a smile her way. He had helped relieve her moments of weariness. With only a few hours' rest, Hitler's men rained down another tonnage of bombs upon Birmingham, and Kitty drew upon the strength the old man had given her to support Robert and the rest of the team.

The man was still a war hero in her eyes, no matter what his enemy had taken from him.

## Chapter Twenty

K itty gave a tentative knock on the office door. Being called to attend an interview with the visiting recruitment officer meant only one thing: her days living in Birmingham were numbered. They'd all come to know changes were made after such a visit. So many staff left with only a few hours' notice. Kitty hoped it was a welfare visit, nothing more.

'Come,' a voice called out from behind the door.

With a frown, Kitty placed her hand on the door handle. She'd not expected a man to be on the other side. Pushing open the door, she entered and faced a stern-looking middle-aged man with endless chins seated at the desk.

'Pattison. We have nae met, but I've heard you have the capabilities of someone we could do with at—'

Kitty took a step forward to stem his rushed flow of words she had barely understood. Scottish accents often caught her by surprise. 'I'm sorry sir, and you are?'

Rising to his feet the man appeared not much taller than

167

when seated. With a red flush across his face he gave a slight shake of his head.

'It's nae matter who I might be. I have a busy schedule and am here to inform you we are moving you to a new base.'

A flip of her stomach unnerved Kitty. The news was not unexpected, but not overly exciting considering she would be parted from Jo – the one person keeping her sane during these sad times.

'You said base, not hospital. Where exactly are you sending me, sir?' she said, and gave the man a fleeting smile in the hope his stern personality might show some signs of cracking, but it was a smile in vain.

The man sat down and indicated she should do the same on the chair at the far end of the table.

'Miss Pattison, during wartime decisions are made, and those who choose to fight also make a commitment to protect …'

Kitty held out her hands in question.

'Have I failed in some way? I thought I'd done enough for my assessments. Are you saying I'm not accepted for further training? Please, I—'

The man sighed and shifted in his seat, waving his hand in an impatient manner for her to stop talking.

'If you would let me finish. I was saying that during wartime, nae decision is made lightly. We are in need of trained staff for… let's say, off-the-grid medical care thanks to our enemy and their ferocious attacks, which leaves the important cottage hospitals or other major ones, in need of help.'

Kitty absorbed his words.

'Sir, do I get a choice? To remain here or work elsewhere?' she asked.

'I'm afraid not, although you will remain on home soil. I am sorry a trip abroad is not on the agenda.'

Kitty let out a sigh of relief, unconscious of how loud she'd expressed it.

'I see. We appear to have made the correct decision for you, if the relief on your face is anything to go by,' the man said, and this time there was a twitch of approval around his mouth.

'I'd go anywhere to serve my country, but yes, I am relieved to be staying in England,' Kitty replied.

Gathering up his battered brown briefcase, the man moved from behind the desk. He looked her up and down, and Kitty felt a sense of discomfort. She shifted from one foot to the other.

'Our choices have to be made to suit the ability of the untrained nurse. Your recommendations do you credit, and you will be of value to the hospital waiting to receive you,' the man said.

Kitty gave him a smile.

'I expect most people are selected carefully, and I consider myself educated by this hospital to a high level, and honoured to be chosen for a new position. Where am I going, sir?' she asked, and took a deep breath in anticipation of his reply.

'You will pack your things, and ready yourself for collection at the front steps, 11.30 tomorrow morning.

Prompt. You will be informed of your destination by your driver. Good luck.'

The man held out his hand and Kitty accepted his farewell handshake. Her mind was still confused by the whole affair and she was a little disappointed at not knowing where they were sending her.

'Thank you. For the good luck, I mean. I'm not sure about the rest. There's not a lot of time to prepare myself, is there?'

'Time is not always our friend, Miss Pattison. Your matron asked me to send you her way when I'm finished. So I suggest you do her bidding. The woman is a force unto herself.'

Kitty giggled inwardly. Matron had the capability to make the man feel smaller than he already was, but Kitty always held great respect for the woman, so made her way to her office without dawdling.

---

'Yes. If you could let them know I'd be grateful, Mr Smith. I'll write to them when I'm at the – sorry, the line is bad. Oh, it's not easy here, no. I've got friends. Yes. Take care of yourselves and I'll see you all when I'm on leave next,' Kitty called down the telephone to the postmaster in her village, asking him to inform her aunt and uncle she was moving out of Birmingham.

Matron confirmed Kitty was on the transfer list, and reassured her all of her duties were cancelled, aside from any emergency call-out duties overnight, and her destination was *somewhere in England*.

'Honestly Jo, I'm not going to be packed in time, and what will I need first? Uniform or mufti? Do I travel in uniform?'

Jo's calm voice overrode Kitty's frantic one.

'Slow down. Of course, it's normal clothing as you'll end up a crumpled mess. We'll get you packed, and you'll have time to sit with me awhile, too. I'll go and get us a cuppa from the kitchen, and you carry on folding.'

When Jo left the room, the realisation that they were to be parted hit home. Tears drizzled down Kitty's face and dripped from her chin. She cuffed them away. Jo wouldn't appreciate the soppy mentality; she appreciated the more controlled emotions when it came to saying goodbye. Jo's foot tapped against the base of the door and she stood holding two cups of steaming tea.

'Topped up with a drop of the best thing to cure the miseries.'

Kitty accepted her cup, sniffed the whisky Jo hinted was an addition to the tea, took a sip, and placed it to one side.

'I'm obviously heading somewhere off radar, or they would have told me, surely? It's a bit scary if I'm honest.' Kitty spoke as she continued packing her things. Jo sat on the bed sipping at her tea.

'Get your cup and sit down a minute. You've been flapping nonstop since you got back. It's happening, and we have to deal with it. They are probably not sending you somewhere secret, and are sorting out who has to go where as we speak.

Write to me when you get to wherever, and if it's all hush hush, write a snippet about, um, let's say a fake Auntie Joy to try and give me some idea of where you are in the country.'

Kitty burst out laughing.

'Auntie Joy? I'll remember that.'

Both girls sat in silence drinking their tea, only stopping to sigh out their satisfaction. Kitty soon felt the tension in her body dissipate, and she relaxed.

A loud banging on the door made them both jump, and Kitty shouted for the person on the other side of the door to enter. To her dismay, Belle sauntered in wearing an outfit worthy of a trip to the theatre, right down to white gloves.

'Daddy's in town and I've the evening off. Ward Sister told me you were unavailable due to relocation in the morning. Decent of you not to let me know, Pattison. It was embarrassing when I asked for them to get you to cover my shift. Some friend you turned out to be. Anyway, I'm not one to hold grudges, so came to say *bon voyage*.'

Belle's plummy voice grated on Kitty. The airs and graces were more pronounced than usual, and she guessed it was down to Belle putting on appearances in readiness for meeting her father.

'As always you thought of me giving up my free time to allow you yours. Sorry it didn't go to plan, but I see you must have found someone else. Enjoy your evening, and I'll maybe see you around when I return to visit Jo. Thanks for dropping by, but if you'll forgive me, I've got a bag to pack.'

Kitty watched as Belle glanced around the room, wrinkling her nose with disapproval.

'Yes, I see you are still clinging onto that khaki

monstrosity. Well, *au revoir*, nice meeting you,' Belle said, and waggled her fingers.

Jo leaped to her feet.

'You and I need to talk. It doesn't pay to sneak around ruining lives – writing lies in letters—'

'Talk all you want; I don't have a clue what you are on about. Unless it is about the poor choices in women some Canadian doctors make …' She glanced at Kitty and flicked back her hair, followed by a tweak of the fingers of her gloves.

Jo rushed and pushed Belle against the door.

'You will regret what you've said. Kitty has—'

Kitty tugged at Jo's jumper to stop her friend's arm from swinging out a slap.

'She's not worth it, Jo. A snake, nothing but a snake. Get out, Belle, and I hope you, Eddie, and Michael – if he'll have you, will be very happy together.'

Rearranging her hat, Belle tugged open the door and gave a sniff of indignation, leaving a waft of overpowering perfume which made Kitty gag.

Jo stood with her arms out in question and disbelief.

'Is she from another planet? No shame. No care for anyone but herself. She'll regret it, Kitty. I'll dirty her name around here.' Jo inhaled and exhaled with anger. 'She might think she has Michael in her grasp, but I can soon filter a few stories to the right ears, and he'll learn a few things to make him sit up and take notice. I'm not going to sit around here and let her get away with hurting you.'

'Oh, Jo. Don't get yourself wound up over me and my troubles. I love you for wanting to fight my corner, but if

Michael cannot believe the best of me and decides a flighty piece like Belle is worth losing me over, then he's not the man I thought he was. Do whatever makes you feel better, but don't get into trouble on my account. Please. It's over between me and him.'

Kitty gave her friend a gentle cuddle to show her gratitude, despite knowing Jo would pull back and compose herself against the show of affection.

'She has to pay somehow, Kitty. I've seen what it has done to you,' Jo said.

'I don't want you getting a black mark against your good name on my account, Jo, so leave it alone.'

Long after Jo had left the room, Kitty was comforted by her friendship. Life without Jo around was going to be tough.

## Chapter Twenty-One

Kitty shifted her kitbag to one side with her foot as she reached the exit of the hospital and tucked away the food parcel Matron had produced at their farewell meeting that morning. Although she wasn't one hundred per cent certain which of the three destinations mentioned Kitty was allocated to, Matron said Kitty was in for a long journey and she might be grateful for the cheese sandwiches and flask of tea.

A honk of a horn alerted Kitty to look right. She checked her watch; both she and the driver were ten minutes early. The cool May morning encouraged her to pull the collar of her outdoor cape around her neck and clasp it securely.

'Looks like your transport has arrived, Kitty. It's a posh job. Staff car. I knew you were special, but not that special. Who are you really, Kitty Pattison?' Jo teased.

Kitty cleared her throat. It was tight with emotion and she'd promised Jo not to cry when they said their goodbyes.

'It's not for me, is it? It can't be; it's a bit of a fancy bus if it is. Oh, he's waving me over, so it must be. Well here goes, next stop… anyone's guess. My stomach butterflies have butterflies of their own. I'm so nervous!' she said.

'Right. Take care of yourself. Don't forget me,' Jo said, and Kitty heard a hint of emotion in the last part of the sentence.

'How could anyone forget Joan Norfolk? Oh, here he goes again – yes, yes, I'm coming,' Kitty called back and waved her hand at the driver below, who'd attracted her attention with an impatient blast of the large black saloon's horn.

Turning to give Jo a wave goodbye, Kitty was disappointed to see she'd already returned inside. Good old Jo, not one to allow emotions rule the moment.

'Let's pop your bag in the boot, miss,' the young driver said, touching his cap.

Kitty watched with amusement and hoped Belle wasn't missing this moment. The car would impress her snobbish aspirations and would be a thumb on the nose salute from Kitty as she slid into the back seat. She'd wanted to sit up front, but the driver insisted it wasn't allowed for safety reasons.

'Wait up!'

A male voice called from the main doorway of the hospital, and Kitty spun around to see Robert Keane bounce down the steps.

'I've just bumped into Jo and she said you were leaving us. Just wanted to say have a safe journey and we'll miss you.'

Before she had the opportunity to say anything, Robert reached in and kissed her cheek and gave her a hug.

'I'll miss you, Robert. And the team. I'll come and say hello when I visit Jo. Stay safe and take care.'

'Keep in touch. Write to me,' Robert called out over his shoulder as he bounded back up the stairs.

Seeing Robert leave, she looked around and this time hoped Belle wasn't watching, as she'd no doubt take advantage of reporting Kitty to Michael as having a relationship with Rob as well as Eddie. Then she shook herself with annoyance over thinking Michael would care either way.

'Are you comfortable, miss? Warm enough? I saw you shiver,' the driver said as he craned his neck around to speak to her.

'Kitty. My name is Kitty, and I am more than comfortable, thank you. Just shaking off the goodbye emotions.' She giggled and changed the subject as he turned back around, and they pulled away. 'How many are we picking up? And more importantly, where are we going?'

'We're not picking anyone up, miss. I've important papers to deliver, which means the usual female driver of this car is off duty for once. I was instructed to collect one passenger; a Red Cross nurse allocated to QAIMNS support, which is you. A Katherine Pattison. I'm Bert, by the way.'

'Isn't this car a bit over the top for VIP papers and a Red Cross trainee nurse?' Kitty asked.

Bert laughed. 'I've got to return with three VIP staff, so they are killing two birds with one stone. Our transport team heard you were to head out for Leeds on one of the ambulances, which would have meant an eighty-mile detour to collect another nurse, so for once one of them saw sense, and bingo, here we are.'

'Well, I'm not complaining. This will be better than bouncing around in the back of an ambulance or truck,' Kitty said with feeling.

Watching the city drift away, bomb site after bomb site, Kitty mulled over his words. She'd heard of the Queen Alexandra's Imperial Military Nursing Service, but never met anyone who'd joined up. The prospect was exciting, as well as slightly nerve-wracking. She hadn't a clue where Leeds was or what it was like.

'Did you say we are going to a place called Leeds?' she asked.

'I did. Another city awaiting their Red Cross VIP guest.'

'Lucky me,' Kitty said with a heavy dose of sarcasm.

A chuckle from the front seat made Kitty smile.

'Are you laughing at me?'

Bert's hand waved above the driver's seat.

'Wouldn't dare. I take it you are not a city lover. It's a long drive with you upset in the back. Relax and we'll find a place to stretch our legs in an hour or so. Four-hour drive if we're lucky. Roads are a nightmare nowadays. All craters and rubble,' he said.

'The city is different from what I'm used to, and I would have liked to be shipped somewhere other than another city, if I'm honest. I do miss the community spirit of my home village.'

Bert gave a vigorous nod of his head. 'I'm a Suffolk village lad through and through and love the countryside.'

'Next county to mine. I'm Essex. Near the port of Harwich.'

Bert gave a nod. 'I know it well. We used to collect shrimps from the quayside there. Big old brown ones for Sunday tea.'

'Ooh, don't remind me. What I'd give for a sniff of seaweed in the air, right now,' Kitty said. With a deep sigh, she sat back in her seat and took in the scenery outside the window.

Drab destruction glared back at her. Every now and then they would pass through countryside, and the struggling sunshine attempting to break through the cloud would peek from behind gaps in the trees. One thick area of trees transported Kitty back to running in Wrabness Woods near her home town, when they went chestnut picking in the autumn. Nostalgia washed over her, and she gripped her hands tightly together to suppress the tears. How she wished time could take a few years back. She appreciated her life with her aunt and uncle, and adored her days with her cousin, but she remembered the first time her parents took her to the woods for a day out without her baby brother. She was four, and the day at the woods was a treasured memory she'd tucked away. It was their last trip together. Her father had carried her on his shoulders back to the train station after a fun day running amongst the damp leaves and climbing trees. Once on the train, her mother had wrapped her in the picnic blanket to keep the chill of the carriage at bay. Their bag of chestnuts had sat on the empty seat beside her father, begging to be roasted when they returned home. It was the day she'd realised how loved she was and how much she loved them. Within two months, they were gone for ever, and the love, although it never died, had transferred in a lighter form to her guardians.

'You feeling all right in the back there? You've gone a bit quiet. Not travel sick, are you?' Bert asked.

Bringing herself back to the present, Kitty shuffled in her seat.

'No. Those trees back there made me think about when I played in the woods as a child. The little ones today are not allowed to enter them now. Everywhere is wired off, thanks to the worries of enemy invasion. Even the beach nearby is off-limits. I miss the beach. I miss collecting chestnuts with my family,' she replied.

Bert gave a grunt of agreement.

'You'll do it again one day, I'm sure, and I'll dig over my grandad's allotment like I used to, then enjoy a Sunday roast with him and my gran.'

A sad sigh left Kitty's lips before she had the chance to stop the negative sound.

'I was orphaned when I was four, so sadly that won't ever happen again. I've an aunt and uncle to share things with when it's over, so I am one of the lucky ones considering.'

Grateful Bert didn't gush on about feeling sorry for her, she allowed the new silence to enfold them until he pulled up at an army barracks in order to refuel and enjoy a bathroom break.

'I've got cheese sandwiches and a flask of tea here, so we can share those if you would like – I mean, if it saves travelling time,' Kitty offered.

Bert got out of the car and opened her door.

'We'll regroup here after we've washed and brushed up. I'll find a few more delights from the canteen and we'll eat on the hoof. It will save us a good half hour to an hour, and help get us to Leeds before four.'

---

After two small roadside – behind the hedge – breaks, Bert pulled the car into the hospital car park at 3.45. Kitty gave a small huff of disappointment when she looked out on a large city building which represented a new friendless start to her career. A huge sense of loneliness gripped her – like nothing she'd experienced since the death of her parents. She felt she needed to speak to someone with the authority to help get her back to Birmingham or she'd suffer some form of traumatic breakdown. She had been prepared to support where required, but never dreamed she'd feel so anxious and alone. Bert placed her bag by her feet and gave her a sympathetic smile.

'Hope it all works out for you. Not a patch on the sea or woods, but it is your new home, so be happy, Kitty. Hopefully, our paths will cross again.'

Kitty gave him a look of despair.

'Bert, I hope I will, but it's scarier than when I first started training. At least we were all new and nervous. Here I'll just be the new girl and—'

A woman in full uniform waved her arms at them both as she bustled down a pathway towards them. Bert stood to attention and saluted as she reached the car.

'At ease. I've been watching out for you to arrive.'

Kitty watched as Bert handed her the large pile of letters all wax-sealed and red-franked with 'Private' across the front. She signed his receipt board and turned her attention to them both.

'I'm sorry to say there's been a change of plan. A telephone call arrived an hour ago,' she addressed Kitty. 'You are to move to a new posting. You leave in an hour – from the station.' She gestured off to the right with a vague wave of her hand indicating the general area of the train station. 'Most unsatisfactory, but it appears I have too many nurses arriving today and you are needed elsewhere. Driver, apparently, your VIPs for collection are heading back to London with another car. You have to take your passenger to the train station and telephone your HQ for further instructions. It is most confusing, and I for one have better things to do than be a messenger boy for the penpushers higher up the ranks.'

Kitty and Bert had no choice but to listen to their senior officer puff out her message and grievances. Both gave each other a glance of bewilderment and amusement. The size of the woman's ample bosom suggested she was anything but a boy, and she'd rushed her message so fast it was hard to digest it all.

'So, you're saying Kitty here is heading out on a train. And I'm to ring in for new instructions?' Bert asked the woman.

She nodded with impatience.

'Didn't I just say that?'

'Where am I going? Have I got a ticket? If I'm honest, I'm a bit confused. It's been a bit of a rush since yesterday lunchtime,' Kitty asked, her voice barely a whisper. Nerves were now triggering worries about where she was going next and how to fund the journey.

'I have absolutely no idea. My job is done. Goodbye and good luck,' the officer said as she strode away.

Bert stepped forward and picked up Kitty's bag.

'We'll ask when I ring HQ. It will get sorted, Kitty. I'll help.'

After parking the car, Bert turned around to Kitty.

'I'll go and speak with HQ. There's a telephone box over there. Someone should be able to shed a light on what's happening. Stay here and try not to worry. Shambles. Penpushers and clipboard holders don't have a clue half the time, I'm sure!'

'Thanks, Bert. I appreciate it.'

Kitty looked at her watch and saw it was now 4.15.

At 4.40, a flush-faced Bert reappeared. He pulled open the door and leaned down to speak to her.

'Sorry it took so long! Well, that was an about-the-houses chat. My instructions are that I continue to drive you, and it appears I'm also relocating. I've a new driving job. Good job my bag is in the boot. How about that! You are stuck with me until we reach, wait for it… Scotland! Buchanan Castle. Drymen Military Hospital to be precise. I hope you've packed your long johns; it's cold up there,' Bert said, and followed through with a whistle sound of cold wind.

'Stop it. You are teasing me. Where are we really heading?' Kitty said with a light laugh.

Bert tapped the side of his nose and grinned.

'Go on, where are we really heading?' Kitty repeated.

'I told you, Buchanan Castle, Scotland. I'm told the place was supposed to become a hotel or became one, before it was turned over to the military. It's a majestic-looking hospital now. Some of the nursing staff were shipped overseas recently, and I suspect you Red Cross girls will be welcomed with open arms. I've taken four of you in the past two weeks. None in this little beauty though.' Bert tapped the car roof with affection.

Kitty stared at him in amazement. Scotland!

'How long does it take to get there?' she asked.

Bert stood up and removed his cap to scratch his head. Sweeping back his hair he replaced his cap, lit a cigarette, took a moment to draw and puff on it, then beckoned her out of the car.

'Hours. You're to report to Major Armstrong when you get there. Stretch your legs a minute. Unfortunately, it will run into an overnight drive, and a slow one at that. Dimmed lights and the restricted twenty miles per hour doesn't make for an easy drive. It will be morning before we get there. We'll take the scenic route where we can; no point in wasting the opportunity for a decent view, plus it will save fuel. I've got blankets in the car so you can get a kip. I joined up to drive, and they never disappoint me, I'll give them that!'

'I'm in your hands, Bert. I've not got a clue where I am or where I'm headed. A majestic hospital in Scotland, reporting to a major. Who'd have believed it, because I don't! I still think you are pulling my leg,' Kitty said.

Bert gave a loud laugh. 'Trust me, you won't be disappointed. You got your flask handy? I'll get us a fill-up from the Sally Army over there.' Bert pointed to a group of ladies and a row of tea urns outside a wooden building across the car park.

'I'll come with you and see if they've got a ladies' room of some description.'

When they both met back at the car, they burst out laughing at each other. The generosity of the ladies of the Salvation Army had exceeded both their expectations. Bert was armed with a bag of beef paste sandwiches, two jam tarts, and a filled flask of tea. Kitty's bag was filled to the brim with a jar of blackberry jam, four scones and a generous wedge of apple cake. She'd also been encouraged to take a flask of Camp Coffee sweetened with a spoonful of sugar, and a jam jar half filled with milk.

When questioned about her southern accent, Kitty had told them of her journey from leaving home up to that day, and the mother-hen syndrome had kicked into play for the ladies. They had directed her to the toilets to freshen up, and fussed over her upon her return. Each one had applauded her bravery and fretted Kitty might starve on the route. She had assured them she would be fine as Bert was getting a flask of tea, and being a man, would probably think of his stomach's needs too, but the group had insisted she took their gifts. They checked she had blankets, but not satisfied she'd have enough, they had folded two into her arms and placed the food bag on top. She could barely see them to offer her grateful thanks.

'Blimey, you came out smiling. Delicious,' Bert said as Kitty relayed what she'd been given.

'It's made me peckish,' Kitty said.

Bert laid the goods carefully into the boot of the car and slammed the lid shut.

'Right. It's nearly 5.30. We still have daylight on our side, and I've just remembered, it's May third, so we will lose an hour's darkness when the clock's change at 2am. This double daylight-saving time is on my side for once – just a shame we're not travelling tomorrow as we'd have had more evening light. If I can make good headway, we can picnic before dark somewhere I think you'd appreciate.'

## Chapter Twenty-Two

A s the car rolled and bounced along the narrow roads, they entered a pretty village lined with stone cottages, and the scenery at the bottom of the road developed into the most beautiful Kitty had ever seen. Rolling hills of lush green meadows filled with fresh new spikes of every shade of green sharing their new spring colours played out before her, and all thoughts of heading to Scotland disappeared.

'Oh, Bert, this is beautiful!' she exclaimed.

With a nod of his head, Bert agreed.

'I'll drive a little further to the end of the street and then we'll stop. The village is Appleswick. I only know about it because of my mum's brother. He met a girl from here and when I joined up, he asked me to track her down. Sadly, she'd died, but I did get to find out she'd married and had a child. I often wonder if it was my uncle's, as he was rather upset when I told him she'd gone. Anyway, I come this way when I can just to breathe the fresh air. The Home Guard will probably come and check us out; they always do when I park here. They know me well enough now, but we still have to show our passes.'

Eager not to be delayed once they parked up, Kitty patted her apron pocket to reassure herself she was prepared with her identity card and travel pass.

Bert pulled the car off at a small country road inlet and jumped out to pull open the door for her.

'Here we go, my lady, feast your eyes on the Yorkshire Dales.'

Kitty did feast her eyes on every mile she could see, and absorbed its beauty. 'It's gorgeous,' she said and, as they took a short walk, she breathed in the sweet, fresh air, enjoying the sharp, cool breeze against her face. Bert spread a blanket out on the ground and laid out their food.

'Sit yourself down and eat up. We'll have half an hour here as it can be a bit unpredictable weather wise, and then it's not so friendly. Although it is cloud free at the moment, that doesn't mean a thing,' Bert said, and pointed towards the sky where a hint of dipping sun filtered above the hills some miles away.

'You're the boss. Let's get you fed, and head off,' Kitty said, layering a thick dollop of jam onto one half of a large scone.

Well-fed and watered, they headed back to the car. Bert was right with his guess; the Home Guard had arrived. Two mature soldiers who'd played their part in the Great War stood waiting.

'We guessed it wor theur lad,' one said to Bert.

'It's me, and this is Kitty,' Bert said, shaking their hands.

Kitty listened intently as they held a conversation, with the local men entertaining her with their strong country accent. They made a play of inspecting her papers. She struggled with the odd missing letter and strong burr, but eventually worked out one of them had addressed her and with her rough translation, she worked out his words without embarrassing herself.

'*Bert eear sez theur are off ta nurse i' Scotlan', bur are fra daahn sahth. Theur best off stayin' eear, lass,*' translated into; Bert here says you are off to nurse in Scotland, but are from down south. You're best off staying here, lass.

Kitty gave them a wide smile.

'Thanks for the invitation. I think I'd like to stay, but have a feeling the Red Cross might not be happy about it. I definitely would like to visit again one day,' she said, and slid into the seat when Bert opened the door for her, ready to embark on the next part of their journey.

———————————

Dusk gave way to darkness the further north they travelled. Kitty guessed the time to be around ten when the first threat of frost made itself known across the windscreen. Bert cursed the weather and everything else around him as he judged the dark road ahead. Kitty didn't envy his task and occasionally, a dip in the road or a kerbstone caught them unawares, but she admired his driving skills. She told him she doubted she'd ever learn to drive; it appeared far too complicated.

'I drove tractors before the war, and I've driven

makeshift ambulances during the tough nights in the past year. A bit of rough ground and darkness won't get in my way. We're near a beautiful place and I wish you could see it, but I'll guarantee you'll feel it. The Pennine roads can be tricky in some places,' Bert said with a determined tone to his voice.

The temperature dropped the further along the road they travelled, and soon Kitty wrapped herself into a blanket and curled up for comfort as best she could.

A flash of light whipped across the front of the car and she jumped.

'Searchlights,' she muttered.

'Clear night – dangerous night. Damn, here it goes,' Bert replied, just as a siren resounded around the hills. 'Hold on to your hat. I'm not going twenty miles an hour with the enemy on our tail. It's a straight stretch ahead; I know it like the back of my hand. When I hit the base of the incline, I'll have to slow down, but we'll need more shelter than we have around us now and there's a good clump of trees in that area.'

Several yards further ahead, the clamour of planes overhead drummed up enough noise to unsettle Kitty.

'They're ours – the engine is different. Heading over to Newcastle way I guess by the angle their outline is dipping. Protecting them against the enemy, who must be threatening somewhere close. Go on lads, give them hell!' Bert shouted.

'I second that, Bert.' Kitty huffed and rubbed on the window to get a better view outside; the searchlights played their part and the hum of plane engines dwindled into silence, but soon the *rat-tat* of the defence guns warned them the enemy had arrived in British airspace.

'I'll have to stop, Kitty. I can't keep the lights on no matter how dim. This cluster of trees will shield us. Chuck us one of those blankets and we'll sit it out. I can't even enjoy a smoke. Damn Nazi nuisance,' Bert said, and as he spoke his breath vapour and shadowed outline were all Kitty could see.

Kitty had never smoked a cigarette in her life but felt for Bert not being able to take advantage of the rest. She was grateful to him for not lighting up and alerting the enemy to their whereabouts. Quite a few people had faced fines from the police for just that, although she doubted there were many roaming around the wide-open fields they'd been driving through.

After attempting a nap, Bert decided to scrape the ice from the windows and see if they could make a few more miles. Kitty got out of the car and immediately regretted doing so. The air was icy cold.

'I need a behind-a-tree visit,' she whispered, for fear of anyone else being around.

'Why are you whispering? They can't hear you, you daft thing,' Bert said.

Kitty rushed to a clump of bushes and settled nature's demand just as the skyline changed from black to every shade of red and gold she could think of, and she realised it was the glow of flames. The enemy had found their target, or at least hit somewhere hard enough to destroy whatever lay in their path.

Rushing back to the car, she found Bert huddled under a

blanket draped over a car door. He was puffing on a part-smoked cigarette.

'I'm not driving without a smoke,' he said.

'Well, I couldn't see a light aside from that lot over there, so you are safe,' Kitty said, pointing to the flames in the distance. She tugged a blanket from the car and wrapped it around her shoulders. They stood quietly watching whatever disaster had fallen on the area miles away, which Bert decided was definitely Newcastle or one of the outlying towns.

The thready sounds of the all-clear echoed out, and Bert heaved a sigh of relief. He stamped upon the now finished cigarette and indicated for Kitty to get back into the car. From the boot of the car, he lifted out the remainder of their picnic.

'I'll sit the other side and put the food between us, with this torch on the floor. It will give a bit of dull light whilst we eat. Let's pray the coffee is still hot. Once we've eaten, we'll get on our way again. At least I'll be able to see where I'm going, even if I do have to go at a snail's pace again. We're not far from Carlisle.'

Kitty wrapped her hands around her tin cup and enjoyed the surprisingly warm coffee. The car windows steamed up and she swept her hand across the window. The flames of the burning town or city flickered against the starlit sky. She watched the condensation trickle tear-like down the glass, giving the impression it was crying for the world outside, and Kitty's heart broke for those suffering that night.

'How far away are we from them, Bert?' she asked, fully aware of the emotion in her voice.

'Scotland or Newcastle?'

'The people caught up in the bombing.'

Bert shrugged his shoulders. 'In this light, a good four to five hours. More.'

It pained Kitty to hear they were too far away to help, and she sniffed back tears.

'I'm sorry. I'm so used to being part of an emergency unit for the nights those poor folk experience, and now I am watching from the sidelines. I feel helpless. Useless.'

Bert sat quietly, and Kitty was grateful for his patience at her outburst. He took her cup from her hand and refilled it with the last of the coffee.

'Listen, we both feel useless, but that's what Hitler wants. He wants us all to feel crushed and defeated. You and I have to be somewhere in the morning. Right now, it doesn't seem like an important journey, but we both know once we get to our final destinations, we will not have time on our hands to feel useless. Drink up, and we'll get moving again. We must have faith there is a Kitty and Bert in whatever town or city has suffered tonight, and they are in the thick of it doing their jobs.'

He reached out and touched her hand, and Kitty's upset eased. Bert was right. She couldn't help, nor could he, but there were others out there carrying out their duty to those facing the horrors of the night. She gave a weak smile and packed away the remains of their food.

'We'd best be on our way. Thanks for understanding Bert.'

Bert clambered out of the back seat and into the driver's. He turned around and checked Kitty was ready for him to drive away.

'You've a big heart, Kitty. I hope nobody breaks it,' he said.

Kitty's reply was a silent one: *Too late, Bert. Michael McCarthy has torn it to shreds.*

## Chapter Twenty-Three

'Wakey, wakey sleepyhead.'

Kitty stirred in the back seat to the sound of Bert's voice and prompting with a shake of her arm. Releasing her curled-up limbs, she peered through sleepy eyelids and rubbed them clear.

'Where are we?' she asked, her throat husky-dry from sleep.

'Under an hour away, just outside of Glasgow. I noticed you'd nodded off, so I pulled over and caught up with a heavy nap myself. It's still dark, but daylight won't be long, so I think we'll crawl a way further.'

Remaining huddled under the blanket, Kitty's heart raced with anticipation. Her new home and workplace were closing in on her, and she needed to compose herself. She felt dishevelled and feared the look would not make a good impression. She pulled her hairbrush from her handbag and tugged and brushed it free from snags.

'I'll scare the natives I think, Bert,' she said with a laugh.

A loud chuckle came from Bert.

'I think they'll cope. Besides, they'll grab your bag and set you to work so fast they'll not notice whether you are male or female. Trust me, no one will worry on arrival. Do it again, and they will come down on you like a ton of bricks. Relax. We've been through a night of bombing, by the time I've finished telling the tale, you will have a week's leave before you've had your first shift.'

---

Kitty's breath failed to escape as they drove alongside a large lake bathed in beauty. Bert, ever the tour guide, updated her on where they were on the map he'd given her.

'It's called Loch Lomond. You're lucky it's not raining and misty. It never seems to stop raining here, so it's your lucky day, as I said. Take it all in as another time you might not get a clear view.'

Another gasp came from Kitty when they pulled up at the entrance of Buchanan Castle to show their passes. A magnificent building with tall round turrets, it reminded her of fairy-tale stories from her childhood. The grounds were busy with army personnel going about their business, and it made Kitty smile when they all turned to peer into the impressive staff car for a better view of whichever VIP was paying them a visit.

'Good enough for you, madam?' Bert asked.

'It will do, Bert. It will do,' Kitty said, eventually releasing the breath she'd held.

Unloading her bag and shaking his hand, Kitty's nerves suddenly kicked into play and she took a moment to compose herself.

'Just breathe and be yourself. You'll be fine. I hope our paths cross again one day, Kitty. You've been the model passenger and companion,' Bert said, and saluted her before walking away.

'Thanks, Bert. Take care,' Kitty called out to him, and he gave her a wave in reply.

---

Walking through the vast front door, and following a maze of corridors inside the castle, Kitty eventually found a door stating it was the office of Major Armstrong, and gave it a tap. Nothing. She tapped again. Still nothing. Desperate for the bathroom, she chose to hunt down the lavatory before returning to see if the major had returned.

Stopping a tall woman wearing a sophisticated grey, red and white crease-free uniform, Kitty admired the magnificent starched cap sitting smartly against the shoulder cape around her shoulders.

'Excuse me. I'm to meet a Major Armstrong and I'd rather not get on the wrong side of him in this state. I desperately need to freshen up. Could you point me in the right direction of a bathroom please?'

'A bathroom? There's a large lavatory at the end of the corridor; turn left. Not the warmest room in the building. Brace yourself,' the woman said, her voice dismissive and unfriendly. She strode away before Kitty could thank her.

Pushing open the toilet door, she appreciated the warning the woman had given her. The room had failed to see the sun rising in the morning and retained the frosty air of the previous night. It took courage to sit on the wooden seat. Biting her lip and praying all the washrooms were not that cold, she lingered no longer than required. Splashing her face with ice-cold water certainly woke her up, and to her dismay, a mirror on the wall reported back the horrors of the overnight journey. Shivering with the cold, Kitty stripped down to her underwear and hastily pulled on her uniform. She brushed her hair into a neat ponytail, ensuring her cap sat securely on her head. She pulled out her flat shoes and rubbed them on the backs of her woollen stockinged calves, hoping they looked polished enough. Satisfied she'd done as much as she could to look presentable, she swung her cape over her shoulders and headed back to Major Armstrong's office and tapped on the door. This time a firm, controlled female voice took her by surprise and instructed her to enter.

Leaving her kitbag in the hallway, Kitty wiped her hands on the back of her dress and stepped inside the room. To her surprise, the woman who'd directed her to the toilet was seated behind the large desk. Kitty gave her a smile, but received nothing in return.

'Katherine Patisson. Refreshed from the cool air and brush-up I see. Well done for putting in the effort. I understand you were expecting Leeds. However, I do hope you will be able to make do with the castle. Be warned though, not many of the Red Cross girls stay for too long.'

Kitty assumed the distinguished woman to be the major and tried another smile – all in vain.

'I must say, Major Armstrong, you didn't lie about the cold room, but it woke me up after the long journey. As for Leeds, I think Buchanan Castle may have won me over. It's beautiful here.'

With a curt nod Major Armstrong looked at a sheet of paper on her desk.

'Well, welcome to Drymen Military Hospital. A lot of our QAs were recently mobilised to support our medics on the front line. We have also lost a lot of brave nurses in the atrocities outside of Britain and we appreciate the support of the Territorial Army Nursing Service. You will see a mix of uniforms here, but not many of yours. We rarely need help outside of the armed forces, but appreciate the odd RC such as yourself sent our way. Unlike the girls of TANS, the Red Cross support has not had the rigid training, which means more menial tasks for you, but it is all part of our duty to this country.' Major Armstrong took a deep breath. 'I run a tight ship as you will find out in due course. Listen, learn and carry out your instructions, and you will soon fit in, but understand this: foolish behaviour will not be tolerated.'

Kitty stood in silence. The woman's voice terrified her. She felt the major's hostility was wasted on British nurses; it would have had the enemy running for home with one short sentence. Major Armstrong dabbed her finger hard on the paperwork in front of her.

'It says here in a report from a Dr Michael McCarthy that

you are suited to emergency duties. He states you worked outside of the hospital within a rescue unit alongside him, and are an extremely competent nurse. Do not let him – or me, down.'

At the sound of the major mentioning Michael's name, the room closed in on Kitty. She sensed a flutter of anxiety inside, but felt sure the formidable woman in front of her would strike her record with a black mark for being weak if she shed a tear over a man.

'Thank you. Yes, Dr McCarthy and I became a strong team. He's a Canadian over here training other doctors. I'm glad he noticed my efforts,' she said. Behind her back she dug her nails in the palms of her hands to prevent even a hint of emotion taking over her concentration.

'Indeed. Take a seat outside and someone will show you to your quarters and assist you in finding your way around. No more asking the way; find it for yourself. Dismissed.'

Startled by the last word said in a sharp, firm tone finalising the meeting, Kitty took a moment to remind herself she was attached to the army, and life would probably become very different. She said nothing in response and left the room. Around ten minutes later a young woman in a uniform much like Major Armstrong's approached her.

'Pattison?'

Kitty looked up and smiled. She rose to her feet and lifted her kitbag. 'That's me,' she said, resigned to the lack of a returned smile.

'Follow me. I'll show you the ropes, after which you will

report to the receiving unit where you will be told of your shift duties. I've set you to start tomorrow – the fifth – so make the most of today by getting to know the place,' said the nurse without introduction. Her voice chipped out the instructions with a voice as firm and friendless as the major's.

The young woman marched at speed to the bottom of a narrow hallway and proceeded to the end, where she pointed to rooms as she went, calling out their purpose as they walked. At the end of the longest corridor was a small wooden door and she pushed it open.

'You're in here. We use this room for all visitors not considered VIP. Our nursing quarters are full, and this is the only available space to accommodate you.'

She stepped inside to allow Kitty in, and pushed the door closed.

'Nice,' said Kitty, her response sarcastic as she glanced around at the gloomy room no bigger than a shoe cupboard.

The nurse gave a slight huff bordering on disapproval at Kitty's response.

'Granted, it's small, but in its favour, it is only for one person, plus it is warmer given it backs off the main kitchen. I suspect it was a maid's room when this place had a different life. You have an hour and a half to unpack and find food. Oh, and by the way, your room will be inspected as if you are one of us, so keep it tidy at all times.'

Without any further instructions, the nurse turned on her heel and exited the room, leaving a bewildered Kitty looking at a small window so high up she'd be lucky to see a bird on a branch on the tree outside. The bed had nothing inviting to say, and Kitty suspected the back of the staff car was the more comfortable of the two. On the bedside cabinet was a list of instructions of what was to be laid out and where, which left a flabbergasted Kitty wondering if Leeds might have been the better bet, considering what she might be subjected to within the tight confines of the British army. Unsure where she was to hang her uniform due to the lack of a wardrobe, she took out the folded clothes and placed them in the bottom of the cabinet. She placed her wash things onto the small stand beside the minute sink in the corner of the room, and made a mental note to hunt down another towel. Before she left to do so and, as instructed to look for food, she stood looking at the bed and hoped the blanket folded at the end of the pristine sheets with their angular corners and creased folds beneath a flat pillow, would be enough. Not wanting the room to suffocate the pleasure of her arrival at the castle, she shook out her cardigan and cape, leaving her outer coat draped over the back of a wooden chair, and ventured into the corridor. She peered around the corner of the kitchen and saw a young soldier washing pots at a large sink.

'Excuse me, I'm told I can find food here. I've had a long journey and have under an hour to eat before finding the receiving bay,' Kitty asked him.

The young man ignored her and continued with his pot scrubbing. Another man sitting in the corner puffing on a cigarette beckoned her over.

'Ignore him. He's a strange one – shell-shocked if you ask me, but I'm only the cook around here so what do I know? Food you say. Sit there and I'll find you something. Where did you come in from?'

'Birmingham. Born in Essex though,' Kitty replied, watching the long line of ash threatening to fall into what looked like a potato pie of sorts.

'Here you go. A potato and scrag-end pie.'

'Mutton? Yummy, I've not eaten that since I left home.'

The man laughed. 'You'll not eat it here again, and don't tell anyone else. What goes on in here, stays in here. Understand? I'm only kind to you as I know you won't be here long. They'll move you before your head hits the pillow. Mark my words.'

The mouthful Kitty chewed on became a lump hard to swallow. Twice she'd been told to be prepared to move out sooner rather than later, and resented leaving Birmingham, where she had Jo to confide in and they could enjoy a laugh together.

'That's a shame – you share a good meal. And return a smile,' she said, trying hard to bring a bit of positivity into her frame of mind.

'You'll get used to it. Those at the top are tough nuts to crack, but our boys would be lost without them. Are you taking a walk now?' the cook asked.

Wiping her mouth on a napkin, Kitty nodded. The food had comforted her for a short time, but after she'd finished and washed it down with a welcome cup of tea, she wondered if her wandering around getting her bearings was to be a waste of effort.

'I have to find my way around this place alone,

apparently. So, if I don't return in a few hours, put out a search for Pattison. Kitty.'

'I'll do that. If you head out the way you came, take a quick tour of the inside, get some air across the tennis courts, and the first large hut you see with the odd ambulance parked alongside is the one you want. You've got half an hour and that's plenty if you do as I say.'

'Thanks, that's helpful. See you again,' Kitty said, and left the kitchen.

Doing as the soldier suggested led Kitty up and down corridors and stairs on several levels. Bandaged patients and staff with stern faces gave her indifferent glances as she peered inside each room, all transformed into wards. She watched orderlies wheel men to and from what she assumed were bathrooms and hoped they were warmer than the one she'd encountered earlier in the day. Confident she knew the basic layout on each level, she made her way back downstairs. A staircase to the lower areas was roped off and guarded by two soldiers. Kitty guessed it was the medical storage area and moved on to the outdoors. She enjoyed a brief walk in the gardens and crossed the lawn towards the tennis courts where a group of nurses were enduring a keep-fit session. The looks on their faces and the barking voice of their instructor suggested they were not enjoying running on the spot.

The large hut looked out of place and a carbuncle against the backdrop of the beautiful castle. Several others – she guessed around fifty – were spread around the grounds, and those which surrounded the large one were a hub of activity; the words she thought of were orderly chaos, bordering frantic. Kitty stepped to one side to allow two stretcher-bearers to carry a patient inside the entrance of the receiving bay she was about to enter.

Pulling a fraction of courage from her rapidly depleting supply, she waited for the men to complete their task and followed through.

## Chapter Twenty-Four

W hen Kitty learned she had been allocated to attend the ward housing German prisoners of war, she found it hard to hold back her horror. Never had she thought she'd be made to nurse the enemy, and she shared her concern with the sister showing her the layout of the basement ward – the place she'd originally thought housed medical supplies. She was told in no uncertain terms that her duty as a nurse was to put bias to one side and get on with the job of caring.

Darker than those rooms housing the injured British soldiers, Kitty felt sure she'd never feel warm again, despite the large log fire burning in the ornate fireplace. The ward sister's words about caring were laughable, as she ensured Kitty never came close to a patient. Her one request to assist a man struggling from his bed was shot down by the ward sister in seconds. She made Kitty's position on the ward quite clear and from then on, Kitty kept herself away from any situation which would lead to disappointment. She continued her cleaning duties in silence, watching the German patients receive the same quality of care as those in the rest of the castle. All were senior officers and were treated with respect. Kitty admired the nurses going about their duty, knowing many of their own had possibly died at the command of those in the room. They were dignified in their duties, some of which, Kitty felt sure she would never be able to perform without feeling some kind of rage inside. Not one nurse she watched showed any expression of resentment.

Kitty felt the only person in the ward who resented anything was her. The task of sweeping tea leaves across a floor to create and gather dust balls from underneath the beds, and other menial jobs, frustrated Kitty. Never had she felt so lonely. Even the cook who'd first befriended her never reappeared.

Her early morning wake-up call was five o'clock sharp thanks to the banging of pans in the kitchen, but she did appreciate the warm wall behind her bed and on her first evening alone in her room, she leaned against it to read her old letters from home to gain a sense of connection. Kitty telephoned her aunt and uncle to let them know she was safe in Scotland, but Jo's shift and hers crossed, so instead of having the chat she'd hoped for, she decided writing to Jo at the end of the week was the best bet; a letter in which Kitty would share her comparisons and opinions of army life to that at the Birmingham hospital. After her first full shift, she knew which life she preferred.

Due to being new and working all hours, Kitty only managed to hold a brief conversation with one nurse outside of the working environment. Sarah worked on her ward, but they never spoke. She came across as aloof and shared nothing of her personality to make Kitty feel she was someone to draw into her life as a friend. The other girls were not unfriendly, but their days were extremely busy, and they had their own friendship groups. When they weren't working on the wards, they were taking fitness lessons and hill-walking exercises. From overheard conversations, she gathered that when off duty, the girls enjoyed parties and the company of the recovered soldiers waiting to return to France or other bases around Britain. Kitty knew a new arrival outside of their group was of no interest, and reflecting on her friendship with Jo and Trix, she understood completely. It didn't take away the need to have a decent conversation with another, though.

After her boring shift, Kitty plucked up courage and asked Sarah to join her for a walk. The late afternoon was crisp and cold, but Kitty needed to be in the open space, to put aside the hemmed-in feeling from the POW ward. To her surprise, Sarah agreed to join her.

'How long have you been here, Sarah?' Kitty asked as they ambled past the river at the bottom of the garden.

'A couple of years. Since it opened,' Sarah replied, and then clammed up. Kitty got the impression she was not a talker.

'And you've been sweeping the floors since then? Can't you transfer?' Kitty asked, amazed anyone would want to continue their life sweeping tea leaves around a ward.

Sarah shook her head. 'Nothing would change for me,

and besides, I am doing my bit for the war effort. I'm safer here than most places I know.'

With a loud sigh, Kitty shook her head in bewilderment. 'I don't know how you do it, Sarah. Those men – the Germans – alive when … oh, don't listen to me. I'm going mad and it's only been a day. I miss the action of Birmingham. It was scary, but at least I felt like a nurse, not a glorified cleaner.'

'Everything has to be clean, Kitty. It's an important job. How can you judge when you've only been here one day?' Sarah's voice was quiet and almost reprimanded Kitty for her words.

They continued their walk in silence to a viewpoint, and then sat on a bench. A wisp of cloud drifting across the sky was reflected in the water and looked like a small boat. Watching it move carefree on the minute waves, Kitty wanted to climb on board and float down the river; to feel nothing, to not be dissatisfied with her work life or with how she and Michael ended their brief romance. She wanted to drift away, sleep, and wake up when the war was over. Today was a 'Kitty pities herself' day. With a sudden movement, Sarah jumped to her feet and blocked Kitty's view.

'Do you have a boyfriend, Kitty? Have you ever let him kiss you? Or, you know, touch you?'

Kitty took a moment to absorb the question. Sarah had an innocence in her face which reminded Kitty of Trix. She wondered if Sarah had lived through an extremely strict upbringing. Whatever her past life, Sarah had obviously not quite mastered the art of discreet questions about the more personal details of another being.

However, not wanting to miss the opportunity of making a new friend, Kitty decided now was not the time to hold back; she needed to be more open than ever before. With a shrug of a shoulder, she answered with honesty.

'I did have a boyfriend, yes. And yes, I let him kiss me. We— He left, and we went our separate ways.'

With a dramatic sigh and swinging her body to face Kitty, Sarah put both hands to her mouth and widened her eyes.

'He didn't marry you after that kiss?' she asked.

At that moment, Kitty realised Sarah had a child-like innocence so deep she should think carefully about what she said next. The girl was too tender to hear about a heart-breaking event between her and Michael. She kept her voice soft and calm, much as she would with a young child.

'No. It wasn't a serious kiss. Just a friendly one – you know, a kiss to say goodbye. He left where we worked together, and we weren't meant to be anything more than friends. I realise that now.'

Kitty knew some of what she said was for Sarah, but also to reassure herself in some way. A comprehension of the relationship she and Michael had shared.

'Oh,' Sarah responded, her voice bordering on disappointment. She gave a huff of irritation as she sat back down on the seat.

'Where are you from?' Kitty asked in order to turn the topic of conversation away from Michael and her memories of his passionate kisses.

'I was born in Ireland but have lived in Glasgow since I was around seven. You?'

Grateful Sarah had fallen for the distraction, Kitty told Sarah her life story both in Essex and the few months in Birmingham.

'I'm heading back to get some rest.' Sarah jumped to her feet and started walking along the pathway back to the castle.

Startled by the sudden statement and abrupt end to the conversation, Kitty rushed to catch her up. Sarah had a nervous energy which rose in peaks and troughs.

'Good idea. Wait up!'

As they approached the grounds closest to the castle, they spotted a senior sister from their ward talking to a group of nurses, and she glanced Kitty and Sarah's way.

'Pattison. There you are. My office please.' Her precise and clear voice held such an air of authority, Kitty wondered how many people had ever dared go against her in life. She doubted very many as she watched the straight-backed woman almost march back inside.

'Yes, Sister,' Kitty replied, and felt her sense of calm and peace sink to her boots.

'God, what does the old battle-axe want now?' Sarah asked.

Kitty rolled her shoulders. 'Only one way to find out, and let's hope it is good news.'

Seated outside the sister's office, Kitty thought of how forty-eight hours already felt like a tiresome week. She found it incredible at how quickly her mind became bored and restless.

The door to the office swung open and the sister peered around the doorframe.

'Come in, Pattison.'

Once inside, Kitty stood tall and waited for whatever ticking off or instructions she was to receive. Another sister from a different ward sat at the end of the desk and, without introduction, she addressed Kitty.

'I need you to cover patient transport. One of my usual girls is off sick and the decision is that you are the ideal choice as her replacement.'

'Is her name Belle by any chance?' Kitty asked, the words slipping from her mouth before she had time to counteract their escape.

'I beg your pardon?' the sister said with a stern, puzzled stare, obviously irritated by the interruption.

'I'm sorry, only I thought I heard someone say a nurse by that name was poorly. Of course, I'll cover. I'd be happy to escort your patient.'

The ward sister gave a derisive snort. 'It wasn't a request, Pattison.'

Flustered, Kitty bowed her head.

'Stand up straight girl and listen. You will head out with a patient returning to Queen's barracks in Perth. He's a victim of a training accident and had a severe head injury. He has recovered physically, but mentally he's struggling, and at times needs encouragement to catch his breath as he has a tendency to panic. He'll not remain in the army, but is not aware of his position just yet, so avoid any questions he might throw your way. Understand?'

Kitty lifted her head. 'Yes, Sister.'

'I've been informed you are level-headed and work hard, and although it is your first day, you have not created any issues on the ward.'

Kitty listened to the false praise. She pushed a broom around and worked in silence; there was nothing level-headed about it, and she'd obviously been pushed forward for a task no one else wanted.

'Thank you, Sister,' Kitty said, resenting her for ruining her evening off.

'Discharge ward three. Thirty minutes. Dismissed.'

Heeding the final word, Kitty rushed from the room and to her own. She was furious. The journey would mean she was to miss her meal and much needed rest. Whilst tugging on her uniform and pinning back her hair, Kitty decided to contact the Red Cross department for transfers and see if she could escape the clutches of Drymen Military Hospital, Major Armstrong, and her ward sisters. She held nothing against Scotland; it was the working environment which didn't suit. Even after such a short stint, and as beautiful as Buchanan Castle looked from the outside, inside its walls was a place Kitty knew she could not last for much longer.

Halfway to Perth, the young soldier in the back of the ambulance with Kitty asked for it to stop so he could relieve himself. The driver grumbled but pulled the truck to one side of a large forest and escorted the man to a thicket for privacy. Kitty took the opportunity to stretch her legs and walked across the narrow road to admire the pine trees and inhale their scent on the cool breeze. A hum of machinery and male voices filtered from what appeared to be deeper into the forest. Loud cracks and crashing sounds echoed out, followed by a shuddering of the ground. Kitty ran back to the truck and spoke to the driver waiting for the patient to climb back into his seat. She expressed grave concern about what she'd heard, but did so in a hushed voice, not wanting to upset the patient inside the ambulance.

'There's something going on in there. I think someone is bombing something,' she said.

The driver drew on the last stub of his cigarette, nipped it dead and threw it, and as he did so, he grinned. Not in mockery but in a friendly, reassuring manner.

'Canadian lumberjacks,' he said.

Kitty looked back across the road as another yell echoed, and turned back to him.

'Did you hear that?'

Nodding, the driver got back into the ambulance.

'It's the Canadian Forestry Corps. They're over to chop down and perform magic on those pines.'

Kitty stared at him in shock. 'Cut down our beautiful trees? What on earth for?'

The driver gave a chuckle.

'Needs must. They might be beautiful, but we've run out of wood and Britain needs it to keep the railways running, and the government is crying out for huts and homes for the bomb victims. These chaps are specialists, and we are lucky to have them here. Shame it will be dark when we head back, or I'd have taken you in to meet a few. They'd love to meet a pretty English girl.'

Kitty gave a slight shake of her head.

'My luck with Canadians does not bode well. I think I'll give it a miss, thanks,' she said, walking away to take her place beside her patient, thankful he'd had no reaction to the noises from beyond the trees.

---

With the patient safe in the care of his attendees, the driver and Kitty were directed to the canteen to enjoy a much needed cup of tea and a hot meal. Embracing the opportunity to talk to the driver, Kitty relaxed, and the deep-set loneliness eased for a short while.

The journey back to Drymen wasn't as dark as Kitty expected and the sunset filtering across the mountains, rolling hills, and loch waters kept her company for part of the journey, and Kitty tried to describe the raw beauty of Scotland in her mind. Ochre, sage, silver, burnt gold; she tried to think of colours to write home about, to share the magnificence of what she saw each day. By the time her list of colours exceeded an artist's palette, they were back at the hospital, she reported the patient as delivered and safe, then returned to her room with a determination to request the transfer. Scotland's beauty wasn't enough. The talk of Canadians and her loneliness had brought about an unexpected sadness she didn't know how to address. She wrote to Trix and made the letter as light-hearted as she could, but when she began writing one to Jo, it all became too much, and Kitty curled up on the bed in tears.

## Chapter Twenty-Five

W aking to the sound of a high-pitched noise outside, Kitty sat up in her bed, her head groggy with the sudden disturbance. She was confused. Her tearful bout had obviously given way to a deep sleep, and when she peered at her bedside clock, she saw it was a minute to midnight, which meant she'd managed a relaxing five-and-a-half-hour sleep fully clothed and with her shoes on. Kitty thanked her lucky stars there was not an inspection on the cards. All tension she'd managed to sleep off returned when it registered that the noise came from the sirens warning of an enemy attack once again.

Comprehending the urgency, Kitty snatched up her cape and ran from her room, where she joined other nurses, some heading to their wards upstairs and others towards the front entrance and the wards outside. Kitty's instructions for times where there was imminent threat to life was to attend the outside wards. She ran across the grounds and within minutes of receiving her orders, the familiar ground-shaking, ear-splitting sounds of bombs striking their targets in the distance told her it was going to be a tough night.

Kitty went about her duty of calming patients and packing away precious medication and equipment for swift removal should the need arise. For the first time for nearly a week, she felt useful and back into her nursing zone rather than cleaning. Her sleep had also given her renewed energy, and she worked with great speed, relieving those who'd worked all day to grab respite breaks.

Around three o'clock the sky fell silent of planes and the sad realisation that another day of death and destruction lay ahead for civilians saddened the hospital staff.

When the shout went out for volunteers to join a rescue team in the affected towns, Kitty did not hesitate to raise her hand. She'd seen beyond the castle towards the affected areas now ablaze across the skyline, and she was desperate to get in to help the victims. Kitty was delighted when handed the clipboard to scribble down her name, releasing her for duty outside the hospital.

'Pattison, Katherine. Greenock. Ambulance six. Sign here,' the sister in charge of coordinating the team barked out and pointed to the bottom of a page. With no hesitation, Kitty signed and moved fast before she could be recalled. This was her time – something she knew she could handle, and where she would be able to show off the skills the Red Cross and the Birmingham team had taught her, and the courage Michael had given her. With adrenaline pumping around her body, she clambered aboard the ambulance and sat amongst the other volunteers.

Once they arrived, she jumped down behind the others

and took a moment to assess the situation. The town of Greenock was ablaze. A member of the fire crew pointed towards a building across what had once been a town square, and addressed the group.

'Over there and join the medical staff. We're not done here yet. Not safe enough. Come back, though – there'll be plenty to do here I'm afraid.'

Kitty followed the others in the group and headed for the central point. The noise was deafening, and she stood back, allowing others to receive their instructions, waiting her turn in the queue. Ready. Willing. Undaunted.

'Kitty?' A familiar voice with that one word undid all she'd resolved to control. She froze on the spot.

Michael!

'It *is* you; I knew it. I saw you by the door. Kitty, it's Michael.' Michael's voice, as soft and gentle as ever, sent her emotions sky high, but Kitty held fast. All resolve to never allow him to draw her in and hurt her again crumpled inside. Knowing she couldn't ignore him, Kitty took a moment and with slow deliberate movements she turned towards his voice and saw him standing there. Handsome as always, but more so in the green uniform he now wore, Michael's eyes were wide with amazement. Kitty's heart jumped to a rhythm she had no control over, as she allowed his smile to bring back tender memories, and her legs threatened to give way. Here was Michael, the man she loved and never thought she'd see again, waiting for her response, and all she could do was tremble and try to control the urge to run into his arms. Composing herself, she gave him the widest smile she could muster.

'Michael. Fancy meeting you here!' she said, and immediately kicked herself for making it sound as if they were at a social event instead of in the middle of a search and rescue operation.

'Kitty, you're in Scotland! What are you doing here?' he asked.

Kitty gave a glib laugh, which sounded like something from one of the automated dolls which tell your fortune at the end of a seaside pier.

'Doing my bit, wherever they send me. I went to Leeds on Saturday, but they had other ideas, and the army needed another pair of hands in a castle of all places. I'm happy to be here for emergency support, but I'll not be staying long; this is the first time I'm actually about to do my job. They've had me cleaning for a week!' she said and, realising her voice sounded resentful and contrary, she gave another fortune-teller cackle to make light of it and hoped he thought it a joke. Besides, knowing Michael was in Scotland, and by all accounts nearby, who knew what her thoughts would be in the morning with regard to requesting a transfer. He still had the magical power to make her heart beat faster, but she still found it hard that he'd rejected her, and she never wanted to experience the same pain again. She braced her back and composed herself.

'I'd better join my group. It's been lovely to see you again, Michael. Take care out there.'

A loud crack of a building collapsing nearby stopped them in their tracks. A shout for everyone to work the west side of the area only went out. A call for all medics to attend the front with local volunteer groups also rang out loud and clear. Now was the time for Kitty to take control of all emotions and do what she did best: help those who needed her support.

Waving his arm across the heads of the crowd in front, Michael responded to someone calling his name.

'Here. Two. Dr McCarthy and Nurse Pattison heading out,' he shouted, then swung around to Kitty before she had the opportunity to walk away.

'Come with me, Kitty. Work with me tonight,' he pleaded.

With a huff sounding like a steam train pulling away from the station, Kitty twisted her lips into what she hoped was an apologetic smile.

'Sorry. I'm with the hospital crew. I can't possibly—'

Michael grabbed her hand, and his touch startled her. Tremors of pleasure played havoc around her body, taking her back to when they first met. She slowly slid her hand from his but, before her fingers brushed the tips of his, he gripped firmly, not allowing her to run from him.

'We work well together, you know that, and I'm heading up the first search party. This is a temporary uniform; I'm still civilian. Only you can think as fast as I do, and act on it. I'll clear it with your team. Come, we've got to go.'

He tugged her towards him and for a brief second, she saw a look from the past in his eyes. A need. Love? She inhaled the scent of his soap, his freshness.

Flustered by his sudden reappearance in her life and his demand that she join him, Kitty's courage threatened to become unstable, but Michael was right; they were a good working team, and Kitty could not be certain that she'd find that bond out there with the strangers she called work colleagues. Theirs was a silent understanding with minimum instructions required. With Michael she had the chance to save lives. Make a difference. With the other team she'd never had the opportunity to prove herself, and would probably end up staying behind on clerical duties. She turned to look at the crew she'd arrived with, all chatting amongst each other. One glance was all she needed. Kitty did not feel the pull of comradeship.

'Let's go!' she said, and allowed herself to be guided through the crowd and outside into the frantic mix of survivors and rescuers.

'It's my night – my lucky charm has arrived. Let's go do what we do best, Kitty. You and me together again.' Michael's voice sounded earnest and genuine. Kitty detected he meant more than just going out to help the victims waiting for their attention, and followed him into the street.

---

'I can't believe I lost a shoe!' Kitty said, and perched herself on an upturned wooden crate. Michael laughed – a loud, relaxed laugh. 'I always seem to be on my knees helping your feet in some way, too... Cinderella.'

Kitty wriggled her ankle as he pushed her shoe in place.

'Oh, yes, my hero walking me home in the snow,' she said.

'Not sure about the walking – you hopped most of the

way home. They were good times,' Michael said, a wistful tone to his voice.

Kitty picked up the well-earned tin mug of tea and took a sip.

'We did well tonight. All saved and stitched up. Poor things,' she said, and diverted the conversation back to the present.

Hearing her name and seeing the hospital crew heading towards the transport, Kitty laid down her cup and touched Michael's shoulder.

'Thank you for trusting me out there tonight. I felt valued. Take care, Mic—'

Before she had the opportunity to say any more, Michael's lips were on hers and the fire in his passionate kiss burned throughout her body. Kitty caved in and didn't pull back until a cheer went up around them, and her name was called out again.

'I'll be in touch,' Michael said as he released her.

Breathless, Kitty gave a slight nod and rushed away. The look on her superior's face was that of anger when Kitty checked herself on to the transport.

'Pattison. What happened to you tonight? I find out you abandoned your crew and now see you standing around kissing Canadian servicemen. I assure you, that is not my idea of a rescue mission. You will be on report when we return. Understood?'

No amount of reprimanding would take away the happiness inside Kitty and she threw the woman a smile. Kitty was under no illusion her name was on the list of complaints to Major Armstrong. The sniggering inside the truck suggested her day was going to get worse, and she chose to make a stand for herself and vented out her reply.

'I rescued ten people. Three families. I closed a wound for a doctor so he could save another life, I pressed down on a bleeding artery, and sat with a lady who'd lost her son with dreadful injuries. I climbed through a shattered window and helped an old man to safety. I clambered down a crumpled wall, lost my shoe and saved a toddler. I could go on, but if you want the full report, the head of my old rescue team from Birmingham can give it to you; since he is a medic and ordered me to follow him, I did. Oh, and the Canadian? It was him, and he's my… my boyfriend, and neither of us knew the other was currently stationed so close by, so the kiss was inevitable after such a night. Wouldn't you agree?' Kitty said without drawing breath. She sat on the truck bench, knowing all eyes were on her, some admiring her courage and others showing annoyance at what they considered was disrespect for a ranking officer. To them all she gave a nod and smile with a slice of defiance.

'Tough night,' she said to the weary faces staring back at her.

No one spoke, and Kitty sat back thinking about what she'd just said.

Declaring Michael as her boyfriend was a bold assumption, but she had to say something to prove their connection and the reason for making such a public display of herself. Her aunt would not have approved, but inside her head she heard Trix cheering her on, and Jo warning her to be cautious.

Standing opposite the senior sister, Kitty stood with her shoulders back and her arms to her side. Her apron was covered in blood, her woollen stockings snagged and torn, her hair loose and escaping from one side of her cap, and she suspected her face needed a good wash. This time she'd made no effort to clean up before the order came for her to explain her conduct. She'd sat on the bench outside the kitchen door sipping a glass of water to clear her throat, and made the decision that Major Armstrong would not be met with the polished version of her nurse on loan. She would put in for a transfer before she went on shift. A new boldness swept through her body and Kitty knew some of it was down to seeing Michael again, but she also knew her love of the Red Cross was strong. She needed to leave the castle, even if it meant being parted from Michael again. If their love was meant to be, it would find a way to grow, no matter how far apart they were.

## Chapter Twenty-Six

'... **A**nd that is my version of events, Major Armstrong. Thank you for taking the time to hear me out. As I've said, last night made me realise how much I miss the emergency team at Birmingham, and I am going to request to transfer back.'

Kitty took a breath and a slight step back to allow the trembling in her legs to settle down. From the moment she tapped on the office door, and throughout Kitty's explanation of events the previous evening, Major Armstrong had sat with a face set as solid as stone. When she shifted in her seat as Kitty stopped talking and gave her a broad smile, it unnerved her. It was the first smile she'd seen the major offer anyone, and this one had a self-satisfied edge to it, almost as if the woman had won a competition of some kind or another. A smug sound in her voice confirmed to Kitty she was not genuine in offering up the smile.

'Excellent timing. I'm due to receive several new nurses over the next two weeks, so your name is on the schedule for release in around ten days anyway. Feel free to arrange your transfer and transport at your leisure. Dismissed.'

The smile disappeared, and Kitty was left staring down onto the top of the major's head as the woman made a play of writing something on a notepad. It annoyed Kitty to think the major saw no value in her, which left her wondering what sort of notice she might have received had she not plucked up courage to speak with her today.

Outside the door, Kitty took a moment to run over the conversation, and the thought of a transfer sent a shiver of semi-excitement through her. Michael was a problem she'd not foreseen, but Kitty knew it was time for her to leave. Unsure as to how long Michael would remain in Scotland, and whether he wanted to pick up where they had left off, she was not prepared to put her life on hold waiting to find out. She'd mulled over the idea of their relationship rebuilding, and decided there was definitely a way forward if she and Michael were to take time to talk, and so, despite her tiredness, she reported for duty with a bit more optimism. Although, her mood lost its spark as she descended the dark winding stone stairway.

On the ward there was a discussion amongst the staff about the previous evening and of how the evacuation programme would be handled if necessary. They had not noticed that four patients spoke amongst themselves in an excited huddle by a window. The men pointed outside, and another wrote something down on a scrap of paper. Kitty looked out at the smoke filtering across the hills from Greenock and, although she could not understand what they said, realised they were discussing the bombing.

Unable to bear their gloating any longer, knowing the devastation she'd witnessed, she pushed her broom their way and, in a voice as firm and loud as the ward sister's, she bashed it against a chair leg.

'Excuse me. Work to be done. Move back please,' she said, and pulled out a polishing cloth, making a display of cleaning the window ledge and windows. A loud cough came from across the room, and the ward sister also added her booming voice to the situation, and this time it was in Kitty's favour.

'Nurses, escort the patients back to bed. It appears they are more able than we've been led to believe. Arrangements will be made for removal. In the meantime, do not let them out of your sight. As you were, Nurse Pattison.'

'Thanks, Sister. Oh, and I'd check their pockets if I were you. One of them might have been sketching or note-taking.'

'Impressive. Highly observant of you, Pattison.'

The slight wink which followed from the sister was as surprising as Major Armstrong's smile, but Kitty refrained from winking back. She gave a brief nod and edged the patients further from the windows into the firm arms of the other nurses. The men had obviously pretended to be more injured than they were, gaining all the luxuries afforded to POW officers. Kitty watched as the sister left the ward and returned with the two soldiers who stood guarding the stairway. They placed themselves either side of the entrance, and the scene did not go unnoticed by the staff. Sister was concerned for their safety.

'Did you really see them off with your broom?' Sarah asked as the last of the men were escorted to more secure premises. Kitty's laugh echoed around the canteen and heads turned her way. It amazed her how many people gave her a smile before returning to their meals.

A rumour spread amongst the staff that Kitty Pattison was as fierce with a broom as a soldier with a gun. It was laughable, but Kitty took it in her stride. At least work turned out to be more bearable in the afternoon. She and Sarah worked together on the four empty beds and lockers, and to her surprise, Sister released her from duty early.

Rather than sleeping, Kitty chose to take her first walk into Drymen and purchase stamps from the post office. Kitty took a slow amble, taking in her surroundings. She'd seen beautiful countryside in the past, but this was beyond beautiful. She failed to find words beyond *pretty*, *magnificent*, and *gorgeous* to describe what little she'd seen of Scotland, and if it weren't for such a deep desire to return to the cocoon of friendship with Jo, and the career she loved, she might have been persuaded to stay for a while longer.

As she walked back to the hospital, an army vehicle pulled up ahead of her and Michael leaned out and waved from the passenger window.

The door opened and Michael jumped down to greet her. She watched as a black and white collie also joined him.

'Michael, what are you doing here? And who are you?' she said, giving the dog's head a gentle ruffle as it sat obediently. Its tail wagged back and forth creating a small dust cloud as it sat watching Michael's every move.

'This is the mascot in training. Ben.'

Kitty turned her attention back to Michael.

'How are you after last night?'

Michael made a play of opening his eyes wide with his fingers.

'I need twenty-four hours of undisturbed sleep and I ache in areas I never knew I had, but apart from that I'm much better now I've seen you again.' He reached out and touched her hand. 'Listen, I'm on duty, but I'll break away tonight. I'm based not far from here. I'll get here around ten. Will you be able to meet me in the grounds somewhere, without getting into trouble?'

Kitty gave him a soft smile. 'I'm off duty, and us being here at the same time is meant to be, because I was supposed to be on a much longer shift. Something happened on the ward; it impressed Sister and earned me a break until tomorrow morning. Find the tennis courts and I'll meet you there.'

Michael saluted her and ran back to the truck. 'See you later. Come, Ben,' he waved one more time before he slammed the truck door shut and they drove away.

Seeing Michael gave Kitty renewed energy. Pondering how her heart had managed to forgive his thoughtless rejection of her over the misunderstanding of her walking out with Eddie, Kitty chose to put the past behind her and move forward. Michael had made his feelings clear, and if she wanted him in her life, she must do the same. Although, she had another dilemma to consider: her leaving Scotland. She returned to the hospital preparing her argument to explain why she wanted to leave, even though Michael was only a short distance away. She ate a light meal and went back to her room. Yawning, she debated sleeping before bathing, but then decided the latter was the better option as most staff were out and about or on duty. She gathered her wash things and walked down the long corridor and along another, to the shared bathroom at the end of it. If it was in use, it would be a trek to the outside shower blocks. This afternoon she hoped the bathroom was free; it rarely was, but tiredness was setting in, and her legs ached. She let out a triumphant little squeal when the handle turned, and she stepped inside. No one else had used it since it had last been cleaned, and she wasted no time in enjoying the delights of bathing and washing her hair for longer than a rushed fifteen minutes and endless rattling of the handle or knocks on the door. Once back in her room, she set her alarm for nine o'clock and settled down for a well-earned rest, with Michael as the focus of her dreams.

## Chapter Twenty-Seven

B raving the night air, Kitty buttoned up her coat and congratulated herself for wearing her siren suit underneath. Although the weather was brighter and milder during the daytime than normal for Scotland, according to many who'd lived there since the set-up of the hospital, the evenings were cold. They were not wrong. In her home town during the month of May, Kitty would enjoy spring evenings with the same warmth as the Scottish daytime weather. She shivered and turned her attention to the sky.

The earlier clouds had faded, allowing the stars to shine through the navy blackness. Everywhere was dark thanks to the no-light law, and Kitty was thankful for the moonlight across the gardens. Silhouetted against the large castle, the military buildings looked shapeless and uninteresting, so Kitty turned to look at the outline of Buchanan Castle. Even in the darkness, it shared its magnificence. It gave the evening a romantic touch, until the searchlight party switched on their observation beams, and reality reminded her that romance in wartime was a fragile thing.

Staff walked the grounds and greeted her with good evenings or goodnights, and Kitty waited with nervous anticipation for Michael's impending visit. Going by the changeover of staff, it was after ten o'clock. Any moment now and she'd have the company of someone who knew her, who understood her hopes and fears. Someone who would always have her love no matter what the outcome of her leaving Scotland.

'Loitering on military grounds is an offence, young lady.' Michael's voice, soft and low with its honeyed tones, made her smile.

'I'm so sorry, I'm on a secret mission. Don't tell,' Kitty whispered, and put her finger to her lips.

Michael glanced around before he placed a discreet kiss on her forehead.

'It's good to see you. Smelling delicious as always,' he said.

'The last of my rose soap from my aunt. From now on it will be whatever I can find, so make the most of it.'

With so many people walking to and fro, it was hard to concentrate on the conversation she had rehearsed in her head.

'Let's move away from here. It's quieter behind the kitchen near my room. They only use the ovens for keeping food warm; the main catering units are over there.' Kitty pointed across the grounds.

Keeping a decent distance between them so as not to draw attention to themselves as they walked to the back of the main building, Kitty chatted about general life at the hospital, and Michael told her what he could about his new life as a civilian on loan to the army for teaching purposes. His role meant he moved around a lot. Once they reached the privacy of the kitchen area, Michael took her in his arms, and she gave in to the demand of his lips. Her body tingled with pleasure and it was several minutes before they parted from their increasingly passionate embrace.

'Stop, Michael. We must stop before we get caught,' said Kitty with reluctance as they pulled apart. She patted her hair in place and put her fingers to her lips, blowing him an apology.

Pulling out a small package from his coat pocket, Michael held it out to her. 'A small gift for you.'

With an excited giggle, Kitty took the gift and wasted no time unwrapping the newspaper surrounding it and squealed with delight at the small gold badge nestled in her palm.

'It's beautiful.'

Michael wrapped his hand over her palm.

'It was my grandmother's sweetheart pin from my grandfather. My mother's parents were very much in love and when he left to train in England to fight in the first war, he gave her this to remind her she was loved. Sadly, he never returned. She passed this on to my mother, who was born shortly after his death. I've inherited it and wanted you to have it – and forgive my stupidity over the Eddie business.' He raised his hand to prevent Kitty from interrupting. 'Be my girl again. Take my pin and my love wherever you go and know you carry my heart, Kitty.'

Michael lifted the pin from her hand and placed it onto the lapel of her coat. He smiled when she didn't try to stop him. Once clasped in place, Kitty stroked a finger across the pin and inhaled. Her nerves twitched around her heart – some with excitement, others with love and anticipation of another kiss, and some with concern over what she was about to say.

'Michael. It is a beautiful gift, but I can't accept it. In Birmingham, I thought we were so strong as a couple that we could survive anything. I was wrong. We didn't survive someone meddling and writing letters to you. If we were to walk out together again, we have to have trust and honesty.'

'I understand. We are together again and I'll not let you go – I promise. Trust and honesty – you have mine, sweetheart.'

As he reached out and gently moved a length of hair from her face, Michael's touch spoke volumes. With tenderness he placed his hand behind her neck and stroked the nape, all the while staring intently into her eyes. She saw his love emblazoned by the moonlight filtering across the treetops. Kitty absorbed his actions and felt his love as it surged around her body. Words were weak in comparison. She gave in to his kiss, knowing this time it could be the last time, depending upon his reaction to what she was about to say, but she needed it to give her comfort should they part ways. To know someone loved her with a passion so strong was not a feeling she was willing to push to the back of her mind ever again; it was a pure love.

When they stepped back from one another, Kitty

returned his touch and stroked his cheek with equal tenderness. She felt the stubble of the day across his jawline and then the warmth moistness of his lips as she put her finger across them.

'I need you to listen, Michael. It's not going to be easy, but I must be honest. Until I knew you were here, the days leading up to the bombing were awful. I was alone. Painfully alone. Although it was only a couple of days, I knew I didn't fit in and I hurt so much inside that it became impossible to think I'd ever be happy again… and then you turned up.'

Michael removed her hand from his lips.

'To be fair, I was in Scotland long before you,' he joked.

With a brief nod and a mouthed hush, Kitty continued speaking.

'I've put in for a transfer, back to Birmingham. I miss Jo. I missed you. I miss the emergency team. The sad truth is, I'm not needed here, Michael. I push a broom around a pile of dried tea leaves, I polish and scrub. In Birmingham, I was allowed to study and move forward, encouraged to become the nurse I feel I could be. I have about ten more days left here, regardless of whether I want to leave or not, as Matron told me they don't need me when new recruits arrive.'

Michael pulled her into his arms again and held her close.

'I'm not going to be selfish, Kitty. You are not mine to control, but I do love you. Seriously, adore you. I've also been miserable up here, but my job is extremely important for the future of this war, and I have no choice but to stay.'

Kitty gave a short sigh of understanding and felt

Michael squeeze her gently. Her body relaxed into his and he buried his head in her hair, holding her in silence for a few minutes.

'The thought of you being miserable if I'm shipped out and not here to comfort you saddens me. And hearing you speak of your dream… who am I to take it away? Wear my pin and do whatever brings you happiness. Life's too short for us to debate our love; we both know it exists. This time it will be stronger, and no one can tear us apart – only death has that power, and I pray each night we survive this war. We *will* survive this war,' he said, and Kitty heard his voice crack with emotion.

'We will, and I'll wear my pin with pride, thank you. Let's make the most of the days we can see each other. Let's walk, hold hands in the shadows, and enjoy tonight,' Kitty said, and slipped her hand into his.

They walked hand in hand until they were in the public gaze again and then they strolled as if chatting about work. When they reached the riverside, they sat behind a thicket and huddled together. Voices behind them were distant and no longer distracting. An owl swooped low across the water's edge and hooted. Time stood still, and Kitty felt her eyes grow heavy with relaxation.

'I could stay here for ever. Just like this – in each other's arms, warm and alone,' she said, following through with a soft yawn.

'One day, it will be better than this – I promise. My two hours are nearly up; I must get the supply truck back or my pal will be in trouble. Give me two days, and I'll be back,

Kitty. I've got to train more recruits, so I'm heading further north.'

Walking back to the edge of the gardens, Kitty enjoyed another passionate kiss when Michael drew her in to say goodbye. As he did so, the horrifying sound of sirens rang out and both pulled back in shock.

'What the—! They're back!' Michael shouted.

They turned to see the skies light up and the peace of the evening was shattered by the brutal realisation of how vulnerable they were. Before they let each other go, they drew comfort from an emotional kiss to last a lifetime.

'Get to safety,' Michael said as he grabbed her hand and tugged her along the pathway back towards the castle.

'I'm going to the main hut and I'll volunteer my services there. It will be all right, Michael. Go, get back to your men. Look out for me if they hit a target; we're bound to send down a volunteer group. I'll get on the list. Go, be safe.'

Kitty dropped a kiss on Michael's cheek and ran towards the hospital hut. She stopped to see him run towards the main entrance where he'd parked, and closed her eyes for a few seconds to set the memories of the evening into a solid grounding in her mind.

'Be safe, my love. Stay safe,' she whispered before she turned away and focused on the urgency of the night ahead.

## Chapter Twenty-Eight

R olling the patient over in his bed, Kitty finished the last of his bed bath and patted his back dry with a towel. A deep satisfaction swept over her and she smiled at the nurse on the other side of the bed.

'All done,' she said.

She glanced over at Sarah, content in her work with a mop and bucket, then back at the patient. Apparently, the ward sister had received positive feedback from a member of the medical tent staff following the second attack on Greenock. They had reported that Kitty had an admirable ability to keep a calm head under stress from the attack during the night. Kitty was taken aback when she turned up for work and the ward sister gave her basic nursing duties instead of cleaning, and Kitty gave every ounce of energy she had left to patient care. She tried to put Michael out of her mind when reports of the attack filtered back from Greenock. By all accounts it was far worse than the day before, although word was that the majority of residents of the main areas hit had managed to get to safety by hiding in tunnels at the end of town.

Kitty remained behind under instructions to make safe the new medical tents instead of going with the volunteer group when the bombing started. Although she had wanted to be in the thick of things, she had looked around at the faces of men struggling to survive and known she needed to stay to help. By the morning, the dawn had risen through flames and spiralling smoke, and the memory of the evening with Michael seemed a lifetime away instead of mere hours.

'Good work, Nurse Pattison. Get some rest,' the ward sister said as Kitty finished the shift, and Kitty gave a smile of thanks.

'I certainly need some. See you tomorrow, Sister.'

As Kitty reached the top of the stairs, Sarah caught up with her. She always looked nervous and awkward but was even more so today, and her words came out in a breathless rush.

'Kitty, the post arrived. I hope you don't mind but I grabbed yours to save you time. Lucky old you got two letters. Mind you, my old gran sent me a parcel, bless her. She doesn't have a lot, but always treats me once a month. This time it was a jar of home-made jam – she's with the Women's Institute and a dab hand at producing something tasty from her kitchen, and look, a handkerchief with my initials embroidered across.'

Kitty admired the gifts and took her letters from Sarah. She smiled when she spotted Trix's neat handwriting.

'That's lovely, Sarah. Thank you for thinking of me,' she

said, lifting up her letter. 'I'm going to eat and relax. This is from a friend, Trixie, but we call her Trix, and this is Jo's scrawling handwriting – I'd know it anywhere. The three of us met the day we joined the Red Cross.'

Sarah gave a wistful sigh. 'You are lucky to have friends who write to you. You are lucky to have friends at all. I know I am an odd one out, but until you came along, I didn't really take much notice. Sharing a walk, a meal and chat with you has made me realise I need to put a bit of effort into getting to know people, now you are leaving,' she said.

Her words touched Kitty. She understood loneliness, and how the love of friends can lift spirits. She reached out and touched Sarah's shoulder. Kitty looked forward to showing her the pin.

'I'll write. I promise. Come and eat with me now.'

Sarah hesitated, but encouraged by Kitty, followed her to the canteen where they loaded their trays and sat at a table at the opposite end from four QAs. The girls gave Kitty a smile in return for her greeting them with a nod hello.

'After we've eaten maybe you'd like to come sit in my room, Sarah? I've something special I'd like to show you. Let's get to know each other more, so I can write to you when I'm settled back in Birmingham,' Kitty said.

Kitty looked over at Sarah and she witnessed tears rolling down her cheeks.

'I'd like that, thank you,' Sarah said, gulping back the sobs.

Confused and taken aback, Kitty reached across and touched Sarah's hand.

'Oh, Sarah. Don't cry.'

Sarah made good use of her grandmother's embroidered gift and gave Kitty a wan smile.

'It's that you are the first person to take any interest in me,' she said between sniffles.

Kitty patted Sarah's hand.

'I'm sorry I never noticed your sadness sooner. I thought you liked being alone. You tend to give off that impression,' she said, and glanced down at the four girls looking at them from the other end of the table.

'The girls here are lovely, but they trained together in a different way to us. They are incredibly brave and need to form tight friendship groups. I came in only a few days ago, and to be fair, it's too soon for them to want to draw another into their circle. Let's face it, you are a quiet one and keep your head down, so they wouldn't think you'd be interested in their company.'

Sarah's tears still flowed, and Kitty accepted them as a release. The girl had bottled up feelings of loneliness for too long and she appreciated the courage Sarah had put into trying to befriend her by collecting her post.

'Eat up. Food's getting cold. We'll chat on our walk. Dry your eyes; it will be fine, you'll see.'

Kitty put a spoonful of mashed potato into her mouth and thought about how she could help Sarah. As she ate, she noticed the girls from the end of the table approach them.

'Sarah, are you feeling all right?' one of them asked, her

voice filled with genuine concern.

A startled Sarah looked up at her.

'You know my name?' she asked in a soft whisper.

'Of course I know your name, silly. We work on the same ward, don't we?' the girl said.

Sarah's face flushed and she lowered her head, her shy nature painfully clear. Kitty realised more tears were brewing and decided Sarah needed a bit of support.

With a beaming smile at Sarah, Kitty spoke to the small group.

'Thanks for asking about Sarah. She won't tell you herself, but she's lonely. We've just become friends and I'm being shipped out in a few days, and the realisation she has colleagues in her life, but not friends, has upset her.'

The four QAs looked at Kitty, and a sadness filtered amongst the group. A girl who dwarfed them all stepped around the table and went to Sarah.

'Nobody should feel alone during this ruddy war. Nobody! I promise you can come to me any time I'm free and share a moment. I'd ask you to join us on our escapades up the hillside, but that would be unkind!' She laughed a deep, warm, infectious laugh.

'We agree no one should be made to join us for the hikes. Kitty, we'll keep an eye on her when you are gone. What a lovely friend you are, looking out for someone you've just met,' said another girl.

Sarah moved back in her chair and stood up. She looked at them all with an embarrassed smile.

'Thank you. It's silly really, but I'm not great when it comes to pushing myself forward. When Kitty turned up and asked me to go for a walk, it made me see that a simple act of asking could make a difference. I envied you all, but me being me, didn't feel I fitted in.'

Kitty put an arm around Sarah's shoulders and gave her a gentle squeeze.

'Listen, we're on duty tonight and have to go, but Sarah, you are not alone. Hear me? See you around, Kitty,' the tall girl said, and the others muttered their agreement and goodbyes.

It warmed Kitty's heart to see their genuine care, and she had learned a lesson for herself, too. She would never look at anyone in the same way she had first viewed Sarah. If the girl had never brought her Trix's letter, she would not have put any more effort into getting to know her. She would write to her and uphold her promise, without question.

Wasting no time once back in her room, Kitty tore open the letters from Trix and Jo. Although the length of their friendship only spanned around eight months, it felt like years. Their bond during tough times had created a sisterhood so strong, there was little doubt of it lasting a lifetime. The war speeded up the need for holding on to those who understood your fears and those who lifted you up when the days were so dark that they lowered your resilience towards seeing a brighter future. Kitty missed Jo's blunt manner and Trix's giddy ways. They allowed Kitty to organise them, to keep them on track with their studies, and suddenly, she had been left with no one – a feeling she'd experienced in the past. People moved around her, spoke to her, but their presence was superficial. Sniffling back tears, she read Trix's letter first, allowing the mothering personality of her friend to wash over her.

*C/O Rosehome Cottage*
*Pinchinthorpe*
*9th May 1941*

*Dearest Kitty,*

*Excuse the handwriting as I the postie will take this for me on his return journey, which means you will receive it tomorrow.*

*How wonderful it was to receive your letter. Scotland?! How wonderful.*

*Your journey through the Dales sounds adventurous. I wish you luck for the future.*

*I hope you are keeping well and not injuring yourself by clambering around bomb sites as you tend to do. Your courage is second to none and being part of a military camp, I can see you volunteering for rescue missions, but please don't join up. Always stay a Red Cross girl – it suits you.*

*Do write and tell me more about your Highland adventures. Are there any eligible doctors for you – and maybe one for Jo, up there in your castle? Make lots of friends but never forget us.*

*We are doing well in our part of Yorkshire. Their accent is a hard one to follow. Mind you, I've heard a Scotsman talk a few times, and think you might also have difficulty with the locals. You are always welcome here, so never hesitate to visit when you can!*

*I've news. I have decided to train as a midwife once I've completed my full nurse training. I shadowed one for a short assessment and it was wonderful. The baby I helped to bring into the world was a little boy.*

*If I train it will mean moving to Acomb. There is a training school for midwives there and Gordon will find a General Practitioner post nearby. He is happy in his locum work but wants to settle down to his own practice and patients – unless I train and he continues with working his way around Yorkshire, and then we set up our own practice. It's all dreams and hot air at the moment.*

*We no longer communicate with Belle. She became quite a nuisance with gossipy letters about doctors who are in serious relationships. You will be pleased to know neither you nor Michael were her focus in any of them. And then the cheek of it, she turned up unexpectedly with Robert Keane one weekend. Goodness knows how many bags she brought with her. We got the impression she is working her way through the doctors at Birmingham. Robert confided in Gordon that she had wormed her way in for a visit, but he's not a man I would always trust, either. He certainly enjoyed her attention whilst here, so I don't believe him. I think he encouraged it myself. After talking with Gordon, we decided not to open the letters she continued sending and simply returned them to her. Maybe she'll get the hint! After what you told us she did to you and Michael, I'll never forgive her. She is the cause of your broken heart and that made me angry.*

*The cottage where I live is quaint, and the hospital where I work in the next town is never busy. I think I've treated everyone in our village, which has put me in their good books. I think it is a place I could build my nest and remain for the rest of my days. Each time I walk around and inhale the fresh air, I feel alive. It takes me back to my childhood. The happy times in my life when my parents doted on me and kept me safe. Gordon makes me feel that way sometimes, but it is reciprocated.*

*We are happy – very. I think we'd be happier if we could marry, but I need to fulfil my dream, or I'll never settle. I have to qualify. I hate that marriage would take that opportunity away from me. It is so unfair!*

*I've written all I can for the moment. Take care of yourself. Oh, and notice I no longer call Gordon, Smithy. Everyone calls him Smithy, so I wanted to have Gordon for myself. He's changed, too. He's still funny but far more serious; this war and the loss of old school friends has made him settle down.*

*Take care, my dear friend.*

*With love from us*
*Trixie*
*X*

*1A West Street*
*Bristol*
*8th May 1941*

*Kitty, how the devil are you?*

*Your letter reached me, and I cannot believe you are in Scotland. Do you get out and about? Is it a local hospital? Made any friends? I've got colleagues but nothing like you, Trix and I had in Birmingham. It will be a good day when we are all together again. In fact, I think I might get me a posting in Scotland.*

*I've got news!*

*I struggled with concentrating on nurse training after you left and came to the conclusion I'm not cut out for that side of medical life. After a long chat with a tutor, I made the decision to leave. Don't be mad at me. I moved back home to Dad to regroup and think about what it is I do want to do, but his temper is getting worse. He's aggressive and spoils for a fight every day. I know his injury from work frustrated him and prevented him from joining up, but it isn't my fault. He tries to control my life. He calls me dreadful names and I'm sure that is why Mum ran away. I've had to walk away, too. I tried, but it was not easy being under the same roof as him. Anyway, I did a bit of thinking and decided to ask at the recruitment centre what I could do about finding something new and am now a volunteer driver for the local dignitaries. They drive me insane with their pompous attitudes, but once I'm behind the wheel, I don't care, and when my head is under that bonnet, I am so happy. I can change a tyre in the dark. I've stayed here in Bristol because I know the roads like the back of my hand, and it is useful in the dark when there's a call-out. Plus, I can stay with my aunt until I decide if this is what I truly want. I miss you so much my friend. I miss our silly nights of card playing.*

*Did you hear Belle has transferred to a hospital in Cornwall? She lives in her parents' summer home. I have a feeling the hospital manoeuvred her away from so many scandals. She's lucky they need people willing to tend to the wounded or she'd definitely be removed from the RC register.*

*Take care, my friend. Stay safe in Bonnie Scotland. Be happy.*

*Jo*

Kitty folded the letters away with a satisfied smile. The past hour spent chatting with Sarah wasn't the same as when Trix and Jo used to gather in her room, and their letters made her wistful and even lonelier than before. She couldn't imagine Sarah plastering cream on her face, sipping whisky or sherry, nor playing cards. They had found a common ground discussing the latest medical interventions, and Sarah was extremely knowledgeable about the current state of countries involved in the war. When she spoke, Kitty felt Sarah was wasted sweeping the ward floors; she had a mind which absorbed and retained information like no one she had met before.

During their time together, Sarah had confided her fears of the news filtering through about German confinement camps holding Jews against their will. By the time she'd finished expressing her concerns about Jewish friends in Britain, Kitty realised Sarah was most probably referring to members of her own family. She chose to say nothing. Sarah had a right to privacy, as they all did, and her religious views and beliefs were as sacred as Kitty's aunt and uncle's – and her own. She now understood why Sarah always appeared nervous, especially given the ward she had been allocated.

Kitty sensed in Sarah a loneliness like her own, and she reassured her of her promise to write. As a pen pal, Sarah would probably have more to say writing letters than she did in person – her heart was in the right place, and no one deserved to feel alone.

When she sat in her tiny room, a sadness overwhelmed her, and she became frustrated at not being able to telephone and check on Michael. She just had to live on hope that he had survived the attack and would come to her as soon as he was free to visit.

## Chapter Twenty-Nine

Although tired, Kitty's mood was uplifted by a message left for her on her door from Michael. The message came from the front gates saying Michael had passed by and would they let her know he was hoping to visit at two o'clock the following afternoon.

The past three night-duty shifts had been busy and after getting five hours' sleep, when her night shift rotation finished, Kitty prepared herself to meet Michael. She saw him waiting by a tree and ran into his arms. Their embrace attracted wolf whistles from the guards at the gate and others witnessing the tender moment. They decided to take their time off camp and enjoy a walk around the banks of Loch Lomond.

'Are you warm enough?' Michael asked Kitty as they walked arm in arm along a quiet pathway. A soft drizzle didn't distract from the beauty surrounding them, nor their happiness at being together again.

'I am. I'm also very happy. I do have a little confession to make,' Kitty said, her voice serious, and she stopped walking to face him.

A concerned look crossed his face and Michael pushed his hands into his pockets.

'Is this where you tell me there's someone else?' he asked.

Finding it incredible that he needed to ask such a question, Kitty leaned back slightly and frowned at him.

'You think that back there was a fake welcome and that I was pretending to be happy to see you?' she said with an indignant fling of her arm in the general direction of the castle.

Michael pulled his hands from his pockets and held them palms upward in front of his body as if to ward her off.

'Calm down, Kitty, it was a joke.'

Kitty took a moment to get her thoughts together. Michael's apparent joke – although he didn't realise it, had hit a nerve. A memory of when he'd thought she'd met up with Eddie threatened to turn their afternoon together sour. With a shake of her head, she gave a cheeky grin and put her finger to her lips and gave a wide-eyed look of pretend shock.

'Did I fool you?' she said, and gave a hearty laugh in an attempt to shake off the moment.

Michael tugged her arm and pulled her close, his breath warm against her cheek.

'Don't scare me like that again,' he said, his voice anxious and loving.

Kitty leaned into him and allowed her mind to absorb all that Michael meant to her.

'So, are you going to share your confession?' Michael said.

With a soft sigh, Kitty took his hand. 'I've officially put in for a transfer back to Birmingham. I know you are here, but I don't want to be, and you probably won't be stationed here for ever.'

Michael raised his eyebrows and dropped a kiss onto the tip of her nose.

'You are a free spirit, and it is not my place to tie you down. Just wear my pin and always remember you are my girl, Kitty. Always.'

## Chapter Thirty

P lacing her pretty pin into its box and pushing it to a safe place at the back of a drawer, Kitty changed into her uniform ready for an afternoon shift. Although due on night duty, Sister had asked her to meet her in a private wing of the house for special duties at three o'clock. Kitty managed another five-hour sleep, marvelling at the fact she'd enjoyed ten undisturbed in total over the past forty-eight hours.

Looking in the mirror to check her hair and cap were in order, Kitty noticed her eyes sparkled more than usual. She also noticed the dark rings underneath, thanks to a late night.

She and Michael had walked and talked for hours. They had ended up at a pretty inn, where military staff were greeted with a warm welcome and a large glass of local distilled whisky. It became a celebration for them both, a way of sealing their love for one another.

She pulled her door shut and pushed all excitement

behind her and headed along the corridor. When she neared the stairway for the basement ward, she noted a lot of activity from the staff as they assisted the POW patients outside.

Sarah came into view looking hot and bothered, and Kitty waited while she supported a patient as he limped his way towards a wheelchair.

'*Psst*, Sarah. What's going on?'

Sarah pushed the chair towards Kitty and leaned in to speak out of the patient's earshot.

'I've no idea. There've been a few visits from Major Armstrong this morning and next thing, it was all hands to the pump. We got news to clear the ward and take them to one of the external units and bring the walking wounded – British boys – to the downstairs. They're waiting to go back to their barracks, so only on a night stay. I don't mind, as the army insists they help with ward work when back on the fitness register. Less work for me. Got to go. See you later?'

'I'm switched to a late shift on a new ward upstairs, so you're right, something is going on. Come see me around eleven for a couple of minutes. I've something to tell you.'

Climbing the stairs to meet the ward sister at the top of the far-end wing – a place she'd never seen before – Kitty wondered about the new ward she was to work on and hoped she would be put to good use. The ward sister stood at the end of the corridor and waved when she saw Kitty.

'Nurse Pattison? I'm Sister Vince. I thought I'd wait for you here.' The woman looked so neat and tidy in her uniform, and she had a friendly disposition, which relaxed

Kitty's nerves. It did surprise Kitty to see a senior QA wait for a temporary Red Cross assistant.

'Good afternoon, Sister. Thank you for waiting, I've not been in this part of the building before now. It's a beautiful place.'

Sister Vince nodded her agreement. 'We are very fortunate the duke agreed to the military takeover. You must be wondering what is going on.' The sister smiled encouragingly again, and Kitty gave a small nod of the head.

'You've come highly recommended by the POW ward sister, and I'm reassured you are calm and not known as a gossip.' Sister Vince lowered her voice. 'We are to nurse a VIP, and although his needs are limited, he needs assistance with pain relief. I'm told he is to receive a visit in an hour, so when they arrive, we will take a break when the visitors are here.'

'One patient?' Kitty asked.

'One patient with security status,' Sister Vince said, and began walking along the corridor, pointing out a door which separated the hospital from the private residential side. It appeared the duke and his wife still retained some of the castle, but did not always stay there. Kitty now wondered if the well-dressed woman she'd sometimes seen sitting at the far end of the gardens was the lady of the house, and she was glad she had never made a fool of herself by talking to her.

On their approach to the room, Kitty realised the person inside was indeed of high rank as two soldiers stood either side of the door. They saluted Sister Vince as they offered a clipboard to her. She signed it and ushered Kitty inside.

The room, which had obviously once been a large and luxurious bedroom, judging by the heavy embroidered curtains draped around the windows, was kitted out as a small ward with only one bed.

She looked across at the window where the patient – a middle-aged man – sat in a comfortable armchair, his lower leg set in a plaster cast and supported on a stool. Kitty noticed he wore the tired look of someone in pain. He held a pad of paper and a pen in his hands and she watched them tremble as he clutched them tightly.

He glanced her way, and they shared a brief smile. With a firm nod to the man but saying nothing, the ward sister manoeuvred Kitty to the desk at the far end of the room before Kitty got the opportunity to speak with him.

'Nurse Pattison. I need you to sign these papers, please. They declare that you understand the need for discretion when nursing a patient of importance.' She slid two forms towards Kitty. She briefly glanced over the paperwork and signed in the appropriate place. A quiver of excitement built as she realised she'd been selected for a privileged position.

'You are to ensure the patient receives limited attention as he is capable of most things for himself. Limit your conversation to the weather, and say nothing about the hospital or news relating to the war. Understand?'

It then dawned on Kitty that the patient was a German POW – and obviously high-ranking by the way he was being given this VIP treatment.

'I understand, Sister. I take it he is classified with enemy status like the others I nursed? I don't speak German though, so I cannot ask him anything about his needs.'

The sister gave an abrupt huff, but to Kitty's relief it was not directed at her for her lack of language skills.

'The man speaks perfect English – with only a hint of an accent. And as far as you are concerned, he is English – which is what he claimed to be when captured. It is an extremely delicate situation, and you have signed official documents of the utmost secrecy. This is a position of trust. One of the most important you will fulfil whilst here – or ever, I should imagine. It is a most unusual case.'

Standing tall and with her shoulders back, Kitty made it clear she understood with a serious nod.

'Of course, Sister. My lips are sealed. Can I ask, what is his name? What do I call him?'

Brushing her hands together as if covered in flour or dirt, the ward sister gave Kitty a strange look and then checked herself with a reassuring smile.

'Nothing. You address him as *sir*, as you would any other gentleman patient, until I tell you otherwise. However, when we record anything, we will call him patient X. I'm still receiving orders with regards to his care and personal details.' The sister shuffled papers on her desk and pulled out a rota sheet. She read it through before handing it to Kitty.

'As we are under orders to limit staff contact with this man, we will not be using an orderly for tea-making, so it will be down to you to ensure he is fed and watered. Cleaning of the ward will also be down to you for your shift. I'm splitting the hours between the three other nurses and one deputy sister allocated to this patient. We will rotate our shifts to ensure we are all in fine fettle and can cope with the extra duties. You might even get a glimpse of me with a mop and bucket at some point,' Sister Vince said with a light laugh, and then beckoned her closer to the desk.

She pointed to the place where *Kitty Pattison* was marked on the paper, and Kitty saw an area where a list of tasks and duties was written in a neat hand. Ironically, the floor sweeping and damp dusting no longer fazed her. Kitty understood the importance of the task ahead, and if dried tea leaves played a part, then she would push the broom with professional aplomb, as befitting the situation. Her mind bounced around the wording, absorbing each detail.

Sister Vince stood upright and as she did so, her hand moved slightly from a patient record card nearby, drawing Kitty's attention away from the rota. When Kitty looked to see the patient's name and information across the top of the page, her blood ran cold.

*Horn / Hess / Hitler. $10^{th}$ May 1941 – crash-landing resulting in Talus Fracture/? Tibula /Fibula. Plaster cast. Admitted Drymen MH / $13^{th}$ May 1941: Enemy alien – male.*

She and Michael had spoken about the enemy, about Hitler, his followers, and those who stood by his side. This man looked nothing like the images of Adolph Hitler she'd seen on the newsreels at the cinema in Birmingham, yet his name was on the entry sheet. Surely the German leader, the man accused of forcing the start of World War Two couldn't be sitting by the window inside a British military camp created out of a fairy-tale castle, with a broken ankle. The man she'd received instructions to look after was too tall, if the images of Hitler she'd seen were real. Who was this mystery man? This man who was so much a secret from other staff that he had a coded name – Kitty hoped she would find out more about him when Sister Vince had all the facts.

The ward sister's voice broke into her thoughts and Kitty realised she'd become too engrossed in what she'd seen. She also noticed Sister Vince's face flush with embarrassment when she placed her hand back over the patient's name, before covering it with a pile of other papers.

'What you saw there is extremely confidential and the fact you've managed to see it is a bad move on my part. Understood?' she asked Kitty with a hint of a small plea in her voice.

'It's not *him*. He's too short, isn't he? It can't be him!' Kitty whispered glancing over at the man, expecting a ticking off rather than an answer, but curiosity got the better of her.

'We are not sure who he is, but it should come to light this afternoon. Again, this is in the strictest of confidence and only because you saw the paperwork. Keep your head down and say nothing. For my sake, and for your own. This kind of information is TS, and we must abide by the rules of war,' Sister Vince whispered with such great urgency; Kitty decided they needed to change the subject. She was entering an area she had no control over and knew she could find herself in trouble if she said or did the wrong thing. This man was more than a VIP patient. He supported the biggest enemy of Britain.

'You will see it marked for the fifteenth of May. Are you listening nurse?' Sister Vince's voice cut into her thoughts and Kitty turned her attention back to her duty rota. They continued their conversation at a normal level and behaved as if nothing had passed between them.

'Here, this is your shift for tomorrow – it runs from 7 in the morning until 2.30 in the afternoon. You will finish at 10.30 this evening. Of course, you will have the time away from the ward for the VIP visit, but I suggest you take the time to read about broken bones and their healing process. I will ask questions, so do not waste the time gallivanting with friends.'

At the risk of being found rude or in breach of an army ruling, Kitty said nothing. Her mind did not stop; however, it played around with the laughable suggestion of her gallivanting. Kitty's life was not that of someone who ever gallivanted anywhere.

During the afternoon, she studied the sleeping man from a safe distance and saw no resemblance to the moustached man shown on the cinema screen. Satisfied it wasn't Hitler, but most definitely a spy, Kitty relieved the boredom of working alone by creating scenes in her mind that she, the British nurse from Essex, saved the country from invasion in a variety of ways. First, she envisaged pushing the man from a window, then she ensured his tea was laced with a tasteless poison, and finally, she persuaded the Canadian lumberjacks working a few miles away to build a wooden hut in the middle of nowhere where he was left unattended.

By the time she had finished her list of punishments for the man – one of the biggest enemies of the British Isles – she scared herself with her ability to think so violently and with such cruelty. Her aunt and her class teacher had often told her she had an overactive imagination, and now, standing watching the man droop his head into his chest and snore loudly, she believed them. She switched her concentration to the ward sister. Kitty had nothing but admiration for the efficient manner in which the nurse moved around the ward. Everything had its place, and Kitty compared the level of training she'd seen a QAIMNS nurse receive to a Red Cross or civilian one. All experienced the same level of emotional input when nursing patients, but the regimented order of the QAs required more self-control and learning to become more forceful due to the fact they worked within a large male-dominated environment. Kitty had witnessed struggles between sisters of high rank, infuriated by orderlies ignoring them, when she worked on the ward downstairs. Another thing she had noticed was the eagerness with which the nurses wished to go abroad and into the thick of the fighting – something she baulked at and knew she would fight against should the Red Cross want to send her. Kitty suspected that if she had been trained by the army, her view of travelling to the front line would be vastly different. In the canteen she heard nurses speak of what they'd witnessed and of the types of injuries they were faced with the minute they reached a patient's side. Of the filth and tough environment in which they had to tend to them and then get them back to England alive by travelling hours from France. They were a special breed of nurses with fighting spirit, and Kitty was not sure she'd have their resilience even with the tougher training.

'Nurse Pattison, I think it is time our patient was disturbed with a cup of tea. His visitors will arrive soon, and it is best he is not in a drowsy, crumpled state. I've placed a comb on the table beside him. Oh, you hold the mirror, and no knives or forks – the same as downstairs. Safety first.'

Laying the tray on the table beside the patient, Kitty nudged his arm to alert him to his drink.

'*Danke* – thank you. A warm drink is a good thing always, do you not think?' the man said, overriding his German with English as quickly as he could.

Knowing Sister Vince was watching like a hawk, Kitty said nothing and kept her face as straight and free from expression as she could. She held out the mirror and handed him the comb.

'I will look my best, yes?' Again, the patient tried to draw Kitty into a conversation.

A loud knock on the door alerted them that the visitors were on their way, and Kitty gave a sigh of relief, took back the comb, and walked over to Sister Vince.

'Do I wait, then leave, Sister, or go now?' she asked.

As the door opened and two distinguished men walked into the ward, Kitty became aware of heightened tensions and moved nearer to the ward sister to wait for instructions as to what to do next.

She stood in the shadows and admired the air force

officer she overheard Sister Vince talking to; she watched the woman go out of her way to make them comfortable, pouring tea herself and clearing away the patient's tray. Once satisfied she'd done all required of her, she approached Kitty and took her to one side.

'Be back in two hours and write a short essay on the care of broken bones. And remember, this room and patient are not to be discussed. To do so is a criminal offence. I cannot stress this enough, nurse.'

Kitty gathered her cape and gave Sister Vince a reassuring smile. 'You can trust me, Sister.'

Once outside, she signed herself off duty and rushed downstairs to the canteen. She kept her ears alert to anything relating to the mystery man, but overheard nothing of interest and gave up trying. She made use of the medical library and wrote all she could about bone care and treatments. She also included the history of the use of plaster of Paris, and the woman who first thought to use it to aid bone fusion. Information Michael had taught her in Birmingham was coming in handy.

## Chapter Thirty-One

B ack in her room, Kitty decided to spend the last of her
two-hour break writing letters. She chose to write to
Jo first in case she ran short of time. Her friend had dropped
a bombshell in her last letter, when she told Kitty she had
left nurse training to become a driver and no longer worked
in Birmingham.

Kitty's letter requesting a transfer back to Birmingham
lay on the dresser. Without Jo in Birmingham, she wasn't
sure she wanted to return. It was time to decide where she
could go next, and to see if she could be accommodated
with a transfer request, rather than the department deciding
where she'd end up.

*Drymen Military Hospital*
*Buchanan Castle*
*Glasgow*
*14th May 1941*

*Dear Jo,*

*Well, you have thrown a spanner in my works with your news. Your interest in cars was always something which amused me, so I am not surprised you've chosen to become a driver. Although, you are a good nurse, too.*

*My news is that I was about to request a transfer back to Birmingham, to be near you again. I'm also missing your companionship, my friend! I don't have anyone to set me on the straight and narrow – unless you include Michael in that category. Yes, he's back in my life! We have reconnected with one another, romantically. It's a long, coincidental story, but in short, we bumped into each other during a rescue operation here in Scotland. He's based nearby under top secret status. He comes and goes due to the type of training he is giving to others within the British army, but we grab a walk when we can. He's happy and surrounded by Canadians, so not as lonely for home now. He has given me the prettiest sweetheart pin to wear; it belonged to his grandmother, and he inherited it when his parents died.*

*Talking of parents, as horrid as this sounds, but you know I don't mean it maliciously, I'd rather have no parents than one I cannot love or who doesn't love me. I am so sorry, Jo. Let me know if you move on within the next couple of weeks, as I intend to request leave to go and see my aunt and uncle for a few days, and then take up my next posting. We must not lose touch!*

*I've had a letter from Trix. Not sure if you have too, but she's considering midwifery. She'd make a good midwife or district nurse, don't you think? She said Belle turned up with Robert Keane and he'd had a hard time fighting her off. I'm not surprised she's no longer at Birmingham due to the scrapes she got herself into – some things never change!*

*Right, got to dash. Back on duty.*

*Take care of yourself and drive safely.*

*Always thinking of you.*
*Your friend, Kitty x*

A quick glance at her clock showed she had enough time to scribble out a letter to Trix and drop them into the outbox ready for collection.

*Drymen Military Hospital*
*Buchanan Castle*
*Glasgow*
*14th May 1941*

*Dear Trix,*

*How wonderful to hear from you and I am glad you are doing well. Midwifery sounds a good career move for you. A handy thing to have when you marry a GP, I should imagine! Smithy sounds so grown up when you write his*

*Christian name. I'm not sure I'd ever be able to see him as Gordon, but it reads right when you say his name.*

*The views I saw of Yorkshire were breathtaking and we met a couple of local Home Guards, so I understand you when you mention trying to work out what they say!*

*Brace yourself: Michael is back in my life and we are trying to rebuild our relationship. Can you believe we found each other here in Scotland? Fate has mapped out our paths for sure and I hope they are good ones.*

*I must decide where to apply for a posting soon, as I was going to request a return to Birmingham to be with Jo, but she's also changed her mind about nursing and is living with her aunt in Bristol. I'll leave her to fill in the blanks.*

*I've just written an essay for my ward sister about broken ankle bones. It made me think back to when Michael carried me home and you and Jo looked after me when I injured my ankle in the snow. Happy memories. Such kind friends.*

*Take care and a big hug for Smithy.*
*Your friend with love, Kitty x*

Climbing back upstairs a few minutes early for her shift, Kitty had to step aside for the two visitors leaving the ward. One man referred to the taller, distinguished man by his title, and Kitty gave them both a polite smile.

'Thank you, nurse,' the man she thought handsome addressed her as they approached.

'You are welcome, sir,' she said.

To her surprise and that of the man with him, the airman stopped.

'Don't let him get under your skin,' he said, nodding to the closed door of the room Kitty was about to enter. She assumed he referred to the patient inside, and by the men's expressions when they exited the room, Kitty guessed the meeting had been a frustrating one.

'I'll try not to, sir,' she said, not sure if she was to respond or not, but given the duke, the owner of the castle, had spoken to her, she felt it good manners.

The other man gave a shrug and followed after him. Kitty watched them descend the stairs at great speed. Something odd was definitely happening – there was an edginess about the pair.

Signing herself back into the ward, she thought she'd be polite and speak to the guard as she handed him back his pen. 'Is it safe to go in, no more visitors?'

'No more on the list,' he said. 'Whoever is in there is really causing a stir in the top rankings.'

The second guard spoke as he placed his hand on the door handle ready to open it for her. 'Don't suppose they've told you much.'

Kitty knew they were fishing for information and wasn't prepared to put herself in an awkward position. If she lied, she'd blush, and they would push harder each time they saw her.

'No one has told me anything, except that I'm making

the tea,' she said brightly, and pushed open the door to end the conversation.

Once inside she looked across at Sister Vince pulling back the bedclothes on the patient's bed.

'You're back. Like me, early or punctual. Well done,' Sister said, and stood back to check her work.

Kitty took a side-glance at the patient and saw him wringing his hands.

'Is he still in pain?' she asked.

Sister Vince nodded. 'After he's eaten a meal, we'll let him rest in bed. He's had quite a time of it and needs peace.'

Once again, Sister Vince gained Kitty's admiration. She had a kind heart, and a patient, no matter his background or political beliefs, deserved civil treatment.

'I've written my essay, Sister. I've left it on your desk,' Kitty said.

'Another pat on the back, nurse, but don't get bigheaded – I've not read it yet.' Sister Vince gave an unexpected laugh.

Kitty returned the laugh as she pulled the screen around the bed. 'Oh, I'm certain you will take back the compliment once you have.'

She worked hard during the evening and said only the bare minimum to the patient. When she pulled the blackout blinds and curtains into place, he tutted.

'No. Keep them open. I want to see the sky,' he said with a harsh rasp in his loud, demanding voice. Despite being a captured prisoner of war, he scowled the message across as a man used to giving orders. The respect shown by Kitty and Sister Vince was most definitely not reciprocated in those words. Before the soldiers outside the door had pushed it open to see what was going on, Sister Vince – to Kitty's surprise and then amusement – jumped from her chair, strode over to his bed, and pulled the screen back around without a word. It took only seconds for Kitty to realise that in those moves and actions, Sister Vince had reminded him of his position and of her authority within the room, and Kitty's admiration of her went to the top of the scale. There was a woman she aspired to become: calm in a crisis, in control of her temper, proud of who she was, and not afraid to show that her female status in the world was as valuable as a male's.

'Nurse Pattison. Let us discuss your essay. Highly commendable, I must say,' Sister Vince said, after reassuring the guards all was well, and the patient just needed a reminder of where he was and to readjust his attitude.

Throughout the evening they left the patient to rest, and Kitty mulled over Sister Vince's praise as they discussed her work. When she heard Kitty talk about the emergency team in Birmingham and the lessons she'd received from the doctor, who was now her closest friend, Sister Vince asked her more about her life. Kitty found the ward sister easy to talk to and was surprised at her relaxed manner.

'Do you intend to complete your training or marry your young man?' Sister Vince asked her at one point during the conversation, and Kitty explained their decision to focus on supporting Great Britain in her fight against the enemy. If they were lucky to enjoy a life together when peace was declared, then it was meant to be. Another question was what her parents thought of her war work. Kitty explained how she was an orphan and more or less free to make her own life decisions, gently guided by her aunt and uncle.

'Well, you will certainly have a wide range of skills to take away with you, Pattison. With you being an orphan, you would also be an asset on a lot of the wards filling with injured children nowadays. Poor things.' Whilst she was speaking, Kitty noticed her look towards the patient's bed and saw a fleeting flash of anger in her eyes. With great relief, Kitty realised the woman opposite her was as angry with the enemy as she was, but controlled her feelings so that they rarely surfaced.

'I have a lot to think about when I leave here, such as where in the country do I go next. I hadn't expected to end up in Scotland, so goodness knows if I put in a request whether it will be honoured or not,' Kitty said.

When they'd finished talking, Kitty attended to the linen cupboard and pondered the idea of transferring. With the news from Jo, and Michael down the road for the present, she wondered whether she would be best staying in Scotland and asking the relocation officer to find her a placement in a civilian hospital. With Sister Vince's suggestion that she'd understand the needs of orphans or injured children, Kitty toyed with the idea of seeking out a specialist hospital, but before she made any firm decisions she would speak with Michael about her future. He always knew how to put things into sensible categories to help her work out the answers. She couldn't wait to see him again, but felt it a shame she couldn't discuss her present work in any detail – something else they now had in common.

## Chapter Thirty-Two

'A decoy vehicle? I don't understand,' Kitty said as she stared at Sister Vince and Major Armstrong seated across from her.

Her face burned with anxiety as to why she had received a request to visit the major's office that morning and she wanted to bathe it in cool water, but she remained with her hands clasped behind her back to prevent her from touching her cheeks. Her face often flushed with nerves when she was stressed these days. She released a soft sigh and inhaled gently through her nose to remain calm and able to listen to the major's information and instructions.

'Yes. Patient X is leaving, and we have good reason for what we are doing. As you are about to finish your duties with us here in Drymen, we feel it is the ideal solution. I can tell you where you are headed; you will be travelling to London. As you requested, I spoke to the Red Cross relocation officer and they have granted you four days' leave. You are to telephone them for details of your new posting.'

Rising to her feet, swiftly followed by Sister Vince, the major held out her hand to Kitty. Shocked by the news and Major Armstrong's hand wavering in front of her, Kitty stood up and accepted the firm handshake.

'You did yourself proud, Pattison. Sister Vince and I are impressed and wish you the very best for the future.'

Sister Vince walked to the door and held it open.

'I'll fill you in on all the details shortly. And I agree with Major Armstrong. You are a fine nurse. It has been a pleasure working alongside you,' she said to Kitty before she saluted the major and left the room.

A flush of embarrassment further burned Kitty's cheeks; the praise from both women was pleasant but most unexpected.

'Thank you, Major. I've enjoyed my time here,' Kitty said, knowing full well the only reason she had enjoyed the place at all was because of meeting Michael again.

Walking back to the ward she felt a twinge of sadness because yet again, the opportunity to leave with more than twenty-four hours' notice had been taken away from her. What was it with people willing to push her from pillar to post at a moment's notice? She had to get a message to Michael.

Back on the ward, Sister Vince gave Kitty a rundown of the journey back to London. A patient transfer was happening via ambulance, and Kitty was to travel as his escort. It was not Patient X, although he was the main reason for the decoy transfer. It appeared he would have a military escort and travel in the middle car, behind which would be a support vehicle of armed guards.

'You are in no more danger than a usual nurse – and just a tip from someone who's made this trip before, don't drink too much tea or water before you leave. Don't look so worried. It will be fine, and they will drive as fast as they are allowed,' Sister Vince reassured her when Kitty grimaced after hearing there would be only one comfort stop halfway.

'With all the cloak and dagger stuff, I assume he is a person of concern to the nation, Sister,' Kitty said.

Sister Vince pulled back her shoulders and Kitty witnessed a slight bristling in the woman's manner.

'I know only the same as you, Nurse Pattison. You have the information about tomorrow. Go about your duties, and if there is anything else you need to know for the journey, I'll pass it along.'

Dismissed and well aware Sister Vince no longer wanted to hear any more questions, Kitty carried out her duties and glanced at the clock, willing away the time. At last, she saw it register 1.55. It was time for the afternoon staff to come on shift. She finished her last few chores and wrote a few words on the handover board for items to be replaced in the linen room, and then took a moment to draft a note for Michael.

*Dearest Michael,*

*I hope you get this letter from the guard. If you are to visit tonight, please try and get to see me outside my quarters. I am not on duty. Yet again, I am packing my bag. They are sending me away earlier than I'd anticipated on a patient transfer.*

*I'll be at my home from the 18th, if the trains from London Liverpool Street are running. That's the closest station I can get a train home from – let's pray there are no attacks and I get home at a decent time. You have the address and telephone number. Get in touch as soon as you can. I have four days' leave and no clue as to my next posting. I'll write to your barracks and hope you get my letters.*

*Stay safe and well, my darling.*

*Until we meet again, I send my love and kisses.*

*Kitty xx*

She took the liberty of sneaking an envelope, convinced if caught she would experience some form of army discipline, and slipped it into her pocket. Once the shift was over, she ran to the main gate and begged a guard to give it to Michael the next time he came to visit. The young man smiled and said a truck was taking supplies later that afternoon to Michael's camp. He scribbled the word medic across the envelope and assured her it would reach her boyfriend. Kitty couldn't thank him enough; he'd witnessed their kiss and seemed to understand her pain as she released the pent-up tears she'd held back.

'Don't cry, love. We'll make this happen. My girl's the same every time we have to leave each other,' he said.

Kitty dried her eyes and smiled at him.

'What's her name?' she asked.

The guard looked about to ensure no one could accuse them of idle gossip. He winked and pointed to the village.

'You've probably met her. It's Fiona from the post office. Her old man runs it, but she's the girl on the counter.'

Kitty gave a little frown.

'But you are not far from one another, and yes, I know Fiona. Pretty sandy-haired girl.'

The guard laughed, then his face wore a serious, sad expression.

'We are not near enough according to her, but her father thinks I'm not far enough away. So, when we meet it's a sneak-around job. I'd marry her tomorrow, but he'll not hear of it. Now you know why I'm keen to keep you two lovebirds together.'

Kitty reached out and touched his arm. 'I hope you get your girl, and thank you.'

Back at the front entrance of the castle, Kitty spotted Sarah and called out to her. The girl turned around and Kitty could see by her face that something had upset her.

'Sarah?'

Sarah gave a small twitch of her face. 'Kitty. Have you seen that sky?' she said, and Kitty heard the strain in her voice.

'I take it you've heard I am leaving. You should know I wouldn't go without saying goodbye. As I said before, I'll write. We will remain penfriends.'

'Promise?'

'For as long as I am able to write, I will. If you transfer, send me your address or Buchanan Castle will be where I send my letters.'

Sarah held out her hand, but Kitty drew her in for a farewell hug.

'Don't be afraid, Sarah, and remember, you have friends here. Ask for help if the loneliness gets too much.'

Sarah clung to her and whispered in a sad voice, 'Shalom my friend. You are a good person to know, Kitty Pattison. I hope you have a happy life.'

Before Kitty had the opportunity to respond, Sarah let go and walked away. Suddenly, the atmosphere around her became unbearable and she rushed back to the confines of her room to finish packing. The sadness of parting washed over her, and the morning couldn't arrive fast enough.

## Chapter Thirty-Three

S tretching her legs outside in the fresh air, Kitty enjoyed the warmer breeze around her legs, rather a contrast to the chillier one in Scotland at five o'clock that morning. The journey to London was much shorter than when she'd driven from Leeds as they could travel faster in daylight, but it had still taken thirteen hours. Sadly, the back of the ambulance had not allowed her a view of the countryside, and the patient had slept all the way to London. It was the most bored she'd been for days, and her back ached from the uncomfortable ride.

Thanks to overhearing one of the military police escorts take a handover exchange from another on leaving Scotland, she knew the prisoner was called Hess, and their directive was to transport him to the Tower of London. They were not to draw attention to the convoy by exceeding the speed limit, but to move as swiftly as possible.

After the main vehicle turned off when they reached London to head for the Tower, the ambulance made its way to the hospital, leaving the support vehicle that followed escorting the fleet car.

It was over.

Kitty's history of nursing a senior member of Hitler's governing body would never be known. She'd been sworn to secrecy on a legal document, and all her family and friends would ever know was that she travelled thirteen hours from Scotland to London with a patient.

The driver dropped her at London Liverpool Street station, and she looked about for the ticket office. She'd not told her aunt and uncle she was heading home; she'd thought she would surprise them.

To her disappointment, she'd missed the last train out of London for the evening, so made herself as comfortable as possible on a seat, out of the draught that swirled around the concourse. She'd still got her uniform on and tried to sit in as dignified a manner as she could, but felt herself nodding off every now and then. She was exhausted, and looked forward to a luxurious sleep in her old bedroom, with no restrictions on her time. She promised herself a walk along Dovercourt Bay promenade, with the time to listen to the over-excited gulls. The beach was off-limits, with barbed wire barricades, but inhaling the salty air to clear the mind was just as good as a paddle. The walk was something to look forward to, and Kitty had every intention of making the most of her visit home. A pot of fresh cockles and a chunk of bread haunted her dreams as she whiled away her time until the first train of the morning. She watched people mill about during waking moments. The station remained busy overnight, with every type of serviceman and woman chatting or resting. Someone in a small group nearby played soft tunes on a mouth organ, and another sang a sea shanty she'd heard many times in the past. Those men, Kitty bet with herself, were local to her hometown, and a comfortable feeling came over her. She spotted a seat nearer to them and moved to enjoy their company and that of another person she recognised from school.

'Hazel, isn't it?' she asked the young woman.

Through tired eyes the girl peered at Kitty and gave a smile. 'Kitty Pattison, well I never! How are you? Sit down, I could do with the company; it's going to be several hours until we're home. I assume you're heading to Parkeston.'

Kitty sat next to her and nodded her head. 'I've just arrived from Scotland. Been in the back of an ambulance since five this morning and here since seven-ish.'

Hazel gave a sympathetic sigh. 'Gracious, you still look fresh and lovely in your uniform. I'm a wreck.'

Kitty didn't like to say so, but Hazel looked tired and drawn, her usual ruddy cheeks hollow and pale. The more she took in Hazel's appearance, the more Kitty wondered what had triggered such a change. No doubt the war had something to do with it, and she was loath to ask for fear of creating upset.

'Thanks. What are you up to nowadays?' Kitty asked.

'I'm not working – yet. I'm leaving home for here – London. I'm good with figures and accounts and my cousin has a financial business and is taking me on.' Hazel shifted in her seat. 'I got married to Terry Barwell, the grocer's son, at the start of the war, and took his place with his parents when he was called up. Only trouble is, silly beggar got himself killed last year, and left me pregnant with our first.' Hazel's voice drifted off with a sadness hanging on her last few words.

Kitty allowed the silence to linger for a moment out of respect for the hurt Hazel expressed.

'I'm so sorry. Terry was a good man – kind to my family during our loss. Your baby …' Kitty looked at Hazel's face that was twisted with pain and realised she'd touched on a tender subject.

'She didn't make it through her first week. They say it was weak lungs, but I think Terry wanted her so badly, he had to take her with him. They say I'm mad in the head, but my cousin said leave them and get a fresh start, so that's what I'm doing. It's for the best.'

With that statement, Kitty decided there was nothing more she could say to Hazel, and the comfortable moment she had enjoyed rolled into a sad one. She understood Hazel's need to leave and start afresh. It was almost the same thing she had done – but for different reasons.

'I take it you are not married, not in that uniform. I don't know how you do it, Kitty. You're brave. Did you work in Scotland long?' Hazel broke the silence and her voice sounded more uplifted.

'Not long. A fortnight. I went to Birmingham first. I met my boyfriend there. He's a Canadian doctor. I'll only marry someone when they declare peace, but not before. We're dedicated to our jobs and he respects my position.'

Hazel's shoulders lifted and she gave Kitty the prettiest smile, widening her bright-blue eyes.

'You are just the tonic I needed. At school you were always fiercely independent. What a lovely story, meeting a Canadian doctor. Where will you work next?' she asked.

Shrugging a shoulder and relaxing back into her seat, Kitty flung open her hands. 'Who knows. I had hoped for a post back in Birmingham where I thought my best friend was still working, but she's on the move again by the sounds of things. I'm off for a couple of days to work it out. A bracing walk along the prom will help me decide, I'm sure.'

'That's the one thing I'll miss when I move here – the sea. Even on a howling storm kind of day, it helped me heal. I'll always return,' Hazel said.

'Me too,' Kitty replied, just as the announcement for their train home was called and they scrambled for a seat.

As the train rumbled home, the sun rose across chimney tops and eventually Kitty watched it touch the tips of the trees and green fields which surrounded her village. She was well and truly ready for the comfort of home. She wished Hazel well and promised to leave her next posting address at the greengrocer's for them to pass on. They both said they'd try to keep in touch before they hugged and parted ways.

## Chapter Thirty-Four

Listening at the back door, Kitty heard her aunt chattering to her uncle, and stood for a while.

'Make do and mend they say. I've made do and over-mended your socks so much they are hardly fit to clean the brass.' Kitty's aunt's voice filtered through the open kitchen window and had a merriment about it. Kitty smiled; it was lovely to hear her in good spirits. With care and as quietly as she could, Kitty turned the handle of the door and poked her head around. They were both seated in their comfortable chairs with their backs to her. She saw the smoke from her uncle's pipe rising to the ceiling, and her aunt's mending lying in a heap beside her chair. It was a heart-warming scene and one she didn't realise she'd missed until then.

'Tell him to get his wallet out and buy some more …' she said with a laugh.

With one scream of delight, her aunt had dropped what

she was doing and wrapped Kitty in a loving embrace, and her uncle chuckled out a welcome home.

The house smelled fresh and inviting and Kitty's body told her it was all right to unwind, to allow her aunt to bustle around and fuss over her whilst she told them the various stages of her journey since leaving Birmingham, filling them in on the things she'd not written in letters.

'You take yourself off for a wash-up and rest. I've seen you yawn more than once. The tea and toast will see you through and I'll make a suet crust meal to tempt you out of bed. I'll do it for teatime instead of dinnertime. Frank won't mind, will you?'

Her uncle placed his newspaper on the table and stood up to face them both. He raised his arms as if in despair. 'You come home Miss Kitty and create havoc to my eating schedule without a blink of your eye. What will the neighbours say when we are eating our dinner at teatime, hey?'

Kitty and her aunt burst out laughing. Her uncle's face creased with pleasure, and Kitty experienced the warmest sense of well-being she had felt since Michael's arms were around her.

Aunt Lil shooed Kitty upstairs, and she went willingly. Her room remained as she had left it, but the smell of lavender bags told her it was cleaned on a regular basis, as was Brian's old room. She looked out onto the street and watched the neighbours group into their familiar packs and places. Climbing into bed, Kitty heard the children racing along the path to the school at the end of their row as the sound of the school bell rang out to announce the start of the day. A day of only two hours – another thing the war had tainted – the education of children. Her aunt told her it was their last day in the building, as all the teachers were now enlisted.

The bell was the last sound she heard until her aunt tapped on the door announcing a cup of tea was brewing in the pot downstairs. Kitty looked at her bedside clock and saw she'd slept solidly for seven hours.

Over their meal, Kitty's aunt chatted about the neighbours and their families, and Kitty listened with polite interest. Four of the girls in the street were married and expecting babies, and her aunt gushed on about when it would be Kitty's turn.

'I have a bit of news,' she said, to quell the constant flow of conversation about wool and baby clothes, and of how her aunt couldn't wait to knit for Kitty's children.

Her uncle's brow creased with concern and suspicion as he switched from a glazed, bored-with-baby-talk look to an interested one.

'Which is?' he asked.

Kitty slipped her hand into her pocket and pulled out her sweetheart pin.

She held out her hand, showing the pin nestling in her palm. 'My friendship with Michael, the Canadian doctor I told you about, developed a little deeper. We found each other again in Scotland, after we separated when he left Birmingham, but fate pushed us together during a rescue.'

Her aunt took her hand and looked at the pin. 'It's pretty, very pretty. And you are happy, I can see that, so if it's what you want… but are you sure? Are you in love with the idea of him, or are you *in* love with him?'

'I love him. It took me a while to understand what I felt for him, but I'm in love with him. It's difficult being apart, and he is on a bit of a secret task at the moment, but we are happy when we are together and have a lot to consider when it comes to our future. You don't have to worry, we are fully aware of how the war is changing things, so we're not rushing anything. He's lived in England long enough, and is not looking for a good-time girl. He's in love with me, too,' Kitty replied with a shyness at sharing so much about her feelings for Michael.

She watched her uncle chew his lip. He glanced at the pin and back up at her. A tear slithered its way down his lashes and dropped to the table; he looked at it and wiped it away. Her aunt reached out to him and covered his hand with hers; a gesture Kitty had only ever seen once in her life, when Brian died. She'd expected a reaction, but not such an emotional one.

'Uncle?'

Kitty slid her pin back into her pocket and reached out to him.

'Frank. Speak to the girl for goodness' sake. What's the matter with you? And don't you go hiding that pin either – it's too pretty,' her aunt said in a firm voice.

Kitty shook her head at her aunt. Whatever was upsetting her uncle needed to be allowed its path. Pushing him too hard for a response would only spark a tension she could not handle. Their blessing to be happy with Michael was all she needed.

'We are not getting married, if that's what worries you, uncle. You don't have to dust your best suit off just yet.' Kitty gave a light laugh at the family joke of Frank's dislike of wearing his best suit. Whenever he wore it, her aunt nagged him to keep it clean and not spill hot pipe ash over it, as he was prone to do.

With relief, Kitty saw him lift his head and give her a hint of a tender smile, but he still wore a haunted look. At last, he spoke.

'But if you do, then you will leave us. Go to Canada.'

His voice hiccupped with emotion and Kitty had no words to reassure him. To tell him she wouldn't go would be wrong, as she knew wherever Michael wanted her to live, she'd be by his side. Her aunt and uncle had given her everything from the day she needed them the most, and guilt now pulled her into wondering whether she would be able to cut the ties if Michael asked her to leave England. But she was not going to give false hope; she'd simply tell the truth.

'And I might not. Michael came to England to train as a doctor before the war started. He has no family left in Canada – he's also an orphan, and his grandmother brought him up. She died years ago. If Canada is the end result, we will overcome any hurdles. Maybe you could come too. Who knows what the future might bring. We haven't spoken about beyond the war yet because life has taught us to live for the day. Be happy for me. It's all I ask for now.'

She went to her uncle and held out her arms to comfort him, and the relief Kitty felt when he accepted swept through her body. To leave home knowing she'd upset them was not something she wanted to deal with when so far away.

'Let's take a walk around the village, and then tomorrow, maybe we'll go to Dovercourt and stroll along the prom, just like we did before I left. A typical Sunday. What do you say?'

She spotted a strange glance between her uncle and aunt, almost a panic.

'What? What's the matter?'

Kitty's aunt gestured for them all to sit down again.

'As you know, we've never been very religious, and I can't say we are deeply religious now, but the Methodist Church around the corner has helped us during some dark days since you've been gone. The minister has helped me especially. I'm much happier nowadays,' she said, and looked to her husband for reassurance she'd said the right thing.

Kitty nodded at the last statement. In the few hours she'd been home she'd noticed a difference, from the laughter to the tender gestures. 'I've noticed. I'm happy you have found something that comforts you,' she said.

'We're the caretakers, too. We clean and keep the place running. You're uncle's a dab hand at the repairs and maintenance side of things. It's the best thing we've done together in a long time. We can walk with you after service, but feel free to take my bicycle and go alone if you'd rather go earlier,' her aunt said, and Kitty could see how important it was to her aunt that she didn't disrupt their routines – and realised it would be selfish of her to do so.

'That's a grand idea. I'll take a bike ride. I can help

prepare dinner before I go and save you a job, if that's all right with you?' she asked.

Her uncle rose to his feet and rubbed his stomach. 'So long as one of you serves me something, I'll be happy. I'm off to check the shelter. We had a rough night last night and it will need a clean-up. Another new job I've taken on. Keeping busy is the best thing; a bit of hard work stops you wondering what if, sometimes.'

Kitty and her aunt set about washing and drying the dishes. It felt like old times, but with a lighter atmosphere.

'Your uncle has found a new side of him since we started at the church. A gentler side which has helped me be a better person. Stronger. Brian and your parents will never come back to us, but we feel close to them when we are there.'

Placing the dishes into the dresser, Kitty set about drying the cutlery. She had no need to respond to her aunt's statement, and a gentle silence of contentment fell about them. They pulled the blackout curtains tight and settled down to play a game of cards, when Kitty's uncle burst through the door.

'That attack last night – it destroyed Bernard's clothing factory. By all accounts it's flat.' Kitty and her aunt looked at him in horror.

'Were there any casualties? Anyone we know?' her aunt asked him, but he shrugged as he pushed his feet into his slippers.

'I've not heard yet. Sad though,' he said. 'Charlie reckons the planes were after something else near the port, but I pointed out that the sailors would be naked without their uniforms the place makes, so maybe Jerry is trying to cripple our navy that way.' Her uncle paused and they waited for him to continue. Kitty noticed a new passionate lift to his voice. 'Either way, I've been asked to help with getting them back on their feet, so I'll be going there after my shift on Monday. A helping hand with a broom wouldn't be sneered at, Lil.' The look he gave her aunt took Kitty's breath away. Admiration and love rolled into one soft glance.

'It's all go around here, Kitty. Let's hope we get a break from it all tonight and tomorrow, and we will be rested enough to help them get back on their feet. We'll say a prayer for them tomorrow, Frank,' her aunt said.

'We'll say a prayer for my cousin in Nottingham, too. He telephoned the grocer's shop to let us know they are safe after the bombing earlier this month, and in temporary accommodation. I've told them to get on a train and come here, but his wife won't leave her mother as she's too frail to travel. It's hard for so many. We have to count our blessings, Lil,' Kitty's uncle responded.

Kitty listened to them both. Their lives had changed so much, and a realisation hit her: they did not need her around to bring them back from the brink of despair; they'd managed to do it by finding a new purpose in life.

Tomorrow she would cook for them, and on Monday she'd head for the recruitment office she'd originally signed up with, to discuss which hospitals could offer her the ongoing training she sought. If there was nothing available, she'd take up the offer of a new adventure, preferably near Jo, or back in Scotland near Michael. Leaving Parkeston on

Wednesday would not be so painful or worrisome as she had thought it might be when she originally walked through the door. Aunt Lil and Uncle Frank were survivors, and she no longer had to fret about them finding a way out of their darkness. They'd found a way forward, and now she needed to seek one out for herself.

## Chapter Thirty-Five

Kitty propped her aunt's bicycle against the wall and took her last walk along the promenade before she left town once again. The weather was much warmer than the previous week, but threatened showers. For the moment the rain held off and she embraced the freshness. Kitty wondered if it would be the last time she would see the unique lighthouses her cousin used to leap from into the foamy waters with the other local lads, whilst she stood with her friends screaming with delight as the boys hit the water.

Looking at the sea, with the rugged breakwater peeking through the top of the grey-blue waves, she could see the potential risks and perils. You had to be born in the town to understand what kind of dangers lay beneath the water and so jump in relative safety from the ancient iron towers of the bay. Even then, it was a daredevil game.

She watched with sadness as the uniformed Home Guards roamed along the shore, shooing away young children daring each other to gather winkles and whelks from the rock pools under the barbed-wire defence barriers. It upset Kitty to see the innocent fun she'd enjoyed as a child denied them by the war. Although, a minute later their giggles and laughter made her smile, as they joked cheekily with the soldiers, who playfully put them back in a place of safety beyond the barriers with a gentle warning to stay there. A home by the sea was one she would always want to return to, or to create.

Hypnotised by the seagulls dancing on the thermals, and the sounds of the waves gently receding across the pebbles, she pulled her favourite peach cardigan around her floral-print spring frock and allowed her mind and body to relax. She pulled out the postcard she'd written to Sarah in Scotland, telling her all was well. The image was of the place she now stood in, and she made a mental note to buy another for her own collection for when homesickness drifted into study time and distracted her.

Taking a last look at the area, Kitty collected the bicycle and embedded the memory to savour until she could next taste the salty air and feel the surge of well-being throughout her body. When she reached her new posting in a hospital near County Durham – confirmed at the recruitment office that morning – she would make a concerted effort to find the closest beach to explore during her time off.

The teasing breeze tussled with her hair and she brushed it to one side, then a moment of daredevilry overcame her, and she climbed onto the bicycle, riding along the promenade against the rules. As she did so, she spotted a cyclist pushing a bike and waving from the furthest point of the green, near Earlham's beach. She recognised her uncle's bike, and cycled towards him. The freshness of the air on her face as she pedalled was bracing. Her hair spun out behind her and she felt like a child of four on her first trike once again, free to abandon all restrictions and enjoy pedalling along without a care. Gathering a little speed, she lifted her feet and freewheeled, as she used to when she met her uncle from work after school. She even squealed out the same happy sounds to make him laugh – right up until she saw it was not her uncle.

'Michael!' she yelled as she jumped from the bike and ran towards him.

He threw back his head and gave the loudest whistle.

'Look at you, my beautiful girl. So free and happy. What a welcome!'

Kitty didn't say a word. She flung herself into his arms and gripped him tightly. She felt so small and loved in his arms – muscular arms of comfort filled with pure, raw love.

'Let me catch my breath,' Michael said, and moved her backwards to look at her.

He inhaled and let out the air again.

'Dear God, you are so beautiful. I am a lucky, lucky man. Come here, I've missed you so much!'

Michael wrapped one arm around her and cupped her face with his other hand. Their kiss attracted whistles and catcalls from the young boys who had been chased off by the soldiers earlier, and both pulled back for decency's sake.

'What are you doing here? I told you in my note I only had four days. Never in my wildest dreams did I expect to see you riding my uncle's bike along the beach. I thought you were him!' Kitty said, breathless from the kiss as she leaned into Michael for another cuddle.

'I guessed that!' Michael laughed and hugged her close again. 'I only got your letter yesterday morning. I've been with the lumberjacks; someone had a nasty accident with a saw.'

They propped up the bikes and sat on a small concrete wall overlooking the water.

'By the way, I've got news, which is why I wanted to see you.' When Michael spoke, Kitty heard a little tension in his voice.

'What's wrong?' she asked.

'I've put off telling you. I was asked to consider joining the British army permanently, as a medic. Several of the English guys have been drafted already. I gave it some thought and agreed. I'm heading for a new post in a hospital in the north – not as far as Scotland though, and in truth, I'm not sure for how long, which is why I needed to see you and grab a kiss before I left. I've got forty-eight hours' leave, and have to collect my uniform and papers from London beforehand.'

Kitty looked into his concerned face and, although she also had news to share, she decided it could wait until they had returned home.

'You'll do us proud,' she said and made a small adjustment to his tie, trying not to think about the fact that he could be shipped off anywhere in the world to fight. 'I'm glad you will stay in England, and let's hope the war finishes before they send you abroad. Anyway, let's not think ahead of ourselves. I bet you gave Aunt Lil a shock when you turned up!'

With a quick shake of his head and a grin, Michael chuckled.

'Your aunt is a lovely lady. I thought she was going to faint when I told her who I was looking for; she tugged me inside without a blink of an eye as half of your neighbours followed me to your door. I felt like the Pied Piper of Hamelin without the tin whistle! Your uncle heard the commotion and came from the yard, and boy has he got a strong handshake. Before I knew it, he'd drawn a map of how I was to get here and produced the bicycle. They said you'd be exactly where you are.'

Michael opened his arms wide and inhaled.

Kitty looked him up and down. 'Yes, this is what I call my place, and here you are in it with me. I can't believe it, Michael – it's wonderful. We must go home and spend time with my family. I bet they'll be waiting by the window. As will most of the women in the street now word is out a handsome Canadian visited our house!'

---

Giving Michael a tour of her village before cycling back to the house gave Kitty extreme pleasure. Women stopped cleaning their steps, children waved to her, and younger women tried their hardest to capture her man's attention. Even old Mrs Calver of the corner shop preened and fluffed up her hair as they rode past.

'This is Una Road. My grandparents lived in the end

house before the hill to Granddad's allotment. Lil and Frank lived next door, but gave it up to move into my parents' house. They took over the rent, so I didn't have the upheaval of moving when they took me under their wing.'

They stood a moment looking up and down the street whilst Kitty pointed out various houses of friends from school. Memories of riding in a wheelbarrow and picking fruit on the allotment brought about goosebumps, and Kitty rubbed her arms.

'Come on, I'll show you the church where I was baptised – St Paul's – and then just around the corner we will be back home.'

Large barrage balloons filled the sky in the nearby area, protecting the station and main sea gateway to Holland. They changed the landscape for Kitty, and she chose not to look at them for too long, preferring to watch the feral kittens skit about the wasteland. The war ruined everything. Within twenty-four hours she and Michael would be apart again, and she'd have to wait until who knew when to see him. Sometimes, the war seemed personal – Kitty's battle with the enemy to keep love alive, to keep track of her dearest friends, and nurture the lost souls who crossed her path.

'Brace yourself. Questions and deep investigations coming up,' she called to Michael over her shoulder as they turned into Hamilton Street. Pushing the bikes into the shed, they took the opportunity to sneak another passionate kiss before entering the kitchen.

'Ready?' she asked as she pushed down the door handle, hoping inside would be only her aunt and uncle.

Community spirit in their road was wonderful, but in a small terraced house it could become rather claustrophobic, and Kitty knew the neighbours would probably have done their utmost to find out more about the man in her life.

'Welcome to our home – again.'

Kitty's uncle stepped forward, and for one moment Kitty was convinced he was going to bow as he shook Michael's hand for a second time. Her aunt pulled away her pinafore and ushered them into comfortable seats.

'Where are you from, lad? Tell us more about yourself. I think it is only fair we know, seeing how you've set your sights on our Kitty,' her uncle said, before Michael had the opportunity to sip the tea her aunt had placed in his hands.

'Ontario, sir. I was born in a place called Haileybury. I was orphaned at four – 1922, and homeless due to the death of my grandmother by the age of eleven – I'm twenty-three next birthday. A children's charity housed and educated me until I left for England when I was seventeen. I began my medical training in Birmingham, but the war changed everything. I train civilians and some medics in new methods. I have a new post in the north, and hope they'll keep me there to see out the war as I'm now signed up to serve in the British army. So, there you have it, sir. My life up until today.'

Kitty's uncle rose to his feet and she saw the jut of his jaw, and hoped he would not interrogate Michael further, but her hope fell flat when her uncle drew breath and threw another question Michael's way.

'Did you join up for this doctor training before or after meeting Kitty?' he asked.

Michael set down his cup and threw her aunt a grateful glance.

'Before. It was too late to retract. I tried to stay on in Birmingham after I met her ...'

'And when did you sign up?' her uncle asked. Kitty saw Michael's jaw twitch slightly.

Kitty looked to her aunt and uncle. She had to break the interrogation; she knew her uncle of old, and once he set about asking questions, he would be hard to stop.

'It's true, he did try and stay in Birmingham. Fate brought us together again in Scotland, where we found out more about one another, and he's had no choice about joining up. It was the British or Canadian army, and he chose ours. I trust Michael, Uncle. He's a good man,' Kitty said.

Her uncle turned to Michael and held out his hand.

'I think I speak for Lil and myself when I say that Kitty is a wise girl and not one for making rash decisions, so if she's chosen you as the man she wants to go courting with, we will not step in her way. Besides, I can't see this war finishing by August, and she'll be twenty-one by then and adult enough to know her own mind. I have respect for you, young man and expect you to show the same to our Kitty – I think you understand me well enough,' her uncle said, and followed it through with an awkward cough.

'Trust me, sir. I have the utmost respect for your niece, and I cannot thank the Red Cross enough for sending her my way.' Michael took his hand, and Kitty smiled when they both sealed the pact of understanding.

'You say you are to work in the north, Michael. Did you know Kitty is headed that way, too?'

Irritated her aunt had stepped in with her news before she'd had the chance to tell him, Kitty simply gave him a broad smile.

'It was going to be a surprise, but yes, I'm going to work in a hospital for injured military personnel; Shotley Bridge Emergency hospital. With the village of Shotley across the water from here, I'll feel closer to home by just hearing the name, Shotley Bridge!'

Kitty looked at Michael, who stared at her with an amazed look on his face.

'I believe it's in or near, the county of Durham. Oh, honey, I'm going to Newcastle!'

Not wanting to appear ignorant of where towns and cities were in England, Kitty gave what she hoped was an excited whoop.

'I'm heading for a place called Consett. How far are they apart exactly?' she asked.

Michael scratched his head. He looked to Kitty's uncle.

'No point in looking at me lad. I haven't the foggiest idea of where you're talking about. Geography was never my strong point.'

With a shrug of one shoulder, Michael gave a quiet tongue tapping, tutting sound as he pondered his reply. 'I'd guess an hour – two – or maybe less, depending on which transport you use. I went to Durham three years ago. You must visit the beautiful cathedral. Maybe we can do it together.'

Kitty clenched her hands together and bunched them

under her chin. Her heart rate increased with the knowledge she and Michael were to work in the same part of the country again. 'That's wonderful. What a wonderful thought! We will get to have days out together again. Oh, Michael this is exciting news.'

'Are we able to travel together by train as far as London?' she asked Michael when they stood outside, admiring her uncle's garden and the last of the daylight.

'Oh yes. I'm making the most of my time with you. I must go now. Your aunt was kind enough to secure me lodgings further down the road. Sleep well, sweetheart, and I'll see you in the morning.'

## Chapter Thirty-Six

'This is it then,' Kitty said, as she and Michael pulled back from another passionate kiss behind a stack of luggage.

The announcements at London Liverpool Street station sounded out and people scuttled back and forth around them, no one taking any notice of the tearful young woman and the soldier clinging onto the last seconds of their time together.

'Be safe, my Kitty. Write to me as before and I'll let you know when I am free, and we can only hope our shifts coincide at least once.'

Michael kissed Kitty's forehead.

'I can't wait to see you in uniform. It's been wonderful to have these few days with you. I can't let you go, so I think you'll have to be the one to walk away first. My legs won't move.'

Kitty's heart was beating at a fast and frantic pace. She tried to smile – she didn't want to leave Michael with an image of her snivelling and red-eyed. She wanted the impression to be more glamorous – after all, she was dressed in her best Sunday clothes, with a revamped emerald-green hat that had once belonged to her aunt, which matched her coat.

Their send-off from her home had been a happy one. The whole street had ventured out and cheered them to the station. The journey on the train together gave them time to discuss future plans and what might lie ahead for them both. Michael did his best to tell her what Canada had to offer. When he'd finished, Kitty got the clear message he wanted to return and live in a place called Tofino, on Vancouver Island. It sounded wonderful, as he described his visits to the sandy beaches, but she pleaded her corner for England until they agreed on one thing: wherever they lived after the war, whether it was together or not, they both wanted a coastal home filled with children.

'I envy those injured men about to meet you,' Michael said, snatching another kiss.

'In what way?' Kitty asked.

Michael's sigh was loud and heartfelt.

'Because they will have you to smile at them every day and help them through the darkness.'

Kitty stroked his cheek. 'I know what you mean. I envy any patient receiving your attention. It is so wrong to envy an injured soldier, but I do and will. Oh, look at the time – I'll miss my train! Kiss me and go. Quick, Michael, before I start blubbering. I love you.'

As he held her, Kitty memorised his smell, the feel of his lips and the touch of the hands.

'Goodbye, darling girl. Save your kisses for me. I love you,' Michael said. He pulled away and picked up his kitbag. He kissed his fingers and placed them on her sweetheart pin that was nestling proudly in her lapel.

'I love you more,' Kitty whispered, just as he turned and marched away with his body braced. Although he didn't turn around to wave, Kitty wondered if his face would be as tormented as her own. The two-hundred-mile journey to Durham would be a lonely one, and even harder with a heavy heart. She just hoped Michael wouldn't be shipped elsewhere before they had more time together, but with the war being so unpredictable there was every chance he might.

With the weather suiting her mood, she stepped out of the shelter of the station and chose to walk, despite the damp drizzle. She ignored the whistles from passing groups of sailors and soldiers, and turned her head away from those who stared at the girl with tears streaming down her face fighting against the weight of her old kitbag.

The link between her and Michael became an invisible thread of distant love the further she walked towards King's Cross station. She found it incredible that in only eight months so much had happened in her life, and here she was back on a station concourse travelling towards another life challenge, but without the nerves of the first time on her journey to Birmingham.

When she stepped onto the train this time around, she was surprised to see the corridor empty, and that she was one of the first passengers on board. She entered the first carriage, heaved her kitbag onto the overhead storage, and pushed the slim window above her head closed, knowing full well the fumes and wind would be a discomforting distraction. Kitty settled down in a seat by the window and waited to see who else would arrive to fill the carriage before they pulled away. She rummaged in her bag and lifted out a Red Cross nursing study book with the intention of reading, but her mind filled with the memories of her brief time with Michael. Soon her carriage was filled with seven servicemen puffing on cigarettes, snoring, or chatting about their destinations or recent missions. The noise varied at intervals between near silence to extremely loud and distracting. Eventually, Kitty gave up on the book, and, resting her head against her coat, she watched the world speed past the window.

Around two hours into the journey, one of the men asked if she would mind if he opened a window, and with a grateful shake of her head, Kitty agreed. The carriage had lost its fresh polished smell, and she dared not try to describe what aromas lingered around them. Stale and fresh cigarette smoke filled the carriage with a hazy fog, but within minutes of the window being open, the cold air rushed in mingled with smells of coal smoke. Unfortunately, it also allowed in smut from the train's outpouring chimney. Her destination couldn't come soon enough.

The train lurched its way through towns and cities, suburbs, and villages, until at last her destination was announced and a mad scramble ensued in her carriage and in the corridor outside – other passengers rushing to catch their connecting trains. Fortunately for Kitty, she had time to pick up her coat and bag without incident.

Stepping down onto the platform, Kitty took a moment to get her bearings. The grey sky threatened heavy showers or worse, and she deliberated swapping her rain hat instead for the green felt one perched to impress. Looking around to see evidence of a bus stop, she found the relevant details, and sat on a bench to wait for the half hour the stationmaster had told her to expect.

After a forty-minute wait she bumped along the roads on a bus heading towards the hospital. The driver called out her destination and pointed to the large, imposing hospital ahead of them. She saw a cluster of elongated huts sitting beyond what looked like a main building.

'It used to be for the weak in the head. Now it's for the poor beggars returning from the front. Good luck, lass. See you again no doubt,' the driver said in his thick northern accent. Kitty was thankful he spoke slowly and clearly.

'Thanks,' Kitty said, and watched the bus pull away.

'Well, this is a bit different to a castle, Kitty Pattison. More like an old workhouse. Here goes,' she muttered to herself as she crossed the road and walked through the front entrance. She showed her papers at the gate and followed the instructions of the guard to Matron's office. The grounds were busier with personnel than Drymen, and the gardens not as attractive, but there was a buzz of energy Kitty had missed since Birmingham, and it triggered a surge of excitement within her.

She pondered what sort of room – and life – her next temporary home would bring her way. From the Nurses'

Home room to a cupboard in a castle, anything was possible.

Hesitating in front of the office inside the main building, Kitty drew back her shoulders, composed herself, and knocked on the door.

'Enter,' a female voice called out.

A feeling of déjà vu came over her and she lifted her eyes to the ceiling and pleaded with the fresh air or guardian angel – whatever invisible being she could mutter to – that she was not about to face a dragon of a matron.

After an hour of speaking with a four-foot-nothing version of the enemy without a moustache, Kitty was taken to a large room used as a communal lounge and introduced to a mix of nurses, orderlies, and volunteer staff. One of the junior nurses, Alice Bay, showed her to their room, and Kitty was relieved to hear she had the soft burr of a southern accent and not the deep, stern Geordie one of Matron. For the first time in her life – aside from the overnight disaster with Belle at Ma Smith's – Kitty was to share a bedroom with not one, but three girls. Fortunately, Kitty's tension eased a little due to the fact that Alice reminded her of a more feminine version of Jo, and it made the daunting prospect a little easier.

The room they entered was light and airy, with four beds in two rows facing each other. All were neatly made and identical.

'My bed is by the window, and you are beside me, but I'll swap if you want to. I have no preference so long as I can sleep when off duty. We're lucky as we get the sun – when it bothers to come out – and the room is warmer than some I've heard about. All rules and regs are pinned over there,' Alice said pointing to the wall beside her. Kitty smiled when she saw the regulations of what to put where, on and inside the locker. It was a touch of Drymen, and Kitty hoped that's where the similarities ended.

'You are under my guidance and will be on duty with me tomorrow morning. We are hut thirteen, so I hope you are not superstitious. It's a tight-run ship, but the sisters are fair and kind if you show willing.'

Kitty gave a shy smile. Alice was probably the person always selected to show new nurses around, given her friendly personality, but she had the ability to make Kitty feel as if she was the first.

'I've never shared a room before,' she said, sensing Alice was not the type to sneer or laugh at her.

Alice waved her hand in a flippant manner. 'Oh, you will fit in just fine. The others are great fun. They are on duty right now, but thanks to you I get to give you the guided tour and have an extra cuppa in the canteen. Unpack later, and we'll make the most of the break in the drizzle.'

## Chapter Thirty-Seven

A lice guided her around the living quarters and gave her a tour of everywhere relevant to her work. With her body fighting tiredness from the long journey, Kitty jotted down notes to study in the evening before she fell asleep, in the hope that she retained some of what Alice relayed about who, what, and where.

They stepped out into the damp air. Kitty smiled at anyone who walked by, and she never failed to receive a smile in return. Although she hadn't been treated badly in Scotland, she had always felt out of place and had never been truly acknowledged by those around her. She did feel more confident since leaving, and attributed it to the Hess transfer, and the trust placed in her to carry out the task.

'Enjoying the tour so far?' Alice asked as they approached a long row of huts.

'I am, and am desperately trying to remember your instructions, hence this,' Kitty said, and waved the notebook in front of her.

'A wise idea. I wish I'd done the same. I got myself into all sorts of scrapes when I first arrived,' Alice replied with a laugh.

Each hut they entered housed a mix of military personnel. Huts two and three were for German prisoners of war, and Kitty warded off the chill memories of Buchanan Castle. Several huts were filled with servicemen suffering from infected wounds, gangrene, and major limb loss, and the smell of infection and disinfectant was not a pleasant combination. Kitty did her best to retain a soft smile whilst holding her breath. She'd smelled gangrene before, but with such a large number of patients in a confined space, it lingered.

Hut thirteen patients were treated for broken bones and minor burns, and when they stepped inside, Kitty felt a glow of warmth and welcome. It gave her a boost of excitement for the following morning shift. Although she'd only just arrived, the atmosphere of Shotley Bridge hospital instantly made Kitty feel comfortable and not in the least bit out of place. Alice introduced her as a valued support nurse of the Red Cross, which made Kitty feel good.

Over a cup of tea, she and Alice learned more about one another, and Alice gave her a rough rundown on the other girls in their quarters. By the time Kitty was ready to unpack her bags, they were off duty and welcomed her to her new home. They were a cheery group, and when Kitty finally settled down for a good night's sleep, she no longer felt uncomfortable sharing her personal space.

The rain fell heavily when they finished breakfast and, before they left for work, Kitty made a mad dash to the room for her umbrella. The last thing she wanted to do was look like a drowned rat when presenting herself to hut thirteen for the first time. She made a final visit to the bathroom and carried out a quick critique of her reflection in the mirror. It was time to meet with Alice and begin another chapter in her career.

The senior sister was a gently spoken woman, and Kitty relaxed into the new ward within minutes of meeting the staff. After finding out her new role was to support a young man with severely damaged legs, she received the handover and couldn't wait to meet him.

'He won't need a lot of encouragement to get out of bed, nurse. Stanley is determined to get back into a plane again, with a tendency to run before he can walk. What he will need is someone able to offer firm advice and make him understand he cannot push himself too hard. Don't be soft on him; it won't do him any favours. Understand?'

'Yes, Sister. I understand. It must be frustrating for him,' Kitty replied.

With a dip of her head the ward sister agreed.

'Both legs took shrapnel and suffered surface burns, but one of the legs was too damaged for us to save. They've had fresh dressings this morning, and I think the best thing is for you to get to know him. I rarely allocate one nurse to a patient, but as you are not yet established on the ward, and he needs a bit of help overcoming the recent shock, I think this might help you both for a few days. He's adamant he will remain in the RAF.' The sister gave a heavy sigh. 'But sadly it will never happen, and it won't be long before he will be medically discharged. He's a married man with a lot of pride. You'll have your work cut out in keeping his wounds from splitting open again. We cannot risk another infection if he wants to keep the good leg. See if you can help him, Nurse Pattison.' The sister pointed to the last bed beside a window at the end of the ward. Kitty could see the back of the man perched on the side of his bed.

'I'll do my best, Sister,' she said, and walked towards the patient who was dressed in the forces-issue blues worn by all hospital patients. A uniform for the convalescing injured.

'Good morning. I'm Nurse Pattison. I am a Red Cross nurse on secondment, and you have the pleasure of my company for a few hours – or days depending on how we get along,' she said, and gave him a beaming smile.

The sandy-haired young man with a handsome face and a well-groomed moustache smiled back at her and she saw a flash of excitement ripple across his face. She was a new nurse, and Kitty bet he was already thinking he could pull the wool over her eyes.

He held out his hand. 'Squadron Leader Walker-Fells, or Stanley if you prefer, but not Stan. Never Stan.'

Kitty shook his hand and smiled.

'Stanley it is.'

'I'll wager a guess with that accent you are from the south – Essex. I was stationed at North Weald.'

Glad she didn't have to clarify whether she knew the place or not, Kitty gave a smile.

'I live in Parkeston, near Harwich. By the sea,' she said.

'Know it well. Taken many trips to Holland in the past.

Choppy waters on some of the trips. Give me a bird to fly any day,' Stanley said, and pointed skyward. 'I was a pilot. Darned accident put a stop to that. I may be stitched and repaired, but they tell me my wings are clipped. I'll prove them wrong, you'll see.'

Stanley's accent was upper-class – family money and all the best things in life – but he immediately made her realise he was not elitist. He didn't make her feel inferior, but still had the air of authority about him, and she knew she had to start off with a firm hand to show him that in hospital, she was in charge.

'As I understand it, Stanley, you are in a hurry to leave the ward and will do anything possible to speed up the process. Correct?'

Taken aback by her forthright manner, Stanley's boyish grin disappeared, and his face creased with concern. He adjusted his position on the bed.

'I, um, correct,' he replied, and leaned to one side in an attempt to pull his crutches away from the locker.

Kitty stood and watched him overstretch. She noticed his left leg thigh stump took the strain of his body.

'I think we might start with moving these to a place where your left leg wound is not put under pressure. From now on, they need to be where you can reach from your right side,' she said, and looked about for a suitable place. With a sigh, she realised she had the solution, but it would mean approaching the ward sister and pointing out something which had been overlooked.

'I'll be back in a minute. Stay where you are,' she instructed Stanley.

After explaining the problem to her senior and receiving praise for the observation, Kitty set about moving Stanley from one side of the ward to the other. His cabinet now sat on the right of his bed, and Stanley practised reaching for his crutches from a new angle, leaving Kitty satisfied his stump wound would remain intact. She put a chair beside the bed and faced it towards the window, then assisted him to the seat before she tidied his bed and locker.

'I could do with some fresh air,' Stanley said with a sigh as they watched raindrops trickle down the small pane of glass behind his bed.

'Do you use a wheelchair for outdoors?' Kitty asked.

The response of a sharp bark of a laugh from Stanley in response to her question made Kitty jump.

'Outdoors? I've not been outside in over a month. The wound breaking open prevented me from leaving my bed, and when I could get out of it, I've been on limited crutch time. It's all so damned— Sorry, nurse, I am feeling sorry for myself again,' Stanley said, and gave a deep sigh. Kitty was now attuned to pay attention to a patient's non-verbal expressions, as sometimes they indicated unrest, a troubled mind, or a pending outburst of frustration.

Kitty stopped plumping the pillow in her arms and laid it onto his bed.

'I'll take it as a no to the wheelchair, then,' she said, with a sarcastic raise of her eyebrows and a smile thrown his way.

'No, nurse. I've never used a wheelchair to go outside.' Stanley over pronounced his words and stared at her with a pretend scowl.

'Well, let's focus on manoeuvring around here. Keeping the wound safe and ready for a prosthetic is our priority, but on the next bright day, if I'm on duty, we'll attempt outside with Sister's permission. But no overruling the instructions of your medical support, agreed?'

Kitty smoothed the counterpane into place as she spoke and stood back to admire her work then noticed Stanley staring into space. His face looked pale and the dark rings under his eyes suggested little sleep. Before she could say anything to him, the man in the next bed cried out, his bandaged hands flailing around as he cursed and struggled to remove the bandage from his face. She rushed to his side and spoke in soft tones, waving to Alice at the top of the ward.

'It's all right, you are safe now. My colleagues will get you something for the pain. I'm a new voice, Nurse Pattison, and you have a new neighbour, Stanley, but I'll make sure he's no trouble, although I'm sure he could be.' She gave a laugh, turned, and nodded to Stanley – an encouragement to speak to the man.

'Hey, old chap. Things will get better – we'll get through this. Can't have Jerry beating us down. We'll find a way back,' Stanley said, his voice light-hearted and encouraging, but Kitty had a feeling the words were more for himself than the man in the next bed. She gave him a soft smile and a grateful glance.

The distressed man calmed down and gulped back sobs. Kitty's heart went out to him. Alice and another nurse arrived at the bed armed with a syringe and morphine. Alice indicated with her hands that the man was completely blind, and Kitty silently cursed the enemy for taking his sight. Losing a limb was one thing, but the inability ever to see again must be the most frightening and soul-destroying injury to endure.

At the end of her shift, the senior sister gave positive feedback on Kitty's first day, and on their way back to the nurse accommodation, Alice also gave her a pat on the back. They discussed the different types of injuries, and Kitty expressed an interest in developing her knowledge to help amputees, whilst Alice claimed to prefer caring for burn patients.

---

After supper, she wrote to Michael, expressing her contentment.

*C/O The Nurses Home*
*Shotley Bridge Hospital*
*Consett*
*25th May 1941*

*Darling Michael,*

*I arrived at Shotley Bridge and was given a warm welcome. I'm sure the main building itself would look cheerier on a sunny day. It used to be a workhouse and an asylum, I think. Anyway, it looks eerie in the shadows. It gave me the shivers in one area – a corner of the hospital to avoid after dark.*

*It appears to be a well-run unit and after working at Drymen some things are familiar which makes life easier for me. Matron is a tyrant by all accounts, and my short time spent in her company suggested nothing to disprove the opinion of the girls in my room. I am sharing with three others and they are a friendly, happy group. One is from the local area, the other from Wales and Alice, my support nurse for a few days, is from Plymouth.*

*I hope everything went according to plan in London and that you are now smartly kitted out in a British uniform. I do so look forward to seeing you wearing it and the day cannot come soon enough. It will be a month before I will get a day free from studies. The broken limb is a fascinating topic for free time reading, but I'd much rather be held in your arms.*

*We have a man who has broken nigh on every bone in his body. The poor thing looks hideous in his body plaster and bandages. It is so upsetting to see some of the burn victims and if they are minor ones, I truly hope I don't see any worse! I impressed the ward sister with my Thomas Splint application time this morning. Your teachings in Birmingham for the emergency unit have not gone to waste. I was declared competent. I cannot tell you how much happier I am here than in Scotland. I'm allowed to perform my nursing duties and am actively encouraged to learn something new each day. I've a sneaking feeling they will try to entice me to join the nursing corps, but they'll have a struggle. I'm a loyal Red Cross lass.*

*This part will probably get blacked out, but we also have German POWs here. I've only had a glimpse inside one hut, and it has only got a few men in there at the moment, but they've allocated two huts to house more. They could quite easily be our boys; the ward looks no different. I do hope the same happens in Germany for the British prisoners of war. Every injured person deserves good nursing care, no matter what their status or nationality might be.*

*We have access to a telephone in the lobby, so feel free to telephone me when you can. It would be wonderful to hear your voice again. My shifts for the next two weeks are: early week one, and late week two.*

*I must sign off now as I've a stocking to darn – now isn't that exciting news?*

*Take care, my darling, and stay safe.*

*My love*
*Kitty xx*

When she settled into bed that night, Kitty sensed she'd found a place where she could finally achieve her nursing goal. All she had to do was hope no one at HQ decided to move her elsewhere.

## Chapter Thirty-Eight

S itting enjoying the early morning sunshine, Kitty read through her small pile of letters and delighted in everyone's news. Her aunt and uncle sent gossip of the village and reassured her all was well. Kitty smiled when they spoke of their duties within the various services they now spent their days supporting. They were a couple who had used their grief and loss to find their way forward, and Kitty felt so much pride.

Jo's letter made her laugh when she wrote of her antics driving VIP servicemen to and from their destinations. After a short spell feeling she still had skills to offer the medical world, she'd decided to apply and had been accepted back to the Red Cross as an ambulance driver, and Kitty learned she'd driven onto a ferryboat and transported injured men back from France – a job she knew completely suited Jo.

A glance at her watch told her it was time for her to go

to work, and she headed to the ward. When she arrived, she saw Stanley reading to his blind companion.

'They're both healing physically and mentally. Your dedication to both men has been recorded, Nurse Pattison,' her ward sister said when Kitty received her duties for the day.

'Stanley, at last, has learned to slow down, and told me yesterday his leg pain had eased. It has helped him realise his potential, and he's stopped fighting against our advice,' Kitty said.

The sister nodded and lifted a box of bandages. 'He's a dab hand at rolling these, too. He has a mind which needs to be kept occupied.' The sister beckoned her to the medical cupboard, and they began a stock count. Kitty admired the woman for always working alongside her junior staff and never thinking herself too high-ranking to undertake menial tasks. She could often be found scrubbing down the bedpans and tidying linen. Kitty aspired to be like her once she qualified. The sister climbed a ladder and Kitty handed her the fresh stock of disinfectant bottles.

'We do have another problem, though,' the sister said as she climbed back down, 'and I've given this some thought. Stanley has received word his wife is unwell, and he is keen to return home. She set up a project when he was away fighting, and he is keen to keep it going while his wife recovers. I've agreed to a home assessment tomorrow with the occupational team in readiness for his discharge, and would like you to accompany him. It makes sense, as my other nurses are heading for their final exams and do not need the distraction. I will record it as part of your next assessment. I expect you to keep notes of any obstacles you feel might need addressing. I need your honesty, nurse.'

Placing the last of the dressing packs on a shelf, Kitty felt a rush of excitement. It wasn't often nurses could follow through with their patients, and to have the sister acknowledge her work with Stanley and put it towards her progress report, made Kitty feel even more at ease with her new environment.

'Thank you, Sister. I will do as you ask, and I'll not put Stanley at risk by ignoring any problems. What is the project his wife is working on? Am I allowed to know?' Kitty asked.

'She takes in orphaned children local to her area and helps find them a new home. Stanley will be able to tell you more. We must ensure he returns home with time to adjust, and doesn't rush into overworking himself by caring for several children and a wife. He appears to be the kind of man who puts others first, but he needs to remember he's been through a dreadful ordeal. The burns on his good leg are healed, but it is weak. He doesn't want to lose that one too,' the sister said, and ushered Kitty out into the ward.

'I understand. What a wonderful thing to do, though – helping orphans,' Kitty said, and headed off to assist with feeding the patients who were unable to help themselves.

She watched as the ward sister spoke with Stanley and pointed across to Kitty. Stanley nodded, smiled, and waved at her. When she left her shift that evening, she had four sheets of instructions for the following day. Once she read through them, she set about writing letters to her family and friends.

*C/O The Nurses' Home*
*Shotley Bridge Hospital*
*Consett*
*19th June 1941*

*Dear, dear Jo,*

*I'm delighted to hear your news. Although driving grumpy men all day is not my idea of fun, I will bet you're happy as a hog in a trough – in fact I'm sure of it, and I'll make another bet that there's grease under your nails and oil in your hair. I cannot believe you are based so close! I miss you so much. Hopefully, I'll stay long enough for us to get to see each other again.*

*At one point I seemed to be the mobile missing piece of a jigsaw for the Red Cross, but am settled here in Shotley Bridge. They are a super bunch to work alongside, and you'd fit in well. Sharing a bedroom was a little daunting at first, but now I barely think about it and some days it is good to have cheerful company. Alice is my main friend here, and she's good company.*

*As I mentioned in my last letter, Michael is working in Newcastle and I am so excited as my first month is up and he has managed to get leave to coincide with mine. We are meeting at Durham Cathedral as we always said it would be the place we'd meet first. We need solid places to remind us of our brief times together, not rubble beneath our feet during a dig-out. I envy my aunt and uncle as they've had a life before the war when they could be together every day. He used to sit her on his crossbar and take her home from work. How I'd love to have that kind of simplicity in my life with Michael.*

*I'm rushed off my feet at work, but am also supporting an RAF pilot in his quest to return home. He has managed so much, and, in a few days, we are taking him to his house for a visit with his wife.*

*Have you been to the cinema lately? I'm hoping to go when I see Michael again. Well, I'd best sign off now and get back to the study books.*

*Take care,*
*With love,*
*Kitty x*

*C/O The Nurses' Home*
*Shotley Bridge Hospital*
*Consett*
*19th June 1941*

*Dear Trix,*

*I am sorry I've taken a while to reply to your last letter. I am so pleased you have a definite place to study midwifery after your final exams. You are way ahead of me now due to my excursions around Britain. I'm settling in well in Shotley Bridge and can you believe Jo is living close by?*

*According to the map, you are a train ride or two away, so maybe we can plan our leave together and come visit. Face cream and sherry days once again – or in Jo's case, whisky. I just know we will have so much fun when we meet again, Good old Smithy. I'm glad his knee is recovering since his fall, but am sorry to hear he is not able to join the army – although, I am sure you are happy to have him near. Investing in his own practice is a solid base for your future together and I am sure when men return with various injuries and problems, his patient list will grow. But I must say, his personality suits old ladies and new mothers. He's gentle and understanding, and so patient. Michael's the same with regards to the kind side, but more action and adventure-minded, and I doubt he could ever settle into a quiet village life. Going by his tales of when he grew up in Canada, I often wonder whether he would be happier in a tent halfway up a mountain rescuing bears! Some of the things he told me about his country fascinate me, to the point I've expressed a desire to visit, but on other days I feel exceptionally British and want to remain in England.*

*He's met my aunt and uncle, and won them over, but my uncle worries we will marry and leave them for Canada. I told them not to get ahead of themselves.*

*Take care Trix, and keep enjoying life.*

*Your friend,*
*Kitty*

One letter she hesitated over writing a reply to was from Belle. It was friendly in nature, and mentioned that Eddie was now fighting on the front after a violent brawl at a dance one night. Belle got caught in the middle of it all, and it was thought best she left Birmingham and she was now settled in Cornwall. Kitty wondered if the letter was a form of apology, a reaching out. When she thought back to Birmingham and the friends Belle had, she realised she had none within the nursing sector, and possibly felt isolated. It was her own doing however. Was Kitty prepared to let her back into her life? She held the letter over the waste basket, but after much deliberation, she chose to respond, deciding she was the better person, and it was time to let go holding a grudge. She was taking a risk with the letter, by allowing Belle to see that she and Michael were together again, but something told Kitty it would help the ugly side to her thoughts of Eddie and Belle disappear.

*C/O The Nurses' Home*
*Shotley Bridge Hospital*
*Consett*
*19th June 1941*

*Belle, your letter came as quite a surprise.*

*Thank you for enquiring after me.*

*Robert Keane must be quite a source of information for him to know where I am living nowadays. I suspect he has had communication with Michael. Yes, Michael and I are back together, thank you for asking. It isn't easy being apart thanks to the war, but we fight our battles as they arise and overcome them, as we did after Birmingham. We met up again in Scotland, but of course, I suspect Robert has already told you that in his correspondence.*

*I'm not surprised by the news of Eddie, but did think you would tame him, seeing as you were both so close. I often thought you might marry, but now I look back, maybe neither of you were looking for anything other than fun – often at the expense of others, but hopefully we've all matured enough to have learned from our mistakes. By writing to me, I'll assume you have, which is why I thought I'd reply.*

*I am pleased you still find Cornwall to your liking and will remain there to oversee your parents' property. I cannot imagine what it must feel like when the army commandeers your home, so well done with reopening the village inn and living there instead. I didn't realise it belonged to your mother and she was a Cornish innkeeper's daughter before marrying your father. I thought both of your parents came from banking backgrounds. We live and learn.*

*With the military base nearby and you ensuring they receive local hospitality, I can see you making a high-ranking officer – or two – feel at home. Also, well done joining the WI. I must say that is something of a surprise as I cannot visualise you making pots of jam, but we never*

*really knew much about each other, did we? St Mawnan
Smith sounds a pretty place – thank you for sharing it
with me; it is good to hear of your Cornish lifestyle.*

*My kindest regards
Kitty*

She read over her response to Belle's gushing letter
claiming to be her good friend and concerned for her
romantic connection with Michael and hoping all was well.
She did not feel the need to write anything over-friendly, or
mention Jo was close by, and kept her hidden sarcasm to a
line or two. Whenever she thought of first meeting Belle,
Kitty conjured up the image of Ma Smith throwing her cases
into the street, and giggled; she picked up her pen and
drafted another letter to their Birmingham mother hen.
After that, she settled down to an hour of study, then Kitty
picked up her pen again to write to Michael.

*C/O The Nurses' Home
Shotley Bridge Hospital
Consett
19th June 1941*

*Dearest Michael,*

*How wonderful it was to hear your voice last week, even
though it was a dreadful line. I'm sorry I cried. I was tired
and just hate us being apart. The weather has improved
since that night and I no longer have webbed feet!*

*My amputee patient is due to go home and I'm heading
out with him for a visit tomorrow, so this will be a short
letter I'm afraid. I am keen on meeting his wife, but
understand she's unwell at the moment, so am not sure I
will. She sounds lovely, and has opened their home for
local orphans, a project she started before he was shot
down. The medical team want to see what changes they
need to make to Fell Hall and, as I'm only a support nurse
until my next assessment course starts, I am to escort him.
As you can imagine, meeting other orphans is the ideal
day out for me.*

*You will never believe it, but I've had a letter from Belle. It
appears Robert Keane writes to her about us, which means
I can only assume he has moved on from Birmingham and
you are both together, so I hope he doesn't lead you astray.*

*My aunt and uncle send their love and reassure me all is
well with them. I do miss the seaside, but hopefully, we
can visit one of the north-east beaches together one day.*

*I've heard from Jo and she's living nearby. She's back with
the Red Cross and driving ambulances. I cannot wait to
see her again. We have so much catching up to do, as will
you and I when we meet again.*

*Trix said Smithy's knee is too badly damaged and he
cannot join the army – and I suspect his rugby-playing
days are over, so he is investing some of his inheritance
into his own GP practice. She's been accepted for the*

midwifery programme, so I doubt they'll marry until the war ends, but they seem happy enough.

I've knitted you a new scarf, gloves, and a balaclava for the winter for something to do in my spare time after my studies. Not that there is a lot of spare time with the amount of extra reading regarding new treatments we have to do just lately.

Well, my darling, this won't be the last letter I write to you, but it is the last one I'll write today as it is time to study more about the care of the amputated limb, read Sister's notes for tomorrow, and wash my hair. I lead such an exciting life.

I'll end this letter now and seal it with a kiss.

Stay safe, my darling. Until we meet again.

Kitty
xxx

## Chapter Thirty-Nine

The beautiful house – Fell Hall – commanded dignity always. Kitty could see it just by staring down the driveway through the vast acreage. Stanley called it a house; Kitty only saw a mansion.

The occupational therapist allocated to Stanley gave a low whistle through his teeth as he jumped down from the back of the ambulance and assisted Stanley down the steps.

'You have a beautiful home, sir. I take it you don't mow the lawns yourself,' he said in a jovial, off-the-cuff manner.

Stanley smiled as he rested against the side of the ambulance. 'Obviously, I do not at the moment, nor did I before the war, and I wouldn't dare. My man Jack oversees the garden. Which is just as well, given the circumstances – don't you think?

Kitty heard the nip of pain in Stanley's voice. He had been reminded of his disability in just that short conversation – something a man as proud and energetic as he was would find hard to accept outside of a hospital ward. The visit home would be a strong reminder of any weaknesses, and Kitty needed to be on full alert. Her unusual task was to be presented as a trainee district nurse attendance, and she had every intention of passing the assessment. District nursing appealed to Kitty's sense of belonging to a community. Until Stanley, she'd never given it much thought, but the conversation with her ward sister made her consider a new path to follow, once qualified. Working alongside the army and civilian nurses gave her many insights into the type of nurse she'd like to become, and her list became shorter by the day. Today, Kitty faced a new challenge and she was determined to fulfil it to her best ability. The OT man was a little short on personality in her eyes, and his thoughtless comment about Stanley and the lawn proved he lacked consideration.

'If it is Jack's job, I doubt he'll thank you for taking it away, and I'm sure there are many other tasks to occupy you in such a large home, Stanley,' she said kindly.

'I'd never dare step on his toes, and I am sure my wife will find many things to keep me busy. I will draw the line at embroidery, though,' Stanley said with a laugh, and a relieved Kitty waved him on.

'Let's get you two together,' she said with a smile.

Stanley guided them around a pretty area in front of the house and into a large brick garage.

'It's a beautiful car,' Kitty said when she saw the gleaming vehicle in front of them. Jo and Bert, her driver to Scotland, would give their right arms to drive something so elegant.

'Bentley 4.2. Cream leather seats. Luxury at its finest,'

Stanley said with pride as he manoeuvred himself around the car and opened the passenger door for them to see inside.

'I would like to drive this beauty again, though. Is it possible?' he asked the OT.

With a shrug of his shoulders the man peered in at the front seat and stepped back again.

'I don't see why not. It might take a bit longer than you'd like, Stanley, but you've plenty of space to practise,' he said.

Kitty watched Stanley stroke what looked like tiny silver wings sitting proud on the bonnet. Her heart went out to him and felt it must pain him to be injured out of the war when flying was his passion, and to be facing so many difficulties in his civilian life.

'There's someone waving, sir. Is it your wife?' the therapist asked as they stepped outside. Kitty looked towards the house and saw a woman with a child on her hip and two others standing beside her waving to them.

'No. That's Daphne, our cook. She's a great help and friend to Jenny, even before the young ones came along. Sadly, we've no children of our own, but now the house appears to be filled with them, which is a good thing. Fell Hall is too big for two people,' Stanley said.

'I think it is wonderful you've taken in so many children. One orphan is enough to cope with, going by how I remember my reactions to the loss of my parents. My poor aunt coped with an awful lot of tantrums.'

Stanley turned and gave a sympathetic smile – the kind which made Kitty cringe inside. The pity smile.

'I didn't realise you are an orphan. At least you understand what those you will meet today must be going through. I've not got a clue what to say. I'm fond of children, but—'

A loud bark and the squeal of a child rang out. Stanley laughed.

'Ah, that's Benny causing chaos. Ben, here boy!' Stanley gave a shout and piercing whistle, and to Kitty and the therapist's horror a large black Labrador bounded towards him. To their relief the dog sat by his master's side with one click of Stanley's fingers.

'He's well behaved,' Kitty said, and to her horror, realised the dog registered a new voice and wove himself around her legs, sniffing in her scent. She'd not had a lot of contact with dogs – only Michael's mascot, also called Ben, who was much calmer than the scatter-brained hound nudging and jumping with great exuberance and pushing his nose where it was not wanted. Kitty felt her cheeks burn hot with embarrassment as she smoothed down her coat and skirt.

'Behave, Ben. Find Jack. Go, find Jack.' Stanley chastised his dog and waved his arm towards a hut at the bottom of the garden.

'He's harmless, but if he annoys you, send him to Jack the gardener. Jack puts Ben in his outdoor run when we have visitors.'

Kitty noticed the therapist frown and begin to write furiously in his notebook. Kitty guessed he was writing a negative against Ben in Stanley's life, so made a note for the ward sister's questionnaire, indicating a boisterous dog lived at Fell Hall, but was well trained and considered an underfoot hazard for Stanley no more than a set of steps or stairs. Ben was normality for Stanley, and a companion to walk alongside him when life got him down. She now wondered whether Sister, in her wisdom, had chosen Kitty to counterbalance the OT's viewpoint of Stanley's home life.

Taking a slow, steady walk towards the house, Kitty thought it all beautiful, and couldn't wait to see inside.

'Jenny. Jen! Come and meet Kitty and Mr Evans.' Stanley's voice boomed in the hallway and Kitty felt sure every Jenny in the county of Durham had their ears pricked.

'Stanley Fells, keep your voice to an indoor level. You are not on the flight path now you know. Welcome home, darling. Kitty, Mr Evans, lovely to meet you. Please, call me Jenny, and him, well call him whatever you want. He's going deaf but won't admit it.' Jenny giggled and shook their hands. 'Welcome to Fell Hall, and we are truly grateful for you agreeing to come and help us organise our lives in our hour of need.'

'I'm only here for the day, remember,' Stanley said, and Kitty heard the rumbles of disappointment in his voice.

Jenny took his free hand and gripped it tightly. 'I know, dear, but we're a lot further along than we originally thought. Be grateful for today. Now, let's go and sit down.'

Kitty was taken aback by Jenny. Her age was several years beyond Stanley's and her skin was the palest she'd seen; her thin body looked frail, and her white hair streaked with grey added to the aged appearance. She knew her aunt to be forty-one, and guessed Stanley's wife was late thirties.

Jenny smiled at Kitty, her face wrinkling as she did so.

'The children are outside. Stanley, we are up to six now so it will be a lively home to come back too. Come and enjoy a peaceful tea before you meet them all.'

'I'll join you in a moment. Mr Evans and I have a few things to discuss,' Stanley said, and swung off on his crutches in the opposite direction. Kitty glanced around and could see the lower floor had ample rooms should Stanley need to sleep downstairs. She also guessed there was a closet in the direction Stanley had gone. She made another note, this time to the positive.

Jenny led Kitty through to a large, airy room with the largest dining table she'd ever seen. It was set at one end for four, and she felt sure she'd do justice to a slice of the large sponge sitting on a pretty china cake stand. This was a household which followed through with upper-class standards despite the war. Kitty made no judgement due to the kindness towards others that Jenny and Stanley Walker-Fells offered.

'My word. I've not seen nor had cake since before the war. That's a sight for sore eyes,' Kitty said.

Jenny sat down and pointed to Kitty's seat.

'Well, you will have a large slice tonight as it was made in your honour, and by the time Stanley and the little ones have devoured their share, there'll be nothing left.'

Dainty napkins, patterned silver cutlery and rose painted plates brought something special to the ham sandwich tea party.

Stanley and Mr Evans joined them, and a natural conversation flowed between the four of them relating to the pros and cons of Stanley's living arrangements. It was agreed that a room overlooking the back gardens would be converted into a bedroom. Jenny said they'd been apart for so long and she missed his snoring, and as the room was large enough, she would arrange two of the bigger beds to be brought down from upstairs. This way, they could still be together, but Stanley's legs would be protected.

During the delicate feast of afternoon tea, Kitty noticed Jenny only nibbled on a corner of her crustless sandwich. The more she observed, the more she realised Stanley's request to return home was a necessary event. Jenny Walker-Fells was indeed a sick woman. When she had the opportunity to talk with the therapist in private, Kitty said that in her opinion there was no reason Stanley wouldn't cope with living back at Fell Hall. It just depended on the support he had with regards to the children. Mr Evans, however, wasn't convinced.

---

## Orphans

Violet Stoneway: aged five
Archibald Stoneway: aged seven
Alice Emery: aged four
Christine Tinsdale: aged two
Peter Gaskin: aged eight
David Gaskin: aged six

## Staff

Jack – gardener and handyman
Daphne – cook
3 sisters – cleaners
Eve: 14
Edith: 16
Edna: 16
Mrs Marston and daughter – laundry

Kitty's list of those who were willing to support Stanley and Jenny sat in her pocket ready to hand over to the ward sister. It concerned her that Daphne and Jack were the only live-in members of staff.

She met Daphne and Jack, whose accents convinced her they were speaking anything other than English; she later learned from Stanley it was Pitmatic, and indigenous to the local area. The few Scots she'd met in Drymen were easier to understand, but Kitty adored listening to Daphne express her devotion to Stanley in a tender, soft tone with an elongated sound on the end of each word. Daphne told her, when referring to the orphans, that the *poower bairns needed the love of their mammy*, and Jack said they needed *skewal ya kna*. Kitty rightly translated it as the children needing their mummy and they needed school, with an added – you know.

After a guided tour of the house, both Mr Evans and Kitty were ready to meet the children.

Stanley and Jenny took them into a large, informal sitting room, and Jenny fussed over Stanley, encouraging him to sit down. Kitty wanted to do the same for Jenny – she looked so frail.

'Daphne's gone to fetch the children and will bring them to meet you once they've washed their hands. The Gaskin boys can be a lively pair, and their manners… well, let us say they could do with some improvement. Both Violet and Archibald refuse to talk to anyone but each other, baby Christine is no longer grizzly, but I fear she's latched onto me and it probably is time for her to learn to go to someone else, and little Alice is a sweetheart, but we cannot coax her outside; she sits in the kitchen on a stool, or hides under the bed. They've been with us weeks now, and she is no bother, but there is a deep trouble within her and no tears. I've never seen a child not cry when in pain. She lost everyone – her mother, her gran, her brother – and their deaths followed after news that her father was killed in France.'

They all listened to Jenny give her breathless account of the children. Kitty recognised that the child Alice was the one needing immediate help. Kitty herself had also become very withdrawn when her parents died, and it was only the persistent, quiet company of her cousin Brian that had eventually allowed her to weep and heal. Kitty also knew Jenny needed relieving of the extra worries she'd brought on herself by taking them into her home. She wrote her notes at speed and from beneath her lashes could see Jenny casting worried glances between her and Stanley, then to Kitty and Mr Evans.

'I don't know how you've managed, Jenny dear. You've taken on quite a task. I think we'll agree six is enough, yes?' Stanley asked.

Jenny gave a slight nod of her head. 'Once they've all found homes, we will only take in one or two until I …'

A shushing sound from Daphne in the hallway told them the children had arrived.

Jenny put her finger to her lips and went to the door. 'We'll speak later.'

Kitty heard Daphne and Jack encourage the children to remove their shoes and place them by the front door. She heard Jenny speak with the adults.

'I'll take these two in first, if you wouldn't mind taking the others into the dining room, Daphne.'

From the hallway they heard giggles and muffled whispers.

'Come along you pair of mischief-makers.'

When Jenny referred to the Gaskin boys as mischief-makers, Kitty was reminded of four little Jewish boys at the local camp where she'd once worked, who always giggled and then followed through with a tease or torment. Usually, a dead mouse or a spider. She bet herself either Peter or David would try and scare them.

Jenny ushered them into the room. Both boys had thick thatches of red hair, home-knitted vests in blue and red over grey shirts, with grey knee-length shorts. Their socks refused to stay upright and were lingering around the ankles. The freshly scrubbed faces of the two boys threw confident, cocky, toothless, devilish smiles their way – the image of mischief-makers at their best.

Stanley beckoned them to him.

'You must be Peter,' he said, addressing the tallest of the

pair, 'and you, David. I'm Jenny's husband. You can call me Stanley, and it's jolly nice to meet you.'

'Away aye,' Peter said, and David nodded.

'Remember boys – I said please say, *it is a pleasure* or *nice to meet you, Stanley*,' Jenny said, emphasising what Kitty classified as proper English, not like hers or the local northern accent. Jenny joined Stanley on the sofa.

'It's noice to meet you, Stanl-aay,' they said in practised unison. Their attempt at mimicking Jenny was not an entire failure, and Kitty suppressed the enormous belly laugh brewing inside. It threatened to erupt when Jenny giggled just as the boys gave a sweeping bow.

'Why thank you for trying so hard, boys. I appreciate it,' Stanley said, and Kitty saw the twinkle in his eye and the gentle twitch of a smile from beneath his moustache. 'This is Mr Evans, and Nurse Pattison. They helped me in hospital and have come to visit Jenny with me.'

Mr Evans stood up and stared down at the boys. His face was serious and somewhat disapproving. Kitty guessed he was not a man who tolerated children for very long.

'My job is to decide whether Squadron Leader Walker-Fells is able to come home after his accident. Your job is to behave and show me you will not create problems for him.'

The hairs on Kitty's neck bristled at the sound of his austere voice, and she jumped to her feet.

'I'm Kitty, and it is wonderful to meet you both. I hear you've been very brave,' she said.

Both boys nodded, but the grins never faltered. David

looked to Peter, and Kitty spotted it – the silent communication. She braced herself.

She pretended she hadn't seen David slip Peter something behind his back when Peter held out his hand to her.

'We're pleased to meet you,' he said, his accent back, with a deep richness of pretend sincerity.

Kitty held out her hand, but Peter kept his closed, then rummaged into his trouser pocket.

'We've got something for you. Hold out your hand,' he said, staring at her with wide-eyed innocence.

Jenny, obviously aware they were up to no good went to stand up, but Kitty gave her a slight shake of her head.

'A gift for me? How kind.'

Peter placed their offering onto her outspread palm and moved back beside his brother, waiting for a reaction.

'Oh, a mouse tail. Now that is sad. We will have to find the mouse and find a way to stitch it back on. Or I could keep it as a memory of my visit,' Kitty said, and held the tail up for all to see.

Stanley burst out laughing, Jenny giggled, and Mr Evans scribbled in his notebook.

'Wey if yee leek it, keep it, but cat's got the rest,' David said, puffing his chest out with importance.

'I see,' said Kitty, pulling out a handkerchief from her pocket. She'd not expected to use it for a mouse tail, but she played along with the boys, loving the expression of admiration in Peter's face when she didn't scream. 'In which case, I think I'll keep your kind gift in my memory box. Thank you.'

'Now lads, it's time for the others to meet our guests. Go and tell Daphne, and no more tricks, you little monkeys,' Jenny said, and shooed the boys from the room.

A gasp of laughter came from Stanley on the sofa.

'You had the royal welcome. Kitty not so much. The night they came here they were in shock, and after that the devil kicked in and they've been playing tricks ever since,' Jenny said.

Daphne presented Violet and Archie next, and Kitty was taken aback at their jet-black hair and swarthy skin. Their eyes were wide ovals of glistening brown as they stood hand in hand.

Archie was dressed much like David and Peter, but Violet wore a pinafore dress over a hand-knitted jumper, both navy blue in the style of a school uniform. Both were robust and healthy-looking children. Before the children entered the room, Jenny told them their mother married their father after he brought her back to England during the Spanish Civil War. They ran his family pub, which had been destroyed during the recent bombings; both had been trapped inside, but the children were sleeping in the Anderson shelter at the bottom of the garden – regular arrangement, according to the fifteen-year-old girl paid to sit with them.

Stanley introduced himself, and Mr Evans gave the same address as given to the Gaskin brothers. Kitty dropped down to her knees and spoke to them in a friendlier voice to soften the harshness of the clipped instructions from Mr Evans.

'Hello you two. I'm Kitty. I'm here to help Stanley come

home and be with Jenny again. What lucky people they are to have you around. Will you help them for me when he does come home?'

Four nervous eyes looked up at her, and she saw the depth of sadness within them. She reached out her hands and took one of each of theirs and gently squeezed them.

'It will be all right. I'm someone who understands what you are going through. I truly am,' she said softly, with reassuring emphasis, while resisting the urge to gather them into her arms.

Violet's face looked down at the floor and Archie stared ahead, and she could see them both struggling with emotions they weren't old enough to understand. She empathised, knowing the words adults use when they don't know what to say for the best didn't always ring true with children.

'Jenny told us your sad, sad news. I am so very sorry. I wish I had known your mummy and daddy, and could tell them what beautiful children you are.' She took a deep breath as Violet raised her head to look at her through tearful eyes, 'I was the same age as you when my mummy and daddy went away for ever. They are stars in the sky now and help me feel safe at night. During the day, they are on the wind, playing tricks in the trees, and are dancing sunbeams on a summer's day. It's early days for you both, but one day you will find them again in different ways. Just as you trust Jenny, you will be able to trust Stanley if you need to talk, or feel upset. Understand?'

Violet dropped her hand from Kitty's and cuffed away a

tear. Jenny rose to her feet and led them to the door. She gave Kitty a smile.

'Ah, here she is, little Christine. Now here's a smile worth waiting for – no, to Kitty please, Daphne. I get a lot of cuddles. Don't get too attached, Stanley. She'll probably be gone by the time you come home,' she said, as Daphne held out the little tot to Jenny.

'I think I'm better at handling dogs than babies. How about you, Mr Evans?' Stanley said with a laugh.

'No time for either. I prefer pigeons,' came the blunt reply. Kitty noticed the glance between Jenny and Stanley.

Without hesitation, Kitty took the little brown-haired baby with blue eyes into her arms and was immediately rewarded with a tug of her hair and a dribbled smile.

'Hello, Christine. When does she leave, Jenny?'

'Her aunt is collecting her next weekend. She's only a short distance away, Houghton Le Spring. Her husband is away fighting with the Durham Light Infantry. Second division, if I remember rightly. They have no children, so Christine will be the centre of her attention.'

Kitty settled back in her seat as Daphne took Christine out of the room. They all sat listening to Jack talking to the Gaskin boys in the hallway, and smiled at Jenny when they heard him give them a ticking off for yet another mischievous prank.

'I feel for whoever has to take those little tikes on,' Kitty said.

'My brother's friend has that pleasure. Another childless couple. The boys have no family for us to turn to, so when Samuel mentioned we'd taken in local children, his friend offered to help. He has a farm out near Barnard Castle. The boys will learn new skills and have fields to run and play in to burn off some of that energy. They won't go down a coal mine, which is a blessing in my eyes,' Jenny said.

Kitty nodded; she could not imagine life in the pits, but would always be grateful to those who did keep the coal coming as best they could. They all turned to the doorway when Daphne appeared.

'Alice is asleep, so I'll not wake her ma'am.'

Jenny smiled, then turned to her husband and guests.

'Mr Evans. Nurse Pattison. If you would like to tour the house and make your notes, Stanley and I will have a few minutes alone before he returns to hospital. It has been a long day for him – for us both. I do hope you will see the children will not be a bother, and Fell Hall can continue to be a place of safety for them.'

---

Back at the hospital, Kitty left her report on the sister's desk and said her goodbyes to Stanley.

Outside the ward, Mr Evans took her to one side.

'I personally will not recommend his return while the children are there. I suggest you tell him to get them to an orphanage as soon as possible; they serve no purpose in his home. Orphanages are there for a purpose. A crippled man and a sick woman are not fit surrogate parents.'

Kitty looked at him in horror. The man had only looked at the practicalities of the discharge home, whereas she had tried to see it from the physical and mental welfare side of things.

'I think we differ greatly in our opinion, Mr Evans. On a professional level – and a personal one – I think the children will benefit from having both Mr and Mrs Walker-Fell under the same roof, and Stanley – if Stanley doesn't rush things – will be able to rebuild his life by doing something useful. Sadly, my word will only be heard by my senior sister, but I hope she accepts what I've noted as useful for the discharge meeting with the doctors.'

Mr Evans gave a loud tut and condescending laugh.

'You young nurses. It's all about romance and happy endings with you.'

For fear of slapping his face in temper, Kitty gripped the edges of her cape.

'Sir, it is one thing to have an opinion, but it is another to insult a professional body that fights on the front lines, saves lives, and supports the servicemen when they come home. Nurses do not live for romance,' Kitty drew breath, but gave him no opportunity to speak as she continued with her reprimand. 'As for happy endings, they work towards them and hope they've achieved enough to bring them about. They are a valuable force and I ask you to remember that and show a little respect. I'm proud to be a nurse, proud to serve my country, and proud to have helped Stanley Walker-Fell realise he is not useless.'

Not wanting to be in the man's company any longer, Kitty turned away from him and could only hope they never crossed paths again.

## Chapter Forty

'It's magnificent,' Kitty said, and spun around in the July sunshine, allowing her hair to fall free from the confines of the hat and pins. Her heart had a lightness to it and the world seemed a distance away from the happiness she felt in that one childlike twirl.

Michael grabbed her by the waist and drew her in for another kiss against the wall of Durham Cathedral.

'I'm so happy we are together at last. Stop spinning, and we'll come back to see it properly once we've settled into our room. According to your friend's instructions, we have to turn left at the end of the main street,' Michael said, and gave a nod in the direction they were to walk. He played the gentleman and insisted on carrying her bag, and Kitty admired how striking he looked in his uniform.

His telephone call three days previous telling her he'd been granted leave to match hers, meant they were able to meet in the city for two days, with him returning to Newcastle on the second afternoon. Alice recommended a bed and breakfast where she had once stayed, and which was within a short walk from Durham city centre.

Kitty telephoned ahead and booked separate rooms, but the closer they got to the accommodation and his remark about their room, meant Kitty had to speak out about her reason for booking two.

'I do hope you won't think I'm leading you up the garden path, Michael, but I booked two rooms. We won't be sharing a bed, I'm afraid. I know a lot of girls are giving themselves to their men to pledge their love, but I want to wait for less frantic days. Ones where we can relax and spend longer than a few snatched days in fear of enemy attack.'

Michael placed their bags on the ground and guided her by her shoulders to sit on the bench behind them. He lit a cigarette and tugged a lungful before exhaling. Kitty sensed he was stalling for time, and feared he was composing the words which might end their time together because he was not willing to wait. They sat in silence while he finished half of his cigarette and she watched intently as he nipped off the lit end and placed the remaining half carefully into his tobacco tin. Her heart pounded and she wanted to speak, but felt anything she had to say would be a repeat of her previous words with added pleading tones. He needed to understand her reasons, however, and she had to push embarrassment aside and talk to him.

'I don't want us to reach a point of no return and end up with regrets – with, er, with me pregnant and having to give up my training. I cannot disappoint my aunt and uncle like that – I'm sorry.' Kitty fidgeted with her hands as she spoke and could feel the burning of her cheeks. 'I've never discussed this sort of thing before, you know... um, sex, and although I'm not naïve and I understand the urges of a man, goodness knows we've dealt with enough issues for some of our patients, but I need you to hear me out on this. I agreed to stay overnight only because I cannot bear being apart from you, but our sleeping arrangements are—'

Michael placed his finger across her lips to silence her and Kitty's breathing settled into a steadier rhythm.

'Listen to me, Kitty. Yes, it would be the most wonderful thing to happen between us, but like you, I want it to be something special and not forced because we've chosen to have a holiday together. You get me hot under my collar, and it is hard for me to resist sometimes, but I respect you and your reasons. Let's just enjoy our daytime pleasures without you fretting about the night. Goodness knows, I could do with a good night's sleep, so you have done me a great service – a room to myself. With our troops – and by that I mean both our countries – leaving Iceland and heading back to England, I've a feeling there will be new orders for my unit and we'll be on the move, so,' Michael said in a soft reassuring voice and ended it with a gentle laugh and a light kiss on the end of her nose, 'let's drop off our bags and come back to enjoy this beautiful place. Pretend the war isn't happening, and make memories without worries.'

On their arrival at the bed and breakfast, their two-room situation gained an approving smile from the landlady.

'It's good weather for a walk around the city and rest your bones afterwards. Doctor, I see – and let me guess, you are a nurse?' the landlady asked Kitty, who was not in uniform but wore her peach outfit.

'I am – for the Red Cross. We met in Birmingham last year. Michael's Canadian,' Kitty replied.

The landlady handed them a key each.

'Not married yet, I see,' she said, making a point of looking at Kitty's hand.

Michael picked up the bags.

'Life will be different once the war is over. Roll on Christmas,' he said, and Kitty was grateful for his swift response. The situation made her feel slightly awkward and she knew she'd blushed.

The woman leaned across the reception desk.

'Do you think it will be over by then? They said the same last year.'

Without waiting for a response from either of them, she led them through a small hallway to the stairs.

Once she'd shown them their rooms and left them standing in Kitty's, both Kitty and Michael laughed about the creaking floorboards throughout the house. The landlady had no intention of them sneaking around without her knowing.

Unpacking her bag, far more light-hearted than earlier, Kitty's respect of Michael reached another level. He had made the awkward conversation comfortable, and she knew she'd chosen the right man to fall in love with; they just had to get through the war to appreciate more of what they had to offer one another.

Back in the area of the cathedral and castle the weather was kind to them, and they walked hand in hand around the outer walls, towards the river flowing below. They settled down onto the grassy embankment beneath the magnificent stone building and watched the clouds drift by, and listened to the birds sing. Kitty's heart swelled with contentment. The cathedral dominated the skyline above them and she hoped it survived the war. Coventry had lost theirs, and now, having seen Durham's, Kitty understood it when people said the heart of the city had been ripped away. Although not born in Durham, her visit with Michael had embedded a sense of belonging, and she too would mourn the place if lost to the enemy.

'This will always remain with me for ever – today, our days here,' she whispered, leaning over to kiss Michael.

## Chapter Forty-One

'Happy twenty-first!'

The singsong sound of voices rang out in unison from the common room of the nurses' home, where Kitty had been instructed to be by nine o'clock, after breakfast.

She looked at her small group of friends and smiled. Alice guided her to a table where a note of congratulations sat in pride of place next to the small birthday fruit cake lovingly made by her aunt – an incredible achievement considering the ration shortages – and a small wooden trinket box carved with her initials from her uncle. She'd received them the previous day, but Alice had taken them from her until it was official. A handknitted scarf and gloves, and a small corsage brooch of tiny flowers made from felt, and a bar of Yardley lavender soap were much appreciated gifts from her roommates.

Her most precious gift was from Michael. He had sent her a dainty silver necklace with a seagull charm. It was delicate and a thoughtful present to remind her of home.

He'd telephoned her the night before, as he was on duty and not free to visit her for another three weeks, and she had cried when he said it would only be possible if he was still in England.

Trix and Jo both wrote to congratulate her, and promised they would get to visit when they could. She smiled as she unwrapped their gift – a bright red lipstick wrapped in a note in Trix's handwriting reminding her of their days experimenting creating bow lips in Birmingham with her remaining stub. The girls always promised her they would replace it when they had money to spare and found the right shade – little did they know circumstances would bring about shortages, and when a lipstick was found, it was always a cheerful red.

Another unexpected gift came from Stanley and Jenny. They sent an invitation for her to visit the following day to join them for a celebratory afternoon tea.

By 9.30, Kitty was quite overcome by the emotion of receiving such thoughtful gifts.

When she went on duty that afternoon, the staff and those patients who were able gave a resounding rendition of 'Happy Birthday' and calls announcing Kitty now had the key of the door. She laughed when she recalled anyone in Hamilton Street turning twenty-one, enjoying the ceremonial receipt of their own front door key when they reached adulthood. Kitty wondered how many years after the war twenty-one would still be thought the age of a child turning adult, considering what some of younger people were now expected to do in place of their elders. Especially the young men fighting to defend the country.

During the shift, several extra beds were rolled into the ward and made up in readiness for patients from other hospitals. The victims of enemy attacks were growing in number, and the sharing of patients became commonplace. Kitty's unit was to house only servicemen, and she noticed the number of burns victims increasing. By the end of her shift, all thoughts of a twenty-first birthday had disappeared and she walked back to her room in a melancholy mood. She enjoyed a bath using her new soap and climbed into bed, trying to distance herself from the images she'd witnessed that day.

---

The afternoon tea at Fell Hall was a welcome distraction from the previous day, and when she stepped down from the bus at Brancepeth, she embraced the warm sunshine and short walk along the country lanes. She arrived to see Stanley smiling and the children waiting to tug her inside to join Jenny. Kitty could barely contain her excitement when Jenny and Stanley explained their birthday gift.

'I know you desperately want to see the sea again, and that's just what you will do. I'm taking you to the beach. You can't get close, but you will be able to see it from a distance and sniff the air. Maybe, you might see a seagull or two. But you have to be ready in fifteen minutes.'

At the mention of a seagull, Kitty touched her new necklace.

'What about petrol, do you have enough? I've not got a car, so I don't own a petrol ration book to help out. Don't use your fuel for me. Save it for collecting the children, Stanley. I can see the beach when I go home. It's very generous of you though, and I know you are keen to get back behind the wheel, but …'

Stanley shushed her gabble of words. 'I've saved fuel rations for this day. It is also a necessary trip to Usworth, as I've to call in at 607 Squadron on official business and we need to leave soon. Jack is driving us.'

Kitty moved towards the stairway. 'In which case, I'll fetch my things.'

Although the weather was not as warm as the previous few days, it was bright and pleasant. Stanley and Jack made the drive to the RAF base an informative one – exciting and different considering the state of the country and of Kitty's sadness.

She chose to push her friendship with Stanley to the forefront of her mind and to appreciate the thought he and Jenny had put into taking her to the seaside, but a twinge of sadness filtered through. Suddenly she found herself wanting it to be Michael driving the car, for him to point out the pit villages, the pretty scenes with children playing, and for him to suggest they eat on the terrace that evening and end the day with a glass of fine brandy he knew he'd receive from a close friend that afternoon. Kitty never questioned where Stanley managed to find the finer things in life – probably due to what she'd gleaned from being around Belle. Belle's privileged family and Stanley's appeared to be run along parallel lines and, since visiting Fell Hall, Kitty was not averse to finding out what a step up the ladder could bring during a time of leanness.

She'd tried to push aside all thoughts of the restrictions and limitations wartime imposed, such was her strong instinct to duty and loyalty to her country, but some days she felt she was missing out on life. That at twenty-one, she was forced to endure days of endless fear and forward thinking on how to survive, thanks to jumped-up egotistical men who wanted to rule the world. Kitty decided it was time to turn a blind eye to what she couldn't understand and focus on the things she could, and one of those was to enjoy the company of good friends and colleagues.

As they drove to the airfield, Jack admired the planes lined up waiting to defend the country, and Stanley admitted he had a hankering to return to duty. He also confessed he'd be prepared to take a desk job just to be part of the action again. The only thing which held him back was it would mean drafting in extra support for Jenny, if they were to continue to offer Fell Hall as a temporary safe haven for orphans. Out of earshot of Jack, who was propping Stanley's crutches against the front of the car, Stanley confessed he wasn't sure his heart would be in the project quite so much as it would be tracking down enemy planes.

He shared stories of his near misses, and the deep-seated passion for flying could be heard in his voice.

'Jenny will find a way,' Kitty said in an attempt to reassure him it was not wrong for him to want to return.

'She's tired with this illness of hers, but determined. I'm going to get local help, as neither of us want to see orphans rendered homeless and scared. They deserve one night of comfort at least.'

Kitty gave him a smile. 'You are both so kind and understanding. I'm sure you will find a way, Stanley.'

From the car she watched him limp beside Jack towards the largest hut, where they stopped to admire a row of planes and chatted with some airmen. For the first time for a long time, Kitty thought Stanley looked taller and broader across his shoulders. Without seeing his face, she knew he was smiling and happy.

## Chapter Forty-Two

'Oh, Stanley, I didn't realise how much I've missed this! Isn't it wonderful, Jack?' Kitty expressed her excitement by spreading her arms wide and twirling around on a grassy peak high above the grey waters of the North Sea, so near and yet a frustrating distance away. She wanted to run through the barriers and feel the sand between her toes.

Jack laughed as he unloaded a picnic basket and blanket from the rear of the car.

'Goodness knows what you'd be like if you managed to get really close. Welcome to Roker Beach, so near and yet so far,' Stanley teased with a laugh.

Kitty went to help him.

'It's the same sea as home. It would feel just the same and I would probably make a fool of myself – and not for the first time,' she said, and told the men the events leading up to her seeing Michael at the end of the promenade.

Laughing, and commenting on how he'd wished to have

seen such a carefree Kitty, Stanley set out a round each of sandwiches. Kitty squealed with delight when she found the fresh bread was filled with thin slices of beef; there were generous chunks of cheddar cheese, and a dish of fresh apples, apricots, and a small pot of small blue-black berries she now knew to be bilberries, set on a small wooden tray on the grass. With a theatrical *tah-dah*, Stanley produced jam jars and from a brown bottle poured a small amount of golden liquid into them.

'I raided the RAF kitchen,' Stanley said with a wide, triumphant grin.

Kitty tut-tutted. 'I should report you, sir,' she said with a tease.

Stanley took a bite of his sandwich and gestured for her and Jack to eat.

He chewed and swallowed, and watched Kitty nibble her way around a small slice of beef.

'Good?' he asked.

Kitty nodded. 'Mm, so good. If this is how they feed you, then I might join up, too. No wonder you want to go back!' she said, and devoured the rest of the beef and fresh bread.

'They have to feed the men well to keep them going. They do get a few extra treats now and then. The bilberries are said to help them see in the dark,' Stanley said, and popped one in his mouth.

'Better than carrots, too,' Kitty said, and sipped her drink. She pulled a face to show her pleasure.

'What's this?' she asked.

'Cider. They called it Chipper's Sauce. Apparently, Tony

Chipper, the cook, is a dab hand at making the stuff from windfalls. He said officially it is for cooking tough pork joints, and gets away with it because, well, as you've found out, it is rather a good drop of stuff. Strong, so be careful, and I'm only breaking it out before midday because it's a special day. We'll have the rest at home later. Bottoms up. I'll save some for you, Jack,' Stanley said, and received a grumpy huff as a reply.

Stanley chipped his jam jar against Kitty's and a comfortable silence settled around them. Kitty sensed Stanley had taken another step towards a positive recovery. His injuries and concerns for Jenny's health had put him through so many traumatic moments, but today he walked tall, and his voice held a happy tone.

'There's something going on, Stanley – I've noticed a difference in you today.'

Kitty saw a slow, soft smile form around his lips, and his eyes sparkled. Stanley was definitely happy about something.

'I'm going back, Kitty. They've agreed. I can't wait to tell Jenny. I'll be working with a team on the route maps for Fighter Command, and with the sound of the engines around me, I'll feel useful and back where I belong. I'm ready. More than ready.'

Kitty drained her glass and packed away the remainder of the picnic, handing it over to Jack to place back into the boot of the car.

'I'm not surprised, Stanley. I think it is about time they said you could go back. You are no longer able to fly, but your love of the RAF is apparent, and you have a sharp mind. It will do you good. Jenny will be pleased to see you active again, I'm sure of it,' she said.

Rising to his feet, Stanley stood looking out towards the sea. Kitty and Jack joined him.

Keeping her focus on the horizon and breathing in the air, Kitty remained quiet. She didn't want to commit herself to a promise or agreement of any kind, but the temptation to offer to help Jenny was on the tip of her tongue.

A glint of something in the distance caught her eye, and she was aware of Stanley shifting to gain a better balance and view. The hint of a drone and hum of a plane crossing the water disturbed the chatter of seagulls as they scattered in various directions.

'Over there, Kitty. See it, Jack?' Stanley pointed.

'I see a dot of something, and I can hear it's not a bird,' she replied.

'Oh, it's a bird all right. A graceful machine. Watch him come in, and cruise the coastline. I do miss the feeling of being free up there. I can't quite see what he's flying with this sun in my eyes.'

Stanley put his hands across his brow, shielding the sun from his eyes. Kitty watched as he leaned forward, straining his neck for a better view, then back at the plane looming large ahead.

'He's flying at an odd angle, Stanley – or is it my eyes?' Jack asked, and leaned forward in a squint.

'He needs to make a turn soon and level out – good God, why aren't the sirens going? He's not one of ours, so where's he heading? Kitty, lay low!'

The sudden urgency in Stanley's voice and the sharp

instructions he snapped out shocked her, and Kitty took another look at the plane. Then she saw the emblem of the enemy.

'Kitty, do as I say! It's a Heinkel – a German bomber – and he's come in unseen. Look, he's not rounding off, which means he's not heading for the unit. What on earth is he doing? He's coming straight for us!' Stanley's voice was wild and anxious. 'Get back to the car. Jack, I have to get back to the squadron. There could be more. I'll get someone to drive … Get down!'

Stanley pushed Kitty's shoulder and they both dropped to the floor. Jack crouched beside the car. The ground beneath them vibrated with the pounding of the plane's engine as it flew over their heads. A deep rumble and an ear-piercing scream as the first of its load descended down towards British soil made Kitty feel sick. Both she and Stanley lay with gripped hands waiting for the outcome of the first bomb to hit – the explosive boom and crash.

It was followed swiftly by others they could hear spiralling through the sky and sending out the same menacing sound. Voices joined the noise. Frightened voices, and some loud and instructive shouts mangled amongst the metallic noise of chugging propellers, adding to the sense of chaos.

Pre-empting each impact, Kitty held her breath to the point she thought she'd never breathe again. Her chest burned. Whether he intended to hit a target or cause random destruction, the enemy pilot had succeeded in his mission. He'd dropped the message that the war was not ending any time soon, and they must live in constant fear.

However, Kitty knew the British people better than a German pilot. Resilience and determination to survive would get them through the worst moments.

Kitty shifted onto her knees, whilst Stanley, assisted by Jack, struggled back upright. They saw white plumes of smoke and dust, then the flames in the streets behind the beach. Kitty heard the return fire, far too late. The plane turned, and she watched as it dipped and weaved its way home to celebrate a success.

'Oh, Stanley. There's the warning – it's far too late! Where did it hit? Nobody would have had much of a chance to hide without the warning.'

Jack started the engine of the car. Kitty and Stanley slid into their seats, and Jack drove towards the airfield.

'We'll find out. I have to know. And how did he get through unnoticed during the daytime like that? It was close. How is it possible that no one picked him up out there?'

Kitty sensed the tension in Stanley as he urged Jack to drive faster, and hoped his agitation would ease the moment they headed for headquarters. The gravel swirled as Jack pulled up to the entrance of the base, now on high alert. Stanley flashed his ID, and they were waved forward. Kitty, convinced Jack would drive straight into the building he headed for, gripped the seat.

'Stay there,' he commanded, and as fast as his crutches allowed him, Stanley surged forward towards what Kitty assumed was his new place of work. He returned a few minutes later.

'I'm sorry, Kitty. Someone will come for you soon. Jack

has to take me elsewhere. I'm sorry your birthday treat ended this way. Take care.' Stanley gave a weak smile.

With a nod of reassurance, Kitty returned his smile, knowing full well her face was filled with anxiety.

'Go. Go and help, Stanley. Be safe. Don't worry about me.'

Kitty sat and watched Jack drive Stanley away, and returned her attention to the frantic activity going on around her. There was a scramble of men rushing back and forth towards planes waiting to take off and prepare themselves for either a defensive fight or revenge attack. Kitty wasn't sure if they did retaliate in any way so soon after an attack, but the adrenaline-driven thoughts which raged around her mind truly hoped so.

A young airman drove up in a forces car and tapped on the driver's door window and before pulling it open.

'I'm to take you home, Mrs Walker-Fell,' he said as she climbed into the passenger seat.

Kitty gave him a slight smile.

'Thank you. I'm actually Kitty Pattison, a Red Cross nurse. Anyway, do you know anything about the attack?' she asked.

'Loner, just offloaded onto residential properties. Nothing industrial. Bas— No warning, nothing. All hell has broken out here,' the driver said.

'I can imagine. Can you get me to where the bombs fell?' she asked.

'My orders are to take you to Fell Hall, or Shotley Hospital ma'am. If you try to persuade me otherwise, I am to ignore you. I'm to tell you that if I don't, I'll be dismissed.'

Kitty threw back her head and laughed. 'Yes, I can hear him saying that, but I'll take responsibility for ensuring you are not dismissed. I've experience in rescue after an attack, and can be of valuable service at the site. Drive me to the ARP, and we'll go from there.'

'Yes, ma'am,' the driver said, and did as asked.

As they pulled up near to the bomb site and followed the directions of various uniformed attendees, Kitty's heart pounded. The sight made her stomach rise and a queasy sensation set in when she saw the enemy had dropped his full load onto a residential street.

———————

'Excuse me. Excuse me,' Kitty called over to the back of a member of the Home Guard who appeared to be assessing the fractured walls of a building threatening to collapse at any moment.

The man turned around and picked his way across the mess and muddle to get closer to her. He was middle-aged, with a thin black moustache bearing less hair than his unruly eyebrows, and had a comical look about him, with his stout belly straining at the buttons, but his face was that of someone in authority.

'Sir. I'm a Red Cross nurse. I don't know this area, but am willing to help.'

The man, who was a head and shoulders shorter than her, pulled himself to his full height and looked her up and down. Kitty smoothed her dress to ensure her dignity was intact, such was the look on his face.

'I was on a picnic with someone from the RAF,' she said, justifying the cotton frock she wore. 'What group do you want me in – over there?'

Kitty pointed to a member of the rescue crew talking with someone, both pointing frantically at a brick-strewn area which had once been a house – a home.

He looked down at her feet, and Kitty was thankful she'd worn her sturdy walking shoes, for her sake, not for his opportunity to wave her aside. 'It's not safe over there. Listen, as lovely as this chat is, I haven't got the time …' the man said.

'I've played my part in attacks both in Birmingham and Scotland. All I need is equipment and a team to join.' Kitty heard the slight irritation in her voice and tried her best to keep it suppressed. Kitty was fully aware she didn't look in any way capable or qualified for a rescue operation, so she increased the authority in her voice.

'I haven't got time to offer references, but I can assure you the doctor and emergency team I worked alongside would offer up a good one. Now, where do I go to help?'

The driver remained waiting for his instruction, and gave a low whistle.

'I think you'd best go back to HQ and I'll find my way back home,' she said to him in the same swift, clipped manner.

'Ma'am.' He saluted and climbed inside the car.

Without waiting to continue any further conversation with the Home Guard, Kitty strode over to another group, introduced herself, and accepted the offer of a brown overall from one of the women standing nearby.

'It's my husband's clean one from the grocery store. It's a bit big but will keep your dress nice. Thank you for coming to help,' she said, and gave Kitty a pat on her arm. Kitty smiled at the woman and looked around.

'I'll need bandages, old sheets, blankets. Anything to help when we pull them free. This house, anyone there?' she asked, pointing to another crumpled mid-terraced property.

'A couple and their daughter. The boy's away.'

Kitty gave the woman a smile. 'Thank you.'

Once she'd introduced herself to a policeman nearby, he pointed to a safer area to walk.

'We'll team up. I'm Len.'

'Kitty. I'm based at Shotley Bridge, but have friends at Fell Hall, Brancepeth. They care for orphans, so please let me know about any children needing assistance. Bring them to me if they have nowhere to go. I'll care for them.'

'Will do,' Len said as they tugged at loose bricks for a closer look into a hole.

A *tap-tap* sound resonated from a gap between what was a door and a window frame.

'Listen,' Kitty said.

Without replying, Len pulled at the debris, jumping back each time something tumbled to the ground. Kitty stopped him every now and then to listen out for more noise or voices. The tapping never happened again. They moved slowly along the row, helping others and working as a pair. At the end of the row, the carnage was sickening.

Kitty looked at Len, and his face flinched with horror and revulsion.

'Ready for this?' Kitty asked him. The last thing she needed was to have to pick him up off the ground.

He bent forwards with his hands gripping his knees and gulped in large mouthfuls of air. Kitty walked away, not because she didn't care, but for her own sanity. Her courage to find life amongst the dead would leave her if she didn't continue the search. Len joined her and they worked with another two teams. Kitty's arms ached and her heart filled with sadness, sometimes overridden by the happy sounds of a survivor thanking everyone for saving their life.

'Where do you find your strong stomach? You're so young. I've years on you and still find it hard – facing death.' Len said, wiping his mouth with a rag after another bout of retching, following another tragic discovery.

'I don't know. It's an instinct I can't explain. I'm not hardened to it, just force myself to cope until I'm alone,' Kitty said, as she bandaged an elderly woman's arm.

'I'm grateful you were here today, Kitty. I'll take you home now, and thank you,' Len said and, brushed dirt from the sleeves of his uniform.

'I'd say it was my pleasure, but … ' Kitty said and gave him a sad smile as she thought back to what they'd dealt with for the five hours they'd worked together.

Her journey back to Fell Hall was in Len's motorbike sidecar. It was the most uncomfortable ride, but Kitty was just grateful to still be alive, and each potholed jolt reminded her of just how lucky she was – especially when she climbed out to see Daphne and Jenny holding the hands of two small children, both with soot-black faces streaked with tears. Her day was not over, and Kitty turned to Len.

'Thank you for the lift,' she said.

Jenny stepped forward. 'Please. Put out the word I'm looking for two women to help me with the little ones,' she said.

Len looked over at the children.

'Poor scraps. My sister would be a good candidate. I'll have a word.'

Both Jenny and Kitty threw him a grateful look and then concentrated on the children.

'Kitty, would you look after them while Daphne prepares a bath. I'll see to some food. I think you will know what to say. I won't hold you up too long,' Jenny said.

With a brief nod, Kitty turned her attention to the children. She opened her arms wide and pasted a smile on her face.

'Well look at you. Welcome to the big house. I'm Kitty, a friend of Mr and Mrs Walker-Fell. I'm a nurse, but as you don't look hurt, I'll just be a friend for now. How about that?'

The children drooped their heads towards the ground. Shock and tiredness set in and Kitty ushered them inside.

'We'll go indoors and get to know each other. You are safe here. It's a kind house,' she told them.

Once inside, persuading the children to take a bath was surprisingly easy. The novelty of a large, airy bathroom in a manor house and fresh flannel nightwear won them over.

The pair were not siblings, but both knew each other well and clung to one another as brother and sister whenever either one became fretful. The girl told Jenny and Kitty she was nine and the boy, ten.

Kitty looked at the young girl in her knee-length nightdress, freshly scrubbed and glowing. Her heart skipped a beat when Jenny crouched in front of the girl. She had memories of her aunt doing the same when she was first told of the death of her parents. She drew a calming breath; now was not a time for reminiscing, it was a time to comfort.

'Sally, you understand why you are here, don't you dear?' Jenny asked.

Sally's head drooped and her shoulders sagged with defeat. She nipped her lips together. The question she'd probably dreaded had now been asked and Kitty understood her reluctance to acknowledge it. The moment she did, it meant it was real. The truth would have filtered through the fragile barrier created to protect her heart. A feeling Kitty knew well enough.

'We'll help you where we can, Sally. I need you to promise me something,' Kitty said.

Sally looked up.

'I need you to promise you will ask questions, that you will tell us when you are sad, lonely or your dreams are too hard to handle. You won't stay here for ever, but while you are here, I know Mrs Walker-Fell will do her best to help you through the scary days,' Kitty said.

'Where will I go?' Sally whispered out her question, her shoulders still slumped, heavy with grief.

Jenny stood up and guided her over to a seat. 'We'll wait until Eric is ready and I'll explain it to you both. Daphne will fetch us some warm milk and we'll all have an early night.'

Two hours later, Kitty sat on the edge of a guest bed, exhausted. She had telephoned Alice and explained the situation. Jenny had offered her a bed overnight and Kitty would catch a train back to the hospital in the morning. Kitty was not due on duty until the following afternoon, but she needed Alice to let the house matron know she was off premises.

Before bedtime, she and Jenny both listened to the children's concerns and held them when they cried for their parents. Once again, Kitty questioned whether to offer volunteering at Fell Hall, and failed to come up with an answer. She was torn, but knew an emotional response was not one to act upon that night.

## Chapter Forty-Three

K itty's birthday of three weeks previous seemed like a lifetime away, and her days were extremely busy. Jenny approached her to become a permanent member of Fell Hall's orphan team, but Kitty turned her down. She promised to visit and help when she could, but her nursing career felt like a stronger path, and Kitty was settled at Shotley Bridge. To her delight she passed more assessments and gained entry into the next year of training, which led to a celebration at a local dance with Alice and other colleagues.

When she returned from the dance, one of the girls from her room told her Michael had telephoned the home to say he was on a 48-hour embarkation pass over the weekend and would explain everything if they could meet again in Durham. He left a message with the exact time and place for them to meet and to say if she wasn't able to get leave, he would understand, but it could be a long time before he would get the opportunity to see her again.

Calling in a few favours to cover her shifts and a begging word with the ward sister, Kitty managed to work out her leave to suit, and packed her bag. Sitting on the train, she recalled the first time she and Michael met.

It was a year to the day since she had sat on another train heading to Birmingham, and Kitty marvelled at the things she had been through in those twelve months.

As she approached the cathedral, her heart pounded in her chest. Michael would be around the next corner. She placed her kitbag on the floor and pulled a small mirror from her handbag. She checked her hair and applied another glossy coating of lipstick.

The autumn equinox had arrived, but the September weather was drier and warmer than normal. Slipping off the jacket of her navy wool suit to expose a pretty pastel-pink blouse – exchanged for a green cardigan with Alice – the summery day gave Kitty a sense of renewed excitement, and she followed the path to where Michael said he'd be waiting.

As she turned the corner, she saw only a wooden bench, but no Michael. She glanced around and looked up and down the pathway to ensure she'd not made a mistake and missed another path leading to the embankment beyond the cathedral. With train delays happening all the time, Kitty decided to sit on the bench and wait. As Michael had made the arrangements, she guessed they might be staying at the bed and breakfast they'd used in their last visit, and decided to head that way to check their booking if he was delayed. She'd give him an hour.

Leaving her bag and jacket on the seat, she paced up and

down the riverside. Bored of duck watching, she ventured to the front of the cathedral and eventually back to the seat. In a half hour of looking out for Michael, she saw only one person: an elderly lady who waved and muttered something about the weather and not enough bread to feed the ducks. Kitty gave her as much of a smile as she could muster and went back to the bench to enjoy the midday shade. Her stomach growled and reminded her it was closer to dinnertime than breakfast.

Her excitement no longer held fast and a disappointment set in, and the image in her head of Michael waiting for her with open arms at their new favourite place faded into a mess of sadness. It was now an hour and fifteen minutes since Kitty had arrived in Durham, and she decided to walk to the bed and breakfast.

Getting her bearings, she headed along the road and every few steps turned to look behind her, but the result was always the same: no Michael. Hesitating on the steps of the pretty guest house, she waited for a few minutes in the hope he might suddenly appear, but with no success. She pushed open the door of the guest house and gave the small bell on the reception desk a light tap.

'Ah, Miss Pattison. Welcome. Your young man has left instructions for you to have the same room as your previous visit.' The landlady appeared from the small dining room, wiping her hands on a floral pinafore. Kitty gave her a smile.

'Is Michael – Dr McCarthy – here? He wasn't where we were supposed to meet. I waited over an hour.'

With a flourish the landlady produced the guest book for Kitty to sign.

'No doubt his train is delayed. It is such an inconvenience for so many. I'm flattered you assumed he'd booked with me again, and you did the right thing by coming here.'

Kitty gave the woman a smile. 'We were made so welcome on our last visit, we now call Durham, and your guest house, our special place. I didn't doubt he'd try and stay here. I just wish I knew where he was.'

The woman patted her hand in a motherly fashion and Kitty thought of Ma Smith. Were all landladies the same – caring and understanding?

'Be patient, dear, he'll turn up. Have a nice cup of tea in the dining room. The pot and cups are on the side, and I'll put your bag in your room. Go on.'

Kitty did as the woman encouraged and sat in the quiet of the room. Her worries and concerns for Michael overwhelmed her the longer she waited until she could no longer bear sitting around. It was over two hours since they were supposed to meet. She went to her room and freshened herself before taking a walk back to the riverside bench. She roamed along the riverbank, around the cathedral and castle area, and debated waiting at the train station, but decided the river was a better option.

The late afternoon sun dipped and ducked behind clouds, and Kitty resigned herself to the fact that Michael had not managed to catch the train. All warmth from the sun disappeared, and Kitty's stomach growled, despite her having no appetite. With reluctance she rose to her feet and walked back to the guest house.

Behind the reception desk the landlady gave her a sad smile.

'Not turned up? Aw, bairn, don't take on so.' The woman rushed to Kitty's side when her resolve to cope broke down and she let her tears free.

The woman placed her arm around Kitty's shoulders and guided her into the empty dining room.

'I've only you as a guest and we can sit in here in peace. I'll fetch you one of my pies, and then you go to your room to rest. Your doctor might get word to me, and if he does, I'll fetch you.'

Daylight faded completely and a flash of light grazed the sky. Kitty watched the searchlights flicker across the city through her window. Michael was out there somewhere, and she hoped he was safe.

Her eyes stung through crying and no matter how hard she tried to stop, the tears kept falling. The landlady – she now knew as Nelly – encouraged her to believe Michael had missed the train or was held up with his duties, but inside, Kitty began to sense a smouldering fire of doubt. What if Michael chose not to come to see her after all? What if he no longer wanted the burden of a long-term relationship torn apart by the war, which was worsening by the day? Her stomach churned with anxiety and she paced the floor, giving thought to getting back to Shotley Bridge. Tomorrow was Sunday, and the trains and bus es worked a reduced service. She'd seen a notice in the ticket office stating certain trains on the Sunday timetable were for service personnel only, but Kitty knew if she explained she was Red Cross contracted, and showed her pass, she would be able to travel. She was not wanting to wait around until Monday morning. Durham had lost its shine.

Nelly fussed over her at breakfast, desperately trying to persuade Kitty to stay until the Monday.

'I'm in need of the company, Kitty, so you won't be a burden. Take a walk after breakfast and clear your head. Your doctor – Michael – won't want you miserable. He would want you to rest and refresh before going back on duty. Goodness knows, from the few conversations you and I have had, you deserve some time off.'

Kitty pondered her words.

'I'm afraid I can only afford to pay you for my room and board, Nelly,' she said.

With a loud tut and a frantic rush of fussing over the teapot refilling Kitty's cup, Nelly bustled around the room.

'I don't expect anything more. You are good company, and since my daughter married and moved away, I've been lonely. Most of the guests I get here now are military and males. You are a breath of fresh air, Kitty. Now, finish your tea and worry about catching the train tomorrow, not today.'

As she walked towards the river, Kitty wondered about the city and of how little of it she'd actually seen. From the station to the cathedral to the bed and breakfast was the extent of both her visits, and without Michael by her side, the river, cathedral and castle no longer appealed. She hesitated whether to continue, and argued with herself for a few seconds before choosing the river over an area she didn't know. As she headed for the bench she'd sat on the day before, she heard someone cough behind her, and spun around.

The man touched the brim of his hat as he walked by and wished her good morning. With a sigh, Kitty returned the greeting. She pulled out her well-read Mills & Boon romance novel and settled down to take her mind off a ruined weekend by investing herself in a fictional love affair.

'Excuse me, miss ...'

Opening her eyes at the sound of the male voice, Kitty's heart skipped more than one beat when she stared up at Michael. He looked down at her and his eyes softened with affection, then his face took on a studious look.

'Sleeping on a park bench?' he asked, as Kitty scrambled to her feet with a squeal of delight.

'Michael McCarthy, I've sat here for more hours than I care to think about, so don't you dare question me – just kiss me. Where have you been?' Kitty's words came thick and fast as she tried to catch her breath from the excitement of seeing him again.

He pulled her to him and burned her lips with a fierce kiss. His hold was firm and reassuring, and Kitty pushed all her questions to one side as she focused upon his attention. Breathless from the passion they shared in the shadows of the tree sheltering the bench, they pulled apart and Kitty frowned. Michael held up his hands in surrender.

'I'm sorry, Kitty. We had so many surgeries, due to the heavy bombing of late, and my leave was cancelled. I'm only here because I explained my situation and was reprimanded by a man with several daughters for leaving a Red Cross nurse alone in the city. He's granted me time to catch a train here and the next one back, so I don't have long.'

Kitty's excitement faded fast and she pulled a face to show her disappointment. Michael gave her no opportunity to speak by placing his lips on hers again. Realising she had to be grateful for what short time they had together, Kitty put aside any sniping remarks. Michael had no choice in what had happened, but he had chosen to rush there to be with her, and he deserved her love, not an upset tantrum.

What happened next happened so fast she didn't have time to think of anything to say. Michael took a few steps backwards, dropped to one knee, and produced a small box from his pocket.

'I don't have time to offer up small talk, Kitty. Hear me out. You made me a happy man when you accepted my pin, and seeing you wear your lucky seagull makes me smile. Now, I have one more thing I'd like to give to you ...'

He lifted the lid of the box and in the light of the intermittent afternoon sunshine reflecting from the water, she saw a small gold ring nestled inside.

'... if you promise to marry me after the war is over. The ring was my mother's. The stone is Canadian jade, but we can get a different one if you don't like it,' he said, looking up at her.

With her breath catching in her chest, Kitty stood looking down at him. His face earnest with anticipation and his eyes fixed on hers, Michael projected his love for her, and she held out her hand for him to slip the ring into place.

'I promise. Yes, yes, I'll marry you after the war, and the ring is perfect, thank you,' she whispered; her throat tight with emotion. 'Just hold me, Michael. Hold me for ever – for our for ever.'

'I wish it was for ever sweetheart, but for now will have to do.' Michael's words faded as Kitty placed her finger against his lips.

'It *will* be for ever. Fate had a plan when it brought us two orphans together and I *know* we will have a lifetime of love. Some things are meant to be; *we* are meant to be, Dr McCarthy.'

# THE
## *Red Cross*
# ORPHANS

Glynis Peters lives in the seaside town of Dovercourt. In 2014, she was shortlisted for the Festival of Romance New Talent Award.

When Glynis is not writing, she enjoys making greetings cards, Cross Stitch, fishing and looking after her gorgeous grandchildren.

Her debut novel, *The Secret Orphan*, was an international bestseller.

www.glynispetersauthor.co.uk

twitter.com/_GlynisPeters_
facebook.com/glynispetersauthor
instagram.com/glynispetersauthor
bookbub.com/authors/glynis-peters

## Also by Glynis Peters

*The Secret Orphan*
*The Orphan Thief*
*The Forgotten Orphan*